# E.R. PUNSHON

# FOUR STRANGE WOMEN

With an introduction
by Curtis Evans

## DEAN STREET PRESS

"Take it, dear, the book and me together. Where the heart lies let the brain lie also." Slightly paraphrasing Robert Browning's poem "One Word More" ("Take them, love...."), E.R. Punshon inscribed this sentiment to his future wife, Sarah Houghton, in a copy of his novel *Constance West* (1905), published a half century after Browning's poem first saw publication, in the collection *Men and Women* (1855). The couple wed that same year, 1905, and their union would last another half century, until Punshon's death, at the age of 84, in December 1956. Sarah Punshon survived her longtime spouse by fewer than six months, passing away in May 1957.

Correspondence between the Punshons and Dorothy L. Sayers held at Wheaton College in Wheaton, Illinois indicates that the couple had a close marriage (though no children came from their union), with Sarah Punshon taking an interest in her husband's writing and attending Detection Club events with him until the end of his life. Christianna Brand, another prominent mystery writer who became a member of the Detection Club after the Second World War, recalled seeing the elderly couple at Club dinners in the 1950s. In a typical example of what might most charitably be termed her affectionately catty reminiscences, Brand noted that Mrs. Punshon (now an octogenarian like her husband) tended to doze during long-winded guest lectures, even though the husband and wife always made sure of getting good seats at the High Table so they could hear everything.

Despite the evidence that his marriage with Sarah Houghton was quite a contented one, E.R. Punshon in his fourteenth Bobby Owen detective novel, the masterfully bizarre *Four Strange Women* (1940), portrays darker potentialities in romantic relationships between men and women. As one character tellingly observes, "there's nothing sends a man to the devil so quick as when the wrong woman gets hold of him." Like *The Bath Mysteries* (1936), *Four Strange Women* is a serial killer novel, one ahead of its time in its determination to plumb the darker depths of human nature, without flinching over what unpleasant things might be encountered in the murk.

*Four Strange Women* follows immediately upon the events of the previous Bobby Owen novel, *Murder Abroad* (1939). Having successfully performed for the well-connected Lady Markham a private commission involving the investigation of a murder in France, Bobby has been rewarded by this consummate string-pulling lady with the position of inspector in the Wychshire county police force. This post includes duties as private secretary to Colonel Glynne, chief constable of Wychshire; and when the novel opens, Bobby, having returned to his London flat after a date with his fiancée, Olive Farrar, plans to turn in for the night in order to be ready for an appointment with Colonel Glynne in Midwych, the county town of Wychshire. His sleep is forestalled, however, when he is visited by Lord Henry Darmoor, the polo-playing second son of Lord Whitfield, and Darmoor's fiancée, Gwen Barton, from whom he learns the strange circumstances behind the recent mysterious deaths in the hinterlands of young Viscount Byatt and millionaire's scion Andy White. The former was "found dead in his car....right away in the middle of Dartmoor" while the latter was discovered expired "in a cottage miles far from everywhere in Wales." In both cases there was no indication of the cause of death of either man, both of whom had been spending freely on jewelry and passing time at the Cut and Come Again, the notorious West End nightclub (now ostensibly reformed) that features in three earlier Bobby Owen detective novels, *Mystery of Mr Jessop* (1937), *The Dusky Hour* (1938) and *Suspects – Nine* (1939).

Darmoor and his fiancée tell Bobby that they fear another young man, an old prep school friend of Darmoor's named Billy Baird, may meet a fate similar to that of Byatt and White. He too has been recently throwing his money about, spending more than he can afford both on jewelry and a caravan that he has driven up to lonely Wychwood Forest, near Midwych, in Bobby's new jurisdiction. Attractive young women have been linked to the three men, all of these women friends of each other with connections to Wychshire: Hazel Hannay, Lady May Grayson, and, most inconveniently of all for Bobby, Becky Glynne, daughter of his new employer. Confronted with this disconcerting assemblage of odd facts, Bobby finds himself beset with foreboding about his future:

> It was simple fact, with no trace of fantasy or imagination, that two young men of wealth and position, Andy White and Viscount Byatt, had died in strange circumstances strangely resemblant. Now it seemed another young man, this Mr. Baird, was traveling by the same road, perhaps to the same destination....Again that thought occurred to him which once before had flashed though his mind, that Colonel Glynne had not merely been requiring some pleasant and amiable and well-recommended young man to help him in the routine work of his office, but rather was seeking even desperately for help as he felt drawing closer about him strange forces of darkness and terror.

When Bobby arrives in Wychshire he finds ample ground for his fears. During his consultation with the sorely-troubled Colonel Glynne he learns that an incinerated corpse has been discovered in the ashen remains of Billy Baird's burnt-out caravan. Has some sort of serial killer of males struck yet again, like some remorseless angel of death, and are more killings meant to follow? Bobby once again goes in pursuit of the truth, traveling to various far-flung rural locales on the island as well some very dark corners of London indeed. In the course of his investigations, Bobby encounters yet another "strange woman," an enigmatic and elusive singer of Welsh ballads named Jane Jones. What does she know about this singular case, surely the most outré of Bobby's career?

With its grim plot that in many ways resembles noir rather than garden variety classical detective fiction, *Four Strange Women* is one of the most intriguing and accomplished of E.R. Punshon's crime novels. The book reads rather like Agatha Christie's famous serial killer mystery *The ABC Murders* as darkly reimagined by, say, modern crime writer Val McDermid. Fans of Punshon's Detection Club colleague John Dickson Carr also should readily detect resemblance to the memorable Grand Guignol found in Carr's shuddery shockers. Punshon himself was a great admirer of Carr's detective fiction, during his years as a book reviewer for the *Manchester Guardian* repeatedly heaping praise on the expatriate American mystery writer for the scope of his imagination. "Mr. John Dickson Carr's special gift is his power by the sheer magic of his writing to create an atmosphere so full of wonder and of dread that in it we are willing to believe almost anything," Punshon admiringly observed in his review of Carr's *The Hollow Man* (1935) (*The Three Coffins* in the US), placing his finger on the source of much of Carr's perennial appeal to generations of mystery connoisseurs. Of another Carr novel, *The Burning Court* (1937), Punshon declared that "as an adventure in diablerie it is a remarkable and outstanding achievement," while of Carr's *The Reader Is Warned* (1939), he avowed that "the manner in which is conveyed an unearthly atmosphere of wonder and dread" proved that Carr possessed the precious "gift of imagination."

E.R. Punshon possessed such a gift as well, and it is this gift that enriches the narrative of *Four Strange Women*, where Bobby Owen finds himself involved in a bone chilling case of unusual moral dimension that provokes him to meditate, as he envisions his impending nuptials with Olive Farrar, on the strange mystery that is love:

> Was it really this strange passion or instinct or necessity of life, or what you will, which men call love....that had traced the dark and dreadful pattern of secret murder now slowly taking form and shape before his eyes? Was it really, he asked himself, of the same kin and kind, coming under the same category, as the steady and tranquil force of his own feeling for Olive?... Was love, then, he asked himself bewilderingly, a tree like that other one which bore upon itself the fruit of good and evil—fruit of both life and death?

Curtis Evans

# CHAPTER I
## BEGINNINGS

Detective-Sergeant Bobby Owen had spent a most enjoyable evening—dinner, theatre, dance, supper—with his fiancée, Olive Farrar, and was now on his way home. In his pocket was his application for permission to transfer to the Wychshire County Police, and on the morrow—or to-day, rather, for now it was in the small hours—he was travelling up to Midwych, the county town of Wychshire and a busy manufacturing centre, there to interview Colonel Glynne, the chief constable.

The fortunate conclusion of a recent semi-private investigation on which he had been engaged had put money in his pocket, won him influential friends, and gained him the promise of an appointment as inspector in the Wychshire county force, with special duties as private secretary to the elderly Colonel Glynne, and with the additional prospect, therefore, of some day succeeding him as chief constable. Indeed the rich, enchanting words, 'deputy chief constable', had already been breathed to Olive by Lady Markham, who, in gratitude for Bobby's services in the semi-private case already mentioned, had been busy pulling those necessary strings by which such comfortable appointments are generally to be obtained in our happy land of England.

Bobby, therefore, was in a very contented, not to say complacent mood as he strolled along. He wondered a little what his future chief would be like. Lady Markham had described him as both efficient and considerate to those working under him, though with a bee in his bonnet about football pools, against which he had been conducting a kind of crusade. He had indeed obtained a certain notoriety by an attack he had delivered on them in public, in which he described them as a menace to society and produced figures to show how badly trade in Midwych was suffering from the diversion to the pools of money that would have been so much better spent in other more productive and useful ways.

Bobby wondered if his future work would include taking part in this campaign. He would be quite willing to do so. Not one of the ways in which he wasted his own money, and every policeman, like every social worker, knows well what harm is done by unrestricted gambling. A little awkward though, if it were true, as he had heard, that a son of the chief constable's, a young man who had occasionally himself played as an amateur in first division football, was rather a devotee of those same pools. However, that, Bobby supposed, would be papa's trouble, not his. He turned into the street in which he lived and noticed without interest a large, imposing-looking car standing near his door. He supposed vaguely that perhaps the doctor occupying the next house had bought a new car and was now suffering under the doctor's tenth plague— a night call. As he passed it on his way to his own door, he was aware of an odd impression that some one from within the car's dark interior was watching him intently. It was almost like a physical sensation and one curiously disturbing, this idea he had that from out that darkness so intent a gaze was fixed upon him. He almost turned back to ask who was there and why such intensity of interest, but then, putting aside an idea he felt absurd, he inserted his latchkey in his door and entered. To his surprise his landlady, who should have been in bed long ago, made a prompt appearance. "There's a man to see you, Mr. Owen, sir," she announced.

"At this time," protested Bobby, for by now it was less late than early, nearly two in fact, since theatre, supper, dance, escorting Olive back to her little hat shop where she lived near Piccadilly, had eaten up the night.

"I couldn't get rid of him," the landlady explained resentfully. "Said he was going to stop if it was till the milk came. I don't like his looks," she added, "and me all alone, and should have been in my bed at a Christian hour long ago."

"Too bad," said Bobby, "I'm sorry."

"As villainous looking he is as ever I saw," the landlady went on, "so I asked him if he would like a drop of beer, and I gave it him in a glass with a bit of butter rubbed on it so as to leave his fingerprints and then you'll know who he is."

"By Jove," said Bobby admiringly, "that was smart."

"I won't say it wasn't," admitted the landlady complacently; "but then I've not had a Scotland Yard gentleman with me so long without picking up a bit of how it's done."

"We shall have," Bobby told her gravely, "to get you a job on the staff at Central. Did he say what his name was?"

"His sort," sniffed the landlady, "has as many names as a cat has lives."

"So they have," agreed Bobby, "Smith to-day and Brown to-morrow. You run along to bed. I'm sorry you've been kept up. Most likely it's only an old 'con' trying to borrow the price of a bed because he's sure of an honest job to-morrow and wants to look his best. Half a crown will get rid of him."

He bade her good night and opened the door of his sitting-room. One of the ugliest men he had ever seen was there and got up as he entered. A low forehead; a long, crooked nose; a mouth framing teeth too widely separated and irregular in shape, and stretching, it seemed, almost from ear to ear; ears themselves enormous and standing out nearly at right angles; eyes small and hidden, indeterminate in colour, the left eye with a cast in it; all that combined with a squat, ungainly figure and sprawling hands and feet to produce an effect so remarkable that Bobby found himself reflecting that fingerprints would hardly be required for identification if the Records Department at the Yard knew anything of him. He appeared to have omitted to shave, but this unfortunate impression was, in fact, due merely to an abnormal growth of beard, so that a shave twice a day at least was necessary to avoid an appearance of not having shaved at all. His hands, his brows, his ears, all showed, too, the same strong growth of hair, and Bobby noticed that though his clothes looked of good cut and material, they were old and worn, and as shapeless as if the coat had never known a hanger or the trousers a press. He was smoking a short pipe full of some exceptionally vile tobacco, so strong that Bobby, getting a whiff of the smoke, nearly choked. But when the stranger spoke from behind the vile, odorous cloud that half hid him, his voice was singularly pleasing, of a rich, musical tone—organ tones they might have been called. He said as Bobby came in:—

"Mr. Owen, isn't it? You must think it awful cheek, my hanging on like this, but I had simply got to see you."

"It is a bit late, isn't it?" Bobby agreed, none too cordially.

"Yes, I know. I do apologize. Only it seemed the only chance, if you're buzzing off in the morning."

"How do you know that?" Bobby asked sharply.

"Cripes," answered the other, "everyone knows it. I've been waiting hours with poor old Gwen hanging on outside like grim death." He dashed to the window, let the blind up, stood there, waved both hands above his head and went back to the chair in which he had been sitting when Bobby entered but that Bobby, himself still standing, had not invited him to re-occupy. "That was to tell Gwen I shan't be long now," he explained confidentially. "She must be fed up, waiting out there, but she wouldn't come in, though it's her idea really. You see, she gets her hats or something from Miss Farrar and so she's heard about you."

"Look here," began Bobby with an impatience slightly controlled by this information that he was talking to a friend of a customer of Olive's—and Bobby had long since learnt how sacred is the aura surrounding that word 'customer', more especially when the customer it refers to is the customer of a small West End hat shop, "it's jolly late and—"

"Yes, I know," the other pleaded in that rich, deep voice of his, "but don't throw me out, there's a good chap. It's important and I've been waiting hours with nothing but a glass of beer they gave me here. Nice woman and nice beer but glass a bit greasy outside. I had to wipe it." And Bobby perceived a glass polished till it shone again by aid of a large linen handkerchief lying near that its owner now put in his pocket. Certainly on that glass no trace of any finger-print would remain. Bobby reflected that not for the first time over-subtlety had defeated itself, and he wondered if this stranger had suspected the purpose of the slightly greasy exterior. He said:—

"Do you mind telling me who you are and what you want? Sit down, won't you?" he added, partly under the influence of that magic word 'customer', but still more under that of the other's deep, resonant tones, that really it was hardly an exaggeration to compare to the tones of a distant organ.

"My name's Darmoor, Henry Darmoor," the stranger explained. "My old man's Lord Whitfield, you know, the diplomatic bloke. He wanted me to go in for it, too, but you couldn't have an ambassador with a mug like mine. Couldn't be done. He did see that at last, so he pushed me on the Stock Exchange, not that I ever go near the beastly place. But I'm supposed to be a bit of a dab at polo. Oh, and I'm engaged to Gwen Barton."

He brought the name out so shyly and yet with such deep pride that Bobby's heart warmed to him. A kind of wondering delight was all about him as he spoke, as though even to himself the thing still seemed incredible. He said presently, his low voice now like a chant of gratitude and praise:—

"Me with my mug and she as lovely as the dawn."

So she might be, Bobby thought, but she lacked the one essential all the same—she wasn't Olive and never could be. Not that the name, Gwen Barton, meant anything to him. A pretty chorus girl, very likely, only there had been a depth in Lord Henry's voice that had set in him sympathetic chords vibrating. Now, though, he did remember vaguely recent news items about the well known polo player, Lord Henry Darmoor, second son of Lord Whitfield, having found the expense of financing the Whitfield polo team too heavy and having decided to withdraw from the game.

"Giving it up now though," said Lord Henry. "Engaged, you know, and all that."

"You haven't come here at this time to talk about that, have you?" Bobby asked.

"Cripes, no. It's about Billy Baird."

"Who is he?"

"Pal of mine. We were in the sixth together. He went up to Balliol. They wouldn't have me, but Billy and I stopped pals all the same. He is going in for politics now after a spell at banking. Standing at next election for some god-forsaken London suburb, and the other day went caravanning on his own."

"Why shouldn't he?" Bobby asked. "If there is a point, please get to it. If there isn't—"

"Get out," interposed Darmoor, to show he knew what Bobby meant. "Don't get shirty, old man," he begged in those organ-like notes of his. "You know what it is when you're engaged. You are, too, aren't you?" he added hurriedly as Bobby looked more impatient than ever. "Gwen says she doesn't half like it. You see, she knew poor old Byatt, you know, Viscount Byatt of Byatt, and she says it's all happening again just the same way."

"Byatt?" Bobby repeated. There had come into the other's voice as he pronounced the name a note that even against Bobby's better judgment impressed him with a curious sense of dread and of foreboding. He began to search his memory. "There was something—a year or two ago," he said. "Wasn't there?"

"Found dead in his car," Lord Henry's deep, expressive voice replied. "Right away in the middle of Dartmoor. No one knew what he was doing there. Not the usual exhaust pipe business. Car all right. Nothing to show cause of death. Just dead. That was all. Been dead a week or two before he was found, the doctors said. He left piles of money but he had been getting rid of a whole lot and nothing to show how or why."

"There was an inquest?" Bobby asked.

"The last time he was seen," Lord Henry went on, "was at a night club. Well known place. The 'Cut and Come Again'. You chaps raid it sometimes, but you've never got anything on it."

"No," agreed Bobby. "I know the place. What about the inquest?"

"He was at the 'Cut and Come Again' with a Miss Hazel Hannay. They had supper and danced. He drove her home. He was never seen again till they found him way out on Dartmoor."

"The inquest?" Bobby asked once more.

"Wash out," answered Lord Henry briefly. "Just said there was nothing to show what had happened."

"Who is Miss Hannay?"

"Then there was Andy White," Lord Henry went on, unheeding this question, too, as seemed to be his habit, perhaps because he was so intent on what he wished to say that questions made small impression on his mind. "Rich bloke. In the millionaire class or thereabouts. You know. White's Fish Cakes, White's Pocket Vitamins, all sorts of dodges like that. Andy's old man started the show. Andy himself played a jolly good game—polo I mean, in goal. That's how I knew him. They found him in a cottage miles from everywhere in Wales. Nothing to show what he was doing there. Nothing to show what killed him. Been dead a month, the doctors said. Or more. Nasty business. Rats and all that, you know. Door had been left open. No sign of violence. No trace of poison. No disease. He had been getting rid of pots of money, too, buying jewellery and that sort of thing. One extra swell necklace was worth a fortune, twelve or fifteen thousand."

"What did he do with it?" Bobby asked.

"No one knows. No trace of it. An uncle or someone heard of it, though, asked him what he was up to, splashing his money about like that. He said it was a present for Lady May Grayson. Lady May sticks to it she never had a thing from him—friendly they were all right, she says, but nothing more, and anyhow she didn't take presents like that from her friends. She's rather a night club bird and often at the 'Cut and Come Again'. She used to dance with Andy there sometimes. No one knows exactly when Andy went off to his Welsh cottage, so no one knows who saw him last."

"I remember the case," Bobby said. "We were notified he was missing, but we didn't handle it except in the usual routine manner. It only looked like a rich young Mayfair playboy going off on his own affairs. Afterwards the Welsh police dealt with it. I don't remember this Lady What's-her-name being mentioned."

"Lady May Grayson. No. They kept her name out of it. Her old man's the Earl of Merefield. Old family, big pot in his way, owns castles and things all over the show, but hasn't a penny to bless himself with. All mortgaged up to the hilt or else tied up in settlements or something. Lady May doesn't do so badly herself though. Gets photographed smoking somebody's cigarettes or washing herself with somebody's soap and a whacking big cheque for it. Two or three of her photos were in the cottage. Nothing much in that. Lots of her photos about—she'll always sit for one if she's paid enough. The photo goes in the weeklies and the man who took it gets known. A woman had been seen there—at the cottage, I mean. No one had seen her close enough to say anything. No one lived very near. One story said she was tall, another that she was short and another that she wore a mask. There was something about her coming on a motor bike, too, but no one was very clear about that or anything else. There you are."

Now the name had been brought to his memory, Bobby recollected enough of Lady May, prominent as she was in society circles, to know that she was a tall woman. Divinely tall, a daughter of the gods, and so on, were epithets no self-respecting writer of a gossip column ever failed to use in speaking of her.

"Who is the Miss—Hazel Hannay, was it?—you mentioned before?" he asked.

"Daughter of General Sir Harold Hannay with a string of letters a mile long after his name. Her mother's dead. Two or three brothers all abroad. Their place is Crossfields, just outside Midwych. He's chairman or something of the Wychshire Watch Committee. She's pally with Lady May. Gwen says they like to go about together, because of being an effective contrast. She's tall and dark, and the other, Lady May I mean, she's tall and fair. Colonel Glynne is a neighbour of the Hannays. I believe their grounds touch or something. Old Glynne has a daughter, too, Becky Glynne. Becky and Hazel Hannay play a good deal of tennis together, Gwen says."

Bobby sat up abruptly. He had been wondering where all this long rambling tale was getting to; he would have cut it short long ago but for a note of urgency, even of alarm, he seemed to be aware of in his visitor's deep, rolling tones. But now abruptly he saw deep water ahead, and it flashed with absolute conviction into his mind that here was the explanation of why he had been offered what on the face of it had seemed so easy, so comfortable, so snug, so altogether desirable an appointment. Colonel Glynne was looking for no assistance in his everyday routine, for no aid in that football pools suppression campaign of his, for no suitable young man to be trained in his methods to carry on in the same way after his own death or retirement. Now it seemed to Bobby that the offer he had received was like a cry for help from one who felt the powers of darkness encompassing him around. Bobby was silent. Darmoor got up and went to the window where again he raised the blind, signalled with his hands, lowered the blind, returned to his place.

"Poor old Gwen's been waiting there for hours," he said. "That was just to tell her that now we shan't be long."

"I don't think I caught the lady's other name," Bobby remarked, thinking to himself that she must be a meek, self-effacing little person to be willing to wait so long out there, so patiently.

"Barton, Gwen Barton," Darmoor answered, with again that note of shy adoration in his voice. "It was partly her idea, my coming here. Last new hat she bought, she heard all about it. I mean all about how Miss Farrar was giving up because you and she were getting spliced now you had got a job in Midwych and how the assistant—she talked Gwen into paying twice what she had meant to give, and Gwen hasn't too much of the ready, and she never runs bills—how she was going to carry on the business, and she told Gwen all about it, and how you were seeing Colonel Glynne to-morrow to fix it all up, and then Miss Farrar would join you, only that didn't mean the shop was going to shut down."

"But why did Miss Barton want you to tell me all this at this time of night?" Bobby asked. "You understand I shall have to report to Colonel Glynne, to Scotland Yard as well. They may want to see both you and Miss Barton."

"That's O.K. with us," his visitor answered. "There's nothing more, only Billy Baird."

"What about him?"

"Well, we're pals, you see, me and Billy," Lord Henry explained; and if his rich, deep tones that seemed almost a language in themselves, did not now tremble with the deep adoration that before had vibrated in every syllable, yet none the less they showed a deep and genuine emotion, "we've been pals ever since we were kids at the same prep school. It was through Billy I met Gwen. Gwen likes him, too."

He paused. Bobby, looking at him, saw that he had become a little pale, saw that enormous mouth of his quiver at the corners, saw a small bead of perspiration trickle down the side of his nose and hang there, ridiculously suspended. Why, Bobby did not know, but the close air of the room seemed filled suddenly with dark and strange forebodings, and the shadows in the corners, as it were, to hide monstrous and incredible things. He said sharply, for he knew well there was more to come:—

"Yes. Well?"

The answer came almost in a whisper, yet every syllable full and clear.

"First there was Byatt and then there was Andy White and now Gwen thinks that perhaps Billy is going the same way."

## CHAPTER II
## ACCIDENTAL

Bobby remembered ruefully that Olive had sent him home with strict injunctions to get a good night's rest so as to be sure to be looking his very best and brightest for his forthcoming interview with Colonel Glynne. It was fortunate that the arrangement was for him to dine at the colonel's house in the evening—'so that we can make each other's acquaintance', the colonel had written—and for the formal interview to take place the next morning. He could therefore leave London by a comparatively late train, so that he would be able to lie late in bed, provided, that is, he ever got there, which was beginning to seem to him increasingly doubtful.

"Miss Barton is waiting outside, you said, didn't you?" he asked. "Will you ask her to come in for a moment?"

"Right-oh," responded Lord Henry with alacrity, making for the door, and on the way knocking over a chair with a crash that Bobby fully expected would bring an indignant and protesting landlady on the scene.

In the hall Lord Henry fell over the door mat, got the door open, called in what he meant for a whisper but that sounded like the leader of community singing giving out an announcement:—"I say, Gwen, old girl, can you come in for half a sec?"

Further sounds suggested that Lord Henry had fallen either up or down the front door steps; and Bobby was a little glad to think he was leaving and would not have to face the reproaches of his landlady and his fellow lodgers over a nocturnal disturbance that was beginning to sound like a minor air raid. Then Lord Henry returned, ushering in a small, reluctant figure in a neat, close-fitting tweed costume.

Bobby somehow had been expecting someone of what is called the 'glamour' type. His first impression now was of a shy, hesitating, rather ordinary-looking girl, not noticeable in any way except for the unusual pallor of her complexion. She did not seem to be much made up, except that her lips were unnaturally crimson. Like a small curved splash of red they showed against that strangely pale skin, and behind them he caught a glimpse of two rows of white, regular teeth, small and pointed. Her features seemed to him small, regular, undistinguished; and when she came into the room she gave him first a shy, embarrassed, almost apologetic smile, and then seemed to be trying to efface herself in a corner of the room, as if offering mute apology for being there at all. Bobby was aware of a momentary amusement as he contrasted this timid, insignificant little figure with the almost passionate adoration Lord Henry's tones had managed to convey. Strange, he felt, that a girl whose presence could be so easily forgotten, as he indeed was already almost forgetting it, could awake so much devotion. He remembered vaguely a case he had once heard of in which a man of experience and social standing had fallen wildly in love with a little typist who struck everyone else as entirely insignificant, who had entirely failed to understand the man's passion, who had indeed been merely frightened by it, so scared, in fact, that finally she had disappeared in a panic, whereon the man had committed suicide. Apparently this was a similar case, with the fortunate exception that Gwen Barton, whether she understood or not, appeared at any rate to be accepting the devotion offered her. Bobby hoped it would not turn out badly, that she would have sufficient character and self-control to live up to the part for which she had been cast, though he was not sure that the frightened air with which she seemed to wish to hide herself in the nearest corner was altogether promising in that respect. But Lord Henry had no idea of letting her efface herself like that.

"Now then, Gwen," he said, "don't look so scared even if Owen is a policeman."

She came forward then, and Bobby noticed that she moved with an unusual, silent speed and certainty, hovering for a moment in her corner as if afraid to issue from it, and then across the room and by his side almost before he knew she had moved. Lord Henry muttered the usual formula of introduction, and she held out a small hand with long, curved, pointed crimson-tinted nails—coloured finger nails being apparently the only concession apart from the use of her brightly-coloured lipstick, she made to the prevailing craze for cosmetics, since the thin, almost transparent pallor of her skin seemed untouched by powder or rouge. Hitherto he had not noticed her eyes, hidden behind heavy, half-closed lids, and now when she looked up at him he thought how dull and almost lifeless they seemed, and yet with a pin point of light somewhere safely tucked away in their dark depths as if at any moment they might blaze into sudden, unexpected life. He took her hand and felt a kind of heat run through him from her grip, as from equally unexpected hidden fires. The vigour of that grip told him, too, that for all her slight build she possessed plenty of strength, nervous though, perhaps, rather than muscular. Something unusual about her, Bobby thought, if only one could find it out, but whatever it was, probably explaining and no doubt justifying the evident depth and sincerity of Lord Henry's devotion. Now his deep voice boomed out:—

"Beauty and the Beast, eh? that's what you're thinking, isn't it?"

Bobby wasn't thinking anything of the sort, for 'beauty' was the last epithet he would have thought of applying to Gwen Barton. 'Ordinary, insignificant, commonplace' were more appropriate adjectives, he thought, except for that hint of something hidden in her, 'burning bright' within, as it were, that no doubt explained Lord Henry's—'infatuation', was the word that came to Bobby but he felt it so obviously unfair that hurriedly he changed it in his mind to 'passion'. Gwen was saying in her quiet little voice:—

"I've heard such a lot about you, Mr. Owen. At darling Olive's. The girls there can't talk of anything else; only when they stop, you find you've spent twice as much as you meant to. Only you don't mind, because they always find something to suit you better than you ever thought anything could."

Bobby was not pleased. He knew enough of the powers and capacities of Olive's head assistant to believe what Gwen said, and he did not wish to think of himself as a selling point in a campaign for more and better and ever dearer hats. He said:—

"Miss Barton, Lord Henry tells me—"

He paused abruptly. He had hardly seen her move, and yet now she was back across the room at Lord Henry's side. As she reached him she looked up at him, and he, though brought up in all that tradition of restraint and self-control so strong in the British governing class, went pale and was visibly shaken. There was indeed as it were a flame of passion passing between the two of them that quite startled Bobby. She seemed to feel this, for abruptly she veiled her eyes behind those dark lashes of hers and those heavy lids, and then turned and facing Bobby again seemed once more to be the small, pale, hesitating ordinary-looking young woman she had appeared on her first entrance. She said softly:—

"Mr. Owen, if ever I tell this stupid boy I won't have anything more to do with him, it'll be because he will keep on about Beauty and the Beast. I'm no May Grayson, worse luck, and if Harry's a beast, he's rather a nice one. Only if he keeps on calling himself one, I shall make him wear a collar and chain and go about on his hands and knees."

"Right-oh," said Lord Henry, and promptly dropped on hands and knees at her feet. "Anything you say."

"Don't be ridiculous, get up," she told him sharply, yet with a note in her voice that showed, Bobby thought, she was gratified by his prompt obedience. "Mr. Owen, isn't he just too silly?"

"Lord Henry has been telling me," Bobby said, unheeding this and thinking it was time to get to the point, "that you are disturbed about a friend of his. Will you please tell me why? You know, of course, that I am a police-officer. I believe that is why you've come?"

She flashed—there is no other word to describe the swift, sure silence of her movements—across the room again and was once more at his side. Her head hardly came to his shoulder, her eyes were hidden, she spoke quickly and clearly.

"It's Billy," she said. "Billy Baird. He's such a nice boy and Harry's ever so fond of him and so am I, too, though of course I only know him a little, and Harry's been friends with him all his life—shared the same cradle, didn't you?"

"Same prep school and stuck to each other ever since," corrected Lord Henry, quite seriously.

"And Billy hasn't too much money, not if he's going into politics, because that does cost lots and lots, doesn't it? and then he's been spending oceans, hasn't he, Harry?"

"Cripes, I should think he had," confirmed Lord Henry. "He bought some sort of swell ruby thing at Christie's the other day for three thou. Three thou, I ask you, and him needing every blessed penny he's got if he's to nurse any constituency properly. Bought it on the q.t. through Higham's, of Bond Street. Old Higham let it out himself when I was in there the other day. It's only the big deals the old man takes an interest in himself, you know."

"May Grayson was awfully disappointed," Gwen went on. "She told me so herself. She's crazy about jewels and wanted to buy, only of course she couldn't afford all that."

"I asked Billy what was the game," interposed Lord Henry, "and he said he had a market and hoped to make a good profit."

"May said it was an awfully outside figure," remarked Gwen. "I don't think she believed any one would ever give more."

"If you ask me," declared Lord Henry, "he's got mixed up with some woman and he bought it for her." He gave a little nod of defiance at Gwen. "All right, Gwen," he said, "you needn't believe it. Gwen says," he explained to Bobby, "it isn't that, because if he gave it to any woman, she wouldn't be able not to show it off, and then every one would know."

"Well, don't you think so, too, Mr. Owen?" asked Gwen, but Lord Henry swept on unheedingly.

"It's not only that," he said. "Billy's bought a slap up motor caravan—swell affair, jewelled in every hole, that sort of thing. It must have cost him a packet. I've backed two bills for him, too—three hundred altogether, and he used to get shirty if I even hinted at stumping up to help him along till he got going in politics. Gwen said I ought to, and all he said was I ought to have more sense than to start throwing my beastly money about. Next thing I knew he was touching me himself for coin. Not that I mind, he's welcome—only it's so damn funny, if you see what I mean."

"All that is surely his own private business, isn't it?" Bobby asked.

"Well, if you put it like that," said Lord Henry doubtfully. "Only there it is, isn't it? I mean to say. Going off caravanning all by himself. Not like him. Never cared for motoring even. Bridge at the club was his best bet. Now here he is, all on his own and no one knows why. In Wychwood Forest. That's near Midwych, you know."

Bobby nodded. Wychwood forest, dating from the days when William the Conqueror ravaged great areas of Yorkshire and Mercia, extended still for many miles north and east of Midwych. Of late years it had become a favourite centre for 'hiking' and other holiday parties. Even one or two holiday camps had been founded on its outskirts, but generally its dense and ancient woodlands, alternating with bare, open expanses of high moor, were as lonely and deserted as in the days following the passage of the Conqueror's destroying bands. Abruptly Lord Henry said:—

"Billy told one or two chaps at the club he was in love with a girl. Not like him, either. He wasn't a chap to talk about things like that. He never let on who it was. He started going to the Cut and Come Again. He never went to places like that before—serious sort of johnny and dead keen on politics. Wanted to reform everything, only not Bolshevik, you know. Just reform." Lord Henry emphasized the word with a wave of the hand that seemed to include the universe. "Sound conservative, of course, he was. Night clubs something new for him. It was Becky Glynne he used to dance with there. You know. Old Colonel Glynne's daughter. Set people talking."

"It's all happening," Gwen said softly, "just the way it seemed to happen with Andy White and the Byatt boy."

"Gwen's a bit scared," Lord Henry said, and he put an arm around her with a gently-protecting gesture. He had the look of one guarding something infinitely precious, infinitely fragile, a look that Bobby never forgot. Gwen snuggled up against him, as if she felt the comfort of the safety that his strong embrace offered, and Lord Henry said again: "Gwen's got the wind up, haven't you, old girl, eh?"

Gwen smiled faintly, timidly, almost, and snuggled closer still. Bobby said:—

"Is it certain it was Miss Glynne?"

"A girl I know told me," Gwen answered. "She described her and it did sound like Becky—Becky's small and fair and she generally wears blue and very often a striped pattern to make her look taller. I've seen her playing tennis. She plays doubles with Hazel Hannay. I play, too," Gwen added with a faint smile, "but I'm not in their class."

"It's this caravanning stunt worries me," Lord Henry repeated. "It's not like him. And it wasn't like Andy White to go off to some god-forsaken cottage in Wales, or for Byatt to go motoring all alone on Dartmoor. Andy's idea of a country cottage would have been a place with thirty bedrooms, all with their own baths—gold plated taps, most likely. It wasn't natural, that cottage business, miles from the next place. And it isn't natural, Billy's caravanning all alone in Wychwood Forest. I'm a bit scared too—scared," he repeated, and Gwen pressed his arm comfortingly as once more he said—"I'm scared."

"Harry wanted to go and see about it himself," she said, and added, "Billy's such a nice boy."

"Well, I did think of chasing up there," admitted Lord Henry. "Only of course it wouldn't do. Even Gwen saw that."

"I don't know why you've come to me," Bobby said resentfully, for it was no such introduction as this that he had desired to his new appointment. "If you can't do anything, when you are his friend, what do you think I can do?"

"Well, you see, you're police," explained Lord Henry. "All right for you to keep an eye on the silly ass and see he's O.K."

"How do you suppose I'm going to do that?" demanded Bobby. "We can't go interfering with people. I'll report what you say to Colonel Glynne, especially as Miss Glynne's name has been mentioned. I don't suppose he'll be pleased."

Bobby wasn't pleased himself. It depended of course on what sort of person the Wychshire chief constable turned out to be. He might quite well be seriously annoyed, and a fair part of that annoyance might very possibly be turned upon Bobby. Not too auspicious a beginning, Bobby feared, and one that might even cost him his chance of this new appointment on which he had been building so many hopes. These vague hints pointing in the direction of the chief constable's neighbour and chairman of his Watch Committee, the mention of his own daughter's name, might well disturb him. Of course, he might refuse to take it seriously. Bobby hoped so. Gwen and Lord Henry were whispering together, and, having received instructions, Lord Henry said:—

"What we thought was you could send one of your chaps round—there's always a blue bottle buzzing about when you're motoring. You know. Lights or speeding or causing obstruction or one blessed thing on top of another, brakes perhaps. Well, there you are. Couldn't you let on it was something like that, and send a chap along, sort of nosing round?"

"Yes," said Bobby bitterly, "and have your friend writing to the *Times* about needless persecution of motorists and the Home Office asking for explanations. Thank you. I think not."

This seemed to depress them a good deal; and Lord Henry said it was jolly awkward; and Gwen apologized very prettily, and said it was all because they did feel so anxious and they both knew what a shame it was to have troubled Bobby so late at night. So Bobby said it was quite all right in a funereal tone of voice he hoped would make them both feel it was anything but all right, and then they departed. At first Bobby thought the car outside could not be theirs for he heard them walk away, the tap-tap of Gwen's high heels loud on the pavement in the stillness of the night. But then they came back and he guessed they had merely been walking up and down, talking and wondering what to do.

Soon he heard them drive off and he went up to bed to seek such sleep as he could hope for in the brief remaining hours of the night. Yet he could not, as he would have wished, dismiss what he had been told as mere fantasy or imagination. It was simple fact, with no trace of fantasy or imagination, that two young men of wealth and position, Andy White and Viscount Byatt, had died in strange circumstances strangely resemblant.

Now it seemed another young man, this Mr. Baird, was travelling by the same road, perhaps to the same destination? Even more disturbing did Bobby feel it that so much of this seemed vaguely connected with the places and the people where he was hoping to take up his new appointment.

Again that thought occurred to him which once before had flashed through his mind, that Colonel Glynne had not merely been requiring some pleasant and amiable and well-recommended young man to help him in the routine work of his office, but rather was seeking even desperately for help as he felt drawing closer about him strange forces of darkness and terror.

One of Bobby's greatest gifts, however, was a capacity to close his mind for a time, to shut up, as it were, his worries and his problems in a drawer by themselves. He liked to remember having read somewhere that Napoleon had once described his mind as resembling a series of drawers, so that he could shut up by themselves, or take out as desired, the different questions he had to consider and answer.

Besides he had enough to occupy him in getting what sleep he could, finishing his packing, getting himself and his bag to the station in time for the fast afternoon train. Not even in the train did he allow himself to open that compartment of his mind in which he had packed away last night's conversation. Arrived at Midwych he went to the hotel where he had booked a room, and then, according to plan, dressed and waited for the car which he had been promised would call to take him to Asbury Cottage, Colonel Glynne's home in the half village, half Midwych suburb, of

Asbury. There he was to dine, and, as the colonel put it, 'get acquainted', or, as Bobby expressed it in his mind, 'be vetted'. The more formal interview and provisional appointment, subject to the approval of the Watch Committee, was to take place the next morning.

Punctually at the time arranged the car arrived, driven by a tall, lean, thin-faced chauffeur, an uncommunicative and suspicious person, who admitted reluctantly that his name was Biddle, and that the car, privately owned by the colonel, had come to fetch Bobby. With some indignation he denied, when Bobby put the question, that he was a member of the police. Certainly, he agreed, there were police cars and police chauffeurs, and the colonel employed them on official work, but he never used them for private purposes, though often enough he did use his own car and his own petrol for what were really duty errands.

It took all Bobby's tact to get even this much out of the taciturn and somewhat sullen Biddle, and Bobby finally gave up all effort to make conversation with the depressing conviction in his mind that Biddle had already determined to be as hostile as he dared. He was evidently a very good driver, for once he took a risk that only a man sure of himself and his car would have run, and at another time he avoided by skill and cool judgment what might have been a nasty collision, with another car, for which the blame would have been entirely the other driver's, since he came out of a side turning at full speed and without warning.

"Good driving," Bobby said, "but that fellow ought to be reported."

"Copper's job, not mine," grunted Biddle, "don't believe in doing coppers' work for 'em. No good neither bringing in the guv's name." Then he added, "One blighted fool more or less on the road makes no difference."

Bobby did not attempt to dispute this dictum. They had passed, by now, through the Midwych main streets, and through the far-stretching suburbs, and had entered charming country, as lovely as is the English scenery at its peaceful best. Once he took an opportunity to ask the silent Biddle in which direction

Wychwood Forest lay, and was answered by a jerk of the thumb towards the north, and the brief comment:

"Over there—miles of it."

"Nice place for picnics and so on," remarked Bobby.

"For them as likes it," grunted Biddle, plainly not of the number.

They were passing a large house now, standing in what seemed extensive grounds, the entrance guarded by a lodge. Bobby asked who lived there and Biddle looked as if he didn't want to say. Bobby repeated the question with a touch of authority in his tone this time, and Biddle mumbled that it belonged to General Sir Harold Hannay. A little further on Biddle gave another proof of excellent driving, by neatly avoiding a cow that chose that moment to emerge from behind a tree, and then turned the car into a gravelled drive of which the entrance gate bore the name 'Asbury'.

The house was much smaller than the imposing residence of General Hannay they had just passed, the grounds much less extensive, but they were well kept and the house had a pleasant and attractive air. Bobby told himself Colonel Glynne was a lucky man, and he allowed his mind to play agreeably with the thought that one day perhaps, when he, too, was a chief constable, he and Olive might have a home like this.

His thoughts were busy enough, but his eyes were still alert and watchful as they swung round the circular drive and passed a gap in some flowering shrubs and trees through which they both saw plainly a girl and a young man facing each other. There was no mistaking their attitude. It was that of furious hostility. The young man had his hand raised. There was something in it and Bobby almost thought he was about to strike. The girl was crouched and tense, her attitude that of one about to spring. A threatening tableau, Bobby thought. Instinctively he raised himself in his seat. At the same instant Biddle jammed his foot hard on the accelerator. The car shot forward with such speed that it flew past the door of the house they had almost reached and plunged straight across a bed of mingled dahlias and chrysanthemums towards a small glass-house at a few yards distant. Biddle tried to swerve, swerved too much, the car overturned, Bobby found himself prone on another flower bed, his eyes, nose, mouth full of mould. He had a vision of a pair of gaitered legs raised in the air at a little distance. He recognized them as belonging to Biddle. He twisted round and sat up. Biddle resumed an upright position and stared in dismay at the ruined flower beds.

"The guv's dahlias gone west," he said aloud. "I'll get the bleeding sack."

Bobby, much annoyed at this concern for the dahlias, this indifference for his own safety, began to get to his feet. He saw an elderly man, red-faced, white-haired, come running out of the house. Biddle stood to attention and saluted. The newcomer looked at Bobby, now on his feet, and seemed reassured.

"Not hurt? no bones broken?" he said, and then very quietly to Biddle, "Drinking again, I suppose? Very well. You have been warned before. Pack up and then come to the study for your month's wages."

Biddle, standing very stiffly to attention, saluted and made no answer, no attempt to excuse himself, offered no plea for leniency. Colonel Glynne, as Bobby assumed him to be, turned to him again.

"I can't tell you how sorry I am," he said. "You must be shaken pretty badly. Come along to the house. It is Mr. Owen, of course? A bad beginning, I'm afraid, but lucky it's no worse."

## CHAPTER III
## INTERCESSION

Still full of apologies, Colonel Glynne escorted Bobby to the house where Bobby removed as far as he could the traces of his contact with the flower bed, of which, however, the soft earth had served very effectively to break his fall, so that, except for the effects of the slight shaking he had received, he felt none the worse. The scarf and light overcoat he had been wearing over his dinner jacket had suffered most, but the dry earth brushed off fairly well and his host brought him a choice of clean shirts and collars.

Unfortunately one of the two shirts offered him had too much in breadth and too little in length. Bobby guessed it belonged to the colonel, who was some six inches less in height than Bobby but fully a foot more in circumference. The second shirt seemed to be the property of someone about Bobby's own height but of much slighter build. The collar band would not meet round the neck just as the other overlapped by inches. Bobby decided he would have to be content with his own shirt and to put up with the stained and crumpled condition of it and of his collar.

He made his way downstairs and was met by the still apologetic colonel, who led him into a large, pleasant room, of which the french windows opened on the garden. Bobby thought the room was empty at first, and then a small, fair girl rose from the arm-chair in which she had been completely hidden.

"My daughter," the colonel explained. "Becky, this is Mr. Owen you've heard me speak about."

Becky Glynne acknowledged the introduction by a curt nod, an inaudible murmur, and a hostile stare. She was hardly a pretty girl, for her features were too irregular, but the prominent nose, the firm lines of the closely shut mouth above the square little chin, the direct look, all suggested considerable force of character. The eyes were a light clear blue with a certain depth of penetration in the steady gaze, and Bobby felt that they took in his crumpled shirt and stained collar with an air of having expected that sort of untidiness from the sort of person her father would go on inflicting on them. Her best feature was her hair, of a light, almost golden brown with a fascinating and obviously natural wave to it such as no hairdressing expert could ever have achieved. But the general expression was bitter, hostile, angry, and Bobby wondered whether this hostile attitude was particular towards himself or general to the world at large. Suddenly it dawned upon him that the arrangement of her hair had something odd about it, something not quite neat or becoming, and then he saw that on the left it had been hastily dragged down and forward to cover a freshly made bruise.

She saw where his quick glance rested, and if her expression had been hostile before, now it grew deadly. Unfortunately, too, her father noticed the change in her expression and noticed, as well, that she raised her hand to pull still further forward the lock of hair with which she had hoped to hide the hurt. The gesture made him look still more closely and he said at once:—

"What have you been doing to yourself, Becky? Had a blow?"

"It's nothing," she answered, "a tennis ball—caught a hot service full, too near the net, I suppose. It was an awful whack."

She turned as she spoke and began to move away, but before she did so she gave Bobby just one look—a look that suggested daggers and poisons and even more unpleasant things.

"Put my foot in it good and hard," he reflected ruefully; and tried to look unconscious as if he thought bruises from tennis balls the most natural, ordinary things in the world.

He noticed, too, that as she moved away she showed something of that light grace in movement and ease in action he had noticed also in Gwen Barton. It came, he supposed, from the tennis at which, apparently, both girls excelled. But the deepest impression his new chief's daughter made on him was of a strong, vigorous, angry personality of which it would be well to beware. Disconcerting in the extreme, he thought, for though he had known the colonel had a daughter—'one d. one s.,' was an item in the *Who's Who* paragraph—he had taken it for granted she would be the ordinary young woman, interested in her own affairs, concerned, no doubt, for her father, but entertaining for his subordinates only that vague, polite indifference a girl in her position would be likely to feel. But 'vague', 'polite', 'indifference', were not the words that came to the mind in thinking of Becky Glynne—especially not the second of the three—and indeed the colonel himself seemed slightly embarrassed by his daughter's behaviour.

"What will you take?" he asked, moving towards a small table on which various glasses and bottles were set out. "You'll need something after your spill." To Becky, or rather to her back, he explained, "We welcomed Mr. Owen by doing our best to kill him. Biddle drove right over my dahlia bed and overturned the car. Drinking again, I suppose. It's the last time. He might have killed Owen—and he's ruined the dahlias."

Becky was round in an instant, facing them both and looking more angry than ever. Those clear, penetrating eyes of hers glared at Bobby with an expression that told she considered it was entirely his fault and she wouldn't forget it. To her father she said:—

"Biddle? drinking? it's not true, I'm sure he wouldn't. What happened?"

"What I told you—" the colonel began and she interrupted him rudely.

"I'll ask Biddle," she said, and disappeared through the open french window.

"Biddle's a favourite with Becky," the colonel explained as he proceeded to pour out the glass of sherry Bobby had asked for. "I've told her before he would have to go if he started drinking again. She'll be upset. He is a good driver as a rule."

"If I may say so, sir," Bobby said, "he struck me as an unusually good driver. But for the way he handled the car we might easily have had a collision with a fool who charged out of a side turning without warning. I'm pretty sure he hasn't been drinking at all."

The colonel grunted.

"What did it then if it wasn't drink?" he asked. "Sane and sober, no one would drive like that. He might easily have killed you. It's a mercy there are no bones broken. My dahlias—"

He left the sentence unfinished and took refuge in a drink, and Bobby was aware of a faint suspicion that the colonel was more distressed over the fate of his dahlias than over the risk to which his visitor had been exposed. Tactfully but not altogether truthfully, Bobby said:

"I noticed those dahlias even while I was doing my double summersault."

"They made a fine show, didn't they?" agreed the colonel sadly. "Ruined now. I expected another first prize this time. Washed out. Hannay will be as pleased as punch, confound him."

Bobby went on:—

"I think what really happened was that as we came up the drive here we passed two people. They were some distance away, but we had a clear view of them through a gap in some flowering trees on the left of the drive. I think Biddle didn't want me to see them, and accelerated quickly to get by as fast as he could, and he overdid it."

The colonel listened gloomily. Then he said:—

"Why shouldn't he want you to see them? I suppose you mean one was Becky?"

"I only had the merest glimpse," Bobby answered. "Biddle accelerated all right."

The colonel made no comment. He was evidently quick in understanding, for he had realized at once the meaning of what Bobby said and the significance of his failure to deny that it was Miss Glynne he had seen. The silence continued. Bobby had nothing to say and the colonel was deep in thought, not pleasant thought either to judge from his expression. A tall, slim youth came into sight, crossing the lawn in an oblique direction towards the rear of the house. He bore a strong resemblance to Becky but was much better looking; his features more regular and better shaped; his hair, where hers had been a light golden brown, almost of a pure gold tint and with the same fascinating wave to it; his eyes, though they lacked that clear fire of penetration hers had seemed to show, large, soft and luminous, with long, silky lashes. A young Apollo, he looked, as he came with long strides across the lawn, and yet with little about him of that air of strength and dark resolve his sister showed, even though his expression at the moment was fully as hostile and angry. From the window the colonel called to him:—

"Len, have you and Becky been quarrelling again?" The young man halted and looked angrily at his father. "I'll lay her out for good one of these days," he said. "I'll not stand that tongue of hers. Let her mind her own blasted business. I'm fed up, her and her dirt." He walked on. He had not seen Bobby or probably he would have spoken less freely. The colonel turned round and seated himself. Bobby was absorbed in his sherry. One would have thought his glass of sherry was an object of such interest as never before had the world presented to him. There was silence for a moment or two. The colonel said abruptly:—

"I suppose Biddle was trying to hide our family skeleton."

"I'm sorry, sir," muttered Bobby, more embarrassed than ever, and he wondered what demon of bad luck was presiding over the beginnings of this new appointment from which at first he had hoped so much but that now he felt was going to turn out a complete fiasco. Most likely Colonel Glynne was already considering how best to get rid of him. He would have to go back to the Yard with his tail between his legs and of course every one would always for ever inevitably believe that he had failed to show he possessed the qualifications needed for a responsible post. More sensible, he supposed, to have held his tongue about the little family scene of which he had been the unlucky witness. But that would hardly have been fair to Biddle, who had plainly been trying to be loyal to his employers, and again, if he was to act as confidential assistant to his chief, he mustn't start by keeping things hidden from him. The colonel said:—

"The tennis ball was a lie. Len did it."

Bobby felt more awkward still. He supposed he might as well go back to London at once. The colonel went on:— "You may as well know the whole story, Owen. It's no secret, and anyhow you would have heard all about it before you had been here a month. Len used to be in the R.A.F. Becky met one of the other men in Len's flight—Cadman, his name was, Charley Cadman. They fell in love rather violently. They got engaged. Len didn't like it. He never said why. He and Becky quarrelled—badly. He told her he wasn't going to allow her to marry Cadman. She asked him how he thought he was going to stop it. He told her to wait and see. A week later Cadman crashed. He was killed. At the inquiry it was proved that the machine wasn't in a fit condition for use, that Len ought to have known it, and ought to have stopped Cadman. He was found guilty of neglect of duty, made worse by proof that he was the worse for drink at the time. He was allowed to resign. Now he has taken up commercial flying. He doesn't do much. He doesn't seem to want to. The accident has warped both their lives."

Bobby made no comment. There was none he could make. A tragic story, he thought, and he felt he could do nothing but receive it in silence. He wondered why the colonel had told it in such detail, but supposed he knew that, as he had said, Bobby would be sure to hear the tale sooner or later and so had thought it best to give him the truth. Bobby wondered, too, if it was the truth, or rather, all the truth, since all the truth even the colonel himself might not know. Anyhow the violent antagonism between brother and sister was explained, as also Biddle's attempt to keep all knowledge of it from the visitor.

"Thank you," said the colonel suddenly, and Bobby, at first surprised, understood he was being thanked for the silence he had preserved.

It continued for a moment or two and then Becky came back into the room, small, swift, and angry. She said:

"I've been to Biddle. He's packing. I told him not to. He's not been drinking. If any one told you he had, it's a lie." This last sentence was accompanied by a fierce look at Bobby that was quite plainly an accusation. "Biddle won't say a word, but he's no more been drinking than I have," she asserted.

"He upset the car," the colonel said, "and nearly killed Owen. But Owen tells me Biddle struck him as a very good driver and he doesn't think it was drink, whatever else it was, made Biddle play the fool the way he did. You can tell Biddle he won't hear anything more about it and he can thank Mr. Owen for that."

The girl turned again her angry, unplacated eyes on Bobby. They said as plainly as possible: 'What's the game? Trying to suck up? ' Without a word of acknowledgment she went away. The colonel remained silent. Bobby continued to interest himself in his sherry. He wondered again if he had better offer to take the next train back to London. He asked himself even if it would not be wiser to do so, for certainly it did not look as though things were going to be easy here. The colonel got up and with a muttered apology left the room. Bobby, now alone, sat down, and felt depressed. A sound of footsteps approaching from without made him look round. There came to the open window a tall, striking-looking woman, one who could almost have been called beautiful, though even Bobby's untrained masculine eye could tell that some of that beauty was due to a careful and a skilful art. Still the classic regularity of the features, the perfect oval of the face, the graceful bearing, were all nature's gift; though possibly the exquisite complexion, the pencilled eyebrows, the long, curling lashes, even the soft lustre of the large, dark blue eyes, might all have received a certain encouragement. In any case the effect, combined with an exquisitely thought out toilet most admirably expressive of the innocence and peace of the country—it made you think of nymphs and milkmaids though somehow of Bond Street and Piccadilly, too—was sufficiently striking to bring a somewhat dazzled Bobby to his feet at once.

In a voice less pleasing, for it was a little harsh, even coarse in its undertones, this vision said:—

"Oh, I beg your pardon. I came across before the others. I walked through the shrubbery and round by the rosery. I thought Len was here. Or Colonel Glynne?"

"Colonel Glynne was here just now, I expect he'll be back in a moment," Bobby answered, slightly confused. "You are Lady May Grayson?"

She gave him a smile, a dazzling smile, showing lovely teeth, but all the same Bobby thought it would have been more dazzling still had it not been so plainly mechanical, taken from stock, as it were, and swiftly returned for future use as required.

"A society beauty," he told himself, "only that and nothing more. If you pricked her, she would bleed cocktails and small talk."

"Now, I wonder how you know who I am?" she said, obviously expecting the obvious reply Bobby promptly made.

"Every one knows Lady May Grayson," he answered. "There was the portrait in the last Academy for instance."

"And those perfectly, too utterly awful things they put in the papers," she sighed, "and you can't stop them either." She lifted long, white, slender, perfectly manicured hands as she spoke, and Bobby was a little startled to see how there shone and glittered on the middle finger of her right hand a diamond that seemed almost as big as a pea, and that gave out a peculiar soft bluish brilliance. It reminded Bobby of what he had heard of the famous Blue John stone, recently withdrawn from public auction as the reserve price of £3,000 had not been reached.

An angry, impatient voice shouted from a distance:— "Hi, May, is that you? I'm over here."

"That's Len," Lady May said, and with another mechanically dazzling smile mechanically designed to complete Bobby's capture, Lady May hurried away.

Bobby, watching her go, found himself remembering that story Lady May had so hotly denied of Andy White's present to her of an extremely valuable diamond necklace. But at any rate Andy White could not have given her the famous Blue John diamond, since the auction sale had been subsequent to his still unexplained death.

"Most likely it wasn't the Blue John at all," he told himself, "though it looked pretty valuable," and he remembered, too, that Lady May was generally supposed to have so little money—her father, the Earl of Merefield, being one of the fraternity of the hard up peers—that she could only afford to go about as she did because she got her frocks free on condition of telling all her friends who dressed her; her gloves and stockings free because she allowed it to be known what brands she wore; her dinners free on condition of allowing paragraphs to appear saying what restaurant she patronized; her car as a reward for being photographed by its side. As for cigarettes, she not only got them free but as much as many a man earned in a year besides for simply allowing it to be known that if she did offer you a cigarette in the unlikely event of your meeting her, then it would be one of such and such a make.

Great are the uses of advertisement, Bobby reflected, and found himself oddly worried by the thought of that softly-shining diamond on her lifted hand.

## CHAPTER IV
## CONSULTATION

Colonel Glynne came back into the room. Accompanying him was a tall, grey-haired man, with a thin, intellectual face; a shy, retiring manner; mild, blinking blue eyes. One could have taken him for an Oxford professor who had never known a danger more deadly than that of making some slip in a learned article and so exposing himself to equally learned criticism. In fact he was, as Bobby learned to his surprise, General Sir Harold Hannay, with the right to tag most of the alphabet to his name. He had the reputation of being the cleverest man in the army—it was said he read Professor Whitehead for recreation and had discussed on equal terms mathematical problems with the gentleman who does not wish to be known as Lord Russell. He had, too, to his credit a series of reckless exploits in the last war, on the North-West frontier, in various other quarters of the globe, and yet in independent command he had not always been a success. Apparently he lacked that fierce, untiring energy of will great commanders need, and he was also always more willing to risk his own life than the lives of others. Bobby regarded him with a good deal of awe, and was reduced to speechless embarrassment when he found the general appearing to regard it as a high privilege to meet a young man of such promise and achievement as he knew Bobby to be.

With him was his daughter, Hazel Hannay, in many ways an odd contrast to her father. Where he was fair, tall, and lean, she was tall, dark, bigly made, with dead black hair, and, beneath heavy, strongly marked brows, dark, passionate eyes whose glance seemed to engulf and absorb all it rested on. Nor was there much that was shy or retiring in her manner, or in the heavy, questioning, somewhat haughty gaze she directed full upon Bobby. In her dress she seemed more inclined to bright and contrasting colours than is usual and a jacket she wore of glittering gold sequins had a striking effect. Bobby noticed also that in her movements she showed much of that grace and ease he had observed both in Becky Glynne and in Gwen Barton and that he supposed they learned from playing tennis.

There was a little small talk. The general refused the sherry his host offered him, but Hazel accepted a cocktail and drank it eagerly. Bobby thought her manner strained and uneasy, and he began to think, too, that in the way in which she still looked at him, there was something not only questioning but both doubtful and defiant, as though she were asking herself whether he were friend or foe. He was conscious of an impression that with her it had to be very completely either one or the other, and that where she gave either her love or her hate she gave it wholeheartedly. He remembered having heard that her mother was a Spaniard, so possibly it was from her she had inherited her hair that seemed like night itself, those dark and passionate eyes under their heavy brows, that intense manner as of bubbling fires beneath. Bobby felt he could understand better now he had seen her the references tennis commentators often made to the fierce intensity of her play, and their criticism that until she learned not to throw all she had into her first games, keeping nothing in reserve, she would never win the championship.

But then, Bobby reflected, if she ceased to give her all at once, if she thought about guarding reserves, she would cease to be herself, and those who cease to be themselves lose far more than they gain. He reflected, too, how entirely and utterly different were these four types of modern girlhood he had met in the last twenty-four hours—Lady May, the society beauty; Becky Glynne, bitter and frustrated; Hazel Hannay, dark and passionate, caring evidently very little for the conventions; Gwen Barton, something of an enigma with her apparent insignificance, her devotion to her lover, the odd fascination of her own to which that lover had so plainly and so utterly succumbed.

Dinner was announced and they went in. Len Glynne and Lady May were already in the room and Becky Glynne appeared just as her father was asking where she was. She and her brother exchanged scowls, and Bobby would hardly have been surprised to see them start throwing the plates and knives at each other's heads. Bobby found himself seated between the general and Lady May, who was next to their host and opposite Len Glynne. The general, noticing that Len had his thumb bandaged, blinked at it mildly and asked how it had happened, with much such an air of concern as a maiden aunt might show over a small boy's damaged knee. Len answered loudly that he had been bitten by a vicious cat. Bobby, busy with his soup, saw how Becky went first red and then white with rage, and the general seemed quite distressed and said that was bad, because a cat's bite was often infectious and might lead to blood poisoning. Len answered that he knew that, that it was because cats were fond of raking dirt over, and therefore he had been very careful to have the bite carefully disinfected. Becky said nothing and appeared to take no notice, but Bobby was very certain that it was all she could do to control the pale fury her features showed. He noticed that she did not finish her soup but put down her spoon and hid her hands under the table, and he knew this was because she could not master their trembling and did not wish it to be noticed.

"Looks like bad trouble brewing," Bobby told himself uncomfortably; "and what's more, their father knows it. A nice hornet's nest I've got myself pushed into."

In fact the only two at the table who seemed unaware of the feeling between brother and sister were the mild- mannered general, whose short-sighted eyes appeared to notice so little, and Lady May, who had not, Bobby thought, much of that quick and ready intelligence and alertness of mind most of the others seemed to possess. At any rate she remained quite placid, showed considerable interest in her food, now and again gave a gentle smile round the table, and occasionally lapsed into contemplation of her ring. Half way through the meal Colonel Glynne made some comment on it, and Lady May held up her hand for all to admire.

"Isn't it marvellous?" she said. "I daren't tell you how much I gave for it, only it was less than half what it cost because it's such a perfect model. It's an exact reproduction of the Blue John diamond they couldn't sell the other day. No one offered the reserve. Highams made it to show at the Paris Fine Arts Exhibition because they didn't want to risk sending the real thing."

"It looks awfully genuine," said Becky, speaking almost for the first time, and Bobby thought so, too, and shared the doubt Becky had made little effort to keep from her voice.

"I had to give nearly all I'm getting for being photographed holding a glass of Neo-champagne (British make)," Lady May explained. "Isn't it awful? Neo-champagne, I mean. I don't know how people can. But they write marvellous cheques."

"I wish you wouldn't do that sort of thing," growled Len.

"Why not, darling?" inquired Lady May, to whom all the world was darling. "If people are such sillies and drink the awful stuff because they think I do, I think it serves them right. Don't you, Mr. Owen?"

Bobby, thus suddenly appealed to, choked and stammered out something to the effect that it was only natural for all to follow where Lady May Grayson led, which earned him, from Lady May, one of those famous smiles, of which it has been so rudely said that she always kept them on tap; from Len, a formidable scowl; and a strong mental impression of his own that every one else thought it awful cheek for him to have said anything at all. Fortunately Becky relieved his embarrassment by remarking that most people would have thought it was the genuine Blue John, but no doubt Len, as an expert, would have been able to tell at once it was only a sham.

"I'm not an expert," growled Len very angrily.

"You spotted old Lady Train was wearing artificial pearls anyhow," Becky pointed out. "Cost you an invite to the Train shoot, too," she added, not without satisfaction.

"Any fool could see those pearls were Woolworth's," snarled Len, with whom the loss of the Train invitation was evidently a sore point. "And any fool could see that isn't the genuine Blue John—the tint is far too pronounced. You don't get the delicate colouring of the real thing."

Len might not be an expert but he certainly spoke with authority, Bobby thought. After that the dinner, much to Bobby's relief, passed without further incident. The meal finished, they went into the drawing-room where Sir Harold Hannay, who had a passion for bridge, Lady May, who by some odd freak of nature possessed what is called 'card sense', and the two young Glynnes sat down to cards. Hazel went to the piano and played there softly and contentedly, choosing, as Bobby noticed with surprise, exactly those sugary, sentimental tunes he would have expected to possess for her small attraction. Having seen his guests comfortably settled, the colonel took Bobby into his study, a large room with two big writing tables, a card index cabinet, a big safe, a book-case containing many law books, easy chairs and so on. On the whole a comfortable though somewhat severe and official-looking apartment.

"I get through some of my work here," the colonel explained, producing cigars and a box of cigarettes. "You understand card indexing?"

"I've never had to keep one, sir," Bobby answered, "but I know how important they are. I've heard it said that card indexing is to organization what newspapers are to publicity."

"Well, there's something in that," the colonel agreed.

He lapsed into silence and for a little they sat and smoked, the colonel with his cigar, Bobby with the cigarette he had preferred. Then Bobby said:—

"I think there's something, sir, I ought to mention. Lord Henry Darmoor—his father is Lord Whitfield—came to my rooms in London last night, rather late. I had never met him before but I knew his name from seeing it in the papers—he is a well known sportsman; polo, I think. He brought a Miss Gwen Barton with him. He said they were engaged."

Bobby went on to describe briefly the interview. Colonel Glynne made no comment, never interrupted, sat so still, his eyes half closed, his neglected cigar smouldering on the table near, one might have thought he was not listening, but for the hard pressure of his clasped hands upon each other, so that the knuckles showed white; but for the air of tension that somehow his humped-up figure in the big arm-chair seemed to show. When Bobby finished he sat for a time in the same silence and immobility, almost as .if he did not even know that Bobby had ceased to speak, and then he got slowly to his feet and went out of the room, coming back in a moment or two with Sir Harold Hannay.

"Might have been a slam," the old general sighed, blinking mildly around, "if partner had played up. Probably she wouldn't. Becky's not as good at bridge as she is at tennis, Glynne."

He settled himself comfortably in a chair, refused a cigar the colonel offered him, remarked that he had already smoked his day's ration, except for the one cigarette he reserved for the last thing before bed, took out a pair of spectacles and fixed them on his long, thin nose. Colonel Glynne said to Bobby:—

"I think you know General Hannay is chairman of the Watch Committee. I consulted him when your appointment was first suggested. I believe Sir Harold intends to recommend its confirmation at the next meeting. Of course, your appointment is outside ordinary routine."

"Good record," said the general. He took off his spectacles, looked at them with distaste, and replaced them. "We all come to it," he sighed. "Lady Markham pressed it. Your father, Lord Hirlpool, isn't he? I don't think I ever met him."

"Not my father, sir," said Bobby uncomfortably. He knew that to admit any relationship meant that he became instantly open to an accusation of snobbishness, that he at once exposed himself to a suspicion of nepotism, in fact that he would have to suffer all those disadvantages aristocratic birth imposes when there is no cash to support it, since, curiously enough, no blood is blue for long unless its hue is sustained by the yellow glint of gold. All the same, the connection was there and had to be acknowledged. "My uncle," he explained.

"Good birth," said the general approvingly. "Nothing in it," he added, sternly now. "My family's got a pedigree goes back to the Conqueror. Faked, of course. None of us ever done a thing except nose out good land and buy it up cheap."

"I want you," the colonel interposed, speaking to Bobby, "to tell Sir Harold what you have just told me."

Bobby repeated his story, as nearly as possible in the same words that he had used before. Both men listened closely. Bobby had the impression that every least word he uttered was to them full of a dark and horrid threat. Neither of them moved or spoke, moved not a finger, breathed not a syllable. The room was brightly lit. There was the ceiling light, a floor lamp, a table lamp. Yet Bobby had the impression, though he knew it was only fancy, that as he talked a darkness crept about them, that his slow speech, for he spoke deliberately and with care, called up strange powers of evil that lurked in the darkness of the night without, that hid in the corners of the room, menacing and mocking. As he finished, the clock on the mantelpiece struck the hour, and Bobby heard the clear, silver chimes as though they were the muffled drums of doom. To his astonishment he found that he was trembling slightly. Colonel Glynne remained motionless, immobile in the frozen tension of his attitude. General Hannay took out a handkerchief and wiped his forehead and his wrists. They had been damp with perspiration. He said, or rather whispered:—

"I think I'm afraid."

Neither Bobby nor the colonel answered. General Hannay said again:—

"Done anything to your clock, Glynne?"

"No. Why?" answered the colonel, surprised.

"Nothing. There's a tale in our family that when we are threatened with death or disgrace, we hear muffled drums, the drums the General Hannay of that time had played when he shot a number of prisoners after Sedgmoor."

"What's the connection with my clock?" Glynne asked. "Nothing," the other answered. Then he said abruptly:—"Nice ring that of May Grayson's. You remember? She showed us. You saw it, Owen?"

"Yes, sir," said Bobby.

"Imitation, she told us," mused the general. "Jolly good I thought." '

"Yes, sir," said Bobby again, as the other was looking full at him.

"Shouldn't have thought it artificial, the way it sparkled," the general insisted. "Would you?"

"No, sir," said Bobby.

"No business of ours you mean, eh?" observed the general. "Quite right. It isn't." He turned to the colonel. Both men seemed more normal now. General Hannay was polishing his spectacles and blinking around like a benevolent grandparent, approving the younger generation. Colonel Glynne had helped himself to another cigar, his first having gone out and one of his pet beliefs being that a relighted cigar is unsmokable. The general went on:—"Better come clean, Glynne, as they say on the films. I like films," he added thoughtfully; "the sillier they are and the worse they are, the more I like 'em. Only they are never so silly or so bad as life. Carry on, Glynne."

The colonel seemed to have some difficulty in beginning. He said to Bobby:—

"Very likely you've guessed by now I felt I wanted help .I had a feeling—" He paused without completing the sentence or explaining what the feeling was. Then he said:— "Mr. Owen, I shall think none the worse of you if you consider you've been brought here on false pretences, that the job isn't what you expected, if you decline to have anything more to do with it—or us. I will let London know I fully understand and that you are entirely justified in refusing an appointment of which the conditions were wholly different from those you had been led to expect."

"What conditions do you mean, sir?" Bobby asked.

Neither of them answered him. They looked at each other. General Hannay replaced his spectacles on his nose. He said in the mildest, most commonplace tone imaginable:—

"The powers of hell have broken loose and they are all about us."

"Yes, sir," said Bobby.

The colonel said again:—

"I shall think none the worse of you if you say you will take the first train back to town to-morrow morning."

"I might think the worse of myself, sir," said Bobby.

"Good lad," said the general.

"Thank you," said the colonel; though whether he spoke to Bobby or to Sir Harold, Bobby was not sure. "Well, then, to begin with, you can take what Darmoor told you as being pretty accurate. What he said is mostly what I meant to tell you myself."

"Byatt was a nice lad," General Hannay said. "I heard in a roundabout way that he was attracted by Hazel. They were about together a good deal. No objection on my side. He had a title, money, position. I liked what I saw of him. I dropped a hint to Hazel that I rather fancied myself as a grandpapa. Hazel only laughed. Said Byatt bored her stiff. It was fun at first, she said, but she was fed up and she was going to choke him off. Afterwards stories got about that he had committed suicide for Hazel's sake, and there was more talk when it came out that the famous Byatt sapphires were missing and there was only a paste duplicate at the bank. It had been made years before for Byatt's mother when she wanted to show off a bit but not to have the risk and worry of wearing the real things. It's a common dodge, of course. You had better know, too, that Byatt called at Higham's—the big Bond Street jeweller—with the genuine sapphires and wanted to know their present- day value. A lady was with him. He addressed her as Hazel. He referred to her as Miss Hannay. Higham's can give no satisfactory description of her. Probably they don't want to. They say they didn't notice her much, no reason why they should. It was the sapphires interested them and she was muffled up in a big fur coat with the collar turned up. She wore a veil, too. Sometimes the ladies—men, too—who go to Higham's don't want to be recognized, and Higham's aren't very keen on recognizing them, either. Saves trouble and better for business if they can say they don't know. By the way, the fur coat was good Persian lamb. Hazel has one. Hazel was never at Higham's or anywhere else with Byatt alone. I believe that because she says so and she's my daughter and I believe her. I have no proof to show you or any one else. Well?"

"I don't think I can make any useful comment, sir," Bobby answered, even though he well understood what a depth of emotion lay beneath the old man's calm and level tones.

"There was nothing we could do," the general continued. "We knew gossip was going on, but legal action would only have spread it further even if there had been anything we could get hold of. I suppose," he added, blinking at Bobby, "you're thinking of alibis and clues and all that."

"You've suggested some useful clues, sir," Bobby answered. "I don't see where they lead. I don't see at the moment what to do. I'll try to get a full report of the inquest. It's not like being on the spot. The evidence and the witness are very different. Truth and lies look the same on paper, not in the eyes or on the face. Of course, identity is always important—I mean, establishing time and place."

"Place is known all right but not the time—dead two or three weeks the doctors said, and that seemed as near as they could get," the general told him. "Hazel is always rushing about from one tennis tournament to another. She was playing at Bath about that time. People don't forget that."

"The place where Lord Byatt's body was found may be known, but it doesn't follow necessarily that the death took place there," Bobby pointed out. "Probably it did but it might not. Miss Hannay is friendly with Lady May Grayson?"

"They were at school together."

"Lord Henry Darmoor said that Mr. Andy White paid marked attentions to Lady May, that he was last seen in her company, that a girl is known to have visited the cottage he rented in Wales. She is said to have arrived on a motor-bicycle. Can I take that as accurate?"

"Yes," said Colonel Glynne. "I made inquiries. Lady May has a motor-cycle she uses sometimes. It was given her by the manufacturers. She made excursions on it, got photographed at hotel doors and no bills to pay, published articles on week-end trips into the country someone else wrote and she signed."

"Times change," said the general. "In my young days, that sort of thing would have shocked people out of their lives. Now they think it smart. Hazel does. I suppose I'm old-fashioned. I don't like making money out of your social position. Hazel laughs. Men always did, she says, guinea pig directors and so on, so why shouldn't girls?"

"According to Lord Henry," Bobby went on, "Mr. White bought an extremely valuable diamond necklace shortly before his death. Nothing is known as to what became of it. Can you tell me if that is generally known or talked about?"

"Not that I know of," Sir Harold answered. "Do you, Glynne?"

The colonel shook his head and before all three of them rose a vision of Lady May's white and slender hand, on the middle finger a gem it was not easy to believe was only artificial.

The colonel said:—

"There's a Count Louis de Legett, well-to-do young fellow well known in London. It's a Holy Roman Empire title. The family say it was given an ancestor of theirs during the war of the Spanish Succession and that George I gave them permission to use it."

He paused as if reluctant to continue. General Hannay said:—

"He's been running after Hazel. She was rather taken with him at first. Then she got the idea that he only wanted to flirt, and she turned him down. Apparently he is still trying to hang on. Apparently he has mentioned Hazel's name, told someone in confidence at the club he would marry her or no one. Hazel sticks to it he wasn't serious. It seems he talked about buying the Blue John diamond when it was put up at Christie's. Apparently that didn't come off."

"Is it known," asked Bobby, and his voice was heavy and troubled, "who did in fact buy the Blue John?"

"It was disposed of by private negotiation," answered the colonel. 'We have no grounds for making closer inquiry."

"No," agreed Bobby. "Is anything known about Count de Legett being fond of lonely cottages or long lonely motor rides or solitary trips in caravans?"

Both men shook their heads. Colonel Glynne said:—

"You are thinking of the Mr. Baird Darmoor spoke about. I have never met him, but Becky has done so several times at tennis tournaments and at friends'. She told me she had the idea he was following her about. She said she was deliberately rude to him once or twice but it made no difference. A few days ago he met her in Long Dene—that's a little place near the outskirts of Wychwood Forest. Becky goes to see her Aunt Agnes—my sister-in- law. Becky got the idea that Baird was there on purpose, that he knew about her coming and was waiting for her. He told her he was caravanning in the forest. He was odd in his behaviour—nervous. He asked her to have lunch with him. She refused, and went off. She thought it rather cheek. Once or twice he has sent her flowers or chocolates after tennis matches when she's come out on top. Now you say that according to Darmoor he is buying valuable jewellery and telling people he is in love with an unnamed girl."

"It's like poison gas, impalpable, invisible, deadly," Sir Harold broke out. "What can you do?"

"I think the first thing," Bobby said slowly, "is to get in touch with this Mr. Baird. One could judge better after having had a talk with him."

The telephone rang. Colonel Glynne answered it. He listened for a time. The message seemed a long one. Presently he put the receiver down and turned to them.

"That was a report from the inspector on duty," he said. "A badly burnt-out caravan has been found in Wychwood Forest with a dead body inside it. Nothing to identify the body but it is known that a gentleman from London had a caravan thereabouts and had given his name as Baird."

## CHAPTER V
## MURDER?

When he had said this Colonel Glynne lifted the receiver again.

"Carry on," he said unemotionally. "I'll be with you as soon as possible." He touched the bell. To Bobby he said:—

"You are taking it on? Good. Get your hat and coat." A maid appeared. To her he said:— "Biddle having his supper? Tell him to get the big car round at once. Tell him, urgent. Quick as you can." To Hannay he said:— "Will you tell the others?"

Hannay nodded and followed Bobby into the hall. Bobby went across to the small cloakroom where he had seen his hat and coat deposited. When he came out again the general was still there, his hand on the knob of the drawing-room door, and Bobby had the impression that he was afraid, that he dared not enter, that some dark, unknown terror held him in its grip. Bobby began to put on his coat. The general looked at him, and very plainly did Bobby see the fear in his eyes, those eyes that in other days had watched death draw near and been unafraid. He saw how Bobby was looking at him. With an effort he drew himself together, flung open the door and marched in rather than entered. So, Bobby thought, he might have looked and walked had he gone to offer to a triumphant enemy a shameful surrender. Colonel Glynne came from the study, crossed to the small cloakroom, came out again with his hat and coat. He nodded to Bobby to follow him. They stood outside, waiting for the car. The front door the colonel had been careful to close, opened. Becky came out. She said:—

"Why is General Hannay afraid?"

Colonel Glynne did not answer directly. He said:—

"They've rung me up from the office. I've got to get along."

"What has happened?" Becky said again. "Why does General Hannay look like that?"

The arrival of the car gave her father an excuse for not answering. To her he said:— "Go back indoors, it's cold." To Bobby he said:— "Jump in," and to Biddle:— "Fast as you like."

Becky said:—

"You're frightened, too."

Then to Bobby's astonishment she laughed; if, at least, so harsh and bitter, even cruel a sound can be called by the kindly name of laughter. The colonel, as he was taking his place in the car, looked over his shoulder and said:—

"Don't let any one wait up for me."

Biddle started the car. The light of the headlamps fell full on the girl as she stood there, heedless of her father's injunction to go back indoors, her light, yellowish hair making in the bright rays of the car lamps a kind of halo about her small and angry face. Bobby did not soon forget the impression she made as she stood there, the tragic intensity of her pose, the stamp of despair upon her features. As a lost soul turned from the closed door of Paradise she stood without her father's house and he saw her lift her arms in a gesture he did not understand but that had in it something of a wild abandonment. Then the light of the car lamps swung on and again the darkness took her.

"Does she know what's scaring her father and Hannay?" Bobby asked himself. "Is it frightening her, too?"

Biddle was obeying to the full the colonel's order to drive fast. At a reckless speed they swung along and, as Bobby guessed, by side roads that avoided traffic controls. They came into Midwych, the suburbs, first. At cross roads they had to wait a moment or two. Near by was a large public-house. At the door a woman was singing. One or two of those passing in or out gave her money. Bobby, deep in his own thoughts, would hardly have noticed a sight so common, so much too common, had he not happened to catch a word or two and recognized a modern version of Gruffudd ap Maredudd's famous lament for the death of Gwenhwyvar of Anglesey. Bobby's acquaintance with Welsh was small, merely the few words and phrases an old nurse had taught him, but he knew enough to recognize both the language and the song. An odd incident, he thought idly, and an odd choice of a song outside a public-house door in the English midlands. The car moved on and soon Biddle drew up. The colonel got out, telling Bobby to wait. He came back presently with a uniform man, a sergeant, who took his place beside Biddle. The colonel got in, too. The car started. The colonel said:—

"They've done as much as they can. Inspector Morris is on duty. He is on the spot. Sergeant Rich knows where it is and he'll take us there. Morris rang up the superintendent—Oxley his name is. I expect he'll be there before us."

The colonel took out a cigar, relapsed into silence. Bobby asked no questions. He wondered if it was only fancy that made him feel his companion's uneasiness was increasing, increasing in proportion as they drew nearer the scene of the fire. Was he dreading what they might find there? To Bobby it seemed that the whole interior of the car throbbed, as it were, with wave upon wave of anguished terror. He stole a look at the colonel's face, calm enough to all appearance; indeed, Bobby thought, almost unnaturally so with a calmness that gave an impression of fierce and intense effort.

"He'll see it through, whatever it is," Bobby told himself; and in his thoughts used the French phrase 'jusqu'au bout,' telling himself again that what that end might show itself to be, would make no difference.

The car left behind the lights of the town, of the suburbs. It was travelling through complete darkness now, along unlighted country roads, and yet at a high rate of speed. There were no stars visible, the moon had not yet risen, the clouds hung low and heavy, letting escape now and again a splutter of rain. The only light came from the headlamps, throwing their powerful beams before as the great car crashed through the still darkness of the night. Presently the car left the smooth and well made road which hitherto it had followed and began to swing and lurch on a rougher track. Its speed did not diminish. The lamps picked out great trees that stood on each side, crowding in on them, bending above them, stretching down their branches as if to clutch at them as they sped by. The colonel muttered suddenly:—

"This damn cigar won't draw."

Bobby thought it might be more tactful not to point out that this was because the cigar had never been lighted. The remark had not been addressed to him and he need not have heard it. The colonel said in a surprised tone:—

"Oh, I never lighted it."

He put it back in his case. A specially severe jolt nearly threw them into each other's arms. Bobby could hear the sergeant appealing under his breath to his Maker. They had left even the rough track they had been following before and now were bumping over what seemed merely a footpath. Colonel Glynne leaned forward and said gently:—

"I don't want a spill, Biddle, but if you can go faster, do so."

"Very good, sir," said Biddle, and charged and smashed down a young tree in quite the best manner of the tank corps.

Bobby held firmly to his seat and hoped for the best, little as he expected it. Sergeant Rich's appeal for the protection of heaven grew more audible. The car, probably thinking it had been entered for a hurdle race, did its best to show what it could do in that way. In a voice full of relief, Rich said:—

"There we are, over there, look. Steady on, mate, we're nearly there."

Biddle's response was to accelerate. His headlamps had shown him a comparatively open stretch of ground. He charged straight across it; hitting, Bobby was convinced, every stone, every tree stump, every hole or mound that existed in the whole world. Nevertheless, everything held, not a single spring broke. A tremendous tribute to the workmanship put into the car.

They drew up. The colonel jumped out. Bobby followed, rubbing the back of his head where it had come more than once in contact with the hardest part of the car's roof. Sergeant Rich said very fervently:—

"Thank God."

Biddle was looking at his tyres. He said proudly:—

"Not a sign of a puncture."

Before them, at a little distance, was a kind of bay, or inlet, in the forest, surrounded on three sides by trees. It lay low and seemed damp. An odd place, Bobby thought, to choose for camping, especially so late in the season, and even though the caravan, from Lord Henry Darmoor's description, was apparently of an expensive type and presumably fitted with every possible comfort. Two or three cars were standing near, the rays from their lamps converging on the centre of the glade, so that it was like an island of light in the midst of that enormous sea of darkness, darkness intense and primaeval as in the days of long ago. The lamp rays were focused on a dark, shapeless mass that lay crumbled there. Men were moving to and fro around it. Near one of the cars lay on a stretcher, covered by a rug, something that had no longer human form, but that Bobby knew instinctively had once been the habitation of a living soul. Even those busy in this far and silent glade, going about their various errands, occupied with their different duties, lessened their haste as they passed near. Two men, separating from the others, came across to meet the colonel. He greeted them as Mr. Oxley and Inspector Morris. He introduced Bobby, whom they both greeted civilly enough but with a certain reserve, which, Bobby feared, concealed some hostility, though he hoped not very deep-seated but only the instinctive hostility always felt when a new-comer joins the pack. Not improbably they resented his sudden appearance as their chief's confidential assistant. Still, that was something he had known he might have to reckon with.

Oxley, the superintendent, was beginning his report. There was not in it very much that was enlightening. Information had been received of the discovery of the burnt out caravan. Evidently the fire was not recent. It must have taken place two or three days before, possibly even longer. Impossible to say for certain. It had plainly been very fierce while it lasted. The caravan was drawn by a small trailer, perhaps there had been an extra petrol store to account for that. People sometimes kept by them more than was either prudent or permitted. As far as was known, the fire had not been seen by any one. Certainly no report had been received. If it had happened in daytime, the flames would not have been clearly visible; and any smoke seen might have been taken for the burning of rubbish on one of the small scattered farms or holdings in the neighbourhood. Not that there were many of these, for it was a thinly inhabited district. In any case so fierce a fire as this had plainly been, must have burnt itself out very quickly. The discovery had been made by a Mr. Eyton, a journalist on the staff of the *Midwych and District News*—not to be confounded with that much more important paper, the *Midwych Herald*. Mr. Eyton had been cycling through the forest and had come upon the scene of the fire. He had rung up from a public-house near, and had waited to guide the police to the spot. He had made a statement and then had gone off to write his report for the next issue of his paper. It was, the superintendent remarked in a slightly offended tone, what journalists called 'a scoop', and Mr. Eyton had flatly refused to wait Colonel Glynne's arrival, apparently thinking it more important to get his story through, not only to his own office but to one of the big London papers, for which he acted as occasional correspondent and in which he hoped this time to 'hit the front page'.

"I did think of detaining him, sir," Oxley said, "but thought it better not to."

"Much better not," agreed the colonel, "can't be too careful with the press—a touchy lot, journalists. Too big for their boots most of them."

"That's right, sir," agreed Oxley with a touch of ancient bitterness in his voice. "Think all they need do is to say 'Press' and then you've got to go down on your knees. He told us straight out he was going to play it up big. 'Mysterious Forest Tragedy—Is it Murder?' Nothing to show it isn't accident, but he had the cheek and impudence to say an accident was only worth a par., while a murder, especially when mysterious, was worth a column and more. He said the torso murder was worth hundreds to some of those who were in on to it early."

"Did he know who the caravan belonged to?" the colonel asked.

"Oh, yes, had it all pat; it was he gave us Mr. Baird's name. Said he had tea with him last week and looked him up afterwards in *Who's Who*. Political gentleman it seems. Of course, it may turn out to be someone else and not Mr. Baird at all. Identification won't be too easy. Mr. Eyton said he was going to risk that. It wasn't libellous to say a man had been murdered."

"Did Mr. Eyton say what he was doing here?" the colonel asked.

"Said he was doing a series of articles on the forest at night time," the superintendent explained. "Going to make a book of it seemingly. Said he was going to call it *Ghosts of the Forest*. Well, after this there ought to be a ghost about here all right."

The colonel asked a few more questions. Oxley answered them, appealing now and then to Morris for further details. Bobby took no part in the conversation. He was content to listen, and he felt, not without amusement, that this modesty was making a good impression on his future colleagues.

"We rang through to Mr. Baird's London address," Oxley added, "but there was no answer. We can't do much more till morning. I'll have the debris raked over again when it's daylight. There were just a few things we got together. There's a photo, of a lady that's not been damaged at all."

He pointed to where a small pile of miscellaneous objects lay, none apparently of much importance, some so damaged by the fire as to be almost unrecognizable, mere melted lumps of metal. The photograph to which Oxley referred had somehow escaped all damage. Bobby picked it up carefully by one corner, using his handkerchief to make sure he disturbed no possible finger-prints. It was an almost mechanical action. There was a small gold badge, too, which also seemed to have escaped damage, though gold melts easily. Like the photograph, it must somehow have escaped the heat of that blaze which had destroyed so much. Odd, Bobby thought, and more odd still, he thought it, when, on inquiry, he learned that both objects had been found close to, but apart from, the heap of charred and twisted wood and metal that was all that remained of the caravan. He went back to where the colonel was standing and showed him the photograph.

"I thought you ought to see this, sir," he said.

The colonel looked at it. He did not show any surprise, but it was a minute or two before he spoke. Then he said:—

"May Grayson, isn't it?"

"Yes, sir," agreed Bobby.

"Would that be a relative, sir?" asked Inspector Morris.

"I don't think so," the colonel answered, "but I believe she was a friend of Mr. Andrew White's."

The name did not seem to convey anything to either Oxley or Morris, nor had there been anything in the colonel's slow, indifferent tone to attract their attention. Only Bobby thought he could detect an undercurrent of a deep unease. The colonel noticed the gold badge Bobby was holding. He put out his hand, took it, looked at it carefully.

"Oh, yes," he said in the same indifferent, almost uninterested tones. "The last eight at the Southpool tennis tournament this spring were given them. Becky had one. I wonder how this one got here." He gave it back to Bobby and spoke to Oxley:— "Nothing else we can do to-night. Carry on, Oxley. You had better leave two men here for the rest of the night, I think. You can spare them somehow. In the morning we'll have another look. Nothing to show it's not been an accident, I think?"

"Oh, no, sir," agreed Oxley. "Accident almost certainly. Not that a blaze like that would have left much to go on in any case. We'll get the doctors on the job, of course, though there's little but burnt bones for them to work on."

The colonel nodded and turned back towards his waiting car. His shoulders drooped. He had the air of a very old man. He said to Bobby:—

"I'll drop you in Midwych. I want you to get in touch with Eyton."

"Yes, sir," said Bobby, who had the same idea but who had preferred to wait for instructions, for it was beginning to seem to him that these were slippery paths on which now their feet were set.

"Find out what he is putting in his articles; if there is anything more he has not told us," the colonel continued. "Try to make out whether he has any real reason for talking about murder or if he only wants to work up a sensation. I expect there'll be someone still at the office of the *Midwych News*, and very likely they'll be able to give you his address. Oxley and Morris are taking it as an accident, but you think it's murder, don't you?"

"There is no proof of that as yet, sir," Bobby answered cautiously.

"No, I know, but it's what you think," Glynne answered. After a pause, he added: "So do I."

## CHAPTER VI
## JOURNALIST

The *Midwych News* does not go to press at so early an hour as do those 'national' papers, whose endeavour is to appear on the universal breakfast table from one end of the country to the other. Their offices were still in full activity when Bobby, duly deposited in the town by his new chief, arrived to ask for Mr. Eyton. He had gone home, but Bobby got his address. Fortunately it was not far, and the constable of the city police, with whom he had been provided as guide, took him there by a short cut through side streets.

The hour was late by now, but a light in the window, the rattle of a typewriter, suggested that Mr. Eyton was still busy, making the most of his 'scoop'. Bobby's knock brought him to the door in person, the other inmates of the house having probably retired for the night. He was a small, plump, middle-aged man, rather prim in dress and manner, with small, inquisitive eyes behind large, rimless spectacles. He seemed a little surprised when he saw Bobby's tall form.

"Oh, I thought it was someone from the office," he said, blinking up at him. "Are you police? I've told everything I know, I think, but come along in."

He led the way into a small room, fitted up much like an office, with two large card index cabinets, an enormous stationery cabinet, shelves filled with row upon row of box files, all neatly labelled, and a few, but not many, reference books. On the gas fire a kettle was boiling, and on the oak writing table stood a tin of cocoa, a cup, milk and other requirements, as also a typewriter, a pile of newly-completed scrip and another pile of fresh paper.

"You look busy," Bobby observed.

"I am busy," said Mr. Eyton seriously. "When a thing like this comes your way, you've got to make the best of it. I suppose it's what you've come about?"

Bobby nodded.

"Colonel Glynne," he explained, "thought perhaps there might be some further details you could give us— more especially why you seem to think it's a case of murder."

"Don't you?" asked Eyton simply, and that rather silenced Bobby for the moment. "Of course," Eyton went on, "if there is anything more I can tell you, I'm perfectly willing. But I don't think there is. Anything special, do you mean?"

"Well, if you wouldn't mind going over it all again from the very start," Bobby said. "Then I might ask a question or two to clear up points we aren't quite certain about."

"Just as you like," Eyton agreed. "Only too ready to help, of course, though I think I've put everything in my story. It'll be in the *Midwych News* to-morrow, but there's a carbon here you can look through if you like. It'll be in the *London Daily Announcer* to-morrow, too—front page stuff, fully signed," he added, closing his eyes for one brief ecstatic moment at the thought. "*Sunday Illustrated* will have it as well, for Sunday, and *Weekly Pictures* next week—with photographs."

Bobby's breath was a little taken away by this hail of announcements, and he perceived that the Great British Public was indeed in for a feast.

"You've lost no time," he remarked.

"A journalist never loses time," said Mr. Eyton firmly.

"You took photographs, then?" Bobby asked.

Mr. Eyton looked at him pityingly.

"Of course," he said. "Do you suppose there wouldn't be photographs? what's a journalist for?"

Bobby was tempted to reply that he hadn't the least idea. Instead he said:—

"I don't think that was mentioned before."

"It was not," agreed Mr. Eyton. "Your people would have wanted to see them, and I wanted to get them off. They'll be in the *News* to-morrow and in the *London Announcer*. The *Sunday Illustrated* will have them too— they pay big," he couldn't help interposing with a deep satisfaction—"and so will *Weekly Pictures* next week—just too late for the current issue, worse luck."

"Are they all the same?" Bobby asked.

Mr. Eyton pondered the question.

"Well, they are and they aren't," he said. "They are all 'exclusive' of course—editors will hardly look at anything that isn't these days. But they're all the same really—just different shots from different angles. Makes them seem different, but they're all much of a muchness. Care to join me in a cup of cocoa?"

"Thanks very much," said Bobby with more gratitude in his voice—he hoped—than in his heart.

Possibly Eyton felt a certain lack of true warmth in Bobby's acceptance for he said:—

"Sorry I've nothing else, but spirits disagree with me and I hate beer. I have to drink the stuff sometimes, because there's a sort of convention that beer's a proof of manliness and good fellowship, but afterwards it always feels to me like a wad of cotton wool inside. Now cocoa"—a touch of enthusiasm came into his voice— "cocoa warms you up, keeps you going, clears your mind, calms your nerves. I do all my best work on cocoa."

While he was speaking he busied himself making that strange brew, and he made it lovingly and with care, carefully measuring the amount he put in the cups—he procured a second for Bobby— mixing it with just the right amount of sugar, adding a little milk, beating it into a paste of exactly the right consistency, pouring on water and hot milk in the correct proportions. As he was thus occupied he said but now without enthusiasm:—

"Smoke, if you like. I don't myself, but I don't mind it." He coughed delicately in a way Bobby accepted as a hint, and so made no effort to produce his own cigarettes. He accepted the cup of cocoa Eyton handed him and said:— "One thing we would like to know, if you don't mind, is how you happened to come across the spot where the fire was, and if you had seen Mr. Baird before? You knew his name, didn't you?"

Mr. Eyton leaned forward in his chair. He looked earnestly at Bobby through the steam rising from his almost boiling cup of cocoa. He said:—

"I am writing a book."

"Yes," said Bobby, and looked as impressed as he could, though indeed he had never known a journalist who was not so engaged.

"Not," said Mr. Eyton sternly, "not a novel."

"No," said Bobby.

"Any one," said Mr. Eyton, this time with deep contempt, "can write a novel."

"They generally do, don't they?" agreed Bobby.

"Two a penny," said Mr. Eyton.

"I thought," said Bobby, "it was one for twopence— if returned within seven days."

Mr. Eyton ignored this. His was a serious temperament, as befits his grave profession.

"Have you any idea," he asked, "how much money *Musings in British Gardens* brought in?"

Bobby admitted his ignorance, though he had often seen announcements of the numberless editions that popular production had run into.

"Have you any idea," Mr. Eyton insisted, "how much *Dreaming 'Midst the Flowers* made?"

Once again Bobby had to admit a lamentable ignorance. "Both," said Mr. Eyton with quiet triumph, "written by journalists. Mine will be *Twilight Thoughts Beneath the Trees.*"

"Good title," agreed Bobby.

Mr. Eyton nearly got up to shake hands, but compromised on an offer of more cocoa. Bobby, however, was able to escape honourably by showing that his cup was still three parts full—or even more.

"I've been working on it for some time," Mr. Eyton explained. "Whenever I can, I take my bicycle and go to the forest. I describe what I see; above all, what I feel. That's the secret," he said, wagging his finger at Bobby. "Any one can see. Few can feel; at least, I mean, few know what they feel till the author tells them. Explain to the average man exactly what he thought when he saw the sunset, the rabbits at play, heard the wind rustling through the trees, that's the secret of success."

"But suppose," Bobby objected, "he didn't feel a blessed thing—except wondering if he could get there before closing time?"

"Ah, the homely touch." Mr. Eyton beamed approval "My dear sir, it is, in fact, the public who never felt anything, who couldn't feel anything, at whom an author aims—that is, if he wishes for a large circulation. You see, it pleases people to know what they would have felt if, in fact, they had felt it. You follow me?"

"Oh, yes," said Bobby, though he felt a little dazed. "Then I take it you were—"

"Of course," interrupted Mr. Eyton, "you mustn't startle your reader by anything he couldn't recognize as his own ideas if he ever had any. All is there."

"I see," said Bobby patiently, "then I take it you mean you were getting material for your book and you came across Mr. Baird?"

"Exactly," agreed Mr. Eyton, though looking a little surprised now, as if he did not quite know how Bobby had reached this conclusion. "About a week or ten days ago. He was making tea on a primus stove just outside the caravan—very smart and expensive-looking affair, too, I noticed. I stopped and we got chatting. I rather hoped to—to—"

"To get material," suggested Bobby, as the other hesitated.

"Well, yes," agreed Mr. Eyton, again looking a trifle surprised at this shrewd guess. "That was in my mind," he confessed. "I expected a fellow lover of the forest—I am one of the 'Men of the Trees', indeed I had something to do with the founding of that admirable society. I felt I might get to know his thoughts in those still and lonely evenings under the rustling—rustling—" He paused.

"Just a moment," he said, "I must make a note of that phrase—rustling—rustling what? ah, yes." Apparently he got the word he wanted. He wrote it down on a card, moved over to the card index, opened it at the drawer marked 'phrases' and filed the card away. Then he turned back to Bobby. "Any ideas he had had, anything he had seen, noticed, all that would have been very useful to me. I take what I want where I find it."

Bobby, who knew his Kipling, remembered those lines beginning 'When 'Omer smote 'is bloomin lyre', but made no comment. After all, isn't all authorship picking other people's brains? He went on listening patiently. He had long learned that with people of the Eyton type it is better to let them talk rather than try to put them through a close examination.

"I was disappointed," confessed Mr. Eyton. "On this first visit, I soon found Mr. Baird was simply bored and lonely. I almost thought that was why he was willing to talk. He was the pure townsman. The forest bored him, puzzled him. He preferred lamp-posts to trees. He hated the silence by day, the darkness at night. He hardly knew the difference between—between a robin redbreast and a rabbit, and anyhow didn't care. His spiritual home was Piccadilly Circus round about midnight, noise, advertisements, and neon lights."

"As bad as that," murmured Bobby.

"Worse," said Eyton firmly, "and I must say I wondered what he was doing there in that expensive-looking caravan right in the very heart of Wychwood Forest. I thought it—well, funny. Caravanners ought surely to be lovers of the country and of solitude. Why pitch a caravan in the middle of a great forest if you can't tell an oak from a fir; have no feeling for the loveliness of trees? Did I tell you I was an original member of the 'Men of the Trees'?"

"You did," said Bobby patiently.

"Mr. Baird was plainly out of tune with his surroundings. I sensed a story. Had I not," said Mr. Eyton earnestly, "possessed an intuitive feeling for the human story, I should never have achieved my present position—for some years now I have written regularly the *Midwych News* second leader—I sign 'Z.Z.' and some of my readers have been good enough to say they prefer ' Z.Z.' to ' Y.Y.' — a quite unintentional rivalry, I assure you."

"You went back again another time, then?" Bobby asked.

Once more Mr. Eyton seemed surprised, and he looked suspiciously at Bobby, plainly wondering how he knew, that.

"Well, yes, I did," he admitted.

"You noticed a change?" Bobby suggested.

Mr Eyton was evidently growing uneasy.

"Well, yes, there was a change," he agreed. "You have had information?"

Bobby waved this aside, not bothering to remind the other that he had spoken of Mr. Baird as apparently bored 'on this first occasion'.

"Please tell me everything exactly," he said. "I'm trusting a good deal to your journalistic sense. Every tiny detail may help. About this change now."

"It struck me very much," Eyton said. "It was remarkable." He looked very thoughtful and still hesitated, balancing his now empty cup on his open hand. "He glowed," he said abruptly.

"He—what?" said Bobby, not understanding at first, and then abruptly there came back into his mind a memory of how Lord Henry had looked up with a kind of bright adoration at his betrothed, of the look of eager happiness that had so transfigured his homely features, making them almost beautiful.

"He—glowed," Eyton said again. He put down his empty cup and got to his feet. He seemed to feel that what he had to say he must say standing. "He seemed to glow," he repeated. "I have never seen anything like it. It was like a brightness all around him. There's a passage in the Bible—you remember? 'His face shone.' Moses, wasn't it? He made me think of that. The first time I was there Baird was morose, gloomy, dull, out of sorts, bored with himself and everything else. But this time—it was almost embarrassing," Eyton concluded abruptly.

"Have you any idea what caused it?" Bobby asked.

"What could cause it?" Eyton retorted, and then answered his own question: "A woman," he said.

"You think one was there?"

"I think he had been waiting for her and she had come and everything was changed," Eyton answered.

"Did you see her?" Bobby asked.

"No. But she was there all right. Everything was different. There were flowers, things like that. Flowers in a vase on the caravan steps and a huge box of chocolates. Someone had been arranging the flowers, and I didn't think it was Baird. And I didn't think he bought those chocolates for himself."

"You didn't get even a glimpse of her?"

"No. I could hear someone moving inside the caravan, but she didn't come near the door. She didn't want to be seen. I sensed that. I'm sure it was a woman, and she didn't want any one to see her. I didn't stop long. It wasn't my business, nothing I could use whoever it was. Baird was very pleasant. He never even hinted he wanted me out of the way. I knew he did, though. It's difficult to explain. He asked me about my book. The other time I didn't think he had even heard what I said about it. Now he said he would look out for it, buy a copy, tell his friends. It sounded as though he really cared. I thought—"

"Yes?"

"I thought," said Eyton, a trifle shyly, "he felt so good, so happy himself, he wanted every one else to be happy, too. It was as if he felt he had so much happiness himself he wanted every one else to feel the same."

They were both silent then. Eyton lost in a memory of an experience that he knew had not left him quite as he had been before; Bobby troubled and thoughtful, for vaguely he seemed to catch a glimpse of strange and dreadful things that hid behind a lovely mask. Eyton said:—

"Well, anyhow, I've seen one happy man. It's hard to explain. I felt as if I had seen a man as we are all meant to be—just happy and wanting every one else to be happy."

"Did you go again?" Bobby asked.

"Only to-night. There was nothing then but ashes—the ashes of the caravan. And he was dead. I knew that even before I looked. The first time he was sullen and depressed. The second time he—glowed. The third time he was dead."

He paused and the two of them looked steadily at each other.

"Murdered," Eyton said loudly and abruptly.

"It might have been accident," Bobby said, but without conviction in his voice. "It might have been suicide."

"It wasn't an accident," Eyton declared. "Why should a caravan like that catch fire? If it did, why couldn't Baird have escaped? Not like being trapped on a top floor. All he had to do was to open the door and walk out. It was no accident."

"Suicide?" Bobby suggested again.

The little man shook his head.

"No," he said. "No man could have looked the way he looked and then killed himself within a day or two." He paused and said again, quietly but with conviction:— "It was murder."

## CHAPTER VII
## EAVESDROPPER

Early the next morning before Colonel Glynne arrived, Bobby presented himself at the county police headquarters. He had sat up to the small hours, writing a report of his conversation with little Mr. Eyton, and now, borrowing one of the office type-writers, he copied it out. He had just finished when Inspector Morris came in and nodded a greeting. Bobby explained what he was doing and the inspector asked one or two questions about Scotland Yard methods.

"Our C.I.D. is a bit out of date," he confessed. "There wasn't much serious crime about here till they started the new factories and got in a lot of Irish riff-raff from Birchespool. Know Birchespool at all?"

"No," answered Bobby. "I was never up here before, but I know at the Yard we used to think the Birchespool C.I.D. pretty good."

" So it ought to be," declared Morris. "One of the biggest towns in the country and fat rates to draw on, not starved like us poor devils of the county force. We used to get them to help us in C.I.D. work, but they made us pay through the nose till the Watch Committee wanted to know why we didn't run a show of our own. I suppose that'll be your job—helping the old man start a real C.I.D. here."

He was looking a little curiously at the long report Bobby had just finished typing; and Bobby explained that the night before he had had a chat with Mr. Eyton, of the *Midwych News*, who had been the first to report what had happened.

"Talkative little chap," Bobby remarked. "He told me all about a book he's writing on the Wychwood forest."

"Talked about it, did he?" asked Morris. "I'm glad to hear he has started again. Looks as if the poor little devil were getting over it."

"Over it?" repeated Bobby, puzzled.

"Wife left him in the spring," Morris explained. "Hit him hard. He got blazing drunk one night. We had to bring him in; he was threatening murder and suicide and Lord knows what. Had to keep an eye on him till he quietened down a bit. Might have been murder if he had known who it was the bitch went off with. Just as well he didn't. I'm glad, too, he's started his book again. He burnt it when she left him though it was more than half done, he told us that night we had him here."

"What made him do that?" Bobby asked.

"I think he had an idea it all happened through the book," Morris explained. "He was dead keen on it, thought it was going to bring in a pot of money and make him famous. I've heard books do sometimes," Morris added, doubtfully, "though it seems queer to me. He used to rush her off to the forest every chance he got, and he would sit and make notes or wander off by himself, getting the air, he told us, or something like that. I don't know what he meant."

"Getting the atmosphere, perhaps?" Bobby suggested.

"That's what I said, getting the air. Anyhow, his wife got fed up. Don't much wonder. I expect my old woman would cut up rough if I wanted her to go and sit under trees all day. But it seems she ran across some chap—camper or hiker or someone like that. Wychwood swarms with them in the spring and summer. They got pally, and while hubby was mooning around, watching the trees grow, wifey and this other chap were having fun on the side. Eyton never noticed anything. Wrapped up in his book. That was last year. In the winter it was much the same, he was either shut up with his writing or busy at the office, or rushing off to the forest to have another squint at the trees. Wifey began to run up to London on one excuse or another—to see her aunt, her sister was ill, a visit to her dentist, all the usual excuses. Eyton went on being quite happy, putting all his spare time into his book. When the spring came he talked about buying a caravan and going to live in the forest. Most likely that put the lid on it. Anyhow he came home one day to find a note saying she had gone and she wasn't coming back, but he wouldn't miss her because he had his book instead. Broke him up. Burnt his manuscript and went on the razzle. We had our hands full with him that night, took three men to bring him in. Talked of murder, suicide. Luckily it couldn't be murder because he had no idea where she had gone or who the man was. He quietened down afterwards, turned teetotaller, and if he's got to work on his book again, I expect he'll be all right now."

Bobby had listened with close attention. Human nature, he told himself, was always unexpected, unpredictable. Even we ourselves do not know what is within us till the test comes. Who could have guessed such a story lay behind the prim, smug exterior of the chatty little journalist? Difficult to imagine him, with his careful brewing of his cup of cocoa, 'on the razzle', or its needing three big policemen to 'bring him in'.

Hidden lives, Bobby thought, and hidden fires. He looked out of the window, watching the Midwych citizens, hurrying to their day's work, with their bowler hats and their umbrellas, their morning papers, their trim little attaché cases and their powdered noses, according to age and sex, and he wondered how many of them hid behind their commonplace exteriors such storms of hate and love and passion as must have raged within the heart of quiet, dull looking little Mr. Eyton.

The inspector, who was not given to such speculations, was going on talking. He said:—

"Did you go into that front room of his?"

"Yes. Why?"

"Used to be his wife's sort of show place," Morris explained. "She was one of the arty sort, design and that sort of thing. She did the setting for the Midwych Amateur Dramatics—jolly good shows they put on, too, what with her settings and Miss Hannay's acting. Up to professional level every time."

"Miss Hannay?" Bobby repeated. "Is that Miss Hazel Hannay, General Hannay's daughter?"

"That's right. It was her pulled in Mrs. Eyton. Eyton was secretary and stage manager. He chucked it after the scandal, and he cleared all her fal-lals out of that front room of hers and turned it into a sort of office. Didn't want anything to make him remember."

Bobby thought to himself that memories lie within, not without, and he seemed to see again the little man sitting there alone at his work, surrounded by memories all the more poignant perhaps for the resolute effort he had made to clear away all sign of the past.

The conversation languished. Morris became busy with routine work, muttering comments the while. Presently he spluttered indignantly over a civilian complaint made against one of the city police, but sent in to the county force, under the evident impression that all police forces are one and the same.

"Nothing to do with us," grunted Morris.

It seemed a woman had been singing Welsh songs outside a public-house. A possibly too zealous constable had told her to move on. A patriotic Welshman had protested. There had been an exchange of pointed comment, and this vitriolic letter was the outcome.

"Nothing to do with us," Morris repeated. "The city blokes can have it."

"I think we passed her last night," Bobby remarked, inclined to be on the side of the woman singer. "I thought she was jolly good, and singing jolly good stuff, too."

Morris, quite uninterested, made no comment. Bobby decided that if he saw the woman again—he felt he would recognize her— he would give her a shilling and perhaps some day, if they got settled here, get Olive to do something for her. Then he forgot all about her when Colonel Glynne arrived.

All the usual routine of such cases was now in full swing. A medical report was already in to the effect that the remains were too badly burnt for anything useful or definite to be said. Death might have been caused by the fire or by anything else almost.

Impossible to say even whether death had occurred before or after the fire reached the body. Equally impossible to say how long since death had taken place. Some time certainly—two or three days or even longer. Fire destroys thoroughly, and this fire had certainly been fierce while it lasted. Identification would have to depend very largely on the teeth—teeth are almost indestructible— and on various faint traces and more or less accurate deductions which suggested that the hair had been plentiful and a light brown in colour, the sex certainly male, the height about five foot nine, the build slender, the age about thirty-five, the features well-shaped and prominent.

"Quite a packet all the same," commented Morris, "to get out of what didn't look much more than a pile of bone and ash."

It all agreed, however, very well with what was known of Baird. Efforts were being made to get in touch with his relatives, and as at the moment there seemed nothing else to do—the arrangements for the inquest being of course in the hands of the district coroner—Bobby received instructions to take charge of the other efforts being made to secure further information from the residents in the locality, few and scattered as they were.

He could only be given one constable to help him, and they started off accordingly on bicycles; Bobby, as befitted his superior rank, being allowed a motor cycle, while the mere constable had to manage with the push bike variety. So Bobby got there first. The day was fine, the ride pleasant; and he had no difficulty in finding his way, for Eyton's articles in the *Midwych News* and in the *London Announcer*, had brought out a host of sightseers in cars, on bicycles, on foot, so that Bobby had merely to join in the procession.

He found the glade roped off, and the harassed constable on duty with his hands full, keeping away curious spectators and eager souvenir hunters, who by this time, had they been allowed, would have carried away every morsel of the burnt caravan— probably even of the turf on which it had stood. Bobby, having succeeded in convincing the at first sceptical constable of his identity, helped in this task of keeping the curiosity-mongers at bay in the intervals of making as close an inspection of the actual spot and the vicinity as the swarming crowd permitted. For efforts to clear the spectators away were a complete failure, since, as some of them pointed out, this is a free country, and Wychwood Forest is public property, open to all. Nor could they be said to be obstructing traffic, so that usual trump card of the police could not very well be played. Indeed they protested they weren't obstructing any one, all they wanted to do was to help, and now and again one of them would find footmarks left by others of them and excitedly draw attention to an evidently important 'clue'.

So they had to be endured, and when presently the official photographers Bobby had asked for arrived, together with an expert to examine the burnt debris more minutely still, Bobby strolled away to mingle with the crowd in the hope of picking up some useful scrap of information—and information, whether useful or not, they were all only too eager to give him.

Evidently it was the general and firm conviction that murder had been committed, which perhaps was not surprising since that had been plainly suggested in Eyton's articles. An opposition theory had, however, been started by a disgruntled representative of the 'scooped' *Midwych Herald*, which had been too late in hearing of the tragedy to do more than include a brief mention of it in their stop press column. Now they had brought out a special edition with many deprecatory remarks about the sensational interpretation certain irresponsible elements in the town, in defiance of every canon of decency and good taste, were endeavouring to put on this most unfortunate accident. A kind of accident regrettably common, it added, since so few people cared to adopt the simple precaution of using the Brown Safety Oil Stove, to be secured at the emporium of Messrs. Brown, in the High Street, as advertised on the front page.

"Trying to make the best of things," Bobby thought, "and after all what proof is there it wasn't pure accident?"

Nevertheless he remembered very clearly the intense and almost passionate conviction with which Eyton declared that murder had been done. He found himself wondering why it was that Eyton had seemed so sure, had spoken with such certainty.

He wandered about a little, made one or two discoveries he thought might turn out to be of interest, and proceeded to arrange for either himself or his assistant to visit every place, farm, cottage, or inn, in the neighbourhood to inquire if anything had been seen of the fire, if any strangers had been noticed, to pick up any other crumbs of information.

Once or twice he rang up to report and to learn if there were any fresh instructions. There were none, so he worked on till nightfall, by which time he and his solitary assistant had covered a good deal of ground and visited every habitation within a wide circuit. It began to rain slightly. He went back to the scene of the fire, where he found a squad, by the light of acetylene lamps, preparing to remove the debris, which the coroner and his officer had already visited. One of the small boys they all considered such a frightful nuisance had made a discovery of some interest and significance that Bobby decided was worth including in his report to headquarters. When he got back to Midwych, however, he found orders to make it personally to the colonel at Asbury Cottage, and thither accordingly, after a wash and a meal, he proceeded.

He was still using the official motor cycle, and as he happened to meet Biddle half way up the drive, he gave it to him and asked him to park it, he himself going on to the house on foot. As he was in the act of knocking the door opened and Becky Glynne appeared. She looked startled at seeing him, and then said with her usual air of bitterness and only half concealed hostility:—

"Oh, it's you. You want to see father, I suppose." She turned and went back into the house and Bobby followed her. In the lounge hall Hazel Hannay and Lady May Grayson were standing, and Bobby thought that the glances they gave him were nearly as hostile and doubtful as that with which Becky had greeted him. She now said to Lady May:—"It's stopped raining."

"I'll run across then," Lady May remarked. "Are you waiting, Hazel?"

Miss Hannay did not answer. She had apparently not heard. She was staring at Bobby with that strangely intense, absorbing glance of hers, as if she meant to beat down whomsoever it rested on by the sheer force of her dark and strange personality. Becky said to Bobby:—

"I expect you had better wait. Some of the Baird clan are there."

Lady May said, but in a not very interested tone:—

"They are worried about my photo. It's business with me, people buying my photo. It's what I have them taken for. I never set eyes on the man."

"I have," Becky said. "I met him at the 'Cut and Come Again'. Then he turned up here. They know that, too. I mean the Baird clan. And I haven't the Southpool tennis badge now. I got rid of it long ago." She continued to watch Bobby with the same challenging and angry air. "I sold it," she said.

Bobby said nothing. This was quite deliberate on his part. He had a strong impression that silence was the most likely way to get anything from this hostile and bitter girl. She flashed out:—

"I expect most of the others did, too, but I don't know. That's why the badges are made gold, so that we can sell them and get full value. It preserves our amateur status," she said with deep contempt. "I wish I had the guts to turn pro. and be honest, I would if I were good enough." The door of the colonel's study opened and he came out with two strangers, a man and a woman; well dressed, typical representatives of the English upper middle class. A little pompously the man said:—

"I need not assure you I am fully content to leave the matter with you. Mrs. Hands and I are both convinced everything possible will be done."

The woman, who was apparently Mrs. Hands, said:— "Billy never committed suicide. He wasn't like that." The colonel took them to the door. Biddle had been warned and had brought their car round. They drove off and the colonel came back and nodded to Bobby to follow him. In the study, he said:—

"That was Baird's sister and her husband. They don't seem to have had much to do with him, but they both had the idea that he was in love with some girl. Mrs. Hands said she had heard from mutual friends that Baird's bachelor days looked like coming to an end, only nobody knew who the girl was. Mrs. Hands came up to town to tackle him—she lives somewhere deep in the country—and he didn't deny it. He wouldn't say who it was though, all he said was she would know in good time. But the funny thing she said was that when he told her this he—well, 'glowed' was the word she used. Odd expression, eh?"

"Yes, sir," said Bobby; and remembered how once before he had heard that same word used.

"You heard what Hands said?" the colonel went on, sitting down at his desk. "That he was fully content to leave it to us. That means he is thinking of going to Scotland Yard."

"Well, sir, they'll only refer him to you," Bobby pointed out.

"I am not going to call in the Yard," the colonel said. "I see no reason to, for one thing. If I did, I should have to explain why."

"Yes, sir," said Bobby and went on:—"I gather Miss Glynne is inclined to think her name and Lady May Grayson's may be mentioned, that there may be gossip."

"If I called in the Yard, I should have to admit that," the colonel said. "It would look as if I believed there might be some foundation for it. I don't and I won't."

"No, sir," said Bobby.

"I have spoken to Hannay," the colonel continued. "I shall leave the whole thing entirely in your hands. You will report progress daily. If at any time you feel you want the Yard's assistance, you shall have it. In that case, I shall resign."

"Yes, sir," said Bobby impassively, though inwardly a little startled at finding such responsibility thrust upon him.

The colonel settled himself comfortably in his chair. There was a small fire burning; the room, well lighted, had a bright and cheerful appearance. From its windows, the curtains not yet drawn, a flood of light poured out into the darkness of a night unillumined by stars or moon.

"Now let's hear what you've been doing all day," said the colonel.

Bobby took out his report. He pencilled a note on the first page and handed it across to his chief.

"Here is my report, sir," he said.

Colonel Glynne, looking a little surprised, took it and read the note. It ran:—

"I think someone is listening at the window. May I see to it?"

## CHAPTER VIII
## SINGER

Colonel Glynne read Bobby's note without allowing to appear any sign of interest or surprise. In indifferent tones, he said:—

"Carry on. You had better look first in the spare room at the head of the stairs, on the third shelf."

"The third shelf? Very good, sir," Bobby answered, guessing this was said to allow him to leave the room without alarming any possible eavesdropper.

He got up and hurried along the passage and into the lounge hall where Becky Glynne and the two other girls— for Lady May had not yet carried out her expressed intention of returning to Crossfields—were sitting round the fire, talking to each other in low voices. They looked up in some surprise as he went quickly by, out through the front door, and round by the side of the house to where from the study window light streamed into the darkness.

There, crouching against the wall, in shadows made deeper by contrast with the rays the study lamp sent out, he could see the eavesdropper, whose faint movements and light breathing his quick ear had caught. He flashed his electric torch and said:—

"What are you doing there?"

He had come up so quickly and so quietly that evidently his approach had gone unnoticed. With a little gasp of dismay the crouching figure straightened itself and stood up. To Bobby's extreme surprise he saw that it was a woman, and, to his even greater surprise, that it was the woman he had seen singing outside a public-house in Midwych the night before; the same woman who, according to the complaint mentioned by Inspector Morris, had been the cause of some dispute between a constable of the city force and a passing civilian.

"What on earth?" began Bobby, quite taken aback.

The window of the study opened and the colonel looked out.

"Anyone there?" he asked.

"Yes, sir. A woman, sir," Bobby answered.

"What's she want?" the colonel inquired unemotionally —he seemed a man hard to surprise, Bobby thought. "Better bring her in," he added, closing the window.

"Very good, sir," said Bobby, addressing, however, only a closed window. "This way," he said to the woman.

She made no attempt to protest or resist—to Bobby's great relief, for if there was one thing he dreaded more than another it was having to handle a woman throwing a fit of hysterics. He could still remember from his uniform days the feel of ten very sharp nails scoring ten distinct and extremely painful channels down his cheeks. He could still remember, on the same occasion, the look on a youthful colleague's face as a most ungentle hand twined itself in his curling locks and pulled and pulled and pulled. True, Bobby also remembered the callous advice given by an old and experienced sergeant on the same occasion that still was mentioned with a certain awe in the district where it had happened.

"Dip the end of a towel in cold water," the sergeant had said, "and apply it to the face hard and frequent." Good advice, no doubt, but then towels and cold water are not always so immediately available as are finger nails and hairpulls, so that Bobby's relief remained intense as his captive continued to walk sedately by his side. He even had the impression that in some way she was pleased, that this was what she had wished to happen, and he found himself wondering if those faint noises he had heard had been less unintentional than they had seemed. He had left the front door open and they passed through, the woman still walking meekly by his side, and on into the lounge. The three by the fire looked up in a surprised way at his return with this unexpected companion. Bobby was walking straight on, but abruptly the woman turned from his side, made a step or two towards the little fireside group, and then stood still in a curiously intent and eager, even challenging attitude, her deep-set, hollow, burning eyes concentrated in turn on each of the three others with a kind of fierce and passionate energy.

It was the first time Bobby had seen her clearly, for, at the door of the public-house the night before, only her white, thin face had shown in the light issuing from the building. He could see now that she was about thirty or thirty-five, tall for a woman, thin and emaciated, with white, pinched features drawn and fine, her cheeks hollow, the skin stretched tight over the bones of the face, the eyes deep sunk with dark lines beneath, the small mouth tightly closed by thin, bloodless lips. She was dressed almost in rags, in an old coat and skirt that once perhaps had been of good material but now was stained and torn. She wore, too, an ancient raincoat, her shoes were worn out, down at heel, altogether deplorable, her stockings sagged about her ankles and were badly and carelessly darned. She had no hat and her hair showed untidy and uncared for, and a woman has indeed gone far into the depths when she neglects her hair. A deplorable figure; and yet, it seemed to Bobby, puzzled and uneasy, showing nothing of that sad acquiescence in defeat which is stamped upon so many of those for whom society has no place. Rather, he thought, there burned within her a fierce and secret flame of purpose, and he wondered, once more puzzled and uneasy, what that purpose could be.

It was indeed as though this homeless outcast dominated and controlled the scene, as though all these surroundings, these comfortable surroundings of middle-class life, had no importance save as a background for her personality.

Bobby did not attempt to interfere. He was conscious of an impression growing stronger every moment that this scene had a significance that he did not in the least understand, but that, if he could grasp its meaning, would explain many things.

For a brief moment the woman stood there in the same attitude while in startled silence the three by the fire looked up at her. Slowly—or so it seemed, though probably it was but the fraction of a second—the passionate intensity of her gaze concentrated itself upon Lady May; and it was as though Lady May's beauty shrivelled and passed beneath those burning eyes as a thing of no account or consequence. Lady May shrank back in her chair and lifted a hand as if to protect herself, that slim white hand on which still glistened the stone that was not, she said, the real Blue John.

The woman's glance passed on and rested next on Becky, and to Bobby it seemed that just as Lady May's beauty had shrunk beneath it to unimportance, so Becky's air of anger and sullen hostility diminished to the status of a little girl's bad temper. Bobby was aware of an impression that Becky herself felt this, and that she was astonished, knowing that in some strange way she had met in this outcast of the streets a stronger than herself. She made a movement as if to rise and then changed her mind and turned to the other a sulky and reluctant shoulder. Bobby was reminded of a child bewildered by a rebuke it did not understand, and he was sure Becky drew a breath of relief when the stranger looked away from her and at Hazel Hannay.

But Hazel, unlike her two companions, met the other's gaze with one as deep, as questioning, as passionately intent as her own, and it was as equal antagonists that their eyes met, in equal search and equal challenge. Hazel spoke, very quietly. She said:—

"Who are you? What do you want?"

But now Bobby thought it was time to interfere. "Colonel Glynne is waiting," he said, and touched the woman on the arm.

Instantly there left her all the strange intensity she had seemed to show, all the fierce restrained passion her manner and her bearing had so strangely expressed. She drooped, she veiled her eyes, she made herself seem small and humble and of no importance, and in doing so she intensified tenfold the menace of her presence, the dark and hidden threat that somehow she had managed to convey. In silence she turned to follow Bobby and they went on and along the passage to the colonel's room; she in meek obedience, Bobby profoundly uncomfortable as he tried to attach some meaning to the odd scene he had just witnessed, that had hidden in it, he was convinced, a warning of ill things to come.

Of one thing only his close observation of what had passed had convinced him—that none of the other three had ever before, to their knowledge, seen this wanderer of the streets and yet that she herself knew something of each one of them. Though how indeed could ever their orbits have crossed, the orbit on the one hand of a vagabond singer at the doors of public-houses, on the other those of three prosperous, carefully brought-up young ladies with all that young ladyhood still implies? How could they ever have come into closer contact than that provided by the stray coppers wherewith the well-to-do express their knowledge that they, too, are indeed their brothers' keepers?

Bobby opened the door of the study. The woman went in. Bobby followed her. The colonel was sitting at his desk. She stood silently before him, her hands folded, her attitude humble and pleading. Bobby, staring at her, could hardly believe it was the same woman whose fierce gaze had but the moment before seemed to challenge the place and life and safety of those other three.

"Now then, my good woman," said the colonel briskly, "what's all this?"

"Please, sir, I didn't mean no harm, sir," she answered in a small, whining voice, certainly assumed.

The colonel looked at her sharply. It seemed he, too, recognized the false note in her voice.

"What's your name?" he asked. "What were you doing out there?"

"Please, sir, I didn't mean no harm," she answered in the same whining tones. "Please, sir, I didn't mean nothing. Please, sir, I'm Mrs. Jane Jones. Please, sir, I only thought if I went to the back door they might give me a little bite of something to eat. Please, sir, they do sometimes, if I sing for it, sir."

"Sing for it?" the colonel repeated in a puzzled way. Then, more sharply:—"You say you are married. Where's your husband?"

"Please, sir, he's dead, sir, a long time ago, sir. At least, I think so, sir. He left me, sir."

"Where do you live?"

"I don't live nowhere, please, sir. At least, I mean, anywhere, sir. That's why I sing, please, sir, to get the price of a bed. I've got that, please, sir." She dived into the recesses of her appalling old raincoat and produced a filthy rag that once perhaps had been a handkerchief and that now appeared to have a few coins tied up in one corner. "I thought if they let me sing at the back door they might give me some supper, sir. Sometimes I get enough for breakfast, too."

"Why were you listening at the window?" the colonel demanded abruptly.

"Oh, I wasn't, sir. Please, sir, I wouldn't never think of such a thing, so I wouldn't. Only sometimes it's a help to know what the gentleman's like, because there's some you could see at once would as like as not set the dog on you or send for the police, even though you ain't doing nothing wrong. And then again there's some as look as if they might listen theirselves, and that's generally good for silver as well as a bite to eat. And sometimes I can see they're Welsh and then I know it's all right."

"Why?"

"I sing Welsh songs then," she answered.

"Do you mean you know Welsh?" the colonel asked; "that you sing in Welsh?"

"Yes, sir."

The colonel looked a trifle incredulous. Bobby, speaking for the first time, said:—

"That much is true, anyhow. I happened to notice her outside a pub last night. It was an old lament in Welsh she was singing."

The woman who called herself Jane Jones flashed at Bobby a glance that reminded him of her other personality, the one she had shown in the lounge. He found himself thinking of little Mr. Eyton. Had everyone, he wondered, a second personality? Did each commonplace, every-day exterior conceal such hidden fires? Bobby continued:—

"I believe a constable told her to move on. There was some sort of fuss and afterwards a complaint was made against the constable for being too officious. Inspector Morris got it, he sent it on to the city police. It was their man and their affair."

"I slipped away, I did," the woman said in the same whining voice she had used throughout, a sort of 'kind-sir-spare-a-copper' voice. "I always do if there's trouble. Not that there ain't nothing wrong in singing nor in kind- hearted ladies and gentlemen giving a copper or two. Why shouldn't they? And me always moving on at once when so told by the police gentlemen."

The colonel was plainly more puzzled than ever. Bobby said:—

"May I ask a question, sir?" The colonel nodded. Bobby said:—"Mrs. Jones, were you in Wychwood Forest the other night, at the 'Green Man', on the Long Dene road?"

There was caution in her eyes now. She said:—

"Is that where they let me come inside? They were very kind. After I had sung a bit, they made a collection for me."

"The landlord wanted you to stay, didn't he?" Bobby asked. "I think he said you could sleep there, said you could have a job if you liked, help in the day, sing at night. You refused. He was annoyed, told you to take yourself off. Is that so?"

"I didn't think he really meant it," she answered, still cautious. "I didn't trust him. He wasn't drunk, but he had had a drop. I didn't expect he would feel the same in the morning."

Bobby looked at the colonel. It was his chief's examination, not his. But Glynne nodded.

"Carry on," he said briefly. "Your pigeon."

Bobby turned to the woman again.

"Was it because you thought he might change his mind next morning that you refused the offer of a good bed for the night?"

"A woman can't be too careful about an offer of that sort," she told him. "I've always been respectable."

"Of course, that's nonsense, as you very well know," Bobby said. "The landlord's married and there are three or four women employees. The 'Green Man' does a good trade, gets all the Long Dene traffic. What was your real reason for refusing? Where did you spend the night?"

She was plainly on the defensive now. She said:—

"I've forgotten."

A familiar phrase, a useful phrase when both the truth and a lie seem equally dangerous.

"Your memory is rather suddenly defective," Bobby said dryly. "Did you spend the night in the forest?"

"Oh, no, why should I? It was a barn somewhere, I don't know where. It was dark; and it was dark when I left in the morning. I always do when I sleep in a barn; I mean, I go before the farm people are up."

"Do you know that was the night when a caravan in the forest caught fire and a man lost his life?"

"Please, sir, I don't know nothing about that."

"For goodness' sake," snapped Bobby impatiently, "don't talk in that idiotic way. Anyone can see it's put on—and not very well put on, either."

"Please, sir, I don't know nothing about that," she answered deliberately, and Bobby recognized the note of mockery in her voice.

"You are merely making us certain you have something to hide," Bobby told her. "I suppose you know this gentleman is Colonel Glynne, chief constable of the county."

"No, sir, please, sir, I don't know nothing about that," came the same response.

Bobby began to get a little red. Colonel Glynne was beginning to look a little amused. Bobby felt his examination was not being a great success. He tried again. He said:—

"Do you know murder is a serious matter?"

"Yes, I know that," she answered; and this time there was that in her voice that startled both men, so did it seem vibrant with a quick and unexpected passion. She saw them looking at her, and instantly she seemed to feel she had betrayed something she had wished to keep concealed. In those whining tones she had begun by using, and then forgotten for a time, she repeated: "Please, sir, I don't know nothing about that."

Bobby looked at her steadily and thoughtfully and for a time there was silence in the room. Then he said more gently than he had spoken before:—

"I think you know that there was murder done the other night and have you then made up your mind you will not help?"

She made no answer, but in her eyes, those deep and hollow eyes, there came now a different look, though one that Bobby could not fathom. He waited patiently and then she said:—

"I have nothing to say."

He was silent, watching her closely, hoping to see some sign of weakening, some sign that she might change her mind. But she stood impassive, patient and inscrutable, and after a time, he said:—

"What is your name?"

"Mrs. Jane Jones."

"I mean your real name."

"I have forgotten," she answered.

"What was in your mind in the lounge?"

"Only what sweet young ladies they looked and if one of them would be likely to give me sixpence if I asked for it."

"That is a foolish answer," Bobby said.

"You'll get no other," she told him.

Bobby looked rather helplessly at his chief. He felt this kind of question and answer could go on for ever. The colonel had told him to carry on and he had done so, with, so far, a conspicuous lack of success. The colonel said now, speaking to Mrs. Jones, since that is the name by which she chose to be known:—

"You said you wanted some supper. Mr. Owen will take you to the kitchen and ask them to give you something."

"Thank you, sir," she said. "I'll sing for it, sir. I always like to sing for my supper."

"I am sure they will enjoy listening to you. I've no doubt I should myself," the colonel answered. "Owen, you might see to it, will you? And you might see if Biddle is there. Tell him Mrs. Jones is waiting for a little as we may want to have another chat with her. You won't mind, Mrs. Jones, will you?"

She dropped him a curtsey and another to Bobby, both full of a scarcely concealed mockery. She said:—

"Mind, when I'm in such luck to meet two such kind gentlemen and be given my supper without hardly asking for it. Why, I haven't had such luck since the night I was at ninety-nine Mountain Street, off the Edgware Road, and they gave me a five-pound note, almost for nothing at all."

She bobbed to them both once more, and then made quickly for the door and Bobby followed her, frowning and puzzled, and more disturbed than he was quite willing to admit, even to himself. He noticed her shuffling, sloppy tread in those worn-out shoes of hers and wondered how in them she managed to move at all.

## CHAPTER IX
## CLUES

What do you think of all that?" demanded the colonel when Bobby returned from depositing Mrs. Jones in the kitchen and seeing that Biddle was there to take care she made no unauthorized departure.

"There's something she doesn't mean to let us know," Bobby answered slowly. "Whether it's about herself or about Mr. Baird's death, I'm not sure. It might be either. It will be difficult to get her to talk."

"You asked her about what happened in the lounge. What was it?"

Bobby tried to explain. He found it difficult. As he told the story there did not seem, even to himself, to be much in it. Colonel Glynne looked merely puzzled. Bobby, either from lack of skill in the telling, or from lack of imagination on the colonel's side, entirely failed to convey the impression of strain, of concealed passion, of an unknown and brooding menace that had affected him so powerfully; so powerfully, he believed, the three young women.

The colonel continued to look puzzled.

"Mrs. Jones didn't say anything?" he asked.

"No, sir," Bobby agreed. "It was the—the atmosphere," he concluded, remembering the word little Mr. Eyton had used to Inspector Morris.

Colonel Glynne looked now less puzzled than unimpressed. He said:—

"Do you mean you think they had met in any way before, any of them?"

"No, sir," Bobby answered. "What I thought—" He paused, trying to put his thought into appropriate words.

"What I mean is—" He paused once more and then plunged. He said:—"I think the idea I got was that they were complete strangers to her, and that was partly why she stared so—Mrs. Jones, I mean—as if there was something she suspected but wasn't sure of, something she wanted to know and that she thought they could tell her, or one of them, and if only she could find out, then something would happen. But all the same she wasn't sure, and I'm equally sure none of them knew who she was or what she wanted."

"It all sounds rather vague," the colonel observed.

"Yes, sir, so it does," agreed Bobby. He added, half to himself:—"I thought Lady May looked frightened, Miss Glynne puzzled, and Miss Hannay angry."

"I'll go and speak to them," the colonel said. "You wait here."

He was gone only a few minutes. When he came back, he said:—

"They say they never saw her before. May says she thought the woman was mad and she was quite scared. Becky says she can't think what was the matter with her. Hazel says she thought her most insolent, and felt like giving her a good box on the ears." He chuckled faintly, in spite of his evident underlying uneasiness. "Hazel is a bit like that, she would go for anyone who offended her as soon as not. A fellow tried to snatch her bag once and she fetched him one with a tennis racket across the face that sent him off in double quick time. Tried to follow him, too, but he dodged away in the traffic." With a gesture he dismissed the incident in the lounge as of little importance. He went on:—"You say this Mrs. Jones, as she calls herself, was somewhere near at the time of the fire?"

"So far as we can tell, sir, when we aren't sure when the fire actually happened," Bobby answered, "but certainly about that time." He paused and then added apologetically:— "I didn't attach any importance to it at first. It didn't strike me there was any connection, I don't think I even mentioned it in my report. It was when I called at the 'Green Man'. We were all busy trying to check up on any strangers who might have been seen. At the 'Green Man' they said there hadn't been many. They told me about those they could remember. Nothing very interesting, but when I pressed them for something more the landlord mentioned a woman who had been singing for coppers. Some of the customers liked her singing and he offered her a job—help in the day, sing at night. He was very peeved when she wouldn't. He told me he supposed it was the idea of doing a job of work that frightened her away."

"She may have seen something," the colonel said. "She was clearly somewhere about at the time. Nothing we can take hold of, and it doesn't look as if she meant to talk. I don't see how we can hold her. There's no charge, is there? What do you suggest?"

"I don't think we can charge her," Bobby agreed. "I think we could justify sending her to headquarters to be searched by the matron. But I don't think it would be any good—if she really had anything to do with Baird's death, or even if she has any knowledge, she would know the risk she was running in coming here, and she won't have anything incriminating on her. My own idea is that the best plan would be to let her go for the present. She may come forward of her own free will later on. Or enough may turn up for us to take action on."

"I don't like the idea of losing touch with her."

"No, sir, I didn't mean that. I think it ought to be easy to keep her under observation. All police forces could be asked to keep a look out for her and note her movements, not interfering with her in any way, but letting her know she is being watched. A sort of continual 'Mrs. Jane Jones, I presume,' everywhere she goes. Hitler's war of nerves adapted to police use. If she does know anything, and I'm pretty sure she does, she may decide she had better tell us and be done with it. Probably, too, if there's any one behind her, we may get some hint of who it is, if we watch her. It may even be important to know if she stays in this part or where she goes if she doesn't."

"She may give us the slip altogether."

"I think we must risk that. I don't see any alternative. We have nothing against her. We can't build anything on the fact that she behaved oddly in the lounge here. It oughtn't to be difficult to keep track of her. A woman singing in Welsh at the doors of public-houses and probably often sleeping at licensed lodging houses ought to be easily noticed. She may fade out altogether, of course. If that happens—"

"Well, if it does?"

"Well, sir, I think it might mean either of two things— either she is in it up to the neck and her rags and her sloppy old shoes and her singing are just disguise. Or else we're on the wrong track with her altogether and she has no more to do with what's happened than any other tramp or street singer."

"Rather my own idea," the colonel said slowly.

"Yes, sir," agreed Bobby, who always said Yes, sir to superior officers to begin with, even if he intended to contradict them flatly the next moment. "I'm hoping myself she may choose to come forward later on. She can't be entirely hostile—at least, if that last remark was meant for a hint, and I don't see what else it can have been."

"What remark was that?"

"She mentioned an address in London."

"Oh, yes, somewhere off the Edgware Road. You think that was deliberate?"

"Yes, sir. Of course, it may not have meant anything particular. Another thing is that a collection was made for her at the 'Green Man'. Not very much perhaps, the landlord didn't know, but he was sure it would be a few shillings, and anyhow enough to carry her on for a day or two. Yet to-night she claimed to have only enough coppers to pay for a bed—ninepence, that would be. I think that suggests she came here for some reason of her own, and that's why she was listening outside."

"I agree we can't hold her," the colonel said. "Especially as we have no actual proof that Baird's death wasn't purely accidental. All rather vague suspicion. If it wasn't for Eyton's articles no one would ever have said a word about murder. Rather makes you wonder why he's so sure."

"Yes, sir," agreed Bobby.

"Someone else to remember," sighed the colonel, "only what can a little journalistic chap"—there was a slight flavour of contempt and pity in the second adjective— "have to do with it? I expect we can wash him out—just out for a sensation probably.

But I think if we let Mrs. Jones go, we might keep a record. There's a camera some\* where about. You might take it to the kitchen. Tell her we've nothing more to ask her, and tell Biddle to get the car out and put her down anywhere in Midwych she likes. Give her half a crown and take two or three snaps. They may be useful for identification."

"Very good, sir," said Bobby.

He took the camera, saw that it was in good order, and went back to the kitchen. Standing in the doorway, the camera held discreetly out of sight, he gave Colonel Glynne's message, asking Biddle at the same time if he could produce the half-crown needed. Mrs. Jones appeared both surprised and relieved. While she was looking at Biddle in somewhat puzzled expectation of the promised half-crown, Bobby brought out the camera and got a snap of her side face. She heard the click and turned sharply. He got two more snaps of her full face before she realized what was happening or had time to put up her hands to cover her face. She said furiously and with fear as well, Bobby thought:—

"You've no right to do that."

"Why not?" asked Bobby amiably. "No law against taking a snap, is there? Haven't you seen those johnnies at the seaside who snap you as you go along? They don't ask permission, do they? These aren't meant for publication, you know."

"You've no right," she repeated, coming angrily towards him. "Give them me."

Bobby shook his head.

"If you think we've exceeded our rights or duty," he said, "you can make complaint to the Home Office. Or you can take action for damages."

"What chance would a poor woman like me have of being listened to?" she asked sullenly.

"Do you know, I'm wondering if you are so poor?" Bobby retorted.

"Oh, I'm poor enough," she answered, this time with bitterness. "No one could be much poorer."

"Anyhow, I notice you've forgotten all that 'please, sir, I don't know nothing, sir' stuff you were so pat with just now."

She gave him another furious look, her pale and sunken cheeks now dark with rage. Biddle was holding out the half-crown to her. She dashed his hand down, sending the coin flying.

"I don't want it or your car either," she said, and turned and almost ran out of the kitchen; and they heard the back door slam violently behind her.

"Shall I fetch her back?" Biddle asked doubtfully.

"No, let her go," Bobby said. "Let me know, though, if any of you see anything of her again." He went over to the table where she had been having her meal, some cold ham and tea. "Get me a tray, will you?" he asked. "I had better take these. There may be finger-prints on them that may be useful for identification. I suppose she didn't talk, did she?"

"No, sir, only offered to sing afterwards, said it's what she did for a living," answered one of the maids.

Bobby collected the used crockery on the tray given him and bore it and the camera back to the study, explaining that he had secured two or three snaps he thought ought to turn out well and that he hoped the crockery might show useful finger-prints.

"She wasn't pleased about the snaps," Bobby added. "She wouldn't take the half-crown or let Biddle drive her back to Midwych."

The colonel was looking very disturbed.

"I don't like it," he said abruptly. Then he said:— "I don't expect finger-prints will help us, I don't expect she's on record. She may be. The snaps may turn out more useful. I'll have copies made for circulation. If they are shown to photographers, we may get an identification if we've luck."

This, of course, was mere routine, but meant that within the course of the next week or two, every photographer in the country would be shown by the police in his district a copy of the snaps Bobby had taken. Just possibly a former client might be recognized. Nation-wide organization has its advantages.

The snaps and the crockery were put carefully aside, to be dealt with in the morning, and Bobby returned to his report on his day's activities the appearance of Mrs. Jones had so long interrupted.

He began by giving a brief account of his interview with Eyton, and he attributed to the little journalist's articles the wide-spread belief that murder had been committed. He thought that idea, he said, was now firmly fixed in people's minds.

"The coroner's jury will go into the box with their minds made up," agreed the colonel. "The verdict will be murder against person or persons unknown. We can be sure of that. Mr. Eyton seems to have made it quite clear what he thinks."

"Yes, sir, quite clear," agreed Bobby.

"I wonder why," said the colonel, and began to scratch his chin reflectively. "These sensational journalists," he grumbled, "anything to make a splash."

He looked at Bobby as if he hoped for support, and Bobby at once gave it—with qualifications.

"Of course, sir," he said, "we have to remember that. Eyton himself said more than once that a sensational murder was worth a lot more than an accidental death. But I thought afterwards it was a way of protecting himself, and it is difficult to understand why, even if the caravan took fire accidentally, Baird seems to have made no effort to escape. He had only to open the door to walk out, one would think he could have done that even if he had been drinking. There's no suggestion that he did drink too much, or that he had been buying drink or anything like that. Not that I could find out much about him, no one seems to have had any reason to take much notice of him. He was at the Green Man once or twice. He had a meal there and another time he called in for a glass of beer. So far as I can ascertain he's been in the neighbourhood about three weeks or a little less. No one seems very sure. No one noticed, no reason why they should. And no one seems to be sure when he was last seen, and no one appears to have seen anything of the fire. I suppose if it took place late at night or early in the morning while people were still in bed, that's quite understandable. It was certainly very fierce and probably flared up and died down again in under two hours. That's another queer point. Why was the blaze so sudden and so fierce? On the face of it, more like deliberate preparation than accident. The Fire Brigade—their report is attached to mine—agrees, but won't go further than 'strong probability'. I can't find anything to show Mr. Baird ever had any visitors. There's one man"—Bobby gave his name and address and that of the farmer for whom he worked—"says he was coming back home late and saw a woman on a motor-cycle going in the direction of the caravan. He said he didn't take much notice, and anyhow she was all muffled up. I pressed him a bit, but he's not very intelligent, and I couldn't get anything more out of him. I asked the A.A. scout on the cross-roads near. He says women cyclists generally wrap up well. What with goggles and so on you don't see much of them; and now they're beginning to wean trousers, he says it's generally a toss up whether it's a man or a woman. He is quite clear he would never know any of them again, unless, of course, they stopped to speak or anything like that. The only thing of interest is that something of the same sort about an unidentified woman having been noticed near by was reported at the time of Mr. Andrew White's death."

"I remember that," the colonel said.

"I had a good look round where the caravan stood," Bobby went on. "Sightseers have been tramping all round so there's not much chance of finding anything, even if there had been anything there. One small boy did come across, and was smart enough to come and tell us at once, a place under a bush where it did look as if someone had been hiding. There were distinct impressions on the ground. Twigs were broken where whoever it was had crawled in. Anyone hiding there would have a clear view of the caravan. Inspector Morris is having photos taken and so on and the spot protected for closer examination. I found some chewing-gum wrappers, and I think it certain it was either a woman or a small man. I am sure if Morris or I had tried to crawl under that bush we should have left more traces and broken a good many more twigs."

"You said Eyton was a small man, didn't you?" the colonel asked.

"Yes, sir. I thought it might be useful to find out if he ever chews gum. I don't remember noticing any about when I was talking to him."

"If it was a woman," the colonel went on, "then, assuming Eyton's story can be trusted, it means there were two women there. One in the caravan and one watching under a bush."

"Yes, sir," agreed Bobby.

"Not much to go on," the colonel said. "If only we could get hold of either of these women—possibly Mrs. Jones was one, but unless she will speak it looks pretty hopeless. Mr. and Mrs. Hands don't seem to have any doubt of Baird's identity, but they evidently aren't going to accept the idea of suicide or accident. I don't think I do myself. They made it quite plain they expected us to find out who is the woman Baird admitted he hoped to marry. I asked them if they had any idea why he was keeping her name secret. They hadn't. They knew, from Eyton's article, about Lady May's photograph—he didn't give her name but he said enough to make it easy to guess her identity. They had heard about the Southpool tennis badge, too."

"I understand," interposed Bobby, for he had asked about this, "that the one Miss Glynne received she melted down before she sold it for its value as gold?"

"That's so," agreed the colonel. "Tournaments used to give a voucher that could be exchanged for jewellery you could buy with the voucher and then sell back again for cash. To preserve amateur status. Now they give a gold badge that fetches full cash value at once. Improvement in technique."

"It might be useful," Bobby suggested, "to find out if the others who got the badges—the last eight, wasn't it?—have them still or sold them, and if so, how many were melted first."

"I don't suppose that will take us much further, answered the colonel. "Follow it up, of course, in case, but it's almost certain all the badges would be sold. The melting down first was Becky's own idea, I think. She didn't want it known about here that she had sold the thing. I don't suppose any of the others bothered. For you to attend to."

"Very good, sir," said Bobby.

"Mr. Hands says Baird appears to have been getting rid of a lot of money lately," continued the colonel. "Selling out his investments and nothing to show what he did with the cash. Another point for you to follow up if you can. I am leaving full responsibility to you. I told you that before. I will give you written instructions. You will have full authority to consult Scotland Yard or report to the Public Prosecutor's office any time you wish or think it in the least desirable. You understand that clearly?"

"Yes, sir," said Bobby. "I propose to begin by going back to the deaths of Lord Byatt and of Mr. Andrew White. There's a curious likeness in some of the details, and we may be able to find other things there was no reason to notice at the time. First I mean to see Lord Henry Darmoor again and perhaps Miss Barton. I may be able to get more now. I didn't take their story very seriously at the time. Now it's different. I'll have a look round the 'Cut and Come Again', too. They've a new manager, and they are making a show of being good, so they may be willing to help. It's not likely, and they mayn't know anything, but I'll have a try. Then I want to see if Mrs. Jones meant anything by that address she gave us. I can't help thinking she meant it for a hint. That will mean making London my centre for the time, if you agree, sir. I thought, sir, with your permission, I could explain to Mr. Oxley in the morning, and ask him to take charge of the routine inquiries and to the trying to keep track of the Jones woman."

"Very good," said the colonel. "Carry on."

## CHAPTER X
## CONCEALMENTS

It would be more convenient, Bobby decided, and probably less expensive, for him to make his former rooms his headquarters during the inquiries in the London area, rather than to put up at an hotel. His landlady, since he had not yet removed his personal possessions— after all, he had not been absolutely sure of receiving the Midwych appointment—and since she had at the moment no other lodger in view, was glad enough to agree, and the day following his talk with Colonel Glynne found Bobby back in his old rooms.

It was well on in the afternoon before he got down to work, partly because he allowed himself the time for, and privilege of, a lunch with Olive. Then she went back to her job of providing that quaint headgear to which women facetiously give the name of 'hats', and Bobby took a 'bus down the Edgware Road alighting at the stop his study of a map had shown him was the nearest to Mountain Street.

Mountain Street was in fact almost exactly opposite where he got down. It began in splendour with on one corner a magnificent public-house, shouting alike its prosperity and the information that 'beer is best'—as undoubtedly the owners of those splendid premises had found to be the case for themselves at least. On the opposite corner stood an almost equally magnificent pawn-shop, its windows crammed with all those relics of defeat left by the vanquished on the battlefield of life that pawn-shops generally display.

From this twin, allied prosperity of public-house and pawn-shop, the street swiftly deteriorated to a dull poverty, its inhabitants too tired by the struggle for food and rent to have much thought or time to spare for the care of their own appearance or that of their dwelling places. As the street stretched on towards the vast wilderness of houses that lies behind the Edgware Road the women grew less tidy, more aimless the gait and bearing of the men, dirtier the faces of the children. Broken windows remained broken or mended only by rags. House doors seemed permanently open, since the swarming inhabitants were so often in and out it was never worth while to close them for that privacy which for the very poor is yet another luxury beyond their reach. The houses, tall, upright, and narrow, had evidently once been intended for the moderately prosperous, and all possessed those deep basements, dark and damp, in which in former days domestic servants were shut up, small improvement though it may be that now those basements serve for homes for families.

Bobby, however, was familiar enough with London scenes to realize that these were all quiet, law-abiding people, hard-working when they were permitted the high privilege of employment, and, when that was denied, suffering with patience and resignation. He walked on, attracting no attention, and noting carefully the numbers of the houses as they grew higher. When he got to the nineties he began to look puzzled and doubtful, for this was near the end of the street, and number ninety-seven seemed the last in it. Then he saw that beyond, at the corner of Mountain Street and of the street into which it ran, there stood what appeared to be a mission hall. A large notice board announced that a meeting for prayer and praise was held every Sunday evening and that all were welcome. There was also a mother's meeting at three on Wednesdays, and on Saturdays various activities of boy scouts and girl guides. There were other announcements of the same nature dealing with different parish activities; all, Bobby noticed, on Wednesday, Saturday, or Sunday, though one aged and tattered bill announced a bazaar and sale of work that had extended from a Thursday to a Saturday. All this was connected apparently with the parish church of St. Jude. A smaller notice board proclaimed that the hall was to let for meetings or social functions, that the caretaker's address was 13, Mountain Street, and that applications for letting were to be addressed to Messrs. Ebbutt, estate agents, in the Edgware Road.

At all this Bobby stared, and reflected ruefully that Mrs. Jones had pulled his leg pretty badly. Apparently she had directed him to this harmless mission hall—careful to describe it by its number so as to give him no hint of its real nature—-just simply so as to have a little private joke at his expense. He felt very annoyed and slightly vindictive, and then it occurred to him that Mrs. Jones's knowledge of the mission hall's exact position showed a fairly intimate knowledge of the locality, and that therefore the locality should know something of her.

Only a slender chance, of course, but his resentment at the joke he felt had been played at his expense, urged him to lose no chance of turning the tables in any way possible. The district police station was not far, so he went there, established his identity, described Mrs. Jones, showed copies of his snaps he had with him, explained that apparently she got her living by singing in the streets and at the doors of public-houses and asked hopefully if anything was known of her.

Unfortunately the district police station had to confess complete ignorance. So far as the inspector on duty was aware no one there had ever heard of any one answering to the description of the woman Bobby was inquiring about. Certainly no such woman had ever come under their official notice, and he was fairly confident she wasn't one of the Mountain Street residents. But he would make more inquiries among the men out on duty or not then on duty, and in any case, he supposed, from what he was told, the Midwych request for information and for a look out to be kept for Mrs. Jones, would be received in due course. He promised that special attention would be drawn to it when it arrived, and all constables warned that the woman referred to was believed to have some connection with that locality. Nor did the inspector seem to know much of the Mountain Street mission hall, except that it was occasionally let for one purpose or another. Again official attention had never been drawn to it.

Bobby retired, feeling more and more sadly convinced that his leg had been very badly pulled indeed by Mrs. Jones. Her idea of fun, he supposed, or perhaps a general dislike of the police expressed in sending them, when possible, on wild goose chases. He nearly lost all interest in the Mountain Street hall for ever; and then he decided, since it is the essence of good detective work to neglect not even the most apparently worthless trail, that he would call at Mr. Ebbutt's estate agency. A very forlorn hope, but it was within the bounds of possibility that they might have something useful to say. Probably only the fact that the office was close at hand, scarcely fifty yards from where he was standing, induced him to carry out this intention. Had the office been a hundred yards distant, instead of only fifty, he would quite possibly have gone away without troubling further. But as it was so near he called in, and said he would like a little information about the Mountain Street hall and if it was to let and on what terms.

A brisk, efficient girl informed him promptly that except when otherwise booked, as so frequently happened, and except on Sundays, Wednesdays, and Saturdays, reserved for St. Jude's parish activities, it was available on the most moderate terms. At, said the young lady earnestly, a really extraordinarily moderate figure, and Bobby could almost see her calculating how much above the normal letting figure she could venture to ask him. It was, she rattled on, in the most excellent repair, new and comfortable furnishings, the fittings quite luxurious, 'replete', she assured him, with every possible convenience. In fact the only drawback was that, the demand being so great, applicants had often to be refused.

"We had," said the young woman, looking him straight in the eye and blushing not at all, "to refuse two lettings last week—dates so often clash. If you will let me know when you are likely to require it, I will see if it is disengaged."

Bobby nearly gave up altogether under this barrage of sales talk, willing though he was to believe it all on confirmation. A certain innate obstinacy of disposition, a certain nagging conviction that Mrs. Jones had not, after all, been merely indulging in a leg-pull, made him persist in his inquiries.

"What I really want to know," he explained, "is who the place belongs to?"

"We have full authority to arrange all lettings," explained the girl stiffly.

"I should like to see, too," Bobby continued, "a list of all recent lettings."

"Oh, we couldn't do that," began the girl, and Bobby laid his official card on the table, whereon she looked very interested and pleased.

"Oh, yes," she said, "we let it to the police minstrels two years ago. It was a lovely show. I went. We should be very glad—"

Bobby interrupted to say he wasn't at the moment interested in police minstrels, however lovely, and perhaps it would be better if Mr. Ebbutt would be kind enough to spare him a few minutes.

Into that gentleman's presence he was therefore now ushered. Mr. Ebbutt proved chatty, quite willing to help, a little puzzled by Bobby's interest in the hall, but apparently hopeful that in some way he would in due time transform himself from a present policeman to a future hirer, or even perhaps a purchaser.

"An excellent bargain," declared Mr. Ebbutt, "for any one interested in real estate development and with a little capital available. The lease falls in shortly—in five or six years, so Mr. Glynne acquired the property at a very low figure, and I believe he would be willing to sell at an even lower. His original idea was to secure a new lease for developing the site, but subsequently he changed his mind— difficulty about finding the necessary capital, I believe."

If Bobby's heart gave a little leap when he heard that reference to a Mr. Glynne as the owner of the hall, his features, his voice, gave no sign of it. But he was aware of an instant conviction that Mrs. Jones had meant no jest but instead something of a strange significance, something, too, that he had nearly missed.

"Do you mean Colonel George Glynne?" he asked.

"The name is Leonard, Leonard Glynne," Mr. Ebbutt answered. "He never used any military title that I remember."

The name of the chief constable's son, the young man who had left the Royal Air Force in something like disgrace. Bobby's looks were dark and grim as he said:—

"Can you give me his address?"

"I am afraid not," Mr. Ebbutt answered. "At present he is in the East somewhere, moving about, I understand. But we have full authority to let or sell—at a figure quite absurdly low," added Mr. Ebbutt, still hopeful.

Bobby felt a little relieved at this reference to travels in the East. After all, a name can be used without the rightful owner's knowledge. He pressed for more information about Mr. Leonard Glynne. He did not get much. But Mr. Ebbutt admitted now that certain features in the original transaction had been unusual. But then in the real estate business that was not unusual, what was unusual was that any transaction whatever should be usual, if Mr. Owen— or should he say, Inspector Owen?—saw what he meant. Real estate seemed to have a special attraction for cranks, eccentrics—crooks, too, he was sorry to say. He often thought he would write a book about the queer things that happened in the real estate business, about the queer people who drifted in and out of an estate agent's office. It would be a best seller, he assured Mr. Owen, and Mr. Owen felt by no means sure that he was not being mentally classed among those same queer people. Gently he recalled Mr. Ebbutt to the Mountain Street hall transaction.

It was, of course, in itself, Mr. Ebbutt assured him, perfectly straightforward and above board. Otherwise, said Mr. Ebbutt severely, they would not have touched it. Not with a barge pole. In two respects, however, it had stood out as unusually unusual, even among normally unusual business deals—if Mr. Owen—or should he say, Inspector Owen?—saw what he meant? Mr. Owen did, and Mr. Ebbutt explained that the first unusual feature was that the whole thing had been done by correspondence. Mr. Glynne was in Ireland at the time—or should one now say Eire?—at a Dublin Hotel, detained there by business. Another and more important real estate deal, Mr. Ebbutt had understood. The second unusual feature was that payment had been made in foreign currency, dollars and francs. Mr. Glynne had sent by special messenger, a package containing dollar bills and franc notes, explaining in an accompanying letter that he had been engaged in carrying out exchange transactions that were now completed but had left him in possession of this foreign currency he wished to turn back into English money and finally into English landed property. Unusual, perhaps, but to all appearance perfectly in order, a conclusion at which Bobby guessed Mr. Ebbutt had been the more willing to arrive since turning the foreign into English money had been a mildly profitable transaction. There had, too, been a considerable surplus, of which Mr. Ebbutt was still in possession, a comfortable little fund against which his instructions were to draw for all necessary repairs, refurnishings, costs of maintenance, should those exceed rents received.

"Which naturally is the case to a considerable extent," explained Mr. Ebbutt, "since Mr. Glynne most generously offered St. Jude's the free use of the hall three days a week."

"Very generous of him," Bobby said aloud, and reflected that the use of a building as a parish hall might be a cunning camouflage for possibly criminal proceedings on other days at other times.

"Very generous indeed," echoed Mr. Ebbutt. "Mr. Glynne was born in the parish and thought he would like to do something to help the people here."

Bobby made a mental note to see if Somerset House recorded the birth in this district of any Leonard Glynne.

"It will be a great blow to St. Jude's," Mr. Ebbutt went on, "if they lose the use of the hall, as they may, of course, if our client sells or when the lease falls in. I believe the Vicar hopes Mr. Glynne's generosity may take another form."

"Perhaps it will," agreed Bobby.

He reflected that the outcome of all these somewhat complicated transactions was that every effort to identify Mr. Glynne or to trace him, had been effectually blocked. No cheque, no address, no personal description available. A complete dead end. With some difficulty Bobby secured one of the letters received from Mr. Glynne. As he expected, it was typewritten. The printed heading was that of a well known Dublin hotel and the signature had to him an artificial look as if written with the left hand. A genuine signature of the Midwych Leonard Glynne could be obtained for comparison, he supposed, and inquiries could be made at the Dublin hotel. But Bobby had little hope of useful results Probably inquiry had been as carefully blocked there as elsewhere, and the very use so openly of Leonard Glynne's name suggested that it had been without the rightful owner's knowledge.

Complications, concealments, suspicions, warnings, on every side it seemed to Bobby. Only suspicions of what, warnings of what? He felt like a man lost in the jungle, doubt and hidden danger and whispering threats on every side. Something more evil, something striking deeper than anything he had ever known before, he felt, and yet why he had this impression he did not know. Perhaps because of the very fact that for the moment the unknown evil he pursued seemed centred about a parish hall, a place used often for religion and good works, as though the wickedness he seemed dimly aware of thought itself so secure it mocked him from the very shelter of the church of God.

He put these thronging, dark ideas from him with an effort, and asked suddenly for the list of lettings of the hall. Perhaps there was something in his voice that betrayed the troubled tumult of his spirit, for Mr. Ebbutt looked startled and without a word of comment, his chattiness leaving him for the moment, he went to find the book in which such lettings were entered.

He was gone some time, and when he returned he volunteered information he had been taking pains to verify, to the effect that a curiously high proportion of the not over numerous lettings had been made by telephone and paid for by one pound notes, sometimes sent through the post, sometimes delivered by messenger, generally accompanied by a few lines in block lettering to explain their purpose. Mr. Ebbutt agreed that this had been noticed and commented upon by his staff, especially as once or twice, when it had been desired to communicate by post with the hirers of the hall, either no answer had been received or the letter had come back through the dead letter office. Indeed one of the clerks had had his curiosity so far aroused that he had gone round to the hall on the occasion of the last letting to have what he called a 'look-see'. All he had seen was a few people arriving generally well wrapped up, some in taxis but most on foot. He had even been curious enough to ask a man who came out for a moment on some errand or another what 'was on', and had been told curtly to mind his own business and clear out, which he had accordingly done. Mr. Ebbutt, when he heard of it, told his staff not to try to interfere with other people, nothing to do with them who hired the hall or for what purpose. A free country, wasn't it? All they had to do was to see that the agreed price was paid and duly credited to the account of the absent Mr. Glynne. Besides the hall was always left in good condition. Everything in perfect order.

Bobby suggested that he would like to see over the hall. Mr. Ebbutt said there was no difficulty about that. The caretaker had instructions to show the hall to any prospective hirer. If Mr.—or should he say, Inspector—Owen, cared to go round, the caretaker would certainly show him over. Mr. Ebbutt would give him a card to view, though, for his, Mr. Ebbutt's part, he had never noticed anything of any interest there.

## CHAPTER XI
## INSPECTION

Bobby had not expected any special result from his inspection of the Mountain Street hall, and was therefore not disappointed. It seemed much like any other parish hall let out occasionally for public or private use, though certainly in a very good state of repair and maintenance, and furnished exceptionally well. But then perhaps the absent Mr. Glynne, if that were his real name, had not wished the clergy of St. Jude's to find his generosity lacking in any respect whatever. Bobby congratulated the caretaker, whom he had discovered not at home but in the bar of the 'Eagle and Serpent' at the corner of the Edgware Road. The congratulations were accepted with complacence.

"Not as Mr. Ebbutt," admitted the caretaker, "is like some as'll let a place go to rack and ruin for lack of a ha'porth of paint. We get a very good class here," he added; "them curtains was fitted at their own expense by one lot."

"Really?" said Bobby, for the passing tenant is seldom so generous, and he had already noticed the dark and carefully fitted curtains, exceptional in days before 'black outs' became necessary.

"Spiritualists," explained the caretaker; "very special tests they were doing for a foreign lady what floated about in the air and such like. What I say is, why didn't she do it at the Coliseum? Made her fortune, so she would."

"Yes, indeed," said Bobby absently.

He remembered having noticed in Mr. Ebbutt's list that the Edgware Psychic Research Society had hired the hall two or three times and had also booked it for the next Friday, and he had made a note of their address and of that of the Honorary Secretary, who lived apparently in Walham Green.

"Do they want you to help while the meetings are on?" he asked abruptly. "I suppose you get something extra for yourself if your help's required?"

"It ain't often," answered the caretaker with a touch of regret in his voice. "Most on 'em seem to think I go with the hall like. My job is to see as everything's ready, and next morning clear up like, and if more's wanted—well, that's for arrangement. Of course, I keep an eye open to see it's all locked up proper and no lights left burning or nothing."

"Yes, I suppose that's necessary," agreed Bobby.

The building included a main hall, a smaller one, what are described as 'the usual offices'. There was also a basement where was a furnace to provide heat, a coal cellar and so on, and under the main hall a large cellar-like apartment, chiefly used, the caretaker explained, for the boy scouts and girl guides from St. Jude's. That explained, Bobby supposed, some ancient looking gymnastic apparatus in one corner and iron hooks overhead from which no doubt ropes could be hung for climbing exercises.

It was a dark, chill, gloomy place, though, no doubt, cheerful enough when filled with the bustling activities of scouts and guides. Not cheerful now, though, and Bobby found himself aware of a curious sensation of discomfort. In the corners, for the caretaker, economical, had turned on only one light, shadows hung heavily, and Bobby could have well believed that some hostile, evil presence lurked there, hiding in the shadows, dodging behind that ancient gymnastic apparatus. The caretaker said suddenly, as if aware of Bobby's discomfort:—

"Fair gives you the creeps, don't it?" He glanced up at the iron hooks beneath which Bobby was standing. "All set and ready for any bloke as wanted to hang himself," he said, and chuckled as if he found the thought amusing.

"No windows, are there?" Bobby asked, ignoring this. "How about ventilation?"

"There's shafts," the caretaker said. "It's a bit deep down for windows." He shivered again. "Creepy like, ain't it?" he repeated; "and there's some of the St. Jude young ladies as won't come down here at no price. Say it makes 'em go all queer like all over. Bad air most like, which," confessed the caretaker in a burst of confidence, "it mostly is down here, shafts or no shafts." Once more he shivered. "Cold as death," he said, and moved towards the door.

"One moment," Bobby said.

He had noticed in one corner, the corner furthest away, the corner where the shadows lay the heaviest, a closed door. He asked where it led. The caretaker, who by now had reached the foot of the stone steps that led to the upper regions, called back that it led nowhere. It admitted to a small room the owner of the hall kept for his own use for storing purposes. It contained various boxes, a case or two of books, a large safe—too much to ask a bank to take care of and yet of insufficient value to make hiring accommodation elsewhere worth while.

Bobby noticed that the door was strong and secured by two locks, a yale and a mortice. Evidently intrusion had been carefully guarded against. Bobby had a vague feeling that a peep within that locked chamber might be interesting and might give some information concerning the identity of the somewhat elusive proprietor. But he had no authority to push his inquiries further, no real reason to suspect anything, the explanation given by the caretaker was reasonable enough. So far as the caretaker knew the room had never been opened since first secured some two or three years ago.

They returned upstairs, neither of them sorry to leave those gloomy vaults behind. Bobby had another look round, noted that in addition to the front entrance there was a back way in from the street behind, whereby, the caretaker informed him, provisions or extra furnishings required could be brought into the hall without the vans entering Mountain Street.

"Saves blocking it up with vans and such like when there's a do," explained the caretaker.

There was also a path running round the hall from Mountain Street to the back, between the building and the busy road into which ran both Mountain Street and those parallel with it. The path was separated from this road by a high fence, in it one gate opposite a side door admitting to the hall.

It followed, therefore, that the hall could be entered and left in three different ways—by the front entrance in Mountain Street, by the back door in the street behind, and by this side door and the gate in the fence into the busy cross road.

Bobby looked a little thoughtful over an arrangement that seemed to him almost too convenient, and as the caretaker was showing him this side entrance and pointing out how handy it was to be able to slip in and out unnoticed as and when desired, a policeman's helmet appeared over the fence and the light of a policeman's lantern shone upon them.

"Oh, it's you, is it?" he said, recognizing the caretaker. "I heard someone and I just wondered, as it's a bit late."

"Showing a gent, round," explained the caretaker. "It ain't Reynolds this time."

"Think you're funny, don't you?" growled the constable and walked off.

The caretaker, who evidently did think he was funny, indulged in a loud guffaw. Bobby asked what the joke was and why Reynolds. It appeared that two or three years ago a man named Reynolds, a chauffeur, had disappeared with his employer's jewellery—especially with two wonderful diamond ear-rings and a diamond pendant valued at a very large sum—'thousands hand thousands,' said the caretaker in parenthesis, adding an extra aspirate for emphasis. A large reward had been offered and the policeman they had just seen had been very excited because he was certain he had noticed a man answering to the description of the fugitive hiding behind the Mountain Street hall fence. 'In the exact very spot where we was', explained the caretaker in another parenthesis. But in spite of instant and careful search no trace of Reynolds had been found. It had got to be quite a local joke, more especially because the constable stuck to his story in spite of official disbelief and a snub from a worried D.D.I., aware that Reynolds had been seen simultaneously in a score of widely separated localities. None the less the constable, still persistent, spent a good deal of his own time for the next two or three weeks, prowling about in the firm belief that the missing man was hiding somewhere in the district.

"Got it on the brain like," said the caretaker, chuckling again. "Everyone was laughing about it."

A local joke evidently. Bobby remembered the case well enough, though he had never been called upon to do any work in connection with it. It had presented no unusual features. The dishonest servant decamping with his employer's jewellery is fortunately rare but by no means unknown. Bobby did remember vaguely some story about the man's wife having protested very violently her husband's innocence when the police called to question her, so violently indeed that she had had to be arrested on a charge of assault—something to do with a rolling-pin, Bobby believed, or had it been a frying pan?—though the assault charge had not been pressed and she had been let off with a warning by a bench evidently sorry for her and ready to make allowances. Bobby felt quite sympathetic towards the constable who plainly thought that his information had been unduly neglected by his superiors and that so he had missed a chance of bringing off a valuable arrest. Then he dismissed the matter from his mind, said good-bye to the caretaker, and went off to eat a solitary and meditative meal.

That there was something odd about the Mountain Street hall he was fully convinced, but what it could be he was quite unable to imagine. These are strange, unsettled times and Bobby's thoughts ranged far. Irish, for example, plotting murder in the name of that liberty in whose name it is indeed true that so many crimes have been and are committed. Then, too, Bobby knew that some of the extreme supporters of fascist and allied movements were trying to get possession of stocks of arms. He wondered if there were arms hidden behind that carefully locked door in the basement of the hall and if perhaps secret drilling was going on there?

He could not think it very likely. Possible perhaps, for there is no folly such extremists may not commit, and already there was a smell of war in the air to make hot heads hotter still. Gambling perhaps! More likely in a way. But generally an empty house or flat is used. Cock fighting?

But that is an affair of the open air and the north country. Prize fighting with the bare fist? Plenty of possibilities, no doubt, for many queer things go on in London, some merely foolish— Bobby had heard tales of meetings held to raise the devil as though that ever-present personage needed any raising—some comparatively innocent, some mildly criminal, like gambling or

cock fighting. He even thought of the Nazis, but in tolerant
England the Nazis had no need for such elaborate precautions.
They could assemble anywhere and plot to their heart's content,
probably with a British policeman stationed at the door to see they
were not interrupted, though also very likely with two or three
emissaries of the Special Branch among them, since tolerance and
watchfulness are riot mutually exclusive, as is often believed.

By the time he had finished his meal Bobby had thought
himself into complete mental confusion. He decided to forget the
Mountain Street hall for the time, but to try to be present at the
next meeting of the Edgware Psychic Research Society, of whom
he had not been much surprised to find no trace in the directory,
as also Walham Green appeared ignorant either of the society's
honorary secretary or even of the street which he had given as his
address. Fortunately the directory had been more helpful in giving
the address of Lord Henry Darmoor.

This was in a large and expensive block of flats overlooking
Hyde Park, on the fourth floor, and so commanding a very
pleasant and extensive view. Bobby was a little surprised to find
two large leather bags standing in the corridor outside the open
door of the flat. He wondered if Lord Henry were on the point of
departure and then noticed that the bags bore the initials 'A.B.C.'
He knocked at the open door and at once there appeared a thin,
elderly, grey-haired man, neatly and quietly dressed. His whole
manner and appearance was that prim, respectful, alert, of the
manservant, and yet that he had been drinking was also perfectly
plain. Unusual, to say the least, since butlers and valets who drink
too much do not keep their places for long. Then, looking again,
Bobby felt that there was more than that, something at once
angry, pathetic, outraged, something oddly reminiscent of the look
in the eyes of the dog that, expecting a caress, has received a kick
instead.

"No one in," he said thickly to Bobby, and tried to push past
him, past a Bobby puzzled and interested and therefore
determined to find out what it was all about, since in this queer,
unusual business, a clue might lie in anything that was also
unusual and queer.

"Are you Lord Henry Darmoor?" he asked, and the other stopped and stared, very much surprised, as Bobby had hoped he would be, and also a little flattered, as Bobby had also hoped.

"My name's Clements," he said. "Been with the family since that high"—he indicated a height of about twelve inches—"and now turned off like—like, like a lost dog."

"Nonsense," Bobby said sharply, and for the moment indeed he felt it was nonsense, for Lord Henry Darmoor had not struck him as a man likely to behave brutally or unreasonably, nor indeed had Lord Henry in general that kind of reputation.

There are still families who keep up the old feudal tradition that between master and man there is a mutual obligation as strong on one side as on the other, and Bobby knew that in the Darmoor clan that idea was still believed in and acted upon.

"Unless," Bobby said deliberately, "there was a jolly good reason."

Clements, who had made a dive for his bags and succeeded in clutching only one of them, straightened himself and glared indignantly at Bobby.

"Call it a good reason," he demanded, "that I wouldn't believe he wanted to do the dirty, even if it was only a bookmaker, and no references, neither, only for Miss Barton, what's as sweet and kind a young lady as ever was, and told him straight out he had got to."

"Let me help you with those," Bobby said, securing one of the bags. "But look here, you know, I know Lord Henry well enough to be sure—"

"Oh, you do, do you?" Clements said, supporting himself against the wall, for he was not finding it altogether easy to stand upright. "Well, let me tell you, he's changed, he's not the same man, he's different. A gentleman as was a gentleman, and so I've often said when others were telling at the 'George and Dragon' about their gentlemen and the way they carried on what would have brought a poor man up before the beaks. That's as may be, I used to say, but my gentleman is a gentleman what is a gentleman, and now turned off like—like—"

This time Clements could find no suitable simile and showed some inclination to weep on Bobby's shoulder.

"Wouldn't have been no reference either," he said, recovering himself slightly, "if it hadn't been for Miss Barton, God bless her, and too good for him, she is."

"What was it all about?" Bobby asked as they made their way towards the lift, Clements carrying one bag and he the other, his help being apparently now accepted as quite natural.

"That I ain't telling," Clements declared firmly. " I know my place and I know my duty even if turned off like a mongrel dog, and I didn't even think he meant it, for it was a dirty trick, and one no gentleman ought to have thought of, nor no one else neither, even if only a bookmaker." He put down the bag he was carrying. "Trustworthy and honest as the day he knows I am, or would he have gone off Lord knows where and left me to pack my own bags and get out, same as he said, and not a thing in them, not so much as a pocket handkerchief as isn't mine and isn't his'n."

He seemed to feel this last sentence wasn't quite right, and then appeared inclined to open the bags on the spot so that Bobby could see the contents for himself. Bobby checked this design, however, for it was neither the bags nor their contents that interested him.

"Changed!" he said. "You say Lord Henry has changed? How do you mean? in what way?"

"In every way," answered Clements gloomily, "and if you want to know what I think, there's some woman got hold of him, and what's more I believe Miss Barton knows it and that's what's troubling her. Crying she was and not my place to ask, but there was a photo she had and it wasn't her."

"Know who it was?" Bobby asked.

"I didn't see it proper, she hid it quick, poor young lady, but what I say is, there's a woman got hold of him and that's what done it, and Miss Barton knows. For," said Clements with dignity, as the lift appeared, "there's nothing sends a man to the devil so quick as when the wrong woman gets hold of him."

Bobby found a taxi for the tearfully grateful Clements, made a mental note of the address Clements gave in case it might be advisable to get in touch with him later on, and then went back into the block of flats to see if he could pick up any further information.

He found the porters suspicious and uncommunicative. They knew nothing about Lord Henry or his movements. They also made it plain that they were not in the habit of retailing gossip to strangers. Bobby did not think it well at this stage to explain his official position or use it to get his questions answered, so he accepted meekly the rebuffs he received from the uniformed giants he spoke to and went back to his rooms, and all the way there seemed to echo and re-echo in his mind those words:—

'There's nothing sends a man to the devil so quick as when the wrong woman gets hold of him.'

Only who was the wrong woman? Plenty of women to choose from certainly. Mrs. Jane Jones, for instance, who certainly was not Mrs. Jane Jones; and Gwen herself; and Hazel Hannay, whose father was afraid; and Becky Glynne, bitter and disillusioned; and Lady May, whose photograph had so odd a habit of turning up near dead men; and perhaps even the vanished wife of the little journalist so interested in the forest where the latest tragedy had taken place; and for that matter all the rest of the feminine population of the country. Clements had no idea of her identity, apparently, and even if Gwen herself knew or suspected anything, it was hardly a matter on which as yet Bobby had any right or ground for inquiry.

In the morning he rang up Lord Henry's flat but got no reply. He took his way there and again there was no reply when he rang. Apparently the flat was unoccupied and a passing porter, one he had not seen before, told him he thought Lord Henry was away in the country somewhere. Bobby had Gwen's telephone number, so he rang her up next, and though she seemed surprised to hear from him and not quite sure of his identity at first, she promised to wait in for him if he would come round at once. Her address was in one of those huge blocks of flats for people of moderate means that recently have sprung up all over London like mushrooms in a field after heavy rain. This particular building, in north London, was, Bobby noticed, of unusual size, and occupied an island site between three busy roads, possessing therefore the advantage that nearly all its windows faced outwards and got a fair share of such light as the dim London skies afford. There was a swimming bath in the basement, a squash court on the roof, shops on the street level, a cinema, a restaurant, so that the management's boast that a resident could obtain amusement, supplies, exercise, all the needs of life indeed, under the one roof, was fully justified.

A maze of a place, Bobby thought it, and managed to get lost once or twice before arriving at number seven hundred and two, Block C, on the second floor, which was his destination. Depressing, too, he found this enormous wilderness of small habitations all piled one on top of another, with its general air of totalitarianism and mass production, of suppression of all individuality, of a heightening of that monotony of life that modern civilization seems to induce. He had the idea that all its inhabitants must necessarily be as much cut to pattern as were the flats themselves, that here every individual must be as utterly lost among the others, as indistinguishable from them, as one bee in the hive, as one ant in the ant heap. He wondered, too, how a dweller in this quintessence of humdrum middle, middle class acceptance of an existence of pattern, regularity and established rule, could ever have come in contact with Lord Henry Darmoor, who moved in such different circles, who in his polo and sporting activities had followed his own line, who even physically stood out from among others by an ugliness of form and feature so excessive that many found it fascinating.

Probably, Bobby supposed, through a common interest in sport, since he remembered now that Gwen, though not even in the second rank of players, played a good deal of tennis, attended a good many tournaments, and so would no doubt meet many leading personalities in the world of sport where there exists a common freemasonry among its devotees.

He knocked at the door of flat No. 702. Block G. Gwen opened it at once. She had apparently been waiting for him. She invited him to enter with one of her easy, rapid gestures. He followed her across a miniature lobby into a small room so ordinary in appearance with its waxed oak furniture, conventionally 'modern' in design, its framed engravings without interest on the wall, its china vases on the mantelpiece, as to resemble almost comically one of those 'model' furnished rooms the big shops display to tempt and instruct prospective purchasers with no ideas of their own. Almost the only sign of any personal existence the room showed was a basket of needlework with a half- mended stocking put down close by. Otherwise it was almost difficult to believe that any one really lived here. One almost expected to see a notice on the wall that the total cost was so and so and that the furnishings shown could be delivered the same day.

Yet somehow, through the very conventionality of these surroundings, Gwen's vivid personality seemed to shine the more strongly. Insignificant as she seemed at first with her small, slight figure, her mouse-coloured hair, and small, dull eyes that heavy lids half concealed, the deathly pale complexion and commonplace features lightened only by the vivid lip stick she affected, yet gradually one became aware of a kind of controlled and hidden eagerness in her, such a sort of suppressed desire as might, if it could find expression, change her entirely. Odd, Bobby thought, that this hidden intensity of hers, of which so gradually one grew conscious, should find expression in a room so entirely resembling that of any other of the thousands of young women who live alone in great cities. Yet all of these have their own possessions to themselves, however limiting their circumstances. Not one but will show in framed photographs, in knicknacks and books and trifles of one sort or another, some clue to private tastes and pursuits. But here was nothing like that, except indeed the basket of needlework and the half-mended stocking that probably spoke more of private necessity than of private taste. Utterly characterless did the place seem, uninhabited almost, even though the actual occupant was there in this small slip of a girl of the pale, undistinguished appearance, the swift and sudden movements, the dull, lifeless eyes that yet made Bobby wonder how they would look if ever it did happen that they lighted up. She was saying now:—

"It's about Henry's friend you've come. I saw it in the paper."

"I was hoping," Bobby explained, "that possibly you or Lord Henry might be able to give me some help. I tried to see Lord Henry last night but it seems he's in the country somewhere."

"Not the country, Paris," she answered, and he thought he caught a low sigh that escaped her after the last word.

"Could you tell me where he is staying?" Bobby asked.

With one of those quick, silent, slightly disconcerting movements of hers, she was at the window, her back to him. He could see her shoulders move, she seemed to be struggling to control herself. Slightly embarrassed, Bobby waited. She turned, moving back to the centre of the room, and he could see that there were tears in her eyes, nor was her voice quite steady as she said:—

"I'm so sorry. I—I forgot for a moment. I'm afraid I can't tell you exactly where he is staying, he only said an hotel. He went in rather a hurry, it was a little unexpected. Of course, he will ring up and let me know or write or something."

Her voice was hesitant. Her long, white fingers with the sharp, tinted nails were twisting together. Evidently she was trying to conceal what she really felt, to put, so to say, a favourable gloss on her words. Bobby felt more and more awkward, and he looked away round the little room so oddly inexpressive of its occupier's personality. She began to talk again, somewhat hurriedly now.

"I'm afraid there's very little I can tell you," she said. "I didn't know Mr. Baird very well. He seemed very nice. Henry seemed worried about him, troubled, I don't know how to put it, almost as if he was angry. He has been a little —oh, I can't explain. Henry, I mean. Different. I think he was really worried, but he would never say why, except that it was about Mr. Baird. He told me about you, only of course I knew already because of going to darling Olive's little shop. I get my hats there and the girls talk, so I thought Henry was right in thinking it would be a good idea to see if you could do anything, and it all does seem so dreadful, doesn't it?"

Bobby asked a few more questions but without getting much more information. She repeated that she had felt just recently that Lord Henry was worried—'changed', was a word she used, and Bobby remembered that Clements also had used the same expression. He made a reference to Clements and his distress at his dismissal, and Gwen looked very sympathetic.

"I was sorry about that," she said. "It was all a misunderstanding, only of course Clements ought to have known better. I expect it will be all right again presently. Clements had been with the family such a long time he was inclined to take liberties. But I'm sure it will be all right if he will write and ask to be taken back. You see," she explained earnestly, "Henry really has been awfully nervous and upset and now there's this about poor Mr. Baird. It was an accident, I suppose, not—not suicide?"

"That's what we want to be sure about," Bobby explained. "The inquest has been adjourned for a week and we are trying to get evidence together. There's a suggestion that a woman visited Mr. Baird just before his death and we should like to get in touch with her. There's to be a broadcast appeal asking her to communicate with us and we thought that possibly Lord Henry might be able to tell us something. I suppose I can take it you have no idea who it is?"

She shook her head slowly.

"No idea at all," she said. "I think what worried Henry was that he felt it was a sort of infatuation, it quite changed poor Mr. Baird." Again that word 'changed', Bobby noticed, and again he remembered how Clements had said that nothing sent a man to the devil so quickly as when the wrong woman got hold of him. "But he had no idea who it was and he said Mr. Baird wasn't letting any one know this and there must be some reason though no one could imagine what. Mr. Baird could have married any one he liked and nobody could have said a word."

"You can't make any suggestion yourself?"

"I'm afraid not," she said, but he fancied there was a trace of hesitation in her voice, and he wondered if perhaps she had not some knowledge she was at present not willing to communicate. She said abruptly:—"I think it's such a pity about poor old Clements and I'm sure Henry will take him back. I shall make him."

She said this very emphatically and yet with still a trace of hesitation in her voice, as though now not really sure that she could 'make' Lord Henry do what she wanted. Bobby went away with the firm conviction in his mind that there was something very wrong between the two young people. Had some other woman come between them, he wondered, and, if so, who could she be, and was it the same who had visited Baird just before his death? A little odd, too, Bobby thought, that Lord Henry had vanished abroad at this particular moment and that his fiancée did not know where he was staying. However no doubt soon he would return and then he could be questioned, though Bobby had no great hope that he would be likely to supply any useful information.

Not that there seemed any good reason to connect Lord Henry's absence with recent happenings. Deep in thought, however, was Bobby as he left Gwen's apartment, for he felt he had learned significant things if only he knew how to relate them.

The rest of the day he devoted to trying to secure more information about Mr. Baird, from his lawyers, from the Mr. and Mrs. Hands who already had visited Midwych, from other relatives, all without much success. For it appeared that there was nothing to be found to explain the tragic fate that had overtaken him. The dead man's life had been open. He had been engaged in many activities. He had many friends and acquaintances, as far as was known he had no enemies, no concealed interests. There was ample confirmation of the fact that recently he had been dropping hints that presently he might be getting married. Also he had been getting rid of a lot of money. Comparatively little was left of what he had once possessed.

"Changed him in a way," said one somewhat distant relative but apparently fairly intimate friend, and Bobby could not help starting at the use again of that word 'changed'. "Sort of exuded happiness, if you know what I mean. Got more—well, he was always a bit standoffish; you felt he was a chap who thought of himself first. Well, I suppose most of us do, so there's nothing in that, but it made you notice it when he got so ready to help other people when he got a chance. Turned a bit religious, too."

All this was interesting, but not very enlightening as regarded what had happened up there in the Wychwood forest. Nor was any hint to be found anywhere of the identity of the woman who had presumably brought about this change. Nothing in his papers, nothing anywhere, either to indicate who she was or to explain why secrecy had been so carefully preserved. Only one hint did Bobby get, from a political acquaintance of the dead man.

"Oh, he was badly hit all right," said this person. "I gathered there was a risk of some sort of scandal developing so the affair had to be kept quiet till things cleared up. Candidates for Parliament can't afford any sort of scandal, you know. No, I've no idea who the lady may be and I don't suppose I should tell you if I did know. What's it matter now? Let sleeping dogs lie."

"We have to be sure they really are sleeping," Bobby said. "Sometimes they wake and bite again."

The other looked at him sharply.

"Surely there's no question of that in this case," he said. "I can tell you one thing, though. Poor Baird was in love all right, head over heels. I called at his rooms once. Rather late. He wasn't expecting me or any one else apparently. Well, the lady was there. He bundled her off into the next room out of my sight. I only got a glimpse of the tail of her skirt. Of course, I didn't say anything. None of my business. But he was all—well, lit up. That's what young fellows say nowadays when a chap's had one over the eight. Well, he had had one over the eight all right— but not whisky or anything like that. Intoxicated, but not with drink. Sort of hit you between the eyes to see a chap like that these days when there's precious little old-fashioned romance going round. Lit up he was through and through, if you know what I mean. Changed."

That word again. It was becoming almost the leitmotif of the case apparently. A puzzling leitmotif, too. Could this woman who had so 'changed' Baird be the same who had visited him in his caravan, the caravan that, it also, had been 'lit up' in yet a third and differing sense.

All this had occupied the whole day—it was eleven at night before Bobby got hold of this final evidence that there really had been in Baird's life a woman with whom he had been on such terms as to permit her to visit him alone in his flat in the late evening. Not that this knowledge, he told himself, as, tired out by his long day of running to and fro, he prepared for bed, brought him much nearer understanding what had happened in the lonely hidden glade in the depth of Wychwood Forest. If Baird had been so much in love as that expression 'lit up' suggested, and if there were truth in the further suggestion that some sort of scandal threatened, then no doubt the theory of suicide grew more probable. If so, there need be no fear that a sleeping dog might wake and bite again, no fear that a foul and hidden crime was to pass undiscovered and unpunished.

The next day was Sunday, but it found Bobby on his way to Devon, and presently in the office of a Devon superintendent of police, who, in accordance with a telephoned request, had ready the full record of the enquiry into the death of young Lord Byatt, concerning which the unquestioned verdict of suicide while of unsound mind had been returned at the inquest. In the superintendent's considered opinion, though, if people wanted to commit suicide, they might at least do it comfortably in their own homes, and not travel down to Devon for the purpose, giving the place a bad name and incidentally inflicting a great deal of unnecessary work upon an already overburdened police.

No, he had no doubt about its being suicide, and he fully accepted the verdict. Beat him, though, why a young swell like that, a peer and all, pots of money even if he had been going the pace a bit, should want to do himself in. Got everything any one could want and then threw it all away. A girl probably. When a man went clean off the rails, there was probably a girl in it somewhere. Packets of dynamite, girls were, as well he knew, having three himself, all busy raising Cain one way or another. One witness had said something a bit odd but didn't seem to know what he meant himself, something he said he had noticed about Lord Byatt the last month or so before his death.

"That he had 'changed'?" Bobby suggested.

"That's right," agreed the superintendent. "How did you know? It struck me as a bit odd at the time, but I didn't think it was in the reports."

"It wasn't," said Bobby, but offered no explanation, and the superintendent repeated that the witness himself had not seemed to know quite what he meant.

There was, of course, the superintendent added, the odd business that came out later, not at the inquest, about the Byatt sapphires and their unexplained disappearance. There had been just one other thing, the superintendent also remembered, that had a trifle worried them at the time. They had tried to follow it up but it had led nowhere. A cyclist who was crossing the moor at the time reported having noticed a large car standing on a path that cars seldom followed. The sole occupant was a man in the uniform of a chauffeur, and the cyclist had noticed him because he had been watching through a pair of field- glasses another car on a lower level in a position roughly corresponding to that in which Lord Byatt's car, containing his dead body, had presently been found. Efforts had been made to trace car and chauffeur, but had failed. The cyclist could give no description of the car and had not noticed the registration number. He only remembered that the car had been a big one. The incident had not interested him much at the time, nor would he know again the man in chauffeur's uniform. He was not even sure of the exact date, only that it had been somewhere about; the time when presumably the tragedy had occurred.

With so little to go on, not much wonder, the superintendent declared, a little challengingly, that their search had failed. Possibly indeed the whole thing had been an invention or a dream of the cyclist wanting to put himself forward. The only confirmation of the story they had been able to secure was from a garage in the district. A chauffeur driving a large and expensive-looking car no one had noticed particularly as the garage had been busy at the time, had stopped in passing to ask if a lady riding a motor-cycle had been there or had been seen passing. On getting an uninterested 'No' for an answer, he had asked that if any such lady did happen to call for any reason, she was to be told that Ted Reynolds had been there and had driven on to Plymouth.

## CHAPTER XIII
### 'CHANGED'

It was too late for Bobby to catch the night train back to London. He had to spend the night in Devon and next day, after a careful study of Bradshaw, he finally arrived by way of Bristol, Birmingham, and Shrewsbury, at the headquarters of a Welsh county police force.

There, too, warned by phone, the authorities had ready for him a full record of their enquiries into the death of Andrew White.

"Nothing to it, really," said the inspector to whom Bobby was talking, "only a lot of fuss because of his being a rich man. Newspaper reporters everywhere, and why didn't we call in Scotland Yard, and this and that and t'other, and all the lot of them with faces a yard long because there was nothing to make a splash about. What's up now? This Wychwood Forest case? Or the family been pulling strings to get it opened again?"

"There are points of resemblance that are rather bothering us," Bobby explained. "With the Wychwood case, that is. At the Andrew White inquest there was an open verdict, I see."

"That's right," agreed the inspector. "Had to be that. Poor chap had been dead as much as three weeks and the weather warm and wet—rats as well. I've seen some things in my time, but—" He paused and went on:— "Dream of it still sometimes, but there you are. Nothing to take hold of. Doctors could tell us nothing. Suicide. Accident. Natural causes. Might have been anything."

Bobby put aside the papers he had been reading with such care, now and again as he did so making a brief note.

"You certainly went into it pretty thoroughly," he remarked. "Jolly good thorough work, if I may say so. People don t realize the amount of work that goes into a case like this with nothing to show for it in the end but an open verdict. I wonder how many statements you took?"

"Never counted 'em," said the inspector, looking a little pleased at Bobby's remarks. "Must have been well over a hundred, though."

"I see," Bobby continued, "it's pointed out there's no record of strangers or suspicious characters being seen in the neighbourhood, except for this one story about a woman on a motor-cycle no one seemed very clear about." He consulted his notes. "She was seen by two different people on different days apparently, but always so muffled up, goggles and all that, no description could be given. Once she was seen actually at the cottage, putting up her cycle outside; once on her motor-bike going in the direction of the cottage; and once near the cottage, doing something to her cycle, some adjustment apparently. Not much to go on. No one noticed the registration number, of course."

"They never do," said the inspector. "We did our best to follow up that line. Wash out. The newspaper boys were keen on that angle. Some of 'em tried to work up mysterious woman slant. They couldn't. Not enough material." Bobby reflected that if newspaper men had been unable to make a story for lack of material, material must indeed have been scanty. He said presently:—

"It's a queer yarn, this muffled-up woman cyclist tale. What's queerer still, the same sort of story has cropped up again. A mysterious muffled-up woman cyclist was seen near Mr. Baird's caravan and we can't get track of her."

"Funny," agreed the inspector. "But where does it get you?"

"I wish I knew," Bobby answered. "I would give a lot to know. I don't like it one little bit. I see at the inquest it was mentioned that White had been getting rid of a lot of money. So had Baird. Mr. White's friends can't think what he was doing in a lonely cottage down here. Mr. Baird's friends have no idea what made him suddenly take to caravanning in the heart of Wychwood Forest."

"Oh, well," argued the inspector, "people often enough think they would like a spell in the country—get tired of town life. White had been splashing his money about and nothing to show for it, but he had plenty left—what he spent was no more to him than half a crown would be to you or me. What about your Mr. Baird?"

"He had pretty well cleared himself out apparently— almost all his capital gone except for a few hundreds. Nothing to show what he did with it except that he bought some very valuable jewellery— a swell bracelet at Christie's. No one knows what he did with it. The motor-cycle woman might be able to tell us if only we knew who she was. Mr. White bought an extra swell diamond necklace in Bond Street. And no one seems to know what he did with that, either."

"Does seem," agreed the inspector uneasily, "as if it was much the same thing happening all over again." Bobby did not answer. He felt cold suddenly, as though at the chill breath of some unknown horror. It was as though he groped in a mist where things vague and dreadful lurked, things threatening and unknown, evil things whereof yet he could obtain no clear knowledge, that might indeed, for all the proof he had to show, be compounded only of imagination and coincidence. Yet it was no imagination that three men had died, died alone with nothing to show how or why. He looked up and saw that the Welsh inspector had taken out his handkerchief and was wiping his forehead. He said:—

"It's—funny." He seemed to find the word inadequate. He said:—"I mean to say—" and once more paused. He fell back on the first word. "Funny," he said, "that's what it is. Funny." Then he said defensively:—"I don't see what else we could have done."

"More do I," agreed Bobby, "and what's more, I don't see what else we can do now. If we could identify the motor-cyclist lady, it would be something, but she seems to have vanished 'without trace'. I suppose you don't remember any one named Reynolds mixed up in it in any way? A chauffeur, probably. Know any one like that?"

The inspector shook his head.

"There's Reynoldses I know," he said, "but none who could have had anything to do with it, and none of them chauffeurs, or likely to be. Why? Any one of that name in your Baird case?"

"No," Bobby answered. "The name cropped up in another connection."

"Name means nothing to me," said the inspector. "Even if there was anything queer about Mr. White's death—or about your Baird case—I don't reckon we shall ever know. Dead end, if you ask me."

"Looks like it," agreed Bobby.

"Well, there you are," said the other. After a pause he added with an air of finality:—"And that's that."

"So it is," agreed Bobby again, "only we don't want any more queer, unexpected deaths of rich young men living alone in cottages or caravans with unknown ladies on motorcycles buzzing about in the distance."

With that he expressed his thanks for the assistance given him and took his leave. What with his long cross-country journey and his talk with the Welsh inspector it had grown late. He found a modest hotel, and, after a meal, spent the rest of the evening making out a list of the other hotels in the neighbourhood. A forlorn hope, of course, but it was just possible that inspection of their registers might show a name that in the light of fuller knowledge might be suggestive in a manner not previously apparent. More especially did Bobby intend to pay attention to any one accompanied by a chauffeur Unfortunate that chauffeurs' names are often not given.

For it still stuck in Bobby's mind that the story of the chauffeur with the field-glasses on Dartmoor might have its own significance. What had, naturally, specially interested him was the coincidence of the name given in the Devon garage about the time of young Lord Byatt's death with that of the absconding chauffeur said to have been seen near the Mountain Street hall. Already he had rung up London asking if all details of the Reynolds case could be got ready for him. A tiny light, he thought, or rather hoped, in the mirk of the bewildering darkness that surrounded these cases, and one that had to be followed up, even though it might and probably would prove the merest will-o'-the-wisp. Anyhow, it would have to be followed until it led somewhere or died away in insignificance.

Searching the hotel registers was, of course, a routine job the county and borough police forces would have put through thoroughly, efficiently and more easily, had they been requested to do so. But that would have meant the delay inseparable from all official proceedings that have to be explained and approved according to the accustomed routine. Also Bobby thought that in the doubt and obscurity enveloping a case in which he did not even know what truth it was he sought, what goal he aimed at, there might be some slight faint indication to be noticed that routine would over-look but that yet might have its own importance. In the country of the blind, the one-eyed is king; in complete ignorance and darkness, the faintest gleam may show the true path.

All that day, a wet and dreary day, he pursued doggedly his tedious task, once as he passed near a bank aware of a feeling of envy for the clerks within who at least had definite figures to add up to a certain assured total—totals, too, different in every separate account—while he had to add up facts of which he was ignorant and was forced always in his search of these hotel registers to arrive at a conclusion monotonously the same— nothing of interest. In none of these lists of visitors during the days about and before the date of the discovery of Andy White's body, was there anything he could discern in any way bearing on the investigation.

The report he sent to Superintendent Oxley that evening ran briefly and simply:—

'Visited hotels in districts named to inspect registers. No result.'

Oxley read it, shrugged his shoulders, and filed it away, thinking to himself as he did so that probably this young busybody from London was merely out for a joy-ride. Oxley didn't much believe in all this sort of free-lance running about away from all official supervision. His idea of police work was solid routine done on the spot and directed by superior officers from headquarters.

But the report he received the next morning ran:—

'Have found in hotel register examined this morning names of two persons who may be connected with case. Am returning to London to-morrow.'

"That's to-day," reflected Oxley, "and why doesn't the young man say what names and what hotel and where it is? Keeping it all to himself. Well, I suppose it's the chief's responsibility, giving him a free hand like this. Their affair, not mine."

He had orders to make no mention of Bobby's reports to Colonel Glynne, save in case of extreme and urgent necessity. Nothing of that sort here, Oxley supposed, and so he filed this report away with the others, expressing dissatisfaction only by a series of grunts and a certain display of ruffled temper during most of the rest of the morning.

It was in a well known, even fashionable resort not far from the scene of the Andy White tragedy that Bobby had found in an hotel register the name of a Count Louis de Legett, and, more interesting, that of Leonard Glynne. They had been together, for the bill had been made out to the Count and paid by him. What, Bobby asked himself, had young Glynne been doing there with a companion at that particular time? Was there any reason to suppose that the woman motor-cyclist could be Becky Glynne? Not very pleasant thoughts, but thoughts all the same to follow up, as indeed was his mission and his duty.

Having thus found something that might or might not turn out to be of real significance, Bobby decided to abandon further effort to trace a chauffeur named Reynolds, who indeed might very well have been neither named Reynolds nor a chauffeur, or, if he were either or both, yet have no connection with the Byatt affair, and to return to London by the next available train. He got to town just in time to tumble into bed—he had eaten on the train—and next morning he presented himself at the Yard where he found: firstly, that no report had been received from any quarter of any street singer answering to the description given of Mrs. Jane Jones; secondly, that all the information available concerning the Reynolds case was ready for him; thirdly, that nothing was known of any Count Louis de Legett, though the directory gave someone of that name as having an address in Curzon Street.

Bobby's reactions to these three several facts were, first, an uneasy fear that he had allowed Mrs. Jones to slip through his fingers and that possibly she had disappeared finally. He had thought at the time that it would be easy enough to keep track of her. Naturally the police tend to keep an official eye on such vagrants. But if she had changed her way of life and retired, so to say, into privacy, it might well prove impossible to find her. Secondly, he decided to devote himself at once to a careful study of the Reynolds case. Thirdly, he would, as soon as possible, look up Count de Legett and have a talk with him. Perhaps ask him outright what business had taken him to that neighbourhood about the time of Andrew White's death and what was his relation to Leonard Glynne.

The study of the papers relating to the Reynolds case showed that it appeared of small interest, presenting no out-standing features save that of the entire failure to trace the fugitive chauffeur. 'Probably left the country' one note ran. Nor had any trace of the stolen jewellery been discovered, though the ear-rings were distinctive, and would lose much of their value if broken up, and the pendant was a diamond of a most unusual emerald green tint to which it owed most of its value and that naturally any dealer would recognize at once.

"Got into a panic and chucked 'em down the drain most likely," observed the Yard man who produced the papers for Bobby's examination.

"Might be that," agreed Bobby, remembering the well known case years ago of a pearl necklace worth £50,000 that in the end the thieves deposited in the gutter of a London street as the only way of getting rid of it—much work for small reward, as was remarked at the time. Yet Bobby remembered also in a worried way that the sapphires of Lord Byatt, the superb diamond necklace purchased by Andy White, also seemed to have disappeared. For a moment a crazy vision came to him of some lunatic collector of precious stones who employed agents to buy rare specimens and then murdered the agents and hid the jewellery. A fantastic idea he forgot almost as soon as he conceived it. "All the same," he added, frowning in a queer concentration of thought, if so vague a mental disturbance as was his at that moment could be called thought, "if only we knew where the stuff was—"

He paused and the Yard man said cheerfully:—

"Then we should know a good deal more, shouldn't we?"

Bobby laughed and agreed, though there was still in his mind as it were a little distant whisper murmuring that if only the problem of what had become of the jewellery could be solved, then all would be solved.

The Yard man was saying:—

"Beat us how Reynolds managed his get-away. We had a full description, photographs and all." He indicated a series of half a dozen, showing Reynolds in various attitudes and in different attire. "But we never got a sniff of him. Kept an eye on his wife, his friends, his relatives, for months. Nothing doing. They seemed all as puzzled as we were. A complete fade out."

Something of a feat, this complete 'fade out', for it is not easy for one whose description, habits, friends are all known to the police, to escape their search.

"He was married, then?" Bobby said.

The Yard man nodded.

"Worst of these cases," he said soberly. "She wouldn't believe it at first. Stuck to it he was innocent. When she couldn't believe that any longer, took the line he was really innocent, only he had been made a tool of. Seemed to suspect another woman, but couldn't name any one, or else wouldn't. Anyhow, we could get nothing out of her." He added musingly:— "I shan't soon forget the way she sat there, pale as death, hardly moving, making creeps go up and down your back the way she stared. She had to clear out of the cottage where they had been living and went off back to her people in Cardiff. She made sure and so did we, he would try to get in touch with her, but apparently he never did, or if he did, it was managed so cleverly it was never spotted."

"Is she still there?" Bobby asked.

"In Cardiff? I believe so. She lives with her sister and helps in the shop—sweets and tobacco, quite a good little business, it seemed."

Bobby took a note of the Cardiff address, asked if it could be arranged for him to have copies of the Reynolds photographs and was promised them.

"Don't think you are going to dig the chap up, do you?" the Yard man asked with a touch of amusement in his voice and Bobby smiled deprecatingly and remarked that once a case began to take twists and turns you never knew where those twists and turns were going to lead you. Then he remarked:—

"You said Mrs. Reynolds had to leave the cottage where they had been living? Do you mean it belonged to her husband's employer?"

"Yes. Nine Elms Park. In Berkshire somewhere I think. Belonged to Mrs. Frayton. She wasn't half peeved we never got her stuff back. Threatened to write to *The Times* about it, and she did go to the Home Office to complain about our inefficiency. Kicked up no end of a fuss, the way these important people do when things don't happen just as they want. We did our best."

"Who is Mrs. Frayton?" Bobby asked. "Any one special?"

"Oh, her old man was an M.P. once and they own a lot of land where they live. She's an Honourable, though she don't use it. Her pa was Lord Byatt."

"The devil he was," exclaimed Bobby, startled.

"Lord Byatt he was," retorted the Yard man. "Why bring in the devil?"

"Because," said Bobby slowly, "I think the devil is not very far away. Rather, I think he is very close indeed. It was Lord Byatt who was found dead in a car on Dartmoor some time ago, and there's evidence a chauffeur who gave his name as Reynolds was hanging about more or less at the same time."

The Yard man rubbed his head.

"I don't see the connection," he remarked.

"More do I," agreed Bobby. "I suppose the Lord Byatt who was Mrs. Frayton's father would be the grandfather of the Dartmoor Lord Byatt. That would make Mrs. Frayton his aunt. If the Reynolds I heard of is the same Reynolds as the one Mrs. Frayton employed, what was he doing on Dartmoor and why didn't he come forward?"

"If he was getting ready to pinch some jewellery, most likely he wasn't too keen on coming under our notice," observed the Yard man.

Bobby supposed that might be the case. An idea had come into his mind. A wild, improbable idea, perhaps, but a possibility.

"Do you know where Mrs. Frayton was at the time?" he asked. "What sort of woman is she? did you ever see her?"

"Did I not?" said the Yard man with feeling. "It was my job to smooth her down when she called to raise hell because we hadn't her diamonds all ready to hand her on a plate. Always pick on me for the tough jobs. Fat old body, about sixty, and thought all the world was there to do what she wanted. She had gone to the south of France for a day or two to see about some tennis tournament arrangements. For all she's so fat and rheumaticy now, she used to be a dab at the game, and it's still her hobby, running tournaments and all that. She came back full tilt though when she heard what had happened. Oh, well, I suppose no one would like to lose a good few thousand pounds worth of jewellery."

There died in Bobby's mind the idea that for one brief moment he had entertained. A woman described as a fat, rheumaticy old body, about sixty, could not be the mysterious feminine motor cyclist who appeared so hazily on the outskirts of these various deaths, seen vaguely for a moment or two, then vanishing into the unknown.

But if his employer had been on the continent at the time, Reynolds—if it were the same man—would have had a greater freedom of action, could easily have known something of young Lord Byatt's movements, and could equally easily have made some excuse to use his employer s car in order to follow to Dartmoor.

Only why?

And was there any significance in the fact that old Mrs. Frayton, too, was interested in tennis—as indeed seemed to be all the women whose names had been mentioned, or with whom he had come in contact, during his inquiries? All, that is, except Mrs. Reynolds, the tragic wife of the missing chauffeur, and, of course, the Mrs. Jane Jones, who whomsoever she might be, was not, Bobby was well convinced, Mrs. Jane Jones.

And of her, an uncomfortable and disconcerting impression was forming itself in his mind that now she had so completely disappeared nothing more would be seen or heard of her—unless indeed it pleased her to re-appear again of her own free will.

A mistake, he supposed, to have let her go, and yet he did not quite see what other action could have been taken? The English law, he told himself moodily, is really very stuffy about detaining people, except for those good, plain, simple, straightforward reasons that appeal to busy, overworked magistrates.

Bobby gave it up, but determined that as soon as time and opportunity served, he would go and have a chat with the Mrs. Reynolds now reported as living quietly with her sister in Cardiff, selling sweets and cigarettes. A placid life, Bobby thought, and one in no way calculated to make creeps go up and down any policeman's back—or the back of any other person. He wondered whether to have copies of the Reynolds photographs sent to Devon to see if they could be recognized as of the man who had called at the garage there and given his name as Reynolds. Then he reflected that an identification, even if obtained, would be of small value after so long an interval and when there had been so brief an interview.

Much inclined to wonder whether he had or had not secured useful information, Bobby went on from the Yard to Count de Legett's address in Curzon Street, only to be told that the Count was at his office in the city. No difficulty was made about giving the office address or the name of the firm, Messrs. Perceval and Wilde, manufacturers' agents, in which the Count was a partner.

Bobby took himself accordingly to the city and on the way, since 'manufacturers' agents' is a term that can cover many activities, decided it would be wise to call at the headquarters of the city police to see if he could get a word with a certain chief inspector, reputed to know more about shady financiers, share pushers, doubtful company promoters, and others of the kidney, than anyone else, even than any financial editor or journalist. When he knew whom Bobby wanted information about, the city chief inspector smiled broadly:—

"Why, he has not been up to anything, has he?" he asked. "I thought he was quite a reformed character."

"Reformed?" Bobby repeated. "In what way reformed?"

"Well," the other answered, "reformed, you know, changed. That's the word—changed. What are you staring at?"

## CHAPTER XIV
## HAPPINESS

Bobby hesitated before replying, a trifle unwilling, unable indeed, to explain in what queer, ominous way that word 'changed' had sounded in his ears. The chief inspector was looking at him curiously. Bobby said:—

"Sorry. It's nothing. Only ever since this business began I seem to have been hearing of nothing but people being 'changed'. And then the next thing is they're dead and no one knows how or why."

"Baird case you mean?" the chief inspector asked. "You mustn't let it get you down," he said.

"No," said Bobby. "There are other things, too," he said. "There was an old boy I was talking to the other day. He said nothing sent a man to the devil so quick as when the wrong woman got hold of him. Is there anything like that has changed this chap?"

"De Legett? but he's not going to the devil, it's the other direction this time. At least, that's what it looks like. Reformed character. Fact. These last months he has—well, changed, if it doesn't give you the willies when I say so. He used rather to go the pace—wine, women, and song sort of bird. You know. Though if that had been all we should never have heard of him. But he was getting mixed up with a shady set in the city. There was one scheme they had on hand—a daisy. We never had to go into it officially because it never came to a head. Nearly but not quite. We were all set to pinch one or two of 'em on a preliminary charge and Mr. Count de Legett would have been the first. Then something happened. Got wind we were on to them most likely. It was called off. We kept an eye on 'em all the same and presently we got to hear the same game was being started again, only in a new form and smarter than ever. Looked like being one of those swindles just on the edge it's old Harry to prove or even to stop. We had a conference about it and no one knew what we could do. Might have run our heads into an action for libel. It looked as if we would have to let her rip till they made some slip up—if they ever did, and it was plain they were going to be jolly careful. Next thing we knew was the whole thing had been called off again. I wondered what was up and I went to a bit of trouble to get a chance to ask the bird who had thought the scheme out in the first place. He was so mad he spilt the whole thing. De Legett had developed scruples—'gone pi', was how the chap put it, and you ought to have heard the way he said it. De Legett told 'em to chuck it, and if they didn't then he would blow the whole thing to the big financial papers. We both felt sure De Legett was playing his own hand. Well, he wasn't. What came out was that he was going to get married; that the girl was an angel on earth, same as they all are, bless 'em; that he felt he had to be worthy of her; and all the rest of the sloppy talk that just naturally oozes out of a man when it gets him on the point of the chin that he isn't fit to kiss the earth she treads on. Doesn't last long as a rule, because he soon gets to know the angel has a tongue of her own—fingernails, too, sometimes, with a good sharp point to 'em. So far, though, it seems to be lasting all right with De Legett. He just sheds sweetness an' light all around, raises salaries before he's asked, wine, women and song cut out for good, works like a horse trying to pull his business together. It's a sound, old established affair—manufacturers' agents— but it had got into a rut, and he's going hammer and tongs to get a move on it."

"Is it his own?"

"Managing director. It's a private company—Perceval, Wilde, and Co. Perceval's dead, but his widow's a director and attends meetings. I don't suppose she counts for much. Wilde is oldish and a bit of an invalid, so it is really De Legett's show. I believe Wilde was getting uneasy over some of De Legett's activities, and was even talking of having a show down, but he seems quite happy again now De Legett's turned over a new leaf."

"Queer story," Bobby said meditatively.

"Queer world," said the chief inspector as one who knew. "Any idea who the girl is?" asked Bobby.

The chief inspector shook his head.

"Never went into that," he said, "not our affair. But now you mention it I remember hearing his staff was boiling over with

curiosity. Neither Mr. Wilde nor Mrs. Perceval had any notion
who had worked the miracle and De Legett wouldn't say. I
gathered Mrs. Perceval was extra keen on knowing because she
wouldn't have minded taking on the job herself—reforming De
Legett, I mean. She seems rather a lively young widow by all
accounts."

"Does she ride a motor-cycle?" Bobby asked abruptly.

"Not that I know of. Quite likely. Plenty of 'em do—girls, I
mean. Why?"

"Oh, nothing," Bobby answered, slightly ashamed of the fresh
idea that had for the moment again fantastically flashed into his
mind. "Thanks awfully for what you've told me. I'll push on and
see if I can get a few words with De Legett. I may get some sort of
pointer from him. He was practically on the spot about the time of
Mr. White's death."

"Not much to go on, have to be careful how you put it," the
chief inspector warned him. "I thought you were on something
different when you asked about him. One of my contacts told me
he's raised quite a good lump of money recently—some thousands.
Rather looked as if he might be starting his old games, but up to
the present there's been nothing to suggest anything like that.
Possibly he wants a good round sum for marriage settlements."

"I suppose he is really a count?"

"Oh, yes, that's genuine enough. It does sound a bit fishy,
counts being what counts often are when they drift about London.
But he's in the reference books. They got the title in the eighteenth
century from some continental johnny and they claim one of our
kings gave permission for its use. No documentary evidence, but
the title has been used in a direct line from father to son for a
couple of centuries or so. Good enough, I suppose. Not legal of
course, in law he is just plain Louis de Legett, commonly known as
Count, etc. You can't call the title a fake in any way."

"No," agreed Bobby. "Well, I'll push along and thanks again."

"You'll find it all O.K. with him at present," the chief inspector
repeated. "Just now he wouldn't touch with a barge pole anything
he thinks his girl mightn't quite approve of. It takes some chaps
that way. A girl mayn't say a word or know a thing about it and yet

somehow she can make you see it all differently. You know," said the chief inspector thoughtfully, "that Kipling chap had it all wrong—it ought to be, down to Gehenna or up to the stars, he travels the fastest who has a girl poking him on. It's funny," said the chief inspector, "it's damn funny, but it's so. Lord knows how they do it. I don't." In a sudden burst of confidence he leaned nearer to Bobby and almost whispered:— "If it hadn't been for my old woman I wouldn't be here. Taking the wrong turning, I was, like the girl in the play, and she yanked me back. That Kipling bloke, he didn't know his onions, not for nuts he didn't. But then he was a poet and only looking for a rhyme likely as not."

Bobby agreed that that was only too likely, poets also being what poets are, and made his way forthwith to the offices of Messrs. Perceval and Wilde. He found them in an ancient, rather out of the way alley not far from St. Paul's. They hadn't a very prosperous appearance, but then in the city of London, among all places in the world, it is never safe to judge by appearance. The staff did not seem very large, and Bobby had no difficulty in obtaining an immediate interview with Mr. De Legett—Bobby noticed that here the 'Count' seemed dropped and the reference was always to 'Mr.' De Legett. He noticed, too, that while he was in the office the telephone never rang, and in a modern office the number of phone calls is often a fair indication of the amount of business done. Still the clerks seemed to have enough to occupy them, and Mr. De Legett's desk, when Bobby was shown in, indicated a fair measure of activity by the number of the various documents strewn about it. 'A sound but not progressive business' had been the chief inspector's description and Bobby thought it seemed accurate.

Sub-consciously he had been expecting to see some one of the foreign manner and appearance appropriate to the title of count. He saw instead a very typical young Englishman, with the high cheek bones and imperious nose of his kind. The only difference lay in his large, imaginative eyes, and a small round chin not often allied with a dominant and beak-like nose. In every other respect, in his neat, well-fitting attire, his carefully groomed appearance, his air of efficiency and authority, he bore the unmistakable stamp of the British public school and university that either forms a boy to its own mould or breaks him in the process. These impressions, however, Bobby was but half conscious of at the moment, he formulated them only later in thinking over the interview. What attracted his attention at the moment was first the very pleasant, friendly, welcoming smile with which the young man greeted him, and secondly the fact that on the mantelpiece, between a small clock and a large calendar exhorting the world to 'Do it now', stood a photograph of Lady May Grayson.

It was about the only object in the room that was not strictly business-like. The phone, the filing cabinet, the shelf of reference books, the basket trays for letters answered and unanswered, all alike were such as can be seen in almost every city office. The interest Bobby showed in the photograph and that he did not attempt to hide, apparently did not attract De Legett's attention. Possibly he was used to seeing his visitors' eyes drawn to that presentation of feminine beauty, a little out of place in this efficient looking office. Evidently he had hoped that Bobby's call had some connection with a business proposition and he appeared both very surprised and a little bit disappointed when Bobby began to explain his errand.

"I saw something about it in the papers," he agreed. "A man named Baird, wasn't it? Poor chap. Hard luck." He paused and Bobby had the impression that he was contrasting Baird's luck with his own, and that this contrast made him more sympathetic to the other's tragic fate. "Some chaps do seem to get it in the neck, don't they? I suppose we can't all be—" He paused then and did not finish the sentence, and Bobby felt convinced he had been about to say '—like me', and then had felt that seemed too much like gloating over the contrast he was drawing inwardly between what had happened to Baird and his own good fortune.

"I thought perhaps there were one or two points you might be able to help us in," Bobby said.

"Me?" exclaimed De Legett looking now very bewildered. "Good lord, how?"

"I think you knew Mr. Andrew White?"

"I don't think so, not that I can remember," De Legett answered, looking more and more puzzled. "Who is he? In what connection? Client, do you mean?"

"He was the head of a big firm in the food products line," Bobby explained. "He was found dead in a cottage in Wales—"

"Oh, of course," De Legett interrupted. "I remember that all right. Made quite a fuss at the time. No one could make it out. But we had nothing to do with his firm— quite out of our line of country. I never met him personally either. He was in a much bigger way, you know."

"There were certain features in the case that are curiously like some of those in the Baird case," Bobby continued.

"Yes. Well?" De Legett said, with the same air of untroubled but friendly interest. He added, as Bobby did not reply at once:— "I haven't seen much about Baird's death. I just skimmed it through. Poor blighter. The paper was trying to hint at murder, but it sounded to me more as if he had done it himself. I remember about Andy White though. If you had said Andy White instead of Mr. Andrew White I should have known at once who you meant. He was always called Andy White. I happened to be in the neighbourhood just about the same time, and I remember being asked if I had seen anything of him. I shouldn't have known him if I had, and anyway I had no idea he was hanging about there." Bobby found himself wondering whether the frank and ready admission was a proof of innocence or whether it had been made because of a guess that the fact was already known and could not therefore be denied.

"Was there any connection, private, business, in any way whatever, between your presence in the locality and Mr. White's?"

"Good lord, no. I've told you I didn't know the chap from Adam. Look here, what's all this about?"

He still appeared to be quite unperturbed, though a good deal puzzled. His manner was perfectly friendly, too; that of a man confidently expecting a reasonable and satisfactory explanation to questions which he did not at the moment understand.

"It's merely this," Bobby explained. "I am trying to clear away the non-essentials so as to get at what really counts, if I can. I would like to say, please, with all the emphasis I can, that I've a reason for my questions, even though you think I'm being impertinent. Impertinent in the sense that they may prove not— pertinent, is likely enough. But not impertinent in the sense of being mere cheek. So I hope you will answer them as fully and freely as you can. If you will give me that help, it may be a very great help indeed."

"Well, fire ahead," De Legett answered, "though I haven't the foggiest what you're getting at."

"Mr. Leonard Glynne was with you at that time?"

"That's right, but what on earth?"

Bobby lifted a hand to check him.

"What was the reason for your meeting?"

"Business," answered De Legett briefly. He was keeping his temper admirably, but a faint note of impatience sounded now in his voice, to remind Bobby that friendly and amiable as so far he had been, his temper was beginning to wear. "Why ask me? Why not ask Glynne?"

"For one thing, you are in London and Mr. Glynne lives in Midwych."

"He has a place up by the Edgware Road somewhere," De Legett answered. "He's often there."

Bobby received this information with no sign of interest, even though it startled him, for the Edgware Road vicinity was beginning to acquire for him a sinister significance. "Can you give me the address?" he asked.

"Well, I think you had better ask Glynne himself," De Legett answered. "I'm not even sure now where it is exactly—though I daresay I've got a note of it somewhere. Still, I think you had better ask him."

"Who was your business with?"

"Well, what do you suppose? I've just told you that's why Glynne and I met."

"You mean it was business between your two selves? But why meet at an hotel in Wales instead of here in your office, especially if Mr. Glynne has a London address, too?"

"It was more convenient, that's all. I run up north fairly often to see my principals and nose around for any chance there may be of a new agency. Glynne knew I was in Liverpool for a day or two and knew it wouldn't be much out of my way for me to stop off where he said. He was helping a Mrs. Frayton run a tennis tournament on the Welsh coast at the time, so it was handy for him, too."

"Mrs. Frayton? Did you say Mrs. Frayton?" Bobby asked.

"Yes. What about it. Why?"

"I remembered the name, that's all," Bobby answered slowly, while to himself he wondered what the meaning might be of the strange way in which this case seemed ever to go round and round in circles. "There was a big jewellery robbery, wasn't there?" he asked.

"Yes, that was her," De Legett agreed. "I hope you don't think that's what Glynne and I were up to?"

He chuckled at what he evidently thought a good joke, and Bobby laughed, too.

"No, I don't think that had occurred to me," he said pleasantly.

"As a matter of fact," De Legett went on, "it was her chauffeur—chap named Reynolds. Got away with it, too. Nothing more ever heard either of him or the loot. I shouldn't have thought it possible when it was perfectly well known who he was. Mrs. Frayton offered a whacking big reward, too."

"It's certainly strange the way he vanished," Bobby agreed. "Did you and Mr. Glynne leave together?"

"No, I came on to town and he went back to his tennis. Miss Glynne, his sister, you know, she's a tip topper, was competing. He wanted to be there when she came on in the finals. It was an idea for a new gadget for preventing ice forming on aeroplanes he wanted to see me about. The idea was for me to put him in touch with some of my principals to help get it launched."

"Did you do that?"

"It hasn't come to anything as far as I know. I believe he's working on a new dodge now. Something about retractors. Besides, he seems to have got hold of backers on his own, plenty of capital now to judge from what he's spending. More than he'll ever get out of it, if you ask me. My own idea is that what he is really keen on is doing something good that'll get him back into the R.A.F. They threw him out over some bloomer he made and he wants to wangle a come back."

Bobby pondered this information. Apparently Leonard Glynne had recently, since at least the death of Andrew White, secured control of at any rate a fairly large sum of money. Also, about the time of that death, Becky Glynne had been somewhere in the neighbourhood. And, if De Legett's story was correct, it was Leonard who had arranged for that meeting in Wales, so near the scene of the tragedy.

Did those facts, Bobby asked himself very gravely, add up to anything significant?

He felt that he had learnt as much as he was likely to, for the present at least, from De Legett, and that now further information must be sought from Leonard Glynne himself. And that young man was little likely to show himself as friendly and as amiable as had done—so far—Mr. De Legett.

"There is just one thing more," Bobby said with some slight hesitation. "I understand you are engaged to Lady May Grayson?"

"Good lord, what put that into your head?" De Legett gasped.

"You have her photograph there?" Bobby pointed out.

"Oh, that," De Legett said. "Well, why not? Easy to look at, isn't she?" He chuckled as if at some secret joke that he found very amusing. "Yes, that's her photo all right, but I've never met her in my life and if you want to know why that photo's there, you'll have to do a bit of guessing. If you guess right I'll stand you a drink any time you come around again."

"I'm not a bit of good at guessing," Bobby said. "In the police, they don't like guesses either. You are engaged?"

De Legett, who had swung round in his swivel chair to grin at Lady May's photograph, swung back again to face Bobby.

"Yes, I'm engaged. I expect I shall be married soon," he said, and as Bobby watched he seemed inwardly to glow, as though the wonder and the glory of that thought had kindled within him a flame of deepest joy.

But Bobby stared at him with a kind of horror, with such a deadly, secret terror as he had seldom known. In a voice he could not keep quite steady, he muttered:—

"Will you tell me who the lady is?"

"Oh, no," De Legett answered, though without any show of resentment, at a question that might well have seemed outside all discretion. "Oh, no, no one knows that but us." He paused and from his inner joy there bubbled up a laugh of such utter and complete happiness as it has been the lot of but few to know. "Why do you want to know?" he asked gently.

"Because," Bobby said, and it was as though the words came from an impulse and a will that were not wholly his, "because I think the answer means your life or else your death."

But the other seemed quite unmoved.

"That's right," he said with the same bubbling laugh of wondering happiness, "it's life and death to me all right. Life or death," he repeated, and with those words still sounding in his ears, Bobby took his leave.

## CHAPTER XV
### CARDIFF

The first thing Bobby did after leaving the office of Messrs. Perceval and Wilde was to make certain arrangements with one of those itinerant photographers often to be seen in London streets, or, in the summer, on the promenades of seaside resorts. After that, he put through a trunk call to Midwych in an attempt to get in touch with Leonard Glynne. The answer, when it came, was from his sister, Becky. She said curtly that Leonard was away, possibly in London, possibly elsewhere. She did not know his London address, no one at home knew it, he had never said what it was, and, anyhow, and very coldly, what was the meaning of such an extraordinary request?

Without waiting for a reply, Becky rang off, and Bobby looked more thoughtful than ever as he, too, hung up. He was aware of a very strong impression that he would get no help from Becky, though in view of the apparent bad feeling between brother and sister, he found himself wondering if it was Leonard or someone else about whom she was troubled. For every tone of her voice had made it plain that she was afraid, afraid of Bobby's activities. He felt sure she would do all in her power to thwart or hinder them.

"But the thing's gone too far," Bobby reflected grimly.

For the next very headachey half hour or so he was busy with Bradshaw, looking up the trains to Cardiff and endeavouring to work out various connections. After that, he just had time to call at the nearest public library where an erudite, astonished, and obliging librarian finally produced for him two books. One was entitled *Tales of Old Paris* and the other *Legends of the Incas*.

"You may find what you want there," said the librarian; and Bobby thanked him, and, by special permission, took the two books away with him to read later.

Next he went on to the little Mayfair hat shop, closed by now, and, taking his fiancée, Olive, to a near-by restaurant, talked over with her his perplexities, his doubts, and his fears.

"It's an ugly case," he told her, "and I'm scared where it's leading, but I've got to talk it over with someone or bust. And there's only you. But for you, I'm all on my own. Colonel Glynne doesn't seem to want to hear anything about it. I'm to go to the Public Prosecutor's office or Scotland Yard if I want help—but only if I have to, sort of last extremity. And I'm not quite there yet, though it's getting to look more and more like it every day."

So he talked and talked, and put forward theories, and showed they were absurd, and put forward more theories, and disposed of them, too, and Olive listened, and said nothing, but thought the more, till she, too, seemed to glimpse behind his words a horror greater than any she had ever dreamed.

The meal ended in silence and then he took her back home and leaving her there hurried on to his own rooms for a few things he wanted. He had run it rather fine, but by taking a taxi he was in time to catch the night train for Cardiff, finding himself about nine the next morning, after a dispiriting breakfast in a restaurant only half awake, hopelessly lost in a busy Cardiff suburb. A policeman appeared presently and directed him to his destination, a small but prosperous-looking shop with well-stocked, well-arranged windows displaying chocolates, chewing gum, cigarettes and so on. Above was the name 'Reeves', and the shop was, he thought, well placed, at a corner where traffic routes intersected and with two large cinemas near by. He stood for a moment, looking at the shop windows, noting their contents, glancing, too, at the windows of the living rooms above, and then as he was about to enter he saw that someone was also looking at him, through the laden shelves of chocolate boxes and boxes of cigarettes that formed the background of the shop window. Who it was he could not tell, for he had but the merest glimpse of a watchful face instantly withdrawn, but it was with uneasy thoughts in his mind that he pushed open the door and entered.

The shop was empty; and though a bell on the door loudly announced his entry, no one appeared. He waited and then knocked on the counter, but still there was a pause before a woman emerged from the door at the back, stood for a moment looking at him with evident mistrust and fear, and then came on to face him from behind the counter.

"She knows who I am," he thought, and, a good deal worried, he asked himself how that could be.

Impossible, he thought, for certainly he had never seen her before and yet it was very certain that she knew him. She was about forty, he guessed, with a pleasant, homely face that at the moment bore a very worried and even alarmed expression, and that he now began to think reminded him vaguely of someone else, though of whom he could not be sure. But there was something faintly familiar about the general cast of the features, especially in the small mouth now so tightly closed above the small, pointed chin. Perhaps only a casual resemblance, he thought, or perhaps one that presently he would be able to identify. He bought a packet of cigarettes by way of a propitiatory opening, and then said:—

"You are Mrs. Reeves, I think?" She nodded and he went on:—
"I think your sister, Mrs. Reynolds, lives with you. Could I have a
few moments' talk with her?"

"I'll go and ask her," Mrs. Reeves answered.

She went back behind the shop and was away some minutes.
No other customer appeared. It was a slack hour, too late for
people going to work, or for children on their way to school, too
early for the morning shoppers. Even the street outside seemed
quiet, with little traffic passing except for an occasional car and
once for the unnecessarily loud hooting of a motor-cycle that sped
by with an arrogant, triumphant 'honk honk' as though it shouted
satisfaction with itself and scorn of all the rest of the world. Mrs.
Reeves came back into the shop.

"I'm sorry," she said. "Jinnie's not feeling very well."

Bobby produced his credentials. Mrs. Reeves did not seem
either very surprised or very impressed, and thought it very
unlikely Mrs. Reynolds would make the effort to see him that
Bobby suggested. He asked what doctor was attending her and
Mrs. Reeves said her sister wasn't one to run to a doctor every
time she had a bad sick headache, but that didn't mean she was in
a fit state to talk to strangers. Bobby said it was very regrettable,
but, in the interests of justice, it was necessary he should see Mrs.
Reynolds. He would therefore, he supposed, have to wait till her
headache was better. In order to lose no time, he would arrange
for a constable to call every hour or even oftener to ask how she
was. This suggestion, of course, was no better than blackmail and
quite unjustifiable—as he made it, Bobby could almost hear
defending counsel thundering a denunciation of police
persecution and every national paper in the land taking up the cry.
All the same it was quite evident that Mrs. Reeves liked the
suggestion of such frequent visits by constables in uniform no
better than Bobby had expected. She said angrily:—

"It's no good your doing that. If you must know, Jinnie's gone.
She's miles away by now."

"Is she, though?" said Bobby. "Well, now then. Miles away, you
said? Quick work."

"She's fed up with your sort and I don't wonder, either," Mrs. Reeves went on in the same angry, indignant tones. "Worrying her out of her life, and me, too, and bad for the business as well, with plain clothes police hanging about in every corner waiting for Ted, as if he would be such a fool as to come here."

"Natural to expect a man to try to get in touch with his wife," Bobby pointed out.

She made no comment on this, but turned away to put some cigarette boxes straight and then said over her shoulder:—

"What's the good? why can't you leave us alone? Ted's safe enough from you, you'll never find him."

"There's no place in all the world where a man is safe from a police search," Bobby told her.

"There's one place where he's safe," she answered in a low voice, "one place where you will never find him."

"You mean he is dead?" Bobby asked, for he believed that he had read that meaning in her eyes. "It's possible. I thought of that, too. Difficult for a living man to disappear so completely as he has done. What makes you think so?"

She did not answer to that, but went on with her work of unnecessarily arranging and re-arranging her stock.

"I thought of it," Bobby told her, "because there are so many dead men in this affair."

"What do you mean?" she said then, pausing in her work to turn and look at him.

"If that's what Mrs. Reynolds believes," he went on, "why did she run away the moment she saw me?"

"She's been driven nearly crazy with questions and questions and questions, and so have I," Mrs. Reeves retorted. "Sick and tired of it we are, and not as if we knew anything, either of us. How could we? I don't and Jinnie doesn't and you lot watching and staring and following, and questions and questions all the time till we were sick and tired. When Jinnie saw you, she came in and told me she couldn't stand any more, and I don't blame her. 'There's another of them outside,' she said. 'It's the Midwych lot this time,' she said, and off she went and no wonder."

"Miles away, now, you said?"

"That's right," Mrs. Reeves answered defiantly.

"Quick work," Bobby said again. "Motor-cycle, I suppose?"

"How do you know?" Mrs. Reynolds asked, looking a little startled this time.

"Well, you said she was miles away by now, and that sounded like a car or a motor bike, and somehow I thought of a motor bike first, because I seem to be always coming across motor bikes in this affair. One hooted rather loudly, too, as it passed a minute or two ago. It almost sounded like a motor bike's way of pulling a face at you. A woman's trick, perhaps, when she feels she's scored for once."

"I don't know what you are talking about," Mrs. Reeves muttered uneasily.

"Well, I don't either, so that's no wonder," Bobby answered. "How did she know where I was from and that I was a policeman?"

"We've had plenty like you here," she retorted, "enough to know when she saw you."

"But she hadn't seen me," Bobby protested mildly. "Oh, yes, she had. Doing the window she was, and saw you staring, and knew at once."

"I see," said Bobby. "Well, will you give her a message from me?" He put a card on the table with his London address. "Tell her I would like to see her. Tell her I'm not looking for her husband. It's not my case. But I think she might be able to help me with another, that of a man named Baird who was found dead recently in Wychwood forest. I daresay you've read about it in the papers?"

"What's it to do with Jinnie?" Mrs. Reeves asked, looking now not only suspicious but puzzled as well.

"I don't know," Bobby answered. "I want to find out."

"Is it a trap?" she asked, more distrustfully than ever.

"No," he answered. "Besides, I think you are right and that most likely we shall never find Ted Reynolds because I think, like you, that he is dead."

Mrs. Reeves said nothing. After a pause Bobby added:— "Only, you see, we don't want any more men dead in the same way."

"I don't know what you mean," she repeated. After a pause she added:—"I expect it's just a clever trap."

"I wish you would get that out of your head," Bobby said. Then he asked: "Was your sister very fond of him?" The only answer she made was a slight affirmative movement of the head. But it carried much meaning. Bobby took a cigarette from the packet he had just bought and tapped it thoughtfully on the counter.

"That makes it bad," he said. "I'm sorry. Funny," he said, "how, when a woman cares for a man it never seems to make much difference what he does."

"He wasn't worth it," Mrs. Reeves broke out. "Men are like that. You can never trust them. I told her so. Never. It's not their fault. Led they are. You'll pay for it, I told her, when I saw how she used to look at him. It's always like that, if you get that way with a man, you'll pay for it. It's the way men are, you can't trust them, but Jinnie always stuck to it, it was her he put first."

"First?" Bobby repeated. "Who was second then?" She did not answer, and for a moment or two they looked steadily at each other across the counter. She said slowly:—

"Jinnie never knew."

Bobby waited. Mrs. Reeves went on:—

"Jinnie knew there was someone, but she was always sure he would come back to her. Because she always knew that she was really first, that the other didn't count, she was ready to wait. The other wasn't real, she said, only a mistake, like getting lost in the dark. But she was the light he would come back to, and she waited, and then it happened about the diamond ear-rings and she knew she would never find her man again."

Again there was a long silence in the little shop, and so softly that Bobby could hardly hear it, she murmured:— "Poor Jinnie."

"Poor Jinnie," he repeated after her, and she looked at him in surprise, as though something in his voice astonished her.

He went away then for he felt that he had learned as much as Mrs. Reeves was willing, or perhaps able, to tell him. One highly interesting detail, however, seemed now to be clearly established, though of its significance, or indeed of its importance, he did not feel at all certain. Nor did he feel certain whether Mrs. Reynolds—

or Mrs. Reeves for that matter—was more likely to prove helper or opponent, or perhaps, and perhaps more probably, merely indifferent.

He found a good and convenient train and was back in London in time to get to Bond Street before the closing hour. Half way down that proud street of luxury and display stand the discreetly imposing premises of Messrs. Higham, who are not so much the 'well known' jewellers as just simply 'the' jewellers. They will, of course, sell you a cheap ring or bracelet for ten or twenty pounds, if you happen to want one for any reason, but they are obviously slightly bored by such transactions they merely carry out for the convenience of their more eccentric customers. They prefer to deal in diamond tiaras, pearl necklaces, rubies at least as large as a pigeon's egg, or indeed, for after all they are tradespeople and have to live, in any form of jewellery of which the value approaches four figures. Transactions over the four figures are, however, those that really interest them, and these, if sufficiently above that kind of dead line, are generally dealt with by the senior partner, old Mr. Higham, a dignitary whom otherwise few customers see.

To-day, though, it was with that scarcely less imposing dignitary, the gigantic commissionaire with a double row of medal ribbons on his tunic, with whom Bobby wished for a little conversation. To him, after producing his credentials, for the commissionaire was not a man to gossip with any casual stranger, Bobby showed that photograph he had instructed an itinerant photographer to secure of Count de Legett—an excellent snap shot it was, too. It was, Bobby went on to explain, important that Scotland Yard should be informed at once if the original of the photograph called at Messrs. Higham's. Especially important was it to know, if the caller came, if he were alone or accompanied by a lady.

The commissionaire listened carefully and promised to report at once any such appearance, and Bobby went on to the Yard. There he explained what he had done, obtained a promise that if the commissionaire did report a visit by Count de Legett in the company of a woman, then every effort would be made to follow and identify her.

"You can trust us for that all right," said the Yard man. "I'll put two of our best men on the job if you really think it so important."

Bobby winced slightly, for the promise to put two men on the job meant there would be two men's time to pay for, and Midwych wouldn't at all like paying for two—especially if 'best men' meant both would be sergeants and so a higher rate of pay and expenses charged. He suspected, no doubt most unjustly, that the Yard was slack at the time, and quite willing to get two men's pay out of a provincial authority. However, it couldn't be helped, and he thanked the Yard cordially and the Yard looked down its nose and said:—

"Mind you, it's your responsibility, and a long shot if you ask me. And don't run away with the idea that we are going to risk getting into hot water, doing your job for you. There'll be strict orders that the lady is not to be interfered with in any way whatever."

"That's all right," Bobby said. "Annoying her or interfering in any way is the very last thing I want. All I want to know is, who is she—and a pretty big all, too. It may mean a lot if I can find out."

"Well, if that's all," declared the Yard man, grinning a little, "it oughtn't to be difficult. That is, if this Count de Legett chap wants to marry her. When a chap's engaged, he generally likes to spill the good news all round, poor devil. Wants 'em all to know he's nibbled the cheese and the trap's shut down."

Bobby requested the Yard not to be so beastly cynical, and the Yard said he wasn't cynical a bit, only he had been through it and he knew, and therewith Bobby took his leave.

His next visit was to the 'Cut and Come Again', that newly reorganized and, at any rate as far as was known at the moment, highly respectable night club supposed to be doing well on the flavour of an ancient though now abandoned wickedness that still clung to its redecorated walls. There Bobby succeeded in obtaining a good deal of miscellaneous information, partly from a prolonged questioning of an eagerly obliging staff most anxious to assist the police so far as unhappily defective memories and a press of business that prevented them from noticing almost anything, allowed them the felicity of so doing.

The books, however, the list of subscribing members, the names of their guests, proved more interesting, and kept Bobby busy to a late hour. When at last he had finished he had a notebook nearly full of information he felt he must submit to careful examination and analysis before he could tell which of the facts he had collected were significant, which irrelevant. But that task had to be postponed, for, as so often happens in such investigations, next morning information came to hand that had to be followed up, that occupied a very great deal of most valuable time, but whereof no details need be given here since in the end it proved to be entirely unfounded and of no value or significance whatever.

Of the encumbrance of this false scent he was not free till the morning of the Friday on which was to take place, during the evening, that meeting of the Edgware Psychical Research Society at the Mountain Street Hall he had determined to be present at, if possible, or, if he could not secure admittance, then at least to watch the arrival of the members. There was also in the post a letter from Superintendent Oxley informing him that his reports were duly noted; that his expenses were, in the superintendent's opinion, unduly high and should be reduced by all possible means, though, on instructions, a remittance was enclosed for the amount claimed and must be acknowledged by return on Form A374-XM; that Inspector Marsh was coming to London on other business and would get in touch with Bobby in order to see if he required further assistance; and, finally, that Colonel Glynne had gone on sick leave, but before doing so had once more given orders that Bobby was to continue his inquiries on his own lines, applying for such assistance or advice as he might require from his own headquarters at Midwych, from the London police, or from the office of the Public Prosecutor, as and when he felt necessary.

Bobby read all this very carefully. Not difficult to see that Superintendent Oxley was worried and uneasy, disliked the whole thing, found it highly unorthodox, and—with good reason— suspected he was not being told everything. The visit of Inspector Marsh, whom Bobby had not yet met, was evidently to be an attempt to find out what was going on. No wonder, Bobby supposed, that Oxley felt sore and angry, and considered that there was not being shown in him that confidence which his position entitled him to expect. Inspector Marsh, Bobby reflected, would have to be handled very tactfully. Perhaps it might be a good idea to take him along to Mountain Street.

He wondered a good deal, too, whether Colonel Glynne had gone on sick leave from necessity or whether it meant that he had heard of the phone call Bobby had put through, of the request for his son's address in London that apparently was known to no one at Asbury Cottage or even perhaps to no one in Midwych.

Uncomfortably, more than uncomfortably, with real distress, for he had liked and admired what he had seen of the colonel and felt a real sympathy for him, Bobby told himself that the second supposition was the more likely. He seemed to have a vision of the old man aware that the hunt was drawing near, that a dreadful possibility was growing every day more and more into the likeness of a probability, yet unable to do more than wait the unveiling of a truth which might well blast for ever all that he valued and held dear. Nor did Bobby feel he had one word of hope or comfort he could utter, since that curtain of darkness and of horror he was trying to pierce might hide behind it things he did not care to contemplate. Only one thing was plain to him, of only one thing was he certain, that his duty must be done and the truth followed wheresoever it led. He put the letter away and set out on his first task of the day, to find Leonard Glynne in his London address that no one seemed to know, or, if they knew it, to wish to tell.

## CHAPTER XVI
## WORKSHOP

London is as good a hiding place as the world has ever known, and to identify amidst its many millions any one individual is no easy task, as the police authorities at least very well know. Normally, of course, there are the directories, but they serve only for the established residents who have no reason for concealment. Nor has London any such 'Bureau de Logis' as the French police find so useful. Naturally the London police have their own methods, but methods that can only be used within the framework of the law—as when a charge is to be laid or for some other substantial reason.

Leonard Glynne evidently wished to remain in concealment, since he kept his address hidden from his family, and yet in order to find him Bobby could ask for no official help. He had no good reason to advance to justify such a request, and besides he felt it important to give as little indication as possible of the lines on which he was working.

There was just one clue to start from. Count de Legett had remarked that Leonard's address was somewhere in that Edgware Road district whereto seemed to lead so many of the threads Bobby was doing his best to follow. Unfortunately the Edgware Road district is as populous, as crowded, contains as large a proportion of transient inhabitants as any in London. But Count de Legett had remarked, too, that Leonard was working on various inventions connected with the problem of flight. Such inventions, Bobby supposed, would be likely to involve the construction of models and for that purpose presumably some sort of workshop would be required. A workshop suggested the use of some kind of mechanical power for the working of lathes and so on. By far the most convenient source of power for small, irregular users is electricity, and Bobby therefore proceeded first of all to the office of the local electricity company. There, though not without some difficulty, and only after a display of his official credentials, he secured a list of the customers in the neighbourhood using power above normal domestic requirements and yet under that of any large commercial concern. In the list supplied him, not a very long one, one name attracted his attention. It was that of the Glinbury Research Company, and 'Glinbury' struck Bobby at once as possibly a combination of 'Glynne' and 'Asbury', of Leonard's surname and his home address. Thither he accordingly proceeded, and arrived presently in a mews whence the horse had long been driven by the car. Several men were busy, washing cars, filling tanks, and so on, and of one of them Bobby inquired if he knew the Glinbury Research Company. The response was a broad grin and a demand to know if this was another 'happy wire'.

"Happy wire?" repeated Bobby, puzzled for the moment, his thoughts turning to birthdays, christenings, engagements, and other such happy and fortunate events. "Why?"

"If you come up with 'em once, you may again," the other answered cryptically. "Why not?" He pointed to some steps near, leading to what had probably once been a hayloft or harness room. "There you are," he said. "Up those steps," and went on with his work.

Bobby ascended the steps indicated and at the top found a door with a brass plate, bearing the legend 'Glinbury Research Co.' He knocked, a cheerful voice bade him enter, he pushed open the door and found himself in a large, well-lighted apartment, serving apparently the dual purpose of workshop and living-room. Along one side ran a work bench, and there were power belts, a lathe, and so on. At the further end of the room was a small electric cooking stove and heater, two or three comfortable-looking chairs, a small kitchen cabinet. Near by was an open door giving a glimpse of a bedroom beyond. On the dressing table Bobby could see various small articles that plainly suggested a woman's presence. Everything looked well cared for and the general effect was of comfort and ease.

Even without the evidence of the dressing table, there was plenty even in this outer room to tell of feminine influence. Few men, for instance, living alone, would have managed to make the living-room corner of the workshop look so cosy and attractive; few men, again, would have thought of placing a vase of flowers on a bench covered with tools.

In the middle of the room, dividers in his hand, stood Leonard Glynne, staring at Bobby with an extreme surprise that was only too plainly swiftly turning to an even more extreme annoyance.

"What the devil?" he began and paused.

"Not at all," said Bobby amiably. "Far from it, I hope. My name's Owen. Surely you remember me?"

"What the devil," retorted the young man, ignoring this, "do you want?"

"I thought perhaps," explained Bobby, "you might be willing to give me a little information on one or two small points."

"How did you know where I was?" demanded Leonard.

"Oh, come, Mr. Glynne," Bobby protested mildly, "what's a detective for if he can't find out a little thing like that?"

"Dad can't have told you," Leonard said, looking blacker than ever. "He didn't know. I suppose Becky gave it away, the little double-crossing bitch."

"Did Miss Glynne know?" Bobby asked. "Sorry to hear it, because that suggests she isn't always as truthful as she might be. And that's bad, because it means one can't be sure of anything she says. You see, she told me on the phone last night that she didn't know your London address. Yet unless she did know it, she couldn't have sent you a wire to warn you I was wanting it."

Leonard stared, so surprised he almost forgot his anger.

"How do you know that?" he demanded.

"Well, you told me, didn't you?"

"I did? what do you mean? I didn't."

"Well, Miss Glynne was the only person I asked for it and you at once thought of her and called her, very unfairly, a double-crosser, which meant evidently that you thought she had both told me and warned you. Or why a 'double'- crosser? And as she sounded a bit excited and upset over the phone it wasn't much of a guess to suppose that she would probably telegraph rather than use the post. I notice you aren't on the phone here."

"I suppose you think all that's mighty clever."

Bobby shook his head, a little sadly.

"No one ever calls me clever," he admitted. "I'm only a two-plus-two detective. I just go on adding two and two together till I find the four they seem to make—it doesn't take brains, merely patience, though sometimes I do think patience is rarer than brains and even at times more useful. The other chap may have more brains than you but it's ten to one he hasn't any patience at all."

"Well," Leonard growled, "brains and patience and all, you can clear out pronto."

"But I've gone to a lot of trouble to find you and ask you for some information," Bobby protested. "Do you mind telling me why you arranged to meet Count de Legett near the place and about the time of Mr. Andrew White's death?"

Leonard's expression changed. The truculence went out of it. He seemed to shrink back, as at some swift and unexpected blow. He became very pale. He muttered:— "Oh, you've got on to that." Then he said:— "Well, what about it?"

"That is what I am asking," Bobby said.

"What? what are you getting at? what do you want to know?"

"What kind of a four that particular two and two make?"

"It was business, a business meeting. I thought De Legett might help me to raise some capital. He acts for some big people. That's all."

"Did he succeed?"

"We didn't go on with it. I got hold of some capital myself."

"Do you mind telling me how and from where?"

"Yes, I do. I think you've a damned cheek to ask."

"Perhaps I have," Bobby admitted, "but Mr. Andrew White's death is still unexplained and the other day Mr. Baird died in Wychwood Forest and no one knows how or why. Other men have died as well and sometimes I think there may be more deaths to come."

"I don't know what you are talking about."

"About deaths," Bobby muttered, "sudden deaths, too many and too sudden."

"Well, it's nothing to do with me. I thought Baird's death was an accident—got drunk and set the caravan on fire and couldn't get out in time. That's what it looked like to me."

"I think that is what it was meant to look like."

"You mean it was murder? Well, you don't think I murdered him, do you?"

"I think you could give me some helpful information if you would," Bobby answered. "I'm not suspicious of any one person at present. I wish I was. It would be a help, show I was beginning to see my way. Only you know a policeman always grows suspicious if people won't answer questions. Automatic, that is."

"Look here—" Leonard began. He was growing more composed now. His eyes were less uneasy, his face was losing its pallor and turning red instead, his stance acquiring a subtle air of menace. "Look here, I've had enough of this. Get out before I throw you out."

"I do hope you won't try," Bobby urged earnestly. "You see, I'm bigger than you and in better training, too, I expect, and then a row—a bit vulgar, I think, don't you? Of course, I can't make you answer questions and if you refuse—well, I'll have to go with my tail between my legs, if you like. Only you might let me ask them. Useful to you, too, perhaps, to know what it is I want to know. Did you know Colonel Glynne had gone on sick leave?"

"What about it?"

"I think perhaps it's worry. I think perhaps it's more than worry. Perhaps it's fear. If you would tell me what I want to know, it might help to take away that fear."

Leonard made no answer. His scowl was blacker than ever, but he neither moved nor spoke. Bobby went on:

"I think there was some reason besides business why you arranged to meet De Legett—or why De Legett arranged to meet you, if it was like that—about the time of Mr. White's death. Wasn't there?"

Leonard made no answer. Bobby went on:—

"I am wondering why you needed capital before you met De Legett but not afterwards."

"Trying to get me hanged, are you?" Leonard said now. "I've had enough of this."

"Another thing, the most important of all," Bobby continued. "At least I think so, but perhaps I'm wrong. Who is the lady who is living with you here?"

"Isn't that going a little far?" Leonard asked, and now his voice was low and dangerous, so that Bobby held himself prepared for an actual attack.

"I know it is," he said, "but then I think this business is going to take us all very far indeed."

Leonard moved across to the work bench and picked up a bit of metal tubing that was lying there.

"You had better go," he said.

"All right," Bobby said, "but remember—we have ways of finding things out. In my judgment, it is necessary to know who the lady is. She is not here now, I can see, but I expect she was this morning, and if I had been half an hour earlier very likely I might have met her. It would save a lot—"

Bobby never completed the sentence. Leonard, swinging the piece of metal tubing, ran straight at him. Bobby was fully prepared though and flung a chair in his path. Leonard collided with it and before he could recover himself Bobby stepped forward and hit him very neatly on the temple, a well timed, well placed blow. Leonard went down before it. Bobby stooped over him, wrenched the piece of metal tubing from his grasp, sent it flying well out of reach through the open door under the bed in the room beyond, said:— "Made rather a bit of an ass of yourself, haven't you?" and took himself off, before the somewhat dazed Leonard was on his feet again.

But the last glimpse Bobby had of him showed him running into the bedroom, pulling violently at a drawer there, and Bobby closed the outer door of the Glinbury Research Company and descended the steps to the mews with considerable haste. For he had an uncomfortable suspicion that in that drawer was a revolver or some such weapon that Leonard in his rage had gone to seek, and the very last thing Bobby desired was to act as target to the young man. Revolver shots are so very difficult to keep out of the police courts, nor did he wish there to be yet another corpse in this case, and more especially he did not wish in any event for that corpse to be his own.

"Hasty and violent chap," he thought to himself as he walked along, and moodily reflected that everywhere in this investigation he seemed to find a woman and yet could never discover her identity. He reflected, too, that sometimes after such interrogations, the person questioned grows nervous and thinks it better to come forward with some explanation. He wondered if there was any chance of that happening this time, but he did not think it very likely. He thought Leonard made of sterner stuff, and also he had an impression that the woman in the background, whoever she might be, would take good care to see that the secret of her identity was preserved. Rather ruefully, too, Bobby felt it would have been much more sensible to have avoided mentioning the signs he had noticed of a woman's presence. If he had held his tongue about that, it might have been possible, by setting a careful watch, to discover who she was. But he had been taken by surprise, and then also, once the secret of his London address had been penetrated, Leonard would certainly have adopted further precautions to protect the further secret of his companion's identity. Most likely Leonard was already ringing her up from some call box to warn her to be careful. The obvious plan, Bobby decided, was to do nothing at all for a few days. Then Leonard and his companion would probably relax the precautions they would certainly now be planning and it would be easier to get her name. But almost as important, Bobby told himself, was to discover how Leonard had secured the money that enabled him to keep up this separate and secret establishment.

He wondered, too, how far Becky was in her brother's confidence. Evidently she knew his address, but did she know how he had secured the money he seemed now so well supplied with or the name of the woman he was living with, or even of her existence? If so, how did such confidential relations harmonize with the ill feeling between them that Bobby had himself seen enough of to convince him it was genuine?

"Another snag," he sighed to himself as he ate his lunch and then hurried back to keep his appointment with Inspector Marsh, of the Wychshire county police. The inspector was there punctually to the minute; an elderly man with a bluff, hearty manner, plainly both experienced and intelligent and even more plainly distrustful of proceedings entirely unorthodox and unexplained. His manner was so distantly formal, not to say hostile, that Bobby thought it better to make a direct approach.

"I know the Super, thinks he is not being fairly treated," he said. "I quite understand that and I expect Colonel Glynne does, too. But then Colonel Glynne, though I don't suppose he is a rich man, has some private means, and so he can run risks a poor man couldn't. And I'm fairly young still and I have a little bit of money of my own now, as very likely you've heard."

"You mean that sort of private business you were mixed up in—first time I ever heard of police officers being allowed to take on private jobs. Of course, you've got swell friends."

Bobby winced. It was quite true, but he didn't like to be reminded of it.

"Wouldn't help me much if I fell down on the job," he said defensively. "The point is, we can afford to take risks. Mr. Oxley, for instance, I should take to be not far from retiring, and if he lost his job and his pension, it would about finish him."

Inspector Marsh fairly gasped.

"What are you getting at?" he demanded. "Why should he?"

"Another thing," Bobby went on. "If Colonel Glynne —well, resigned in a hurry, there would be an awful fuss, and unless there was someone to take hold and carry on, the whole Wychshire force might go to pieces. Mr. Oxley has just simply got to be there."

Inspector Marsh was by this time beyond all speech. He could only gape.

"The simple fact is," Bobby continued, "Colonel Glynne has got on to something so full of dynamite it may explode and blow us both to—well, to wherever sacked policemen go. We aren't sure yet what it really is. It may fizzle out. It may have to be dropped. It may boil down to something quite ordinary. There you are, the plain fact is, the less any one knows at present, the safer they are. Naturally, the moment there's anything to act on, it'll go through the usual channels."

Marsh asked doubtfully:—

"Is all that on the up and up? not pulling my leg, are you?"

"Murder cases don't lend themselves to leg pulling," retorted Bobby. "My own belief is that Mr. Baird was murdered in Wychwood Forest, and that there have been other murders in the past and that there may be more to come. But for the present—go slow's the word. Look here, how about coming along with me to-night? It won't commit you to anything. The Edgware Psychical Research Society is holding a meeting at a parish hall sort of place in Mountain Street, off the Edgware Road. I want to get in if I can."

"What for?"

"To see what happens."

"Spiritualism, isn't it?"

"Apparently. And a spiritualist stance is held in the dark, so specially thick curtains are necessary. This parish hall has them. But specially thick curtains can hide other things than ghosts."

"I've got to be back on duty to-morrow morning," said Marsh doubtfully.

"There's a train at midnight. You could catch that."

"Right," said Marsh, making up his mind.

"The meeting's for eight," Bobby said. "I want to be in good time. I want to watch arrivals. Could you be here about half-past six? It's not more than a quarter of an hour from here by bus."

"Right," said Marsh again and departed, evidently both puzzled and doubtful, a state of mind with which Bobby had much sympathy, since it so closely resembled his own.

The rest of his time before the hour appointed for Marsh's return, Bobby devoted to a careful examination and analysis of the notes he had made in the 'Cut and Come Again' club, now so happily reformed, so zealous to give every possible assistance to the law that an extraordinary pressure of affairs and unfortunately defective memories permitted.

The facts Bobby finally extracted and jotted down separately seemed to him of interest, both for what they did and did not show. Though he was inclined to think that the indications absent were even more significant than those that were present.

For instance, there was nothing to show that Leonard Glynne had ever been near the place. All Bobby's questioning at the club had failed to obtain from any member of the staff any recognition of Leonard's name or the least sign that there he had ever been heard of.

Equally interesting was it to know that Andy White had not only been a member of the club—he had also been a part proprietor and had taken an active share in the reorganization when a decision had been come to to make it respectable and to abandon for ever its former lurid methods. He had been a frequent visitor and more than once had given there supper parties to his friends.

Lord Byatt, apparently, had been one of the first to join the reconstituted and reformed club. An original member, in fact, and again a frequent visitor. He was still remembered with regret by some of the club staff with whom he had been popular. He had often brought friends, especially ladies, especially young and good-looking ladies. Never anything to object to, of course, in surroundings so decorous as those provided by the new 'Cut and Come Again', but definitely a young gentleman with the friendliest feelings towards the opposite sex. It was confirmed that the last time he had been seen alive was at the club when he had danced a good deal with Miss Hazel Hannay. This was clearly remembered because of the enquiries made at the time. Bobby also learned that Hazel had left the club alone some time before Lord Byatt's departure. Bobby took it for granted that this point had been dealt with during the investigation and that nothing further of interest had been discovered.

Lord Henry Darmoor was one of the few who had been members both of the old naughty club and of the new and reformed and respectable—so far—club. But then he had a wide membership of clubs, and it was only recently that he had attended the 'Cut and Come Again* with any degree of frequency. A point that came out through Bobby's questioning was that lately he had begun to drink too much and to show himself excitable and quarrelsome. This had been widely noticed and commented on as it was such an entire change.

"Might be a different man," one of the staff told Bobby. "Used to be as pleasant a gentleman as you could wish for. Something worrying him, if you ask me."

Also in the list of members Bobby found the name of Edward Reynolds, garage proprietor, proposed by Lord Henry Darmoor and duly elected. He had, however, never paid his subscription or taken up membership. His address was given as a West End hotel, but letters addressed to him there, asking for his subscription to be paid, had been returned 'not known'.

Miss Hazel Hannay was a member. She had joined soon after the reorganization, her proposer and seconder being respectively Lord Byatt and Mr. Andrew White. Mr. White, however, to judge by the number of times it appeared, had allowed his name to be in general use as a seconder as and when required.

Lady May Grayson, like Lord Henry, was a member both of the old and of the reconstituted club, but then it was part of her business, as a kind of walking society advertisement sheet, to be a member of as many clubs as possible. She was well known to the staff, as was only natural, since she was well known everywhere, but of late had been an infrequent visitor.

Becky Glynne was also a member, but one only recently elected. She had been proposed by Mr. Baird, seconded by a Mr. Simon, who, Bobby had ascertained, held shares in the club, and had taken Andy White's place as always ready to second a new member when required. When Bobby questioned him, he admitted that he had never heard of Miss Glynne till Mr. Baird brought her to the club one evening. But Baird had vouched for her, her parentage was in itself a guarantee of respectability. "We are extremely careful whom we admit, especially women," Mr. Simon had assured Bobby earnestly, "but of course in Miss Glynne's case we had no hesitation, and then Mr. Baird was a respected member. I rather gathered," admitted Mr. Simon with a faint smile, "that Baird had hopes in that quarter, and you know we have a bit of a reputation here for being matchmakers. Brings young people together. Really, I think we shall have to adopt a slogan: "'Cut and Come Again" for fortunate engagements'."

He laughed a good deal and went off, leaving Bobby wondering whether a reputation for matchmaking was the only one the new 'Cut and Come Again' deserved.

Further enquiry showed that Miss Glynne was quite unknown to the staff.

The name of Gwen Barton, Lord Henry's fiancée, did not appear, and apparently no one knew anything about her, though most had heard of the engagement and some were inclined to believe that something had gone wrong with it since at first Lord Henry had been almost uproariously happy and then had followed the apparent alteration in his character and habits whereof Bobby had already heard.

"Not that he is always that way," the bartender had confided to Bobby at the end of some close questioning. "Sometimes he is like he used to be—-jolly and friendly. And then again—well, you don't know whether it's his own throat or yours he's going to cut."

Over these facts, so carefully and so laboriously extracted from the general mass of information he had obtained, Bobby brooded long and doubtfully, asking himself whether vague, strange outlines of an almost incredible pattern did indeed emerge, or whether it was only his own heated imagination that seemed to see there so grim, so menacing a horror.

He was still deep in thought and fear and wonder, when Inspector Marsh arrived and together they set out on their way to the Mountain Street hall.

## CHAPTER XVII
## PETTINGS

It suited Bobby very well to have a companion on this expedition, since the Mountain Street hall, situated between two parallel streets, had in each an entrance, and yet another side entrance in the busy main road into which ran the two other streets. It happened, too, that each one of these three entrances was badly lighted, all of them lying midway between street lamps. In addition, the rear entrance lay in the shadow of a tree, and the front entrance had before it a small unillumined forecourt, thrown into deep shadow by a tall neighbouring building. Bobby noticed, too, as soon as they arrived, that the side door in the main road boundary fence was unfastened, so that any passer-by could easily push it open and slip through.

Bobby pointed all this out to his companion, and explained that he wanted to watch the arrivals; to pick out the leaden, if possible; and to attempt to trace them home and establish their identity.

"If only we can get a few names and addresses we shall have something to work on," he said.

Also he intended to try to get admittance to the meeting by declaring himself a visitor interested in Psychical Research.

"Which I am," he said grimly, "when it's this sort. If it does happen to be a genuine show, I don't see why they shouldn't let me in, or anyhow tell me enough to make it clear they really are all right. I'll offer to pay my subscription on the spot. That ought to work the oracle. It would with most societies, they can no more resist a subscription than a cat can cream. If it's not a genuine do, then they'll turn me down and we'll know there is something wrong. Only—"

"Only what?"

"Well, it may be some kind of crooked game and yet they may let me in all the same, and if it's like that, then I shan't be sorry to know there's someone waiting outside to see that I come out again."

Marsh whistled.

"As bad as that," he said.

"Oh, I don't know, it's only an idea," Bobby answered. "Just as well to take precautions though, and I know the cellars there had a beastly chill, grave-like feeling about them. There were hooks in the ceiling exactly like some I remember when I was a boy in a big barn on a farm near. They used to sling the pigs up on them for slaughtering."

"Bit nervy, aren't you?" Marsh asked with a touch of patronage in his voice. "They wouldn't dare—not with a police officer."

"No, perhaps not," agreed Bobby. "Luckily there is still a divinity that doth hedge about policemen, even if it has a bit forgotten kings. All the same, if I do get a chance to get inside, I hope you'll wait till I come out again—even if it does make you miss your train."

"I don't want to do that," Marsh said in a somewhat alarmed voice, with visions of the wrath of his superintendent if he were not there at the right time to see the morning duty men duly dispatched. "Besides," he added, "what's it all about? haven't you any idea?" he repeated, for he had asked that question more than once before.

"Not the faintest," Bobby repeated, as he had answered previously. "I've thought of everything I can think of— from Nazis plotting to seize Broadcasting House down to religious revival services. If I didn't go to sleep so quick I expect I should have stopped awake all night worrying. As it is, your guess is as good as mine—and probably better."

They separated then, Bobby watching the front entrance from a shadowy doorway just across the street, Marsh hanging about at the back where no such convenient observation post existed, and both at intervals going to look at the side door where Bobby had looped a bit of string round the handle so that the door could not be opened without displacing it.

The hours came and the hours passed and nothing happened. No passer-by seemed even to give so much as a glance at the hall where it lay dark and silent and solitary in the night. Visits at intervals to the side door showed the loose loop of string still undisturbed. By nine Marsh was growing impatient, Bobby uneasy. At ten Marsh said suspiciously that it looked like a washout, and Bobby felt that by a 'wash out' he really meant a 'take in', such being the intricacies of British slang. At eleven Marsh announced firmly that he must go, or he would miss his train, and at half past he was back again.

"Thought I might as well see it through," he said, "just in case."

"Hope Mr. Oxley wasn't annoyed at being rung up so late," Bobby observed, quite sure Marsh would never have run the risk of being absent from duty next morning, unless he had received permission—and permission could only have been obtained over the 'phone.

"What do you mean?" Marsh asked, disconcerted and a little angry, too. "Been following me?"

"Gracious, no," Bobby protested. "Can't a full blown detective have a 'hunch' as they call it?" He added:— "While you were away, someone lighted up and drew the curtains."

"Did you see who it was?"

"No, they didn't go in this way. The string I put on the side door isn't in position now, though. Look!" A woman who had been coming briskly up the street turned in sharply as she reached the entrance to the hall. "Things beginning to move," remarked Bobby. "That wench had a business-like air."

"I'll go round to the back," Marsh said.

Other people began to arrive—generally on foot, one or two on bicycles, none in cars or taxis.

"Don't mean to run any risk of being traced by registration numbers," Bobby reflected. "Have to inquire if taxis have been putting fares down near or if stray cars have been parked hereabouts."

That precautions, careful precautions, against identification were being taken was sufficiently evident. All the watchers could make out was a succession of dark and shadowy figures, so muffled up that even sex was difficult to decide, faces concealed by scarves or veils, by upturned collars and downpulled hats. Silently they came, one by one, slipping through the night, many of them betraying by their hurried and uneven footsteps their inner excitement and unease.

Bobby, watching intently from his shadowy doorway, became more and more convinced that whatever the object of the meeting, it was one they had good reason for wishing to conceal. One thing he felt fairly sure of was that they all belonged to the prosperous classes. Their clothes seemed well cut, some of the furs the women wore looked expensive in the light of the street lamps they slipped by so furtively, the sound of their footsteps in that quiet street suggested they were well shod, their gait did not show the tired slouch that too much manual labour—or too prolonged a search for it—presently imposes.

Bobby wished he dared stop and question one or other of them. Not difficult to invent some charge or cause for arrest on suspicion. It is a useful procedure at times. One may have to eat a big helping of humble pie afterwards, of course, to grovel in apology. A risk of the profession. There may even be public rebuke, but none the less in this way useful evidence may sometimes be obtained and would have been procurable by no other means. There was, for example, a certain share pusher who was once arrested on an entirely unjustified charge of pickpocketing, who had to be offered the most abject apologies, who even had to be paid compensation, but the examination of whose dispatch case none the less provided that address of the headquarters of the conspiracy which had been searched for so long, so earnestly, and, till then, so fruitlessly.

But that sort of thing can only be done under authority and not in London by obscure police officers from the provinces. Nor, for that matter, was it by any means certain that identification of any of these people would reveal the full scope and purpose of whatever was here going on in such secrecy and darkness.

Leaving his post in the doorway from time to time, Bobby ascertained that other visitors were slipping in through the side door in the fence that ran along the main road. Others, Marsh told him, were arriving by the back, but all alike, it seemed, had to go to the door at the front in order to gain admittance to the hall.

"I'll have a shot at getting in," Bobby told Marsh. "Not that I'm very hopeful. There's something jolly queer going on, though I can't imagine what, and I don't much fancy they'll exactly welcome visitors."

They went together back to Mountain Street, and Marsh waited there, while Bobby walked through the small forecourt to the front door, trying as he did so to look as assured and purposeful as though he knew all about it.

The door was closed, but he had been able to make out that it was not necessary to knock. All that was needed apparently was to push and enter. So Bobby did, and found himself in a small, dark lobby or porch-like entrance, closed by other doors at the further end. A harsh, metallic voice said:—

"Please give your name and address and admission number before entry."

"Oh, you know my name and I never could remember numbers," Bobby answered cheerfully, hopeful that even so crude a bluff might possibly succeed.

Complete silence followed; and when Bobby took out his pocket torch and flashed it around he was slightly disconcerted to find himself entirely alone, though the voice had sounded quite close. Feeling distinctly uncomfortable, wondering what had become of whoever had spoken, he switched off his torch and tried the inner doors. They were securely fastened. He pushed hard, though cautiously, but without result. Something unpleasantly ominous, he thought, in this utter silence after that first brief greeting whereto his response had evidently been found inadequate. It was rather a relief when he tried the outer door to find it was still unfastened so that at least his retreat had not been cut off. Not that he had any intention of retreating, though none the less it was comforting to know that retreat was possible. He would wait developments, he decided. Only there were none, and he was wondering what to do next when he heard someone from without fumbling at the door admitting to this sort of porch or lobby where he stood. He drew back into a corner. The door opened. Someone entered. The same harsh, metallic voice that had greeted Bobby, boomed out:—

"Please give your name and address and admission number before entry."

That was one mystery solved. Evidently opening the door set in motion mechanism operating a gramophone record on the principle adopted in, for instance, some lifts on the London tube stations. The newcomer plainly knew, as Bobby had not, what to do, and at once spoke into a mouthpiece at one side of the inner doors, a mouthpiece Bobby had failed in the darkness to notice. In a voice that was clearly feminine, and that ended in a squeak of amusement, the newcomer announced:—

"George Bernard Shaw, The Adelphi. Number 73."

This was evidently regarded as satisfactory for, after only the briefest delay, the inner doors swung open. The newcomer darted through and Bobby followed into a well- lighted inner lobby.

Luck always plays its part in all police work, and if so far fickle fortune had been distinctly on Bobby's side, as witness the ease with which from Count de Legett's casual remark, he had discovered Leonard's habitation, now she failed him miserably. For bending over a small table was an exceedingly big man, apparently consulting a typed list lying there, and he looked up and said:—

"Here, there was only one name—blimey, it's Mr. Owen."

On his side, and very sadly, Bobby recognized a man named Evers, better known as Batter Evers, partly because of a reputed fondness for batter puddings, partly because he was supposed to 'batter' his opponents, partly again because 'batter' was held to be less 'la-di-da' than his correct name 'Bertram'. Mr. Evers was, in fact, a former heavy-weight boxer who had been at one time put forward by hopeful backers as a pre-destined world champion. That ambition had never been realized, nor had he indeed ever actually been accepted as challenger. To-day he no longer appeared in the ring. But he was still a fit and formidable personage, and once it had been Bobby's duty to escort him— happily in mild mood and unresisting—to an adjacent police station, there to be charged with race-course offences that had resulted in his retirement from the world for nine months in the second division, this last addition meaning nothing at all, but being added as a polite recognition of the fact that Mr. Evers had made no use of his fistic prowess to avoid arrest.

He had indeed been very pleased by so courteous a comment on his self-restraint, and his gratitude had been further earned by certain financial assistance Bobby had helped to secure for Mrs. Evers during a nine months of some financial embarrassment for her and for a baby due to arrive during that period. Incidentally, it would surprise many people who appear to regard the police as a mere invention for the annoyance of motorists, to learn the amount of hard cash that goes out of police pockets to help the many tragic cases of distress of which under the compulsion of their duty they have been in a sense the indirect cause.

It was as a consequence therefore of this earlier acquaintance that Bobby's hopes of wangling a way into the meeting as an interested visitor vanished utterly, but also it was a further result that there was no hostility but only much surprise in Evers's expression as he turned towards Bobby.

"Why, Mr. Owen," he said, "this isn't up your street, is it?"

"Why not?" asked Bobby cautiously. "Pretty queer goings on, aren't they?"

"That's right," agreed Evers with a broad grin, "but it ain't nothing against the law. It ain't a raid, is it?" he asked anxiously.

"Might be," said Bobby. "What's going on? What's it all about? I've had my eye on this place for some time. What's all this rot about admission numbers? why did that girl call herself Bernard Shaw?"

He spoke with a great show of authority and more confidence than he actually felt. For he had no standing, little to go on, it might all turn out to be no more than some elaborate piece of foolery. If Evers told him to clear out and quick about it, he would have no option but to obey. Fortunately, Evers had far too great a respect for the majesty of the law in general, and for Bobby in particular, to dream of attempting any such presumptuous action. He said:—

"Oh, the whole boiling of 'em takes fancy names. I've got a Neville Chamberlain, Downing Street, here." He indicated the typed list on the table near. "And the Bishop of London, Fulham Palace, and a Sigmund Freud"—he pronounced it "Frood"—"and John Smiths and Polly Browns as well. A hot lot, they are, and unless they give a name and address on the list here and the correct number, I don't let 'em in, and how you got in, Mr. Owen, sir, I don't know."

"Walked in," said Bobby briefly. "Now then, Evers, what's it all about?"

"Lor', Mr. Owen, there ain't no harm to it, not what you could call harm. Nothing at all. Real class they are as you can tell at once, and most respectable, and if they choose to behave disgusting like—well, it ain't against the law. I don't say there isn't time I wouldn't like to take a pail of disinfectant to 'em—strong it would have to be, too. But no business of mine and good pay and nothing against the law like, and nothing you can do nothing about, Mr. Owen, sir, now is there?"

"Why not?" persisted Bobby. "What exactly is going on?"

"Petting party, explained Evers simply. "Mind you, I ain't supposed to know. Told very special I was to keep my eyes in the boat. Told if I was caught peeping, it would be all the worse for me. Got a way of saying it, too, that sort of sends a chill up your back like going into the ring against a bloke a stone or two heavier than you and a better record. But there, Mr. Owen, sir, you know what human nature is, I don't deny as I've had a peep or two— Lumme, talk about your lady Godivas. Ain't in it, she ain't."

"Do you mean?" began Bobby.

"I do, said Evers. "I remember the boys took me along to a strip tease act in New York after I won my first fight there and had been matched up for a second I would have won, too, only for a bit of bad luck in not noticing a left hand swing coming along. Only the strip tease act—well, Sunday school it was along of—" He jerked a thumb over his shoulder towards the closed doors behind. "Pay's good and nothing against the law in being like the lilies of the field, if so be your tastes is such. Mind you, down in Hoxton where I live they wouldn't stand for it, but of course West End gentry's different."

Bobby asked one or two more questions. The details he received he found sufficiently surprising, though no man can serve for long in the police forces of London without learning much of human depravity. But it did appear that Evers was very likely right in claiming that there was no actual breach of the law. The whole thing appeared to be no more than the breaking through the ordinary restraints of decency and civilization by those ancient animal instincts that lie deep hidden in man, inherited from his brute ancestry. A sink of corruption certainly, and there might be legal means of dealing with it and clearing it up, but for that greater authority than he possessed would be needed and greater knowledge, too. Perhaps the Home Office would know what to do, but he certainly did not.

"It's the young 'uns she wants," Evers said suddenly. "She likes to get the young 'uns here."

"Who is she?"

"There's times," Evers answered slowly, "I think she's the devil himself turned woman, and a way of speaking so sometimes you feel there isn't nothing you wouldn't do if she asked you in that voice of hers that curls all round your innards like, and then there's times you feel you would rather have truck with a whole bag full of vipers than her. It's she as does it all—and it's the young 'uns she wants, it's the young 'uns she likes to get here."

"Who is she?" Bobby asked again. "What is she like?"

"I've never seen her, only heard her talk," Evers answered. "I get my orders by post—typewritten, they are —and if she is here when I get here to open up, then she talks to me through the door curtains."

"But you see everyone when they get here, you admit them all," Bobby said.

"That's right," Evers agreed, "but I've got no way of telling which of 'em is her."

"Can't you tell by her voice?"

Evers shook his head.

"Some of 'em speak in a disguised sort of way when they give their fake names and their numbers," he explained, "and then some of them come together and only one speaks. No, I've no idea which is her though sometimes I've thought that if I did, it would be a sort of day's good deed to wring her neck for her. But the pay's good and you can't quarrel with your bread and butter, not in these days."

"Then you can't give me any idea how to identify her?"

"No, sir, honest I can't," Evers declared earnestly. "I don't even know for sure it is a woman, only by going by her voice."

"What about her letters? aren't they signed?"

"Oh, yes, but only in typing same as any one could do. Jinnie Reynolds the name is, and an address in Cardiff, only they don't come from there, being always posted in London."

## CHAPTER XVIII
## WARNINGS

Plainly the former heavy-weight boxer knew no more and plainly, too, a fear had been put upon him that smothered in him any desire to investigate further. Then, too, when Bobby hinted that he would like a chance to see for himself what was going on behind the closed door leading into the main hall, a door screened further by heavy curtains in black, entangling velvet, Evers protested that he had been paid to carry out a duty he must perform to the best of his ability.

"My job is to stop any one as isn't their own lot," he said. "You wouldn't ask me to go against my job, Mr. Owen, sir, now would you? I've never double-crossed any one yet, once I've took their money, not even when I was in the boxing game, I never did. You wouldn't want me to start now, sir, would you?"

It was quite a pathetic appeal and as a matter of fact Bobby did know that Evers even if his ethical ideas were slightly confused on some points, had always shown himself loyal to his employers.

"Oh, well, that's all right," he said, "if that's how you feel about it."

"Thank you, Mr. Owen, sir," Evers said gratefully. "I know you run straight, and I knew you wouldn't want another bloke to go crooked. Besides," he added, as an afterthought, "you wouldn't see nothing except a mixed bathing show without the bathing—or nothing."

"Especially nothing, apparently," said Bobby, and after ascertaining from Evers that he had never thought of keeping any of the typed notes he received and extracting from him a promise that for the future he would preserve them for inspection, Bobby retired.

Outside, by the open gates admitting to the forecourt, he found Inspector Marsh looking very worried indeed.

"You were right enough," he said, "though I didn't believe you at first, but dynamite this job is sure enough. Dynamite. You can handle it on your own from now on as far as I'm concerned."

"Why? what's happened? what do you mean?" Bobby asked.

Marsh leaned nearer. In a hoarse and cautious whisper, as though he feared even the night might overhear and tell, he said:—

"Hannay."

"Hannay," repeated Bobby, puzzled.

"I saw him plain," Marsh insisted in the same hoarse and careful whisper. "He stopped to light a cigarette and I saw him plain, plain as I see you. If I hadn't dodged quick as I knew how, he would have spotted me, like as not."

"What did you dodge for?" Bobby asked. "Why didn't you ask him what he was up to?"

"Me?" gasped Marsh, quite overwhelmed at the idea of a mere inspector asking General Sir Harold Hannay, with half the alphabet after his name, chairman, too, of the Wychshire Watch Committee, 'what he was up to?'

It was, however, less Sir Harold of whom Bobby was thinking than of his daughter, Hazel, tall, dark and haughty, with those searching, passionate eyes that told of her southern ancestry. Was it to seek his daughter, was it because he knew or suspected something concerning her, that Sir Harold was here? could it be that Hazel was the unknown 'she' whose identity Bobby desired above all things to discover, of whom Evers had spoken with such strange terror in his voice? Abruptly Bobby asked:—

"Did Sir Harold go inside the hall?"

"He came along immediately after you had gone in," Marsh explained. "He stood looking at the front door and then he went round to the back along that narrow passage between the hall and the fence, and I lost him. I couldn't follow too closely or he would have spotted me. When I got round the corner into the back yard, there wasn't a sign of him. He might have gone through into the street or he might have gone in by the back door. I tried it but it was locked. Of course, he might have had a key. I don't know. No one came when I knocked. What's it all about, anyhow? what did you find out?"

"Nothing much," Bobby answered. "Unluckily 'Batter' Evers was on guard. You know—the old heavy-weight boxer. He spotted me at once and that did for my chance of getting inside. He sticks to it there's nothing going on but a specially hot 'petting party', as he calls it. According to him it's nothing but a lot of young Mayfair decadents amusing themselves in their own fashion."

"Not a police job at all?"

"Seems not," agreed Bobby gloomily.

But Marsh was looking very relieved.

"That explains Sir Harold," he said. "Got wind that Miss Hannay's mixed up with it and wants to yank her out."

"Yes, I thought just possibly it was Miss Hannay," Bobby agreed again.

"Well, then," said Marsh, more and more relieved, "not our business and we can drop it. Eh?"

Bobby shook his head.

"The petting party may be only a blind," he said; "only the meet of the hounds, and the kill yet to come."

"I don't know what you mean, what kill?" Marsh said uneasily. "Anyway, we know what Sir Harold was here for, he's not the only papa wondering what the girls and boys are after. You can wash him out."

"I suppose so," Bobby said, but remembered how Sir Harold had looked, what discomfort, amounting indeed to terror, had shown in his eyes when he had been about to enter a room at Colonel Glynne's where were his daughter and her friends.

In Bobby's memory that had not been the look of a father angry or suspicious of a daughter's conduct, something stranger far must have caused that terror to show so plainly in eyes that on so many battlefields had watched with calm the angel of death pass to and fro.

"I'll have to tackle him," Bobby decided, "but if he thinks his daughter may be mixed up in it, he won't say a word. He is the type who might give her a revolver and tell her to use it, but he would never say a word in public."

He reflected, too, that he had no actual proof to offer that Sir Harold had actually been there that night. He himself was certain Marsh had told the truth, but suppose Sir Harold chose simply to deny it. Doubtful, more than doubtful whether Marsh could be trusted to stick to his story, if it were seriously challenged. Bobby was not much inclined to think the good inspector was quite the type to stand up to a man in Sir Harold's position. After all, the bare possibility of a mistake did exist. Marsh might have been deceived by some chance resemblance. Not that Bobby himself believed that for one moment, but the existence of that possibility would certainly destroy the validity of Marsh's evidence.

Bad luck all along the line to-night, Bobby told himself bitterly. Why had it to be Evers guarding admission to the hall, Evers, who knew him so well, when it could so much more probably have been someone who had never seen him? Why had Sir Harold chosen to make his appearance at the very moment when Bobby was inside the hall? A few minutes earlier or later, Bobby reflected, and he would have been able to stop and question him. No doubt Marsh who knew so much less of the affair and its strange implications, was hardly to be blamed for his hesitation, but for Bobby it might have been a chance, now lost, to obtain valuable information.

"No good hanging about here any longer, is it?" suggested Marsh, evidently longing to be off bedwards.

"You cut off if you like, I think I'll stay around a bit," Bobby answered, and poor Marsh was torn between his reluctance to leave a colleague and his very keen desire for his bed.

Before he could decide, they saw someone coming towards them across the forecourt where the shadows lay so heavily. They stood watching the approaching figure. It was coming slowly and with apparent hesitation. A woman, they thought.

"Show's over, beginning to go home," Marsh suggested, his tone hinting the example was one to be followed.

But that was not what Bobby thought. He was aware of a tightening at his heart, of a dryness in his mouth, as he watched how silently, as it were a shadow among others, the approaching figure came towards them, at times almost hidden from sight in some patch of darkness thicker than elsewhere, then again appearing, always a little nearer, furtive and unreal in some queer way, and always silent as the night itself. At a little distance she stood still.

"Mr. Policeman," she called—the voice was certainly a woman's but pitched unnaturally high, for disguise, Bobby thought, "Mr. Policeman."

"Yes," Bobby said, and began to move forward.

"No, no," she called. "Keep away. Not too near, if you please, or I'll be off where you can't follow. I'm only a messenger."

"From whom?" Bobby asked.

"From—her," came the answer. "She wants to know what you are doing here? She can't imagine any reason why police should be bothering us. She would like to know by what right police come here asking their impudent questions?"

"Now, that's a lot she wants to know," Bobby said. "But who is—she?"

"Just—she," the other answered, and laughed a little and then abruptly shut her laughter off.

"I mean her name, what is her name?" Bobby asked, though a little disconcerted by the sound of that harsh and brief laughter.

Behind him, he was aware of Marsh's heavy and uncertain breathing that seemed to be coming in short, tiny gasps. There came into Bobby's mind a memory of Evers's sudden exclamation:—'There's times I think she's the devil himself turned woman.' To his surprise he discovered he was wondering if this could be true.

"Does her name matter?" the woman was saying. "What's in a name?" she quoted mockingly. "Ask her that yourself if you like and she'll tell you—perhaps. This way."

"Is that necessary? are you sure you are not her yourself?" Bobby asked, and moved towards her.

At that she turned and ran. Swift, swift beyond description, swift and light, she turned and fled on swift and noiseless feet, light as a fawn on grass, and after her raced Bobby at his utmost speed, his footsteps crashing down the silent night like strokes of a hammer, and behind him followed Marsh, though less ready and less swift. Not often had Bobby ran as he ran now, for instinctively he knew that this illusive figure before him might at any moment vanish somehow or somewhere into the unknown. Yet there was also exultation in his heart, for he was very sure that never yet had lived woman born of mortal sire who with so short a start could outstrip his pursuit in such a chase. He was gaining on her already. Already he could distinguish more plainly the form and outline of the shadow that was her among those other shadows that flickered and wavered in that so dimly-lighted forecourt. Already he was preparing to stretch out his hand and seize her. He saw her plainly as she fled past the corner of the main building into that narrow passage that ran by its side, between it and the boundary fence. He increased his pace as a runner increases it with the winning post in sight. He flung out his hand to reach her he judged to be now within arm's length, for indeed he ran more swiftly than ever any woman could, he caught his feet in a coil of wire she dropped at that instant behind her, headlong he went, prostrate and sprawling, he heard her laugh in the darkness and behind him Marsh, unable to stop in time, fell over him as he tried to get to his feet so that they became a confused and struggling heap in that narrow space between wall and fence. The impact, for Marsh was a heavy man, knocked Bobby flat again, and took away all power of speech. He heard Marsh gasp out an oath. He heard again the woman laugh. He felt a sudden blow on his throat, a sharp and heavy blow. He heard the sound of another blow and a muffled exclamation from Marsh. Something fell tinkling to the ground near by. A door opened and shut. He managed to get to his feet. Marsh, muttering and swearing to himself, was still upon his knees. Bobby pulled open the door in the fence and ran into the street. He was just in time to see by the light of the nearest street lamp a figure on a bicycle riding furiously away. He almost thought he heard again a faint laugh floating back to him, but he was not sure. Anyhow, she—whoever 'she' might be—had made good her escape. No hope of overtaking her now.

Bobby went back through the gate in the fence into the passage. Marsh was feeling a bruised knee, a damaged nose, a bump rapidly growing on his forehead. On the ground lay the coil of wire in which Bobby's feet had been caught. It was the kind of trick he himself had played more than once, but he liked it none the better for that. Near by lay a long-bladed knife, ground and sharpened. An ugly weapon. He picked it up very carefully, by the point, using his handkerchief.

Marsh said in a voice that was not quite steady:—

"That was hers, only she used the hilt and not the blade."

"Yes," said Bobby, looking at it.

"If she had used the blade," Marsh said, we would both be dead 'uns by now."

"Yes," said Bobby, once again.

"Between the shoulders," Marsh said. "I can feel it still, that's where she gave it me."

"I got it here," Bobby said. He felt his throat where it was red and bruised from the blow he had received. 'Right over the jugular," he remarked thoughtfully.

Marsh said:—

"It was a woman. Who was she?"

"Oh, just—she," Bobby said.

Marsh was still standing looking at the knife in Bobby's hand. He seemed unable to take his eyes from it; and the more he looked at it, the less he liked it.

"Dead as stuck pigs, both of us," he muttered, "if she had used the other end."

"Dead as stuck pigs," Bobby agreed, "and without being strung up to hooks, either."

"What? what's that?" Marsh asked.

"Oh, nothing," Bobby answered, wondering himself why there had come into his mind so vivid a memory and image of those hooks in the ceiling of the cellar under the hall that had so strongly reminded him of those others in the old barn at home, where at one time the farmer had been accustomed to slaughter his pigs each autumn.

"She could have laid us both out in two ticks with a thing like that and no one been the wiser," Marsh said, his fascinated gaze still upon the thin and deadly blade in Bobby's hand. "What was the idea though? If she only meant to hit us a whack, anything would have done, and why did she leave it behind?"

"Probably meant it for a hint, a warning to watch our step and keep out," Bobby said. "Evers must have told her we were asking questions. He has his own ideas of loyalty. He had taken her pay and so he had to earn it. He will have been told how to get a message to her, if necessary. So then she got things ready for us—a coil of wire and a push-bike all ready to get away on. A push-bike is a lot safer than a motor-bike, motor bikes can be traced sometimes, more likely to be noticed, too. And this nice little tool for use, if required. I expect if I had caught up with her too quickly, I should have got six inches of it under the ribs."

"She could have outed us both as easy as not," Marsh muttered.

"We were safe enough, except in the last resource," Bobby said. "Publicity is the very last thing the lady wants, and two stuck policemen would make quite a fuss."

"All thought out seemingly," Marsh agreed with an uneasy laugh. "Regular plan of campaign—good staff work and all that.

Makes you inclined to remember Sir Harold Hannay is a soldier and a general at that."

"Yes, I know," agreed Bobby, frowning. "It's possible. It was well planned all right. But not beyond her, I think. I think she must be quite good at planning things."

"Who do you mean—she?" Marsh asked.

Bobby did not answer. He was still looking at the knife he held so carefully by its extreme point.

"We'll have a try for finger-prints," he said, "but there isn't an earthly. We aren't up against any one so simple as all that."

"Gloves," commented Marsh. "They all know that answer."

In the darkness the knife blade glimmered with an evil light as Bobby held it up, turning it this way and that.

"All the same," he said, "there is something familiar about a thing like this, something simple, understandable, something human you could almost say. It's not hidden and unknown, not like the lurking hellishness you feel behind what's going on here. For I tell you, Marsh,"—he spoke with a sudden and profound emotion that astonished even himself, "there's enough in this business to turn the stomach of Satan himself."

Marsh did not answer. Something of the same feeling had already stirred in his own mind. Unimaginative man as he was, he was yet aware of a sense of evil things around them that passed far beyond his knowledge or experience.

"I think I feel a little sick," he said. "I suppose it's because of knowing how easy you and me might have been done in."

But both he and Bobby knew well enough it was no physical danger that had so shaken them.

They talked a little longer and then departed, since it did not seem to either of them that now it was worth while, now 'she' had gone, to continue their watch.

Happy to remember that he had no duty hours to keep, Bobby slept late the next morning and was still at breakfast when he was rung up to receive the information he had asked Marsh to obtain. It was to the effect that General Sir Harold Hannay had left Midwych for London the day before and that when in London he often stayed at Hassall's Hotel, an old-fashioned but still flourishing hotel near the Haymarket.

"Better tackle him, I suppose," Bobby decided, as he completed his more immediate business with toast and marmalade, a decision he arrived at in pursuance of his general principle that when a detective wanted information his best plan was to go and ask for it.

To Hassall's Hotel he therefore proceeded, only to learn that the general had left an hour or two previously. He had not said where he was going. Certainly he had left in a taxi, but did Bobby, the hotel asked pityingly, really suppose that an hotel porter, who probably called a taxi every five minutes of his working day, remembered all the directions given to him to repeat to the driver? Two minutes later, he would hardly know whether he had told the driver to go to Euston or Victoria, to an address in the suburbs or to a Pall Mall club. Nor could they say, nor would they if they could, at what hour Sir Harold had returned the night before. The hotel was not a detective agency, as he, Bobby, so evidently and so unreasonably supposed, nor did it in any way attempt to keep any kind of check on the movements of its guests. It was his own affair if a gentleman like Sir Harold chose to stay out till the small hours, chatting with old companions of the Great War, which was in fact precisely what had happened the night before since Sir Harold had chanced to say as much to the night porter, another old soldier, on his return. But there was no reason why that fact should be communicated to Inspector Owen, nor any reason why he should think it any business of his.

Bobby said meekly he was very sorry, and of course the hotel was perfectly right to preserve so absolute a discretion, nor did he stress the fact that now he knew all he wished to know, namely, that Sir Harold had been out very late the previous night and had thought it necessary to offer an explanation therefor to the night porter. A sure sign, Bobby felt, of an uneasy conscience and of something to conceal.

The hotel, unplacated even by this display of meekness, remarked menacingly that Sir Harold would be informed of these very strange inquiries, and, in the opinion of the hotel, Sir Harold was not likely to be pleased. In any case, added the hotel with a touch of malice in its voice, here was Miss Hannay herself, just come in, and perhaps the inspector would be good enough to ask her for any further information he required.

Bobby turned quickly. He had had his back to the door and had not seen her enter. She was standing just behind him. Evidently she had already recognized him, had perhaps heard this last remark addressed to Bobby. Tall and frowning she stood there, her dark, angry eyes beneath the strongly-marked brows, seeming as it were to engulf him in their passionate inquiry. He saw how her hand, a large, capable hand, was fiercely clenched on the small umbrella she carried, nor could he help wondering if so, the evening before, her hand had clenched a bare and shining knife. She looked tired and worn, he thought, as if she had not slept well, or had not been long in bed, with dark rings beneath her eyes to match the dark, straight brows above.

At first she did not speak, nor did Bobby, and they stood intently watching each other, alert and challenging, with growing doubt on his side, with increasing anger or defiance—or was it just simply fear?—showing on hers. But in this mutual challenge of their eyes, it was hers that first turned aside, and that Bobby thought was significant, for he did not much suppose that it would have happened so easily or so soon, had there not been some reason. Abruptly she moved, in a too obvious effort to ignore his presence. To the clerk at the reception desk, watching with discreet interest, she said:—

"Is my father here?"

"He left first thing this morning, Miss Hannay," the clerk answered. "I was just telling this gentleman so." Reception clerks learn to be tactful. But this remark was distinctly lacking in that useful quality. Possibly for the moment professional tact was subordinate to human mischief. Anyhow, the remark made it difficult for Hazel to pretend longer to be ignorant of Bobby's existence. He took swift advantage of the opening thus given to say to her:— "I am trying to find Sir Harold. I am hoping he may be able to help me. Could you tell me how to get in touch with him? "

"You could write, I suppose, couldn't you?" Hazel suggested coldly. "Probably he would arrange to see you when convenient."

"It would mean delay I am anxious to avoid," Bobby said, watching her closely and more and more certain that she was profoundly disquieted. "It may be important," he added. "I don't know, but it may be."

"If you care to give me any message I will tell him when I see him," she said. "Why important? what is it about?"

"There is some information I have," he answered, "Sir Harold may be able to confirm or correct. It would depend on where he was last night." At that he saw her stiffen, her face grow blank like a mask, but a mask through which her eyes burned. He said quickly, on a swift impulse:— "Where were you last night, Miss Hannay?"

She made no answer. She turned and walked away, straight out of the hotel. Bobby watched her go, saw her call a taxi, wondered whether it was fear or anger or what else that had so, as it were, chased her away with such an aspect of flight, a flight he thought not usual with her. The hall porter, an imposing person, one accustomed to speak to the great as their mentor and guide, came up very angrily to Bobby.

"Now then, what's all this?" he demanded accusingly. "You've upset that lady. Miss Hannay, that was. You've upset her."

"Looks like it," agreed Bobby. "I wonder why."

The hall porter stared.

"Miss Hannay," he repeated impressively. "Her father's General Sir Harold Hannay, he is."

"Yes, I know," said Bobby.

"Well, we don't like it, annoying our clients," said the hotel porter. "Annoying our clients," he repeated, as one might say 'committing high treason' and then, seeing how little impressed Bobby seemed, returned to his post to welcome, with an effusion he would not otherwise have shown, a mere second lieutenant who had just come in.

Bobby went away then and all the time as he walked slowly along there wavered before him the figure of Hazel, mingling indistinctly with another figure, one that fled through darkness and shadow down a narrow passage way between fence and wall. Were they identical, he wondered; did they, in fact, merge into one another as, in his fancy, they seemed sometimes to do; and through the roar of the busy London traffic he seemed to hear distinctly the tinkle of steel on stone as a long-bladed knife fell upon a flagged path.

"On the whole," he told himself gravely, "I prefer automatics to knives—you can miss with an automatic and generally do, but a knife thrust is apt to get home. No safety catch on a knife blade, either."

However, he had obtained some useful information, or rather, information that might be useful when he knew how to use it. For the present he had to be content with knowing that Sir Harold had been in town the night before, that he had been out late, that therefore it was at least possible that Marsh was right in his belief. An established possibility is, however, very different from completed proof. Also Sir Harold and his daughter had not come to town together and had not kept each other informed of their respective movements, since Hazel had come to seek her father at the hotel after he had left it. Did that suggest that he had followed her to town for some reason of his own and had not known exactly where to find her? Apparently Hazel, too, had spent the night in town, since no train from Midwych could have got her here so early, and she did not seem to have used a car or to have travelled by the night train. Quite plainly, too, she had found Bobby's question disturbing when he asked her where she had been, nor had she answered it.

All these different points Bobby found interesting, even suggestive, and yet, consider them as he might, and most of the rest of the day he devoted to that task, he could not see that what he had learned took the investigation beyond that domain of vague doubt and suspicion in which he felt himself caught and held.

He wondered whether to go back to Cardiff to make another attempt to interview the Jinnie Reynolds, whose name, like that of Lady May Grayson, seemed so often to crop up in the affair. He decided that such an interview he was unlikely to obtain at present, and that in any case it would be better to wait till he knew more—if that were ever to be the case. Then there was Leonard Glynne, too, who ought to be questioned again, though again, with small prospects of useful results. But he, too, it might be wiser to leave for the present. Time allowed for quiet thought sometimes induced the reflection that speech is wise and prudent—the innocent begin to feel it more honest, the guilty that they must do something to make themselves more secure. Experience had long ago taught Bobby that often it was the best course to wait and watch for the other fellow's next move.

All this had taken up the morning so that now it was time for lunch, after which would begin the universal week-end pause, when in England the general rhythm of life sinks into something like immobility. So having for once a free evening Bobby seized the chance to spend it with Olive, who took him to the cinema to see the latest of the Marx Brothers films in the hope that the antics of those inspired clowns might change and relieve the current of his thoughts. Her idea was that laughter, loud, long, and continuous, might help to clear his mind. As they were coming away she remarked that a Shirley Temple film was always charming, and he agreed absently, and said how much he had enjoyed it, whereat she longed furiously to box his ears, since evidently he had not the least idea what they had been seeing. It seemed to her too bad of him and rather ungrateful as well, besides seven shillings and a whole evening wasted, since for her part she had never been able to understand what any Marx Brothers film was about, or why on earth people laughed so much at what seemed to her merely behaviour entirely lacking in commonsense.

On the Monday morning Bobby presented himself, the world having decided to start revolving once more, at the office of the Public Prosecutor and afterwards at Scotland Yard. To his disappointment, he found neither place very keenly interested in the story he had to tell. It had been well enough known that such a place as he described existed somewhere in London, though its exact locality had never been ascertained. Interesting, of course, to be informed now that it was this Mountain Street hall. Amusing, too, that it should be a place also used for parish purposes. Only neither the Public Prosecutor's office nor the Yard seemed very clear about what action could be taken.

"Corrupting the young," said the Public Prosecutors office, "only what statute makes that an offence? Blowed if I know. The leading case of Socrates does not seem to apply. Put it like this: what offence is committed when a pack of young degenerates get together to behave a little worse than usual? This Mountain Street place of yours," the Public Prosecutor's office pointed out with some severity, "is not even licensed for music and dancing. Private show all round apparently. Of course, if you could show any connection with your Wychwood Forest case—?"

But that was precisely what Bobby could not do, and though he attempted to controvert the suggestion that the Mountain Street hall and Wychwood forest were his personal property, the Public Prosecutor's office remained unimpressed. So Bobby went on to Scotland Yard who listened carefully and rubbed its chin thoughtfully and said:— "Private show apparently. Our job is public order, not private morals. Police have no power to enter private property, no power to do almost anything if you ask me, except say 'Move on there, please'. Of course, if you could show any connection with your Wychwood Forest affair—?"

Bobby was too dispirited even to protest that the Wychwood Forest affair was not 'his' in any sense whatsoever. Scotland Yard, accepting his silence as proof that no such connection was known—or, probably, existed,—promised cheerfully that the Mountain Street hall should be kept under observation, which meant, Bobby reflected gloomily, that the D.D.I. would be asked to send round a plain clothes man to have a look at it occasionally.

Bobby had therefore to be content with the knowledge that the Public Prosecutor's office was busy—more or less—looking up statutes, and Scotland Yard was—more or less—keeping the hall under observation.

He went back to his rooms and sat there, trying to work out a plan of campaign. Finding that task difficult, he attempted to put down on paper a clear statement of his own thoughts, doubts, suspicions, for the vague, almost formless ideas in his mind he did not dare as yet to make explicit to others, hardly even to himself. He was in the middle of this task when his landlady came in to inform him of the arrival of a visitor.

To his surprise, it was little Mr. Eyton, the Midwych journalist whose articles, hinting that the Wychwood forest tragedy had been neither accident nor suicide but murder, had made this investigation necessary.

Bobby had learned, as all good policeman learn, that it is necessary both to be very polite to newspaper men and still more so never to tell them anything, except what it is desired should be proclaimed as widely as possible, strict accuracy, however, no object at all; for indeed it is a poor journalist who cannot, as Sir. Walter Scott said, put a cocked hat on a story, a staff in its hand, and set it walking.

Bobby therefore was ready to tell Eyton as little as possible in as many words as convenient, but as he talked soon became aware of an odd change in the little man, who indeed was hardly listening to him, and who was betraying a peculiar restlessness and excitability of which he had not shown the least trace during their previous talk. Now he seemed unable to keep still, he changed his seat, fidgeted continually, his eyes were feverish, his skin looked hot and dry. Bobby wondered if he were sickening for some illness, but was reminded still more strongly of some of those whom it had been his duty at other times to interrogate when they had been labouring under the consciousness of some secret knowledge.

Abruptly he asked, for an abrupt unexpected question has sometimes unexpected results:—

"Has anything happened? Is there anything you want to tell me?"

Eyton looked startled indeed and hesitated for a moment, but that was all.

"Something has certainly happened," he agreed, "but not to interest you." He paused, his restlessness and excitement seemed to leave him. He sat back in his chair, motionless and silent. He smiled to himself, a tender and a secret smile that changed and illumined his whole countenance, as at hidden thoughts too wonderful for speech.

"My God," Bobby thought, with sudden cold terror at his heart, "is he the next?"

There was an interval before either of them spoke again. Bobby was watching the little man intently, still telling himself his sudden fear was unreasonable and unfounded, a mere result of the strain he had been under these last few days. Eyton, with that strange, distant smile still on his lips, seemed unaware of their silence. Bobby had the impression that he might sit there for hours, lost in whatever dream or vision held him in such abstraction. But presently he stirred, like a man wakening from sleep, and looked around him and at Bobby, as if remembering with difficulty where he was or why. To Bobby, still watching him closely, his eyes seemed aloof and dazzled, as though they had been gazing on a brightness too great for them to bear.

"What has happened?" Bobby asked.

Eyton, looking more normal now, smiled and waved a deprecating hand.

"Oh, I didn't come here to worry you about my private affairs," he said. "I had to come up to town on business. I have a freehold plot of land I've been holding for years, as values were going up all round. I've just made up my mind to sell."

"Land this time," Bobby said heavily, "not jewellery?"

"Jewellery?" repeated Eyton. "Oh, I've no jewellery. It's a bit of land left me by an uncle years ago. It was valued at about £300 then. I'm told I shall get £3,000 now, clear, the purchaser paying all expenses, even my solicitor's fees."

"£3,000 is a lot of money," Bobby agreed.

Eyton nodded complacently.

"I was keeping it as a reserve for old age or if I got the sack—a chancy trade, journalism, you know. I'm chucking it—Journalism, I mean. It's a useful job in its way, of course, but is any one really ever the better for it? Does it ever help any one to a better understanding of life?"

As this was a question Bobby felt unable to answer, he remained prudently silent. Eyton shook his head a little sadly at the failure of journalism to lead humanity ever upward and onward, and continued:—

"I shall devote myself to my book. I believe I told you about it. On the forest. I shall try to show people the spiritual message there is in the forest, in its green beauty, its peace, its solitude. You remember the verse that one is nearer to God in a garden than anywhere else? No. No. It is in the forest one can draw nearest to God. I am sure you have felt that?"

"No," answered Bobby with a certain harsh vehemence. "I don't like forests—hidden places, secret places, places of darkness shutting out the light and the air, places where life is strangled, smothered. Let trees grow to their will and they kill and smother everything else with their dark growth. Why, trees were the first of all the enemies men had to overcome. There's life in the sea, there's light on the mountains, but trees mean darkness and death."

"What an extraordinary tirade," Eyton protested, quite amused and also startled from his abstracted mood, as in fact Bobby had intended to be the result of this sudden attack on what seemed his pet obsession. "Good gracious, no."

"Good gracious, yes," retorted Bobby. "You only know our tamed, trimmed, conquered English forests. Wait til you've seen a real forest in its native state—dampness and darkness and rottenness everywhere." He lowered his voice and said in a quick whisper:— "Did you meet her in the forest?"

Eyton nodded. The question did not seem to surprise him. Perhaps the fact loomed so tremendously in his own consciousness he found no surprise in another's awareness of it. Speaking very slowly, as though each syllable called up in his mind memories he could have wished to linger on, he said:—

"I went there one evening. After my work. To have a look round where the fire was. I wasn't expecting to find anything. It was just to look round. I suppose I thought there was an off chance I might spot something. I hung around till it was dark—the stars were coming out and it was all very quiet and lovely. It wasn't quite dark and she could see me still and she called to me out of the bushes.

"Who is—she?" Bobby asked, using every effort he could summon up to keep all trace of eagerness from his voice.

Eyton was silent. Bobby dared not ask again, but the strain of waiting seemed intolerable. An answer might solve all. But Eyton presently shook his head.

"I do not know," he said. "I do not think I even want to know. Not yet. Not knowing makes it all the more wonderful—more wonderful by far. She called to me out of the bushes. We talked a little. She told me to come back the next day, only later."

"Did you?" Bobby asked.

"Oh, yes, yes, naturally." Evidently Eyton thought the question a trifle absurd, as a soldier might think it a trifle absurd if asked whether he obeyed orders. "She was a little late. It was quite dark, a velvety, all-embracing darkness. She talked wonderfully, things I had never known, never understood, things about myself, too— about the trees, about life, about love."

"Are you sure it was love?" Bobby asked, and a soft, long sigh from Eyton was the answer.

"I never understood before," he said again. "I don't think many people do. We live our narrow little lives from day to day, our cramped, artificial lives. All the time —if only we wanted to, if only we dared, if only we weren't tied up with all kinds of petty taboos and restrictions, if only we could dare to live as Nature meant us to live."

"How did Nature mean us to live?" Bobby asked, and, had he ever heard it, would have agreed with the saying of that philosopher who declared that whenever he heard people beginning to talk about what Nature meant he knew they were beginning to talk nonsense.

"She meant freely and simply," came Eyton's answer, "away from all the stupid codes and taboos we have invented ourselves. Freedom. Simplicity. The direct approach. All is there."

He got to his feet.

"I am a bigger, a braver, a better man since I met her," he said.

Bobby was watching Eyton gloomily, and his thoughts were gloomier still and very busy. He seemed to see a motor car deserted on Dartmoor, and a lonely cottage, and a caravan in flames, and again he seemed to hear the tinkle of a falling knife, steel upon stone. Eyton said, smiling at himself:—

"I was going without having told you what I came about. I want to find my wife now, so as to get a divorce. It's stupid, another taboo, of no importance really, but it's like wearing clothes in towns—stupid, and a great bore, but necessary to avoid a lot of bother. I shall have to trace her to get evidence, and the only private detectives I know in Midwych are a pretty incompetent lot and not too trustworthy. I thought possibly you could tell me of somebody honest and knowing his job and not too expensive."

"Was that your idea?" Bobby asked. "Or hers?"

"What do you mean? Does it matter? It was mine, of course. She had read my story in the *Announcer* and I knew you were working on the case. That's why she wondered if there had been any developments I was going to write about."

"There haven't been any," Bobby said. "We know no more than we did," and to himself he thought that what Eyton said made it perfectly clear that in everything he did he was acting on suggestions conveyed to him so subtly that he believed them his own. "Been like that all the time," Bobby said to himself. Then he said aloud:— "You are getting a good price for your property. Is it all settled, cash down?"

"Settled all right," Eyton answered readily, looking surprised at this abrupt change of subject, "though the cash won't be in the bank for a week or two, I suppose."

Bobby gave a sigh of relief. He knew only too well that no warning he could utter, based, too, on such unsubstantial grounds, would have the least effect, except indeed that of rousing an anger and mistrust it was terribly necessary to avoid. Now he felt fairly confident that Eyton at least was in no danger until the money was actually paid over. He wondered doubtfully if the same could be said of Count de Legett; and suddenly he made up his mind to go again the next morning to interview him. Useless probably; dangerous even to the success of the investigation. None the less Bobby felt the warning must be given, no matter though it brought to the ground in ruins the whole careful structure he was so laboriously building up. On his thoughts broke the voice of Eyton bidding him good-bye.

"Look here," Bobby said, "you wanted to know if there were any fresh developments. If there are I may ring you up, because I may need your help. I might see my way to lay a trap for Mr. Baird's murderer you could be a big help in. Make a good story, eh?"

It was an offer to stir the blood of any journalist but Eyton seemed only mildly interested.

"What's worrying me is how to find my wife," he explained, "and get a divorce without too much delay. Why are people such fools as to marry before they know?"

"Know what?"

"What it—what it really is when you do know," Eyton answered, shivering a little and somehow, in some odd way, not very pleasantly.

He went away then and Bobby saw him to the door and felt very certain that soon he would be back again, so alluring, Bobby felt convinced, would prove to be the ground bait he had laid down in his offer made to the little journalist.

"She—whoever 'she' is," he told himself, "will be keen on knowing what trap is to be laid for her."

He worked a little longer and then went up to bed, for by now it was late, and as he was undressing, in the stage between trousers and pyjamas, he heard someone singing in the streets, a woman's voice and a Welsh song. He tore on his clothes again, he raced downstairs, he had to unlock and unbolt a door fastened for the night. When at last he got into the street, it was empty and silent. For nearly half an hour he raced around in the vicinity but without success, and for once sympathized with the common complaint that never is a policeman there when you want him. In point of fact the constable on the beat had had to go off to the nearest hospital with a bad accident case, but that Bobby did not know till later. In a very bad temper he began to undress again, and this time was actually in bed, and had just put out his light, when once again he heard that snatch of Welsh song in a woman's voice, just beneath his window.

"Oh, it's a game, is it?" he said aloud. "Watching me running round all the time most likely and now thinks it fun to start again. Well, my dear lady, you can have your fun all to yourself this time."

He put his head resolutely on the pillow, and, for once in his life, lay awake for long. But he heard no more, and presently he slept, and next morning when he went down to breakfast, he found by his plate, with one or two letters, a key with a label attached to it, a label on which was written his own name and an address.

"It was in the letter box this morning," his landlady said, bringing in his eggs and bacon. "Someone must have pushed it in, it was there before the post came."

But Bobby was not listening. With a queer, wondering sensation he was staring at the address, that of the flat occupied by Lord Henry Darmoor.

"Now what on earth," Bobby asked himself uncomfortably, "does that mean?"

He began to open his letters. One was a small bill, one was a circular, one informed him passionately that it was his duty to his country and to himself to join a new book club, the last was from the commissionaire employed by Messrs. Higham, the man he had asked to let him know if the original of the photograph given him by Bobby had visited the shop.

It appeared that Count de Legett had in fact called the previous day, and had been granted that interview with the head of the firm only accorded when really big transactions were under consideration. Nothing more had 'transpired', wrote the commissionaire, using the word as he saw it generally used in the popular press, but he was on his guard, and also he would like to see Mr. Owen again as soon as possible with a view to passing on to the firm the warning received.

Bobby did not ask himself what this meant. He felt only too uncomfortably certain that he knew.

## CHAPTER XX
## SHOES

All the time he was eating his breakfast Bobby was looking doubtfully from letter to key and label and then back again. The commissionaire's letter was a development he had anticipated and provided for, but none the less disturbing, ominous in its hint that here, too, drama was developing into tragedy. The key and the attached label puzzled him. What its significance might be, he could not guess, nor who had left it in the letter box, or for what reason, or how it was to be connected with the snatch of song he had heard the night before. That there must be some connection seemed certain, but what that connection might be he could not even guess. One thing alone, he told himself, was clear: that someone was for some reason taking in some way some sort of action—and then he reflected that 'clear' was in this connection scarcely the 'mot juste'. He could not even decide whether the intention was friendly or hostile. Possibly all that was intended was another warning, like that already given at the Mountain Street hall.

Another point he had to decide was whether first to interview Count de Legett or to call on Lord Henry Darmoor to return to him what was apparently the key of his flat. Bobby's plan for the day, even before the arrival of the commissionaire's letter, had been to go first to Count de Legett's office, there to offer that warning which he felt must be given even though he knew well it would be useless, would be resented, was likely to have mischievous consequences. None the less his sense of duty told him warning must be given, since no man may be allowed to walk into danger to life and honour without at least some attempt to save him. Yet such a visit would take consider-able time, and therefore a long delay before the mystery of the key and label could be solved.

In the end, though with some hesitation, Bobby decided to make his first call at Lord Henry's flat. Uneasiness was growing in his mind, and an uncomfortable feeling that strange things might have been happening there. Best to make sure at once if anything was wrong. First of all, though, he went to the Yard. There he left the label to be tested for finger-prints though he was assured it showed every sign of having been carefully wiped. The key also was examined. It, too, had been carefully polished, and though finger-prints were plainly visible on it, Bobby felt fairly certain they would prove to be those either of his landlady or her maid.

From the Yard Bobby proceeded to the Park Lane block of flats. At the door of that occupied by Lord Henry he knocked and got no answer. He had knocked again, and more loudly, when one of the staff employed in the building came down the corridor and paused to tell him there was no one in.

"Must have gone out early, for he was here last night all right," the man added. "I saw him come in myself with a—lady." Bobby noticed a faint hesitation in pronouncing this word, as though the speaker had been much inclined to use another name. "But there's no answer when we phone up, and there's a parcel come by post couldn't be delivered and waiting for him downstairs."

"Do you know who the lady was?" Bobby asked.

"No, nothing to do with us," retorted the attendant, and walked away quickly, so quickly indeed that Bobby felt sure the man scented some sort of scandal or indiscretion and was afraid of being mixed up in it and so getting into trouble himself.

Bobby stared thoughtfully at the closed door and fingered uneasily the key in his pocket. Was that why it had been sent to him, he wondered, that he might secure admission? He remembered, too, the old valet, and his story of sudden unfair dismissal after long years of service, a story confirmed to some degree by what Miss Gwen Barton had told him with such apparent unwillingness and distress. At any rate he decided it would do no harm to put the key in the lock and turn it and see if the door were bolted on the inside. It was not, for it opened at once, and Bobby hesitated no longer, for he was beginning to feel that he trod upon the very threshold of the mystery and yet was perhaps as far off as ever.

The door admitted to a small entrance lobby. Various inner doors faced him. All were closed. He stood for a moment waiting to see if the sound of his entry had attracted any attention. All remained as still and silent as before. He called out loudly:—

"Is there any one here?"

No answer came. His voice died away unanswered in that small, confined space. He called again, and again there was no reply. He opened the door nearest to him. It admitted to a fair-sized sitting-room, furnished like that of any young English bachelor of the upper classes. Commonplace engravings on the walls, no books, plenty of evidence of interest in sport and outdoor games, an exceedingly high standard of comfort and well-being. The room was tidy, everything exactly in its place, with a general air of not being very often used. Bobby left it and went into a smaller room next to it. This one was apparently what is often called a 'study', though study is the last use to which it may be put. But it had a more intimate air. There were papers and magazines, even a book or two, there were college photographs, over the fireplace hung an oar with on it an inscribed plate to celebrate some triumph of the past. On the table stood soda water, whisky, glasses. Bobby noticed that the glasses did not seem to have been used. On the floor, half under the table, so that it was not visible at first, lay a woman's stocking, very neatly filled with sand; and on the thick pile of the expensive Turkey carpet were faint marks, as though some heavy body had been dragged along it.

Bobby touched nothing but looked long and carefully at everything, and then went out again into the corridor. He opened another door, it was that of the bathroom, in normal condition and undisturbed. He tried the door opposite. It gave admission to a large, comfortably furnished bedroom and on the threshold Bobby stood still and gaped at a spectacle as surprising as any he had ever witnessed.

For there upon the bed lay Lord Henry Darmoor, neatly spread-eagled. Each wrist was secured by a length of strong dog chain, such as may be purchased anywhere, to each upper corner of the bedstead; each ankle was secured in a similar way to each lower corner. Round the neck was fastened yet another chain with its other end secured to the head of the bed. It was an arrangement that allowed the victim a certain slight freedom of movement but none the less held him helplessly a prisoner. Over the lower part of his face a towel had been placed and made secure by stitching, so that he was unable to call for help. On a small table, placed conspicuously in the centre of the room, were two or three keys. From above the towel covering so completely mouth and chin Lord Henry's eyes, red and swollen, stared at Bobby, and in them Bobby thought that he could read a kind of wondering and incredulous despair as of one who knew that he had lost all, all and for ever, and yet would not believe it, though he knew it.

Bobby went quickly to the bed and removed the towel, cutting the stitches with his penknife. Lord Henry drew a deep breath and tried with his tongue to remove fragments of fluff that clung to his lips. He did not speak. Bobby took the keys from the table where they were lying. As he had expected they fitted the small, strong padlocks with which the chains had been fastened, and soon he had the prisoner free. Not a word did Lord Henry utter, he watched in silence and the tragic misery in his eyes seemed even greater than before, giving to the ugliness and irregularity of his features a kind of new dignity in suffering. When he was quite free he raised himself slowly to sit on the edge of the bed. *He did not attempt to stand up. In spite of a slight freedom of movement the chains had allowed, he was cramped and stiff and aching in every bone. Still not speaking he leaned his head upon one hand and stared moodily before him. Bobby went back into the other room and poured out a stiff drink of whisky and soda. Returning, he found Lord Henry sitting in an armchair. Bobby offered him the drink. He accepted it and drank, still in complete silence.

"Feeling better?" Bobby asked.

Lord Henry looked at him and seemed to consider the point. Then he said:—

"Have a drink yourself."

"What's happened?" Bobby asked.

Lord Henry looked at him and then looked down again, covering his eyes with his hand as though all at once he feared what might be seen there. Presently he said:— "Practical joke— damn fool practical joke."

"I don't think so," Bobby answered softly. Then he said again:— "What happened?"

Lord Henry was still silent, he still kept one hand over his eyes as though to hide what might be written there. Bobby had the idea that he was trying his best to collect himself and decide on some story. But he was in no condition to think coherently, and after a minute or two he said again:

"Practical joke, I tell you. That's all."

"Who is—she?" Bobby asked.

This so startled Lord Henry that he looked up sharply. "What do you mean?" he demanded, a note of fear now in that deep rich voice of his.

"I mean, who is the woman?"

"What woman? What do you mean? There wasn't one, just pals playing the fool."

"I wish you wouldn't tell such lies," Bobby said patiently. "Makes things so difficult. Of course it was a woman. She got you to bring her in here on some excuse or another. The porters saw you come in together and noticed that she didn't look like an ordinary caller. She asked you for a drink. While you were getting out the whisky she got out a stocking filled with sand and knocked you out. The stocking is lying there under the table in the other room. Then she dragged you in here and fastened you up the way I found you."

"Know it all, don't you?" Lord Henry muttered. Then he seemed to remember and said more loudly:—"That's all wrong, nothing like that happened. There was no woman, none at all."

"The towel you were gagged with was sewn in place," Bobby told him. "A woman's work. It's no good telling lies both you and I know to be lies. Who was she?"

"I don't know," Lord Henry answered then.

"You mean—she was a stranger?"

"Someone I had never seen before—didn't know her from Adam, from Eve I should say, I suppose. She said she had something important to tell me. Next thing I knew I was done up the way you found me. How did you get here?"

Bobby explained briefly.

"I think you had better see a doctor," he added. "You don't look too good and you've had a bit of a rough time. Who shall I ring up?"

"No one," Lord Henry answered with vehemence. "I don't want any one fussing round here. I'm all right."

"You don't look it," said Bobby dryly. "If you won't have your own man, I shall ring up for the police doctor. Police will always send someone."

The threat was sufficient. Plainly the very last thing Lord Henry wanted was police action of any sort or kind. He muttered sulkily a name and address.

"I do feel a bit dicky," he admitted and proved it, for when he tried to get to his feet he could hardly stand.

"Better lie down again," Bobby said, supporting him.

"Don't be an ass," Lord Henry snarled. "I've been lying down all the blessed night. I never want to lie down again."

Bobby thought that very reasonable, and helped him to get seated once more. He asked for another drink, but Bobby, returning from the phone, said the doctor would be round as soon as possible, and he had better wait till then. Meanwhile Bobby offered to put on the kettle to make some coffee, if any were available. Lord Henry received this very ungraciously, declaring that he didn't want slops, but very nearly fainted in the middle of his tirade. So Bobby made him a little more comfortable with cushions, gave him some water with a faint dash of whisky in it to placate him, which it failed to do, and then said:— "Why not tell me what really happened?"

Lord Henry, a little better now, looked at him warily. "I have told you," he said. "Pals of mine. Silly practical joke. That's all. Nothing to it."

"I know a good deal already," Bobby remarked. "It is very important I should know more. What's happened here, doesn't stand alone. It links up."

"What with?" Lord Henry asked, and now his deep voice was harsh and troubled, and once more there seemed to come into his eyes an obsession of some horror they dared not contemplate.

"With the death of Mr. Baird in Wychwood Forest," Bobby answered slowly. "With the death of Lord Byatt, too, and of Mr. Andrew White."

To that Lord Henry made no answer, but he forgot to hide his eyes, he forgot to keep his face hidden, and Bobby could see very plainly how he fought to preserve his self- possession, to crush down thoughts it was as though he dared not entertain lest they might overthrow his sanity.

"I wish you would go," he said hoarsely. "Please go." Bobby shook his head. He felt the other was in no condition to be left alone. Once before he had seen a man look like that, at the moment when he had realized that all in which he trusted had failed him utterly. That man had committed suicide, and Bobby was not sure that Lord Henry was very far from seeking the same sad refuge. He said:— "Look here, if you won't tell me what happened, will you tell your doctor? He won't be long. Or is there any friend I can ring up, any relative? There are things sometimes that are too much for one man to face alone."

"I've got to," Lord Henry muttered in a voice so low Bobby could hardly hear it. Then he said in slightly louder tones:— "Get me a drink, will you? there's a good fellow. I need it. A real drink, I mean."

His face was so ghastly, his expression so strained and tortured that Bobby felt he must obey. It was almost neat whisky that he brought. Lord Henry drank it at a gulp. He sat back in his chair and closed his eyes. A little awkwardly Bobby stood by and watched. It is no pleasant sight to see a human soul lost in a black agony of doubt and of despair and be unable to offer any help, to be in ignorance even of the cause. Silently, almost motionless, as Lord Henry sat, somehow Bobby knew well that he was struggling desperately to retain his self-control, even his sanity perhaps. Without even opening his eyes, he muttered:—

"Please go. Why won't you go?"

"Because I don't think you are in a fit condition to be left alone," Bobby repeated. "I think you would feel better if you would tell me what happened—at least, I can guess what actually happened. I mean the rest of it. You aren't like this merely because you have been knocked out and tied up all night. There's something more."

Lord Henry made no answer.

Bobby went on:—

"I shall have to tell the doctor the condition in which I found you."

"A practical joke," Lord Henry said again. "That's all. What's that to do with him?"

"I shall report of course to the authorities. They will wish to investigate," Bobby said.

"A practical joke," Lord Henry repeated. "No affair of theirs."

"A queer practical joke," Bobby retorted. "What would have happened if I had been away? Suppose I had gone back to Midwych for a week or two and I had never got that key?"

Lord Henry gave him a twisted smile.

"Oh, she thought of that," he said. "She thought of everything. She said she would keep a look out, and if you didn't turn up by noon she would come herself to let me loose."

"Well, it's noon now," Bobby said, glancing at a clock on the mantelpiece. There was a knock at the door. "That'll be the doctor," Bobby said and went to open it.

When he did so, it was Becky Glynne he saw standing there.

"Oh, you, you," he stammered, and she stared back at him with a dismay and a surprise equal to his own.

"Oh, you, you," she repeated, echoing him. Recovering slightly she said:— "It is Lord Henry Darmoor's, isn't it? I wanted to see him. It doesn't matter. I'll come back another time. I rang up but I couldn't get an answer. I'll come back."

She was turning to go but Bobby stopped her.

"Were you here last night?" he asked, and the thought was in his mind that her famous 'cannon ball' service could have been well diverted to the swinging of a stocking filled for the occasion with sand.

From within came Lord Henry's voice in a shout:—

"I won't see any one, I tell you I won't see any one."

Ignoring utterly Bobby's question, though it had plainly startled her, Becky said:—

"I will come another time."

She turned and began to hurry away. Bobby called to her to stop and made a step or two to follow her. As he did so a violent push from behind sent him staggering across the corridor against the opposite wall. His hat and his umbrella came flying after him and before he could recover himself the door of the flat was violently slammed. Lord Henry had seen and seized his opportunity.

Ruefully Bobby picked up hat and umbrella. He felt it was no use knocking for re-admission and he had lost Miss Glynne, who had darted into the lift and was probably already out of the building. There was nothing for him to do but to depart also, deeply puzzled by this new development and as worried and uneasy as ever he had been in all his life. Again and again he was being faced with this problem of an unknown woman, whom he could never identify, about whom all information was always refused or else profession of ignorance made. And if he did seem to find some sort of trace or indication, invariably it was each time someone different to whom that trace or indication appeared to lead. Yet possibly all these hints and indications he had seemed to find, were all misleading, all the creation of his own too active fancy. It might be, for instance, that Leonard Glynne was not really living with any woman. The traces of feminine influence visible in his flat might merely be due to the passing presence of his sister. It might be that Becky shared the flat with him when she came to town. And her recent visit might be entirely unconnected with recent events. Lady May's photograph was widely circulated and no doubt to be found in many odd places. Mrs. Reynolds might have fled from him merely to avoid further police questioning, and the woman who seemed so fond of singing Welsh songs might be merely an ordinary street singer. Nor was there any real proof, for that matter, that it really had been General Hannay whom Marsh had seen the other night. Possibly Marsh had been deceived by some chance resemblance, Miss Hannay had merely been offended at finding a policeman enquiring for her father, and some girl perhaps merely amusing herself with the impressionable little Mr. Eyton.

Not that Bobby for one moment really believed all this, but his head was beginning to go round with the strangeness and the multiplicity of his thoughts. In the entrance hall he found the attendant he had spoken to in the corridor outside Lord Henry's flat.

"Lord Henry is in," Bobby told this man, "but I don't think he is in a fit condition to be alone. I persuaded him to let me ring up a doctor"— Bobby repeated the name and address of the doctor Lord Henry had mentioned—"so I expect he'll be here in a few minutes. I couldn't stay myself because Lord Henry wouldn't let me, and I shouldn't be much surprised if he didn't refuse to let the doctor in. You might give the doctor my card and tell him what I say. I am quite sure myself Lord Henry needs attention."

The man, suitably impressed, promised to do as requested, and Bobby added carelessly:—

"Oh, by the way, are you sure you didn't recognize the lady who came in with him last night?"

"Quite sure," the man answered, and added:—"If there's any funny work, I don't want to be mixed up in it. End up with me getting the sack as like as not. If you want to know anything more, you go and see the manager."

"So I would," Bobby answered, "only I don't think there's anything he could tell me—or you either for that matter."

The man looked relieved, and Bobby, in the act of turning away, shot out another question:—

"Did you notice the lady's shoes?"

"Shoes?" the other answered staring. "No. Why? Why should I?"

"Marble floor," Bobby pointed out. "Heels of lady's shoes rather go tap-tap on it, don't they? I've noticed that. Did hers, do you remember?"

"Well, I did notice," agreed the man, "how quiet she went— there was no one else about, quiet time it was before the tenants come back when they've been out for the evening. I do remember now you mention it how quiet they walked across the floor, none of that tap-tapping from high heels." He seemed suddenly to take alarm. "Look here," he said, "I don't know what's on, but, police or no police, I'm answering no more of your questions. You go and see the manager, if you want to."

Bobby produced half a crown and handed it over. "What you've told me may be very important," he said. "I don't know yet and I don't quite see where it fits in, but I expect I shall dream of high heels to-night."

"But she hadn't high heels," the attendant protested.

I know, I know," Bobby said as he hurried away.

## CHAPTER XXI
## DEDUCTIONS

All this had taken so much time that Bobby's very healthy appetite now asserted itself and he went to look for luncheon. This, he has always felt, was natural and defensible. Even detectives must eat. But he did linger over his meal longer than was absolutely necessary. Coffee and a cigarette are merely agreeable accessories. He knows they could very well have been dispensed with, and so have been saved twenty or thirty minutes that might, though of course also they might not, have meant so much. True, he had much to think over after his recent experience, but the time for thought was later on, not now when action was required. Also he proceeded to Count de Legett's office by bus and even walked part of the way for the sake of his digestion. That, however, was natural, since taxis are luxuries whose appearance in an expense sheet is apt to cause a minor earthquake. Of course, had he known what urgency there was, a taxi there would have been, even if he had to pay for it himself, but on the whole he does not feel that, the cigarette and coffee apart, he can accuse himself of any waste of time.

However, regrets are futile, as regrets always are, and the simple fact is that when he reached De Legett's office, he found it smiling and excited, as gay indeed as an old- fashioned and extremely dingy London office can well be, and learnt that Mr. de Legett had departed about ten minutes previously, that his destination was unknown, but not his purpose, and that when he returned to work in a few days he would return as a married man and would introduce to his staff his newly-wedded wife whose identity, he had said smilingly, must, for certain reasons, be kept a secret till then.

"We are all awfully excited at the idea of seeing her," one of the clerks told Bobby. "He's taken such pains to keep it dark."

"No one has any idea who she is?" Bobby asked.

"Not the foggiest," said the clerk. "He's been as close as an oyster."

"No one knows where he has gone?" Bobby asked again.

"Not the foggiest," repeated the clerk. "We're running a sweepstake—seaside, country, South of France, Italy, Switzerland, Paris, elsewhere, and two blanks, of which," added the clerk ruefully, "I've drawn one—just my luck."

Bobby thought grimly that there was yet another destination that to him, at least, seemed possible—the destination that had been reached already by others in strange and sinister procession.

He left in a troubled and depressed mood, and it was now he began to remember that half-hour or so he had spent dawdling over coffee and cigarette. Now it seemed there was nothing to be done but wait and hope for some sign to show his fears were unfounded.

He went back to Bond Street and there, after talking for a little to the commissionaire, he asked if he could see Mr. Higham. Permission was only secured with some difficulty, Mr. Higham not being much inclined to disturb himself for any official under the rank of superintendent at the least —chief constables and assistant commissioners preferred.

Bobby's insistence prevailed in the end, and Mr. Higham, imposing, aged, and dignified, but still very alert, explained at once that in no circumstances except perhaps in the case of a direct order from the courts, would he even refer to any transaction with any client. Bobby pointed out that he already knew a good deal, and gave details to prove it. Mr. Higham retorted that if clients chose to talk about their own business, that was their own business, but made no difference to the absolute discretion his firm had always and would always observe. Under pressure, however, he agreed, and even admitted that it was puzzling, so far as so Olympian a person could be puzzled, that up to the present nothing had been heard of the missing Byatt sapphires or of those other pieces of jewellery disposed of by the firm in which Inspector Owen seemed so curiously interested. The diamond ear-rings and pendant stolen by the chauffeur, Ted Reynolds, who also had so mysteriously disappeared, had certainly not as yet been offered anywhere for sale. Nothing again had been heard of the wonderful diamond necklace purchased by Mr. Andrew White—a historic piece, of which even the stones would be recognizable should such a vandalism as breaking the necklace up have been perpetrated. Certainly there was nothing known to suggest it was in the possession of Lady May Grayson, for whom ostensibly it had been bought. True, she was known to have a passion for jewels, and a ring she sometimes wore was set with what looked very like the famous Blue John diamond, though she always declared it was only a replica. Naturally the point could only be decided by an expert examination which she had not offered and no one had a right to demand. Mr. Higham showed himself faintly displeased by Bobby's knowledge of the fact that the late Mr. Baird, victim of the notorious Wychwood Forest tragedy, concerning which the more vulgar papers had recently published so many columns, had purchased from Christies through Messrs. Higham a very fine diamond and ruby bracelet.

"A certain Personage," said Mr. Higham impressively, "was negotiating for it. I impressed on Mr. Baird that nothing was to be said of the transaction until the end of this month. The Personage in question might have been—surprised"—Mr. Higham managed to convey the impression that the surprise of a Personage was an awesome thing—"that we had not allowed her further opportunity for consideration. Not, of course, that she would have availed herself of it, but she might not unreasonably have thought that her position entitled her to it."

"Quite so," said Bobby, not much interested at the moment in any Personage or in what she thought her position entitled her to expect. "You have no idea what became of the bracelet?"

"It has not come on the market, if that is what you mean," Mr. Higham answered. "It is hardly our province—the destination of our clients' purchases, I mean. Though I admit," and here Olympus became almost human— "the more frivolous of our assistants occasionally gossip when some valuable piece purchased by Eminent Persons is heard of in the possession of—of ladies of somewhat irregular position. Naturally, such gossip is most severely regarded by the firm, and would entail instant dismissal if repeated elsewhere. To avoid such a risk is one reason why the more important transactions are handled by myself or one of my co-directors."

Bobby said he realized how necessary that was, and under further questioning Mr. Higham admitted that his intelligence service was of a very high working efficiency. Occasionally it had been found profitable to know when to hint to the lady of—er—unrecognized position that replicas of valuable jewellery, indistinguishable from the original to all but an expert, could be supplied at a reasonable figure, and the original itself purchased at a very liberal figure.

"We have," admitted Olympus, grown quite human now and indeed indulging in a sort of Jovian chuckle, "in our possession at this moment a fine piece we have twice over sold at a satisfactory figure and then re-purchased from the recipient—also at a satisfactory figure, supplying at the same time a perfect replica. Only the other day indeed a certain elderly gentleman of some standing came to see it—er—not unaccompanied—and appeared so favourably impressed that we have thought it prudent to prepare a fresh replica in readiness for eventualities. You understand, therefore, Inspector, how necessary it is for us to exercise an absolute discretion."

Bobby said he quite understood, and, continuing his questioning, learnt that the firm had trustworthy agents and connections all over the world. It was hardly too much to say that no important piece could be offered in any quarter of the globe without Messrs. Higham hearing of it. That applied especially to the Byatt sapphires and the diamond ear-rings and pendant. Naturally, since for them not only dealers but police were everywhere on the watch. Mr. Higham thought he could say quite definitely that neither sapphires nor ear-rings, nor pendant, could be shown, either publicly or privately, without his firm getting to hear of it.

"As well," said Mr. Higham, growing suddenly poetical, "hide the sun at noon as those sapphires."

He admitted, however, that these pieces, having been obtained dishonestly—there had been no authority to dispose of the sapphires and any purported sale or gift would be invalid, as the late Lord Byatt must have well known—might still be kept in concealment. Stolen pieces were sometimes put by for years. The actual thieves would sell them to a receiver for a mere trifle compared with their real value, and the receiver would keep them locked up in his safe till he thought active search was over and the whole thing more or less forgotten.

"But we never forget," said Mr. Higham in parenthesis. Ted Reynolds, for example, the chauffeur who had succeeded so cleverly in disappearing, had very likely sold his loot for fifty or a hundred pounds or so and the purchaser might still have the pieces in his possession. In a year or two he would make a journey to China or South America, and there dispose of them; for half or two-thirds their proper value perhaps, but at an enormous profit all the same.

"Supposing that happened and the sale took place to some rich Chinese or South American, would you be likely to hear of it?" Bobby asked.

"Undoubtedly," said Mr. Higham firmly. "Jewellery is bought for display, it is displayed—and we hear."

"The odd thing," Bobby remarked thoughtfully, "is that Ted Reynolds has disappeared too."

"Probably means," Mr. Higham suggested, "that he has not as yet attempted to make a sale. I've known such cases. Men who have brought off a successful coup and then not dared to try to dispose of their booty. They may be tramping the roads, starving, begging, doing odd jobs, with pieces in their possession worth thousands of pounds they yet dare do nothing with. That may be the case here."

"It's not only his loot," Bobby observed thoughtfully. "Reynolds himself has vanished. We had recent photographs, we knew his friends, habits, family, he had no start—the theft was discovered at once. He had no passport. Yet we've never been able to find the least trace."

Mr. Higham smiled tolerantly.

"Been too smart for you apparently," he said. "But you may be sure of one thing—if those ear-rings and, or, the pendant turn up anywhere, we"—there was a faint emphasis on the 'we'—"we shan't fail to hear of it." He added, Bobby accepting this snub to the police force of the country in meek silence:—"It is more difficult to guess what has happened to the diamond necklace Mr. White purchased. The ruby bracelet we sold Mr. Baird, too. I can't imagine any woman in possession of either the necklace or the bracelet keeping it hidden. Her first instinct would be to visit a theatre or a restaurant and let all the other women see it. The pieces were paid for. Everything was in order. There might be some complication in the shape of a husband, but even so somebody would know and we should soon get to know too. Besides, that could hardly apply in both cases. I'm afraid I can't think of any explanation," concluded Mr. Higham, ceasing for once to look omniscient. "It's a complete mystery to me."

"A mystery," Bobby agreed, "and yet everything seems to link up."

"Link up, link up what, in what way?" asked Mr. Higham, and Bobby said he didn't know, it was in fact what he was trying to find out, and therewith departed.

Returning to his rooms, he occupied himself with writing out a full account of the day's happenings for his own record, a briefer account for his customary report to Midwych, and then, these completed, he sat and brooded as uselessly as ever over them and the significance that might in them lie concealed.

Later on, since he felt there was nothing in connection with the case wherewith he could usefully occupy the evening, he rang up Olive and asked if she would come and dine with him at a small restaurant near by, where the food was tolerable—the proprietor did his own marketing and his own cooking, and put no faith in refrigerators—and where they could be sure of a quiet corner in which they could talk undisturbed. For to talk over every aspect of the affair and so clarify the ideas running wild in his mind was the chief need Bobby felt at the moment.

Not that Olive allowed any such discussion until the meal was over. Till then she kept the talk strictly to personal chatter, the increasing difficulty of selling hats, the distressing habit of going about without any hat at all which was slowly breaking her chief assistant's heart, the unpredictable changes in style, and the proof of original sin provided by the evident innate depravity of all errand boys. Insensibly Bobby found his attention diverted from his own worries and presently he was listening with attention to some of Olive's tales about the whims and fancies of her customers.

"You've got me a new customer by the way," Olive added. "Miss Glynne. I expect it was because of you she wanted one of our hats."

"Has she been to your place to-day?" Bobby asked, very interested.

"No, is she in town?" Olive countered. "It was a 'phone message last Friday evening, just as we were closing. We do business sometimes with a Midwych firm, exchange stock if

Midwych wants what London doesn't or the other way round, or sometimes it's a special model we supply 'exclusive to Midwych'. Miss Glynne wanted one of our creations she had seen and she went to them for it so they rang up and I had quite a long talk with her, making sure what she really wanted."

"I saw her in town to-day," Bobby said, wrinkling his brow. "I'll tell you presently. Last Friday, you said? Are you sure?"

"Last Friday," Olive repeated, "I remember she said she had just seen General Hannay off at the railway station before she rang up about the hat. She had been talking to him about her father, I don't think she believes he is really ill. I think she thinks he is staying away on purpose and I did wonder if what she really wanted was for me to tell you that."

"I don't see why," Bobby said, frowning more deeply even than before. "I don't see that has anything to do with me—unless it's to let me know again I shan't be interfered with."

"I expect that's it," Olive said. She added:— "Now tell me all about what you've been doing. Stuck, aren't you?"

Bobby nodded.

"Stuck, and badly stuck," he agreed. "The general pattern and idea is growing fairly plain. I've looked up French history and legend and the Inca legends too. The book I got hold of seemed to think the French yarn was only a yarn and very likely the Inca legend is that, too. But the idea is there, it's old, old as evil itself, and I believe there's always been some foundation for it, though one didn't expect it to be turning up again in modern days."

"I've forgotten all my French history," Olive said, "except Joan of Arc. The Incas had something to do with gold, hadn't they?"

"Yes, but Joan of Arc and gold don't come into it," Bobby told her. "Let's go over it all from the start. The thing I want to do is to pick out the essentials."

Rapidly he went over the history of the case in full detail as he knew it. Olive listened intently. She knew the whole story well enough, of course, but she noted now the points on which Bobby laid the most stress and made him explain fully the deductions that he drew. When at last he finished, she said:—

"It all comes to this; you feel sure you know who she is and the explanation of it all, but you have no proof you can act on."

Bobby nodded gloomily.

"Three lives depend on what I do," he said, "and I haven't the right to do anything—De Legett, Lord Henry Darmoor, Mr. Eyton, any one of them, all three perhaps, may go next, and there it is. It's like one of those nightmares when you know you must do something but there's a great weight holds you helpless."

"Don't you think," Olive suggested, "that just because Lord Henry told all those lies, it means he has some plan of his own?"

"I did wonder if that was it," Bobby said. "If so and if half what I suspect is true, he has about as much chance as a rabbit has with a rattlesnake."

"One does rather feel like that," Olive agreed, "though he may be less of a rabbit than you think. Isn't it likely Mr. Eyton is in greater danger?"

"No, he'll be all right for the present."

"Why?"

"He won't get his cash for a day or two. It always takes a few days to make sure that a title to land is secure, and purchasers don't part till they are sure. He's safe enough till the cash has been handed over."

"Mightn't he get an advance from a bank or his lawyers?" Olive suggested.

Bobby looked uneasy. It was a possibility he had overlooked, and one which he did not much like.

"There's that," he admitted. "Still, it's a land transaction, and even a bank would have to make sure there wasn't a prior charge of some sort—a mortgage or something like that. 'Once mortgaged, always mortgaged' lawyers say sometimes."

"You didn't say anything to him about being careful?"

"No. I wonder if I ought to. I should have to go to Midwych to see him. I could make a report direct to Colonel Glynne if I did. It's just possible that what Miss Glynne said when she rang you up was a roundabout sort of hint. Though I don't much think he is awfully keen on seeing me."

"Why not?"

"Well, he's in a very awkward hole. Leonard Glynne's name has been mentioned and so has Miss Glynne's. On the one hand, if he resigns, which, strictly speaking, I expect he feels he ought to, then he is as good as saying publicly that he thinks they may be guilty. Not quite fair to them and if the business is never cleared up, it might mean they would be under a cloud for the rest of their lives. In their case, his resignation would point them out at once. On the other hand, if he runs the investigation himself, he feels he might be influenced, even unconsciously influenced, in their favour—failing to push home points telling against them and so on. It's a very awkward dilemma and he's solved it in a way by leaving it all to me, with orders to consult the P.P.'s office or the Yard at my own discretion."

"I suppose it is difficult," Olive agreed. "For General Hannay, too. You really think it all links up?"

"Sure of that much, anyhow," Bobby answered with decision. "Three men dead: Byatt, White, and Baird, all in similar circumstances. One man, Ted Reynolds, vanished—circumstances similar again. Three men in danger: Darmoor, Count de Legett, Mr. Eyton, and still the same general pattern clearly apparent. And four strange women, Becky Glynne, Hazel Hannay, May Grayson, Gwen Barton; not to mention Mrs. Ted Reynolds I can't get to see, and, dodging about in the background, the street singer woman, who may or may not have something or nothing to do with it."

"There may be someone else," Olive said, "someone you know nothing about."

"No," Bobby answered. "It's one of them. I'm sure of that much at least."

"Yes. Yes," Olive said. "One of them," she almost whispered, "and I've seen them all and it doesn't seem possible." They were both silent, looking at each other across the table, and it was as though a cloud of horror rose there between them as from the heart of evil itself. "How could a woman—any woman?"

"How could any human being for that matter?" retorted Bobby. "Only once you get going—once you get playing with hell..."

He left the sentence unfinished. Olive was looking round, she seemed to draw a sort of comfort, a kind of re-assurance from her commonplace, familiar surroundings, as though they told her the ordinary framework of everyday life still existed, that in and around and about it still moved ordinary, everyday people, people whose lives touched no such dreadful depths as those of which now they two seemed to have caught a glimpse. She said musingly:— "Saints seem incredible, too. If some of us can be saints, then I suppose others—" She paused, and only by an effort did she control herself. "Do you know," she said in a surprised tone, "I think I feel a bit hysterical."

"Well, that's no good," Bobby told her. "Take a hold on yourself. Of course, I do, too, sometimes," he conceded.

"No good kicking and screaming, I suppose," agreed Olive. "Bobby, it can't go on. Surely you know enough to do something?"

"If I go to the P.P. with a yarn like this and no more proof than I've shown you, they'll have me certified," Bobby answered. "If I go to the Yard, they'll call up Midwych and suggest that a senior officer of greater experience should be appointed to handle the case. You see, it's so entirely, so awfully, outside ordinary knowledge."

"There's what Henry Darmoor told you about his having been to see Higham's, in Bond Street?"

"Yes, that's how I got my first hint of the truth," Bobby agreed. "Not much by itself, though."

"There's what Mr. Higham told you about the jewellery vanishing?—"

"The deduction is plain to my mind," Bobby agreed again, "but other people would call it a bit thin to act on. Deduction isn't proof, not by a long way."

"There's all that about May Grayson's photographs...?"

"All of which might bear another interpretation," Bobby said.

"Even together with what you saw when you went to Gwen Barton's flat?"

"They would just say that amounted to nothing," Bobby said. "Which of course is quite true."

"There's Mr. Eyton's story?"

"Yes, thank God," Bobby said. "I think even the P.P. would admit that that clears one—but only one. Negative, you see, not positive. Same with your 'phone message. What I want is something clear and hard and concrete, something calculated to impress the official mind. Not mere reasoning from this to that. They are right in a way—there can always be a flaw in reasoning. You want facts to hang people on, not logic."

"Well, what the porter at Henry Darmoor's flat told you is definite—I mean about heels. Isn't that direct evidence?"

"It's more the sort of thing I need," Bobby admitted, "but it's not much by itself. Defending counsel would have the time of his life poking fun at the fatal proof of the high heels that weren't worn."

"But surely there must be something?" she urged once more.

"Very likely," he answered grimly, "but I haven't found it. I feel I know who it is and why, and just possibly I could make out a sufficient case for her to be watched in the hope of more proof turning up somewhere or somehow. But there's no immediate proof, and the question is—how to stop it happening again? If I put my theory forward, and if, after that, what I expect happens and there's another death, as in my belief is certain, then some notice of my ideas would be taken. She would be questioned perhaps. She would know she was suspected and she wouldn't dare go on. That would be something. In the meantime, there are Darmoor, De Legett, Eyton, and for one of them at least, it will be too late."

They had been sitting there talking for so long that by now it was nearly closing time. They rose to go and as they left the restaurant, Olive, holding Bobby's arm, said:

"It's all like some awful nightmare, you feel you must wake up presently and find it's morning and it's just been a dream. What makes it even worse is that it's all mixed up with love—is it love?"

"Love gone wrong," Bobby said slowly, "love gone wrong and bad, worse than bad."

Next day Bobby took the first available train to Midwych and all the journey long he found his mind less occupied by the errand he had come on or by the details of the investigation, than by a memory of those last words he and Olive had exchanged as they left the restaurant the night before and by the confused and troubling thoughts to which they had given rise.

Was it really this strange passion or instinct or necessity of life, or what you will, which men call love, which irresistibly draws together the two sexes, on which indeed depends the existence both of the individual and of the race, which may in the last analysis be best defined perhaps as the urge to completeness, was it then this mystery of mysteries that had traced the dark and dreadful pattern of secret murder now slowly taking form and shape before his eyes? Was it really, he asked himself, of the same kin and kind, coming under the same category, as the steady and the tranquil force of his own feeling for Olive?

He found himself wondering a trifle uneasily if this emotion he himself experienced was the weaker or the less intense because it burned steadily, controlled and yet strengthening, rather than consuming utterly all things else? A difference, he thought, like that between the fire upon the hearth that warms the house and makes life possible and the fire that consumes all, even to the burning the house to the ground. A greater fire, no doubt, a fiercer heat, but one the sooner over and leaving behind it only death and a handful of cold ash.

Was love, then, he asked himself bewilderedly, a tree like that other one which bore upon itself the fruit of good and evil—fruit both of life and of death?

He remembered how continually there had been mention in this case of that excited restlessness he had himself noted both in Henry Darmoor, when he had first met him, when he had been inclined to attribute it to drink, and again and more recently in his recent talk with little Mr. Eyton. He himself had never felt like that in Olive's company, he had felt instead repose and gentleness and a freshness of the mind, and afterwards a clearer insight into other things.

He reflected that Love seemed like a gate opening on two different roads. Well, he supposed birth was like that, a gate to life, and each man's life was his own, duality of the necessary body and of the controlled and yet directive mind to be shaped into such common form as the will might choose. Was Love, too, a kind of birth to a fuller, ampler life, a duality again of physical and spiritual, of the necessary body and the dependent and yet directing mind, to be shaped into such form as again the will might choose?

Puzzling thoughts, and troubling, and the riddle one that Bobby felt beyond all powers of his own, though it was one that each must solve in his own way. A riddle, he reflected again, that had been too much for wiser heads than his own, and he remembered with a smile having read somewhere that Martin Luther had once expressed a wish that God had asked his advice and arranged to continue creating fresh members of the human race direct from clay, and so saved all the trouble and worry and confusion caused by what the philosophers have sometimes called the 'most troublesome of all the passions.' Then, too, there was that common phrase 'Sacred and Profane Love'. Perhaps that was it, and just as life can choose, if it will, to follow the paths of hell, so also love can make the same choice. Perhaps that was the sign of its supreme value, that it can turn to evil as well as to good, even as the greatest gift of God to man is the right to sin.

With a start he realized that he had reached his destination, and indeed he had only bare time to collect himself and his belongings and tumble out on the platform as the train started off again. At the county force headquarters he found that Superintendent Oxley, now acting deputy chief constable, was not there, having been unexpectedly called away on unexpectedly important business. Bobby, who had rung up from London to announce his coming arrival, was inclined to suspect that this 'unexpectedly important business' was chiefly important because it saved Oxley from too close contact with an affair which he did not understand and which threatened uncomfortable repercussions. Besides, Bobby had to admit that there was also the excuse that Oxley probably felt he had been so far deliberately excluded from the investigation and that therefore those engaged in it could clear it up for themselves as best they could.

From the county headquarters Bobby went on to Asbury Cottage, where he was told that Colonel Glynne, on the advice of his doctor, had entered a nursing home for a few days' complete rest and quiet. He could be reached on the 'phone, naturally, but it was most undesirable that he should be worried. The doctor had declared that only matter of life and death could be sufficient justification for disturbing him. Bobby said grimly that this was precisely that—a matter of life and death. So, after some more argument, he was given the 'phone number of the nursing home, and, when he got through, heard his request for speech with the colonel received with undisguised horror and amazement. Quite out of the question, he was told, but with that quiet persistence which was one of his most valuable characteristics, he explained that he was going to ring up again and again, every five minutes if necessary, unless and until he got a direct refusal from Colonel Glynne himself. He did not quite succeed in obtaining that, but he did get from the doctor in charge a personal statement that his message had been given to the chief constable who had replied that Inspector Owen had his instructions and if he felt himself in any difficulty must consult the Public Prosecutor's Office or call in the assistance of Scotland Yard. The doctor also added that he was to tell the inspector that Colonel Glynne felt himself so near a complete breakdown that he had actually written out his resignation though as yet he had not sent it in. This, of course, was confidential, and only for Inspector Owen's own private information.

Not much help there, Bobby thought, as he put down the receiver. He went back to Midwych very doubtful what action he could take next, and yet stronger every moment in his deep instinct that immediate action was required. He had, of course, still to attend to the other of the two errands that had brought him to Midwych. But when he tried to find little Mr. Eyton, to deliver to him that warning he had been too late to give to Count de Legett, it was only to be informed that Eyton had resigned his post on the Midwych paper he worked for, had given up his house and sold his furniture, and that no one knew his present address.

"He just said he would find some place in London but he didn't know where yet," one of his journalistic colleagues told Bobby. "I expect he'll ring through some time and let us know. He's been a bit queer lately, all raggy and nervy. Needed a rest cure all right."

Bobby went away, trying to console himself for this second failure with the reflection that this warning, too, would almost certainly have been ineffective and might have served merely as a warning not to the victim, but to that dark unknown of whose identity he was growing more and more certain, but against whom so far he had been able to secure so little of the proof that a court of law requires. Not an uncommon dilemma, of course, for again and again police authorities know very well who is guilty but cannot act for lack of material, definite proof.

"A rest cure," Bobby repeated to himself uneasily, remembering the last casual remark Eyton's journalistic friend had made, and he found himself hoping that it was only his own troubled imagination which had felt the phrase so ominous, though indeed there were too many names in his mind of those who had reached a 'rest' lasting beyond the confines of this present world.

He returned to the station to take the next train back to London and there was surprised, so far as the developments of this case were not removing from him all capacity for surprise, to find Lady May Grayson. Apparently she had learned of his visit to Asbury Cottage and of his attempt, and of its failure, to get in touch with Colonel Glynne. Guessing that he would be likely to return to London she had come here on the chance of meeting him. Very evidently she was troubled and alarmed. For one thing she knew of Bobby's visits to Leonard and its result and evidently she feared consequences.

"Becky's in London, too," she said, "though her father's so bad. When I ring up she is either out or she won't answer, and Leonard hasn't heard either."

"Would he be likely to?" Bobby asked. "I understood they were not on very good terms."

"You mean about me?" Lady May countered, and then when she saw that Bobby looked surprised, she added quickly:—"Oh, you mean about poor Mr. Cadman. He had behaved very badly to Becky and it set her against every one almost. She seems to think it was all every one's fault, and especially Leonard's for finding out and telling."

"I suppose it was a great shock," Bobby agreed, wondering if he knew all the story, or if Lady May knew it, and, if so, if he could induce her to tell it.

"You see," Lady May said, "she always felt that it didn't matter so much about what Mr. Cadman had done—she thought she could change him."

Bobby winced. 'Changed' was a word he little liked to hear in connection with this case. It had acquired an ugly sound. He said:—

"Have you any idea why Miss Glynne has gone to London?"

Lady May did not answer at once. She was looking at him very closely and attentively, and somehow it seemed as though she had ceased to be the professional beauty and had become simply human, beset by secret doubts and fears, troubled by some deep misgiving. Bobby had an idea that what she was about to say might be of great importance and yet he dared not press her; for how easy it would be, in this crowded railway station, for her simply to turn and walk away. She said:—

"I think Becky wants to find Hazel Hannay."

"Oh, yes," Bobby said, hoping more was to come.

"Her father's in London, too," Lady May went on. "Hazel's, I mean. That's what's upsetting Colonel Glynne." It was a remark Bobby found unexpected and that he did not understand. He did not see why Sir Harold Hannay's presence in London should disturb Colonel Glynne so much as to make him seek refuge in a nursing home, as Lady May's words clearly implied. It was another explanation Bobby had had in his mind.

"Oh, yes," he said vaguely. "Yes."

"Becky's changed herself," Lady May said. "She wants to change every one else too, I think."

"Lady May," Bobby said. "I think you know very well—"

"No," she interrupted, "no, I don't; nothing." She was looking at him with quick alarm. "I don't know anything, I must go," she said.

"There's one thing you do know," Bobby told her, checking her with a gesture as she began to turn away. "Will you tell me—it's whether the ring you wear sometimes is really the genuine Blue John diamond."

"Why do you want to know?" she asked, astonished.

"Because, if it is, then I would like to know how it came into your possession?"

But she shook her head.

"I don't see that that matters," she answered. "You know I tell every one it's only imitation. One man said he didn't need me to tell him that. He could see it for himself. He was an expert."

"Did he say anything else?" Bobby asked. "Did he say, for instance, that owners of valuable jewellery sometimes have replicas made for them to wear instead, as a sort of safety precaution?"

"Detectives do know a lot, don't they?" she retorted. "I keep my secrets. The more people go on guessing, the more they talk, and the more fuss they make, the more publicity, and the bigger fees for me." More gravely, she added:— "I wish you would find Becky and Hazel. I'm—I'm afraid."

Then she was gone swiftly and lightly, and as Bobby watched her tall form passing through the bustling crowds that filled the station, he wondered gloomily what this meant, if it had been a genuine attempt to express uneasiness about Becky, or a warning about Hazel, or simply an ingenious effort to divert his energies.

Lady May had given him the address of Becky's hotel. It was late when he got back to town but he went on to the hotel at once—he had his dinner on the train—and found it to be small, not very attractive in appearance, and situated in a not very savoury neighbourhood. When he asked for Miss Glynne, he was told she was not in. She had a room there, but she did not use the hotel services very much, explained the hotel with a knowing, faintly unpleasant smile. The evening before she had rung up rather late to say she would not be back that night—she had explained she was staying with a friend in the country, added the hotel, again with that knowing and this time distinctly more unpleasant smile. She had also said that it might be very late when she reached the hotel to-night, as she was motoring up from her friend's place in the country. So it was not much good Mr. Owen's trying to wait, unless, suggested the hotel, he also booked a room. Oh, yes, Miss Glynne's belongings were still there, she had taken nothing with her when she went out the previous morning. Bobby guessed it was a point on which the hotel had assured itself and made certain also that their value was more than enough to cover the bill.

Plainly no use to wait, so Bobby left his name and his address in London and his 'phone number—though not his profession. He had no intention of telling the hotel that, though in point of fact they already strongly suspected it. He left also a message asking Miss Glynne to ring him up as soon as possible on her return, and then, deciding it was too late to do anything more, made his way home. On the way he bought an evening paper and there found in the 'stop press' column a brief note to the effect that much uneasiness was felt over the fate of a visitor who had hired a motor launch at a small East Coast watering place and had not since been heard of. It was feared an accident might have occurred.

Bobby read it over twice. More or less it was what he had been expecting. He got down at the next stop and proceeded to the nearest police station.

There he showed his credentials and got permission to use their telephone. It was not easy to establish communication, but by midnight evidence gathered from the owner of the missing motor launch, from the local inn, and from what the local police already knew, made it clear that the missing man was De Legett. To Bobby this was no more than confirmation of what he had been gloomily anticipating, and all through the greater part of the night he drove in a hastily-secured car to the scene of this latest tragedy, or rather to the spot where the beginning of the final act had been staged. He arrived in the small hours, was able to snatch a little sleep, and then in the morning began his enquiries.

He learnt little and all that he did learn merely confirmed his expectations. De Legett had arrived alone, he had been alone when making the arrangements for the hire of the motor launch, nor had he said anything about expecting any companion. A local youth reported that, lounging on the quay where the launch was lying, he had seen a woman walk briskly to the launch and go on board, without hesitation or question, entirely as if the boat were her own or she knew she was expected. The young man had not thought much of it at the time, he certainly would not know the woman again, he could give no useful description of her, he had only seen her back, and that from a distance. His impression was that she had been well wrapped up but that was about all. No one else seemed to have seen her, or if they had seen her, they had not paid her any attention. Shortly after her arrival the launch had started off and it had not since been seen. Nor had any one remarked what course it took, except vaguely, as out to sea. It was a fair sized boat, the weather had been calm, there had been no reason to suppose anything but a brief pleasure trip, only the failure to return had caused alarm. Probably, said the local people Bobby questioned, no one would ever know what had really happened.

"I suppose not," agreed Bobby, though a clear vision had risen in his mind and he had seemed to see a man lying drugged and insensible in the cabin of a launch that was slowly sinking somewhere out there in the wide and lonely sea, sinking into depths from which never would it rise again, the while a little boat pulled steadily away towards the shore, towards a point where probably lay hidden a car or a bicycle to make escape easy.

In answer to further questions he learnt that the launch had naturally, and as a matter of course, carried a small collapsible boat. Necessary both for safety and convenience. Other questions brought the information that nothing unusual or abnormal in De Legett's behaviour had been noticed, except a certain excitement and restlessness that had at first given rise to some suspicion that he had had too much to drink. But then it became apparent that he was merely a little nervous and expectant, as if waiting for someone whose coming was eagerly anticipated. A chambermaid, remembering a former case and hearing that a woman had been seen boarding the launch, had at once openly expressed her conviction that here was another romantic elopement.

The local police, when Bobby finished his enquiries, asked uneasily:—

"What's in your mind? do you mean you think it's one of these suicide compacts?"

"I think it's murder," Bobby answered, "but I don't think we shall ever know."

He drove back to London and on the way made up his mind that, incomplete though his case still remained, difficult though it was to see what could be done, ardently though he wished for more time to try to secure the further proof he needed, yet now he must ask higher authorities to act.

In view of what might happen next—and soon—he dared not run the risk of the further ill that further delay might mean.

## CHAPTER XXIII
## CONFERENCE

Even so there were delays and formalities to be gone through, and it was not till the next morning that Bobby was able to present himself at the offices of the Public Prosecutor, where there was awaiting him one of the staff, a Mr. Findlay, known as the author of a leading work on jurisprudence and one of the assistant directors of the department, together with no less imposing a functionary from Scotland Yard than that high personage known as a chief constable, a personage so exalted that in all his years of service at the Yard Bobby had never seen more than his majestic back. His appearance cheered Bobby considerably, as proof that the report he had submitted was being taken seriously and had not merely been consigned to the waste paper basket as the melodramatic dreamings of an over-excited imagination—a fate he had sometimes feared might overtake it. Moreover, the chief constable seemed in a good temper, which, rumour said, was not always the case, at least not before lunch, and when Bobby put down on the table two books he had previously borrowed from the public library—*Tales of Old Paris* and *Legends of the Incas*—he looked quite interested.

"Well, well," he said mildly, "are these exhibits in the case?"

"Not exhibits exactly, sir," Bobby answered. "More what you might call atmosphere—background."

Both chief constable and assistant director looked puzzled and then settled down to listen to what Bobby had to say and to question him on details of his report, and all the time Bobby had the feeling that they would have refused to give his story serious attention but for that paragraph in the papers, under the heading 'Feared Boating Tragedy', which recounted how a London business man, Count de Legett, had hired a motor launch for a trip to sea and had not since been heard of.

The chief constable said when at last they were at the end of their questions:—

"I've come across some queer things in my time, but never anything like this."

Mr. Findlay said:—

"It's quite incredible but it does hang together." Bobby said:—

"It was a long time before I could get myself to think it was possible nowadays. I don't know why. All over Europe we are going back to the primitive instincts in public life, so why not in private life, too? It spreads."

"Yes, but a woman," the chief constable protested. "You can't think a woman—" He left the sentence unfinished.

"I know, sir," Bobby agreed. "You don't think of women like that. Only sometimes they are."

"Once a woman gets going—" began Mr. Findlay and then he, too, left the sentence unfinished. Then he said rather loudly:— "Unnatural."

"Yes, sir, I know," agreed Bobby once more. "It does seem like that—unnatural, I mean. When the sultan in the Arabian Nights takes a new wife every night and has her beheaded every morning—well, we feel we can understand it in a way. So to speak, it's in character. When a woman turns the tables and does much the same sort of thing— well, it seems out of character."

"Once a woman gets going—" repeated Mr. Findlay, and again he left the sentence unfinished. Then he said:— "You can't believe it, only you can't believe half the things that are going on in the world to-day."

Bobby picked up the two books he had brought with him.

"When I began to suspect what was behind it all," he said slowly, "I went to the library near where I live."

"Looking for precedents?" asked Mr. Findlay with a grim smile.

"Yes, sir," Bobby said. "Somehow it seemed less incredible when I knew something like it had been heard of before." He opened one of the books—the one entitled *Tales of Old Paris*—and showed an illustration. "The tower," he said, "from which one of the old French queens is supposed to have had her lovers thrown into the Seine each morning." He showed the second book: *Legends of the Incas*. "The same sort of story here," he said, "about Inca princesses who disposed of their succession of lovers in much the same way."

"The ancient way," mused the chief constable. "I suppose the modern way is divorce. Some women get divorced half a dozen times. Too slow for this lady, I take it. A throw back as you might say."

Mr. Findlay had been taking notes, and now he said, referring to them:—

"You say the first thing you noticed was that Lord Henry Darmoor knew about these purchases of jewels from Messrs. Higham?"

"I didn't realize that was important for a long time," Bobby answered. "What did strike me was the extraordinary resemblance between all these cases. The 'modus operandi' was always the same, and of course we all know how important the M.O. is— criminals always stick to the same line. I noticed, too, it always happened that the actual cause of death couldn't be determined. The one thing certain was that violence had not been used—even after a body has been burnt a doctor can almost always tell if there is any trace of a bullet or knife wound or of broken bones. That made me think that possibly poison or a drug of some sort had been used and that first gave me the idea that a woman might be concerned. Then when I began to make enquiries, I found there always seemed to be a woman somewhere about, never very conspicuous but always there. That made me remember there was always a mention of jewellery, too, and there's a connection in a way between the two ideas—women and jewellery. It was then I got my first glimpse of the truth. It struck me that if Lord Henry knew so much about these purchases of jewellery, he could only have got the information from Higham's, and that meant that he must have been in touch with Higham's himself and probably therefore buying jewellery himself. Only that didn't prove for whom he had bought it whether for Miss Barton or someone else. Another thing that began to seem significant was that all this jewellery always disappeared. Jewellery is usually bought for display—what it's for. But this wasn't, because it wasn't displayed, and when I tried to think what it could have been wanted for the only answer I could find was—a trophy."

The two others looked startled.

"You mean," the chief constable asked, "she wanted a sort of souvenir of each of her victims?"

"I think so," Bobby said.

The chief constable made no comment, but even he, man of long and varied experience as he was, had become a little pale, and taking out his handkerchief he wiped his forehead and his wrists that had grown damp. Bobby went on:—

"As soon as I felt sure it was a woman, I knew it must be always the same woman. There were four, and four only, who seemed in various ways to have known or been connected with each of the dead men—Lady May Grayson, Miss Becky Glynne, Miss Hazel Hannay, Miss Gwen Barton. In addition I had to remember Mrs. Reynolds, the wife of the absconding chauffeur—"

"You don't mean you think he was another victim?" Mr. Findlay interrupted.

"Yes," Bobby said, "though I'm not sure whether partly at least he didn't suspect the truth—perhaps even he had helped. I don't know. But there is evidence he was hanging about in the vicinity at the time of Lord Byatt's death. Anyhow, I feel sure he is dead, and that is why the search for him was a failure."

"No body has been found, has it?" the chief constable asked.

"No, I think it was hidden. Probably there had been less time for making the necessary arrangements for passing it off as suicide or accident, as was done pretty successfully in the other cases."

"Can't do much unless we find the body," remarked the chief constable.

"I think I know where to look," Bobby answered. "I'm not sure, of course, but I've a pretty good idea." He went on:— "So I had to think of Mrs. Reynolds as a possibility, and then there was the street singer who kept turning up as if she had something to do with it. Also I had to remember the statement made by the old butler or whatever he was Lord Henry sacked—rather brutally, it seemed. Incidentally, it was noticeable that all the men concerned seemed to have their characters changed—developed perhaps would be a better word—by their contact with this woman. I took it that was another proof of the strength of her personality she seemed able to impress on everything and every one near her. That fact became an important indication."

The chief constable nodded.

"Some of your line of reasoning is new to me," he remarked, "but I did notice how that stood out."

"To go back," Bobby continued, "to what Lord Henry's old serving man said—that someone had come between Lord Henry and Miss Barton. Miss Barton herself more or less confirmed that. But again there was nothing to show who it was. It might, for all they seemed to know, be any one, one of those I was already considering, or someone I had never heard of, or, again, they might both be wrong in making the suggestion. Obviously the first thing was to try to rule out those I knew of. I took first the street singer who called herself Mrs. Jones. I was sure she came in somewhere and I thought, too, that probably she was up to something on her own. I didn't feel too easy about that, either, and I felt we had better know what it was and stop it, if possible. I remembered she sang in Welsh and I knew Mrs. Reynolds lived in Cardiff. It seemed suggestive, so I went there to try to see if Mrs. Jones was also Mrs. Reynolds. But she cleared out before I got the chance, as soon as she saw me outside the shop. A sweet shop, selling chewing gum it was. Only a detail, but there had been chewing gum wrappers near the burnt caravan in Wychwood Forest. Well, I thought her flight conclusive. Next thing Lord Henry's key turned up in my letter box and when I went to his flat, he had been knocked out and fastened up. The thing to be noted was the knocking out—the first piece of physical violence in the case. I thought the difference in technique suggested a different— well, operator. The porters at the flats where he lived had seen him bringing in a woman, they had specially noticed because she didn't look his class. I made a point of asking about her shoes because I had noticed that the street singer woman wore very sloppy, down-at-heel shoes, part of her rig out, I thought. The other women concerned all wore the usual high heels that make a tap tapping sound on marble floors like the one in that entrance hall. This woman's didn't. I thought it looked like the street singer woman turning up again and still working on her own for her own ends, and I thought it pretty clear she was really Mrs. Reynolds. Only I couldn't prove it, and as usual, Lord Henry wouldn't say a word, no one in the case ever would say anything."

"You don't mean Mrs. Reynolds is the woman you've been looking for?" Mr. Findlay asked quickly. "You've no real proof Reynolds was actually one of the victims?"

"Only that he disappeared, that in his case also there is a history of jewels, and that he deserted his wife with whom previously he had been living on perfectly good terms. At any rate, she seemed greatly distressed when he vanished, and it is pretty plain she had nothing to do with it or she would have disappeared, too."

"What was Mrs. Reynolds's idea—if it was Mrs. Reynolds —in this Darmoor business?" asked the chief constable. "Why should she want to fasten him up like that? Her idea of a joke?"

"No," said Bobby. "I think she wished to warn him, and I think she knew very well he would not listen to a word unless she made him. So she knocked him out with her improvised sand bag made out of a stocking, fastened him up, and then, when he recovered consciousness, told him her story. Then she went away, leaving him to think it over, and sent me to release him."

"Yes, but I mean, why tell him?" insisted the chief constable, "why not tell us what she knew—if she did know anything?—"

"I think," Bobby said gravely, "she kept away from us for the same reason that has made her keep away from us all the time. I think she is playing her own hand because she means to take the law into her own hand."

"Oh, we can't have that," said the chief constable hurriedly; "we can't have that, that must be stopped."

"Yes, sir," agreed Bobby. "If we can," he added. Then he said:— "I think she knows more than we do, and I think she will trouble less about—well, procedure."

"Must be stopped," the chief constable muttered, looking very uneasy. "Must be stopped somehow."

Bobby did not ask how. He continued:—

"I suppose she didn't want to risk there being another victim, so she took her own way of making sure Lord Henry listened to her. She gave him the warning I was too late to give De Legett and that Mr. Eyton ought to have, too. Only no one knows where he is and it may be too late again."

"Oh, not another," the chief constable exclaimed, almost flurried now. "Not another, for God's sake."

"I think every effort must be made to find him," agreed Mr. Findlay.

"I'll see to it," the chief constable promised. "We'll broadcast an SOS if we have to. Only will he reply?"

No one answered that. Bobby said:—

"It was what Eyton said the other night when he came to see me that finally gave me proof it wasn't Miss Hannay. I knew he had been mixed up a good deal in private theatricals with her. It was pretty certain he would have recognized her had it been she who talked to him in Wychwood Forest. For that matter she would never have risked such recognition. It had to be someone Eyton had never met and didn't know—therefore not Miss Hannay, with whom he had a good deal to do over amateur theatricals. It's true he told me he never got a glimpse of her all the time they were talking, but I didn't believe that for a moment. It wasn't probable in itself and it was so evidently what he was told to say. I never seriously suspected Lady May. I felt the way her photographs kept turning up showed they were being used as red herrings to confuse the trail. At a guess, too, there was a touch of feminine psychology in that. If I am right, the woman responsible for all this is not strikingly beautiful—I think she is one of those women who can walk down a street and no one will look at her twice, only if you do, you're lost. A sort of inner flame in her, a flame of desire. I remember reading somewhere that none of the portraits of Cleopatra show great beauty—an inch more or less on her nose would have made no difference, it was her, not her looks, that did the mischief. I think there was a sort of jealousy, or rather, an extra zest in triumph behind these photos of a really beautiful woman she gave her lovers to put up in their rooms, like the one I saw in poor De Legett's office. So I soon ruled Lady May out. I was a good deal worried about Miss Glynne for a time. Little uncomfortable things kept cropping up. I think now some of them were introduced on purpose to confuse us—the gold tennis badge, for example, and Baird's clumsy show of efforts to meet her. He had been told to put on a show of interest in Miss Glynne, just as previously another man was persuaded to pay open attention to Miss Hannay. Kind of a smoke screen. In each case the man was so infatuated he was ready to swallow any yarn, and do anything he was told. Finally I got information from a friend that showed Miss Glynne wasn't in London the Friday night of the Mountain Street meeting, the night Marsh saw General Hannay. So I felt she was out."

"What was General Hannay doing?" the chief constable asked.

"I take it he knew something of what was going on and suspected Miss Hannay was mixed up in the proceedings. I think to some extent that was so, and she has been in deadly fear of it being found out. Not that it amounted to much, only she was scared of her father knowing, and he got it into his head that possibly there was something in the stories associating her with Andy White's name. The Mountain Street hall itself was only a kind of—well, try out, a hunting ground, bait, a place where suitable young men could be picked up. Probably most of them simply went for what they thought was just a bit of fun, meaning by 'fun' a chance to behave rather worse than at the average night club, with the further advantage of nothing to pay, lots of free drinks, and so on. It was all paid for out of the money obtained from Byatt and White and the others. There is nothing to suggest most of those who went there had any idea what was behind. Some may have suspected something. I don't know. I expect it was there Lord Byatt was picked up and probably the others, too. General Hannay must have got to hear something."

"I'm glad Miss Hannay is cleared," said Mr. Findlay slowly. "Very awkward for your chief constable," he added to Bobby, "if it had turned out that the chairman of his Watch Committee—" He paused as a new idea struck him. "Is that why it was left so entirely to you?" he asked.

"I think so now," Bobby agreed. "I thought at first the colonel was afraid that Leonard Glynne or Miss Glynne might be involved. Both Colonel Glynne and General Hannay felt the thing was somehow beginning to concentrate on Midwych. They both made that plain in their first talk with me. I suppose it was because of that, because they felt they needed independent help, that I was sent for. Only now I expect it wasn't so much Leonard and Miss Glynne the colonel was worried about, as Miss Hannay. I didn't realize that."

"I thought you said you had a complete alibi for Miss Glynne?" Mr. Findlay remarked.

"That only came later on from a casual remark a friend of mine happened to make," Bobby answered. "Before that, I couldn't help feeling Miss Glynne's behaviour was—well, curious. You see, I hadn't fully allowed for the effect of her disillusion over the man she was engaged to. He was a bad lot. Leonard Glynne knew it and said so, and then he got killed in an accident, for which Leonard Glynne was held partly to blame. I did consider the possibility that Miss Glynne might be, so to say, working off her disappointment and disillusion on other men, but it didn't seem a very plausible idea, and now it seems what was upsetting her was that she thought the same sort of thing was happening to Leonard. She got the idea that Lady May was playing the same kind of trick with him that Cadman had with her. That was all wrong, but it resulted in a violent row between them. He boxed her ears and in the scuffle she bit his thumb. She had got wind that Lady May was already married and that was right enough, only it was Leonard Glynne himself she had married. Apparently, they didn't want it known till she had wound up her contracts and he had completed some invention he is busy with. There were two complications worrying me. He had got hold of money and that seemed suspicious till I looked him up one day and got asked if I was bringing him another happy wire. I didn't realise at first what that meant. It's an expression the football pool people use when they send a wire to the winners of big prizes. Leonard Glynne won a half share in a £20,000 prize last year. He kept his own name out of it and said nothing about it at home because Colonel Glynne had been running a sort of crusade against the pools. A bit difficult for him if it had come out that his son had won a half-share in one of the biggest prizes. That explained where young Glynne got his money from, and it explained the Blue John diamond business, too. Both he and Lady May are keen on jewels. It may have been what brought them together in the first place. Leonard seems to be a bit of an expert in precious stones, and has carried out deals in them—probably pays him better than his inventions. He bought the Blue John for Lady May out of his pool prize money, partly perhaps as an investment or reserve. That cleared away the second complication—her possession of one of the pieces of jewellery mentioned. Only, of course, it was always noticeable that she displayed her possession of it, while the other pieces all vanished."

The chief constable was looking at the notes Mr. Findlay had made and had handed across the table to him. He said:—

"A lot of all this is guesswork and theory. It all makes a logical whole all right enough, but where's your proof? The sort of proof you can take into court and plump down before a jury?"

"I know," Bobby answered. "You remember, sir, I said my case was not complete. I felt something had to be done. That's why I spoke. If we can't put her in the dock, we can at least make sure she—stops."

"What do you advise?"

"Questioning her. She won't answer. She is far too clever for that. She knows what safety there is in silence. We can go on asking questions all the same. We show her we know all, but not that we can prove nothing. She'll guess it, but she won't be certain. We shall have to let her go in the end, but we can warn her she will be kept under observation."

"Running a bluff," commented the chief constable.

"Yes, sir," said Bobby. He added:—"I think it's all we can do—yet. It means showing our hand too soon, but I think we've got to. Or there'll be another death and we'll be responsible."

"Yes," said the chief constable. He looked at Mr. Findlay, who nodded and wrote 'I agree' on a slip of paper and then looked surprised at what he had done and dropped the slip into the waste paper basket. "O.K.," said the chief constable.

Bobby rose to his feet, feeling the conference was over. He said:—

"With a bit of luck proof might turn up. I'm thinking of trying a spot of burglary to-night."

Neither of the others made any comment. They did not seem interested or perhaps they had not heard. At the door Bobby paused and looked round. He said reluctantly:

"I don't know if she ought to be warned that she is in some danger herself."

They made no comment on that either, and Bobby went back to his rooms, where he found waiting for him the proof that for so long and arduously and vainly he had searched.

It was in the shape of a long, written statement, signed by Lord Henry Darmoor.

## CHAPTER XXIV
## STATEMENT

I first met Gwen Barton two or three years ago. I don't remember exactly. I don't even remember where it was or how it happened. That's like her. First of all you don't notice her at all. Then you don't notice anyone else.

I never knew when I fell in love with her.

One day we were just ordinary acquaintances. Next day nothing else mattered, only her. You just belonged to her, body and soul. I don't think it was love exactly, it was possession.

She took everything, she possessed you.

One day I got an invitation to a place in Mountain Street, off the Edgware Road. I had heard there was such a place, of course. Every one had. Not where it was exactly, only that it existed, and you were rather out of things if you had never been. If you went you had to swear not to tell, and if you did, you were never asked again. Besides you didn't let your people know if you could help; I mean, of course, if you were still living at home. It was all very mysterious, and every one was awfully thrilled to get an invite, but no one knew who sent it or who ran the show or why. You heard all sorts of stories. Some said it was a group of film stars and the secrecy was to prevent the bosses knowing, because of their contracts. Or else it was an American millionaire, or else a Russian grand duke who had got away with the Imperial crown jewels and didn't dare let it be known who he was for fear of their being claimed. Any tale you liked to tell or believe.

The invite told you a name and number you had to give to get in, and you were advised to wear a mask. It wasn't essential. They let you in without, but most people had one. The name I had to give was Sir Galahad, Camelot Hotel, Cornwall, and my number was 666. I thought that pretty thick. I'm no beauty, I know, but I called that rubbing it in. It nearly put me off, only I thought I might as well see what sort of a show it was, with all the stories going about. I knew plenty of my pals had been, young Byatt, for instance, and Andy White and other chaps, too.

As a matter of fact it was a pretty dull show, night club style, not much out of the ordinary, though some of the women were certainly very much out of their frocks. All a bit second rate, including the drinks, only lots of them and nothing to pay. That was a great attraction, because every one likes a free show, and it's all being so mysterious. When everything is just the same every day, a bit of a mystery does appeal. For instance, no address for reply was ever given on the invites. To accept, you had to put three candles in your window or something like that—spy film style— and then you were rung up and told where to go. All that sort of thing. Good stage management, but the show itself boiled down to a big petting party, with nobody caring much how they behaved because nobody knew who anybody was—no limit and nothing to pay for drinks.

I got fed up and went off early. We met at the door as we were leaving. She was going, too, she said. Good stage management again, good timing. She said it was the first time she had ever been there. She seemed a bit upset, cried a little. She knew how to put it on, she was a wonder when it came to lying. She could lie in a voice so full of truth I think God Himself must have believed her. I walked part of the way home with her because she said she wasn't feeling very well. She wanted a little fresh air, she said.

We talked about the show and we both said it was a dud and we wouldn't go again.

All the same there was something exciting in her voice— something hot and hungry. Even her telling you how flat and dull it had been made you go all excited and restless because somehow she made you understand how different it could have been.

She said every one there had been asleep or dead and that was how she made you see them, too, and that set you longing to be awake and alive and different from them, and you knew that she could show you how.

She said she wouldn't tell me her name or where she lived, though of course I knew, because she wasn't masked, though I was. I had no idea she knew all about me well enough, I never dreamed it was me she was getting hold of. She said we must never meet again.

Only before we separated she promised we would, only the place must be Mountain Street again, when we got fresh invites, because only there could we meet without our knowing each of us who we were. You see, she pretended to be very keen on that, though of course we both knew quite well, though I pretended not to, and I never dreamed she knew just as well as I did.

I spent all my time till the next invite wondering about her and trying to meet her and wondering how to behave if I did. She kept out of my way, though, and then the invite came, and when I got there I thought at first she hadn't come. I was all on edge wondering if she would turn up. The time before the music had been ordinary sort of stuff—jazz, swing, the usual night club programme. This time it seemed all drums—drumming. There wasn't any band, just one of those big gramophone things. Drumming. It seemed to beat you down and down. Some people couldn't stand it and cleared. I felt like that at first. But if you listened long enough it got into your brain, it got into your blood, you felt yourself slipping...

It made you think of dark places in woods, or nights on lonely hilltops, and altars to strange gods, and people dancing round them in and out of shadows, and cutting themselves with knives.

You got to feel there was nothing else in all the world except that unending beat, beat, beat...

Worked you up.

You hadn't any self-control any longer. I knew I ought to go before I lost mine, and I tried to, only then I saw one of the women looking at me and I saw it was her. She had a mask this time, but I knew her all right. Gave me a jolt somehow. I nearly ran for it. I knew very well, as well as I knew that I was standing there, that it was the only thing to do.

But then she beckoned me and I went.

After that, I didn't care any more.

Nothing mattered except her and what she gave me. The things she knew, the things she showed me, things that I had never dreamed of, though before I should have said I knew as much as most.

No one could ever understand who hadn't been the same way. Sometimes she would tell me things just to see how far I was under. I was under all right. She told me I wasn't the first. There had been young Byatt, she said. She said it was on her account he had killed himself. If she had told the truth, and that he hadn't killed himself but she had killed him, because she had grown tired of him when she had got from him all he had to give, and killing him was the only way to keep him quiet and prevent any risk of exposure, I shouldn't have cared.

I think I should have felt it quite natural she should kill when she had—finished.

But I never thought that one day it would be like that with me, too, and with me also one day she would have —finished.

I might have known. I am not sure that in reality I didn't always know. Because it was so plain that nothing could ever satisfy for long her infinite desire.

If there ever was that idea in my mind, I never let it come on top.

Sometimes I would wonder a little how I had changed. Not that I wanted to admit that, even to myself, and when an old chap who had been with us for years, before I was born, page he had been and my father's valet and mine, more like an old friend, when he started worrying I just cleared him out. I wonder what's become of the old chap.

One night lately a woman spoke to me, a woman I didn't know. She said she had been sent with a message. There had been trouble at Mountain Street with the police. It surprised me, because it was always the idea to keep on the right side of the law and give no chance for them to interfere, but I took her up to my rooms because she said it was so important I should hear what she had been told to tell me.

I wasn't suspicious. I remember noticing some of the porter chaps looking, but it was no business of theirs. When we got in my flat I started to get her a drink. Really, I wanted one myself. I was always wanting a drink now to try to cool off on, and out of the tail of my eye I saw her swinging something up to land me one.

I remember thinking quite clearly that Gwen must be through with me, that this was the Byatt finish for me, too.

So, you see, I must have known all the time, or why should I have thought that?

All the time, even when we were in each other's arms, I must have known deep down what she really intended, only I suppose I didn't care.

Next thing I remember I was lying on my bed. She must have got me there somehow after I had passed out. She had me fast with dog chains by the wrists and ankles to the bed posts and she had stuffed a towel into my mouth, and she was bathing my forehead with eau de Cologne. Once she took the towel out to let me have a drink, but she stuffed it back again at once.

She started to talk. She told me about her husband and meeting him and what it meant when you met a man you cared for, and who cared for you, and about their little house—he was a chauffeur getting good pay from the people he worked for—and how he always brought her every penny home, and used to tease her asking if he might have a little back for pocket money, and how he was just her man till another woman came and took him from her.

Gwen, of course.

He knew Gwen liked jewellery—swell jewellery—we all had to buy her some, mine was a diamond tiara I had to sell out all my holding in war loan to pay for—and as he hadn't any money he stole stuff to give her. Diamond ear-rings, and a diamond pendant, I think, belonging to his employers. After that she had to kill him so as to keep him quiet, because if he had been arrested it might all have come out. She hid the body, so that it was never known what had happened to him. Every one thought he had got away abroad somewhere, but the woman talking to me said she knew where his body lay hidden. And she told me about Byatt—what a jolly, bright boy he had been, friendly with every one, till Gwen got hold of him, just as she got hold of me. And how she killed him when she grew tired of him, managing so that it seemed like suicide. She told me a lot more. About Andy White. About Baird. She knew it all, so long she had been watching and waiting.

All through the night she sat there by the bed, talking, telling me. Telling me things I had known all right, even though I never let me know them. But I knew them for a truth, as all through the night this woman I had never seen before sat there by my bed where she had made me fast so that I had to listen, and told all the things I had known so long and never let my knowing matter.

When she had finished she began again. All over again, only this time more about me. You see, she knew it all, watching, waiting. She had managed to get into the Mountain Street hall somehow and she had hidden close by when we thought we were alone, listening just as I listened while Gwen talked.

Also she knew just what Gwen was going to do and how.

She said Gwen was tired of me and growing frightened, too, because questions were being asked. A man named Owen. A policeman. Gwen always laughed at the police. I've heard her say they were too tied up with regulations and red tape to be much good. They often said themselves they knew criminals but couldn't get proof. Gwen said if the police had any sense they would know it was the criminal they had to get, not the proof. She had heard about this Bobby Owen, though, and took me to see him once. She said afterwards she wasn't impressed. Military type, she thought, and he ought to have gone into the army where being a gentleman and having relatives in the House of Lords is a real help. All the same the woman said Gwen was getting uneasy about him now because of the way he was plodding on. The woman said she had seen Bobby Owen, too, and she thought Gwen was right to be uneasy, because he did give you the idea that he would never stop plodding on—not till he got there.

She said she was just as frightened of him as Gwen was, only for a different reason. She said she was afraid he might be first. I don't know what she meant.

She said Gwen had made up her mind to go to America and start fresh there. Only first she was going to kill me so I couldn't make trouble.

She told me just how Gwen was going to do it.

When she had finished she went away and made herself some tea. Then she came back and started all over again from the very beginning, just as if she had never said a word before. She sat and drank her tea, and said it all over again every word.

I had to listen because the way I was gagged with that towel and fastened up. I couldn't move or speak.

I had to listen.

It's strange to have to lie still and listen while one woman tells you how another means to kill you as she killed those others, too.

Always when she had finished she made herself more tea and then began again—right from the beginning.

You see, I couldn't speak or move.

It was like that all through the night.

You see, I couldn't speak or move.

I had to listen.

When it was day she washed the cup and saucer she had been using and put away the tea pot, and then she went away herself.

She said she would send someone to let me loose.

She came back and said very likely I didn't believe her, and if I didn't, she didn't care. I had to be told so as to have a chance to save myself and I could believe her if I liked, or I could disbelieve her and die—like the others, like her husband.

All one to her, she said.

She said her job wasn't me, it was something else.

She went away again then and I lay and thought and thought till Bobby Owen came, the police johnny. She had sent him. He wanted to know all about it. I told him it was a practical joke. He didn't believe me. I didn't care. All I wanted was time to think. God, how I wanted to think.

Only I couldn't.

You see, I knew it was all true, every word, only it didn't seem real. It seemed a truth about other people, another world. Like watching a play of marionettes that had nothing to do with real happenings.

I had arranged to meet Gwen at the Savoy for dinner. I felt rather jolly and high spirited. She noticed that. She said something about my being fey, but I hadn't had anything to drink. I told her so, and she said if I wasn't fey, then I ought to be.

It's strange to sit at dinner and watch across the plates and flowers the woman you know has made her plans to kill you.

It all happened as she had said—the other woman, I mean.

Gwen was never more—I don't know any word to describe it. She pulled you right out of you—if you see what I mean. The other woman said: 'She is a vampire, she feeds on men.' That was true. Unless she was sucking the life out of a man, she couldn't exist. That night I could almost feel her feeding upon me, and it was as though she fed till there was nothing left of me.

That's what I had been told all the night long.

All the night long I had been told, and it was so.

She took me to her own place in Camden Town I had never known about before—one of a terrace of empty houses that are to be pulled down when the lease runs out. Most of them are empty, but she had rooms in one of them. She only took you there when it was the end, when she didn't mind letting you know because you were never to know anything else.

I let her do what she liked. It didn't matter. I went the whole way with her. Why shouldn't I? You see, I knew how it was meant to end—what she meant and what I meant, now I had been told, told all through a long night, over and over and over again.

Next night we started off again, in my big car. I drove. She told me we were going where last night would seem nothing, nothing, nothing compared with what was waiting for us.

She told me where to drive and when we had gone a long way she told me to stop.

There was a hamper in the car with food and wine, a bottle of wine. Only not the bottle she thought because I had changed it.

Not difficult, because she never even thought of suspecting anything.

I was watching though, and I saw her pour away her own glass of wine but I drank mine.

She watched me while I drank, and she smiled a little only, you see, what I drank, it wasn't from the bottle she had prepared.

It is strange to drink the wine a woman has poured out that she thinks will kill you, while all the time she sits and smiles, and sometimes whispers a word or two about what presently you are to share together; other whispers too, whispers about love—of one side of love, I mean, the only side she knew.

When she thought my senses were gone and the drugged wine had acted, she started the car. Then she slipped out of one side and I slipped out of the other, and I lay quiet in the bushes while the car went over the edge of the pit opposite where we had stopped, where she had told me to stop.

It was late and very dark. I lay there quite still, under the bushes in the dark, and she came to the edge of the pit, very carefully, for fear of falling, and when she was right at the edge she stood there and laughed.

I don't know how long it was she stood there, laughing to herself.

It seemed a long time but perhaps it wasn't.

I lay very still. The bushes hid me and the night and I never moved. I might have been dead—like those others. I think sometimes I thought I was. I think I saw her dancing. I am not sure. I could see her against the skyline and it is in my mind that I saw her dancing as she laughed.

But I am not sure. It was like watching a marionette show. It didn't seem real. It didn't seem real that I was dead, though I thought perhaps I was.

It is very strange to lie and watch a woman laugh and dance, because she thinks that you are dead and she has killed you.

She had a bicycle hidden somewhere near. She rode away on it, very silently and swiftly, and I came home again.

There was a letter on my table. Gwen's engagement ring I had given her was lying near. The letter was in my writing and had my name to it. But I had neither written it nor signed it. It said that now Gwen had found out I was deceiving her with another woman and had sent back her ring, I had nothing left to live for and so I was going to commit suicide.

It was a good letter. The writing was just like mine, I could almost have sworn the signature was mine if I hadn't known it wasn't. No one would have had any doubts. They would have looked for me a long time; and when they found me under my wrecked car at the bottom of that old chalk pit, everything would have seemed perfectly simple and plain.

And Gwen would have been provided with a good reason, after such a tragedy, for leaving England for a rest and a change of scene and to get away from talk. Every one would have felt sorry for her, and in America she would have been able to start fresh.

That's all.

Except that there wasn't only the letter waiting for me. Becky Glynne was there, too. She had been rung up, just as she had been once before. The other time was in case Bobby Owen didn't come. This time she was told she was to, make sure I was all right.

It's Becky who has made me write all this. I didn't want to, but she said I must and so I did.

HENRY DARMOOR.

## CHAPTER XXV
## CLIMAX

The first thing Bobby did when he had finished reading this long document was to ring up the Yard to say that he was bringing it to them for their information and action. Then he rang up Lord Henry's flat, but got no reply, and when he tried the manager's office he was merely told that Lord Henry Darmoor was away and had not said when he would return. An attempt to get in touch with Becky Glynne was equally unsuccessful.

Annoying, for though Bobby did not doubt a word of Lord Henry's statement, which indeed told him no more than he had long suspected, he knew the Yard would want personal confirmation. To the Yard it had to be shown at once, however, and there after it had been examined it was considered to provide sufficient ground for action. Inquiries were sent out for Lord Henry and for Becky, as well as for Gwen Barton. Every place that could be thought of was visited, every person believed to be likely to know anything about any one of them was questioned.

Without result. All three of them had vanished utterly without trace. A phone call put through to Cardiff brought presently the reply that Mrs. Reynolds was selling sweets and cigarettes as usual in her sister's shop. It was understood she had been in bed two or three days with a touch of influenza, and certainly she looked ill enough, pale and drawn.

"I wonder if she saw a doctor," Bobby mused, but did not think the point sufficiently pressing to be worth at the moment any further inquiry.

Cardiff was asked, nevertheless, to keep an eye on her, and if she showed any symptoms of departing, to arrest her on any charge they could think of, assault, theft—she had helped herself to Lord Henry's tea, for instance—unlawful entry, anything so long as she wasn't allowed to slip away.

It all took time, and mostly, it appeared, wasted time. One paragraph, however, in Lord Henry's statement had mentioned that Gwen used occasionally rooms in the Camden Town district, in a row of otherwise unoccupied houses destined shortly to be pulled down when certain leases expired.

An urgent message to the Camden Town police brought the information that there were in the district two or three such blocks of houses waiting for demolition, but that houses in Mop Brow Terrace seemed likely to be those required, since one of them was known to be in occasional use by a lady who lived in the country but sometimes spent a day or two there when visiting town. Nothing was known about her, there had been no reason for inquiry, talk in the neighbourhood was merely to the effect that a woman had been seen entering one of the houses, and that local tradesmen occasionally delivered supplies. It was known, too, that the water and electricity charges and so on were paid—paid by money order in the name of George Burton.

To Mop Brow Terrace set out therefore two police cars; the first containing the chief constable himself, for even that dignitary was growing interested, a superintendent to take the responsibility, an inspector to do the work, and Bobby, trying to remember that he, too, was now an inspector, if only of a provincial force, and therefore entitled to feel quite at home, even in such exalted company. The second car contained technical experts, the finger-print and photograph men, and two uniform men who might be required, since a common or garden policeman in uniform often makes more impression than even a chief constable in mufti. Mr. Findlay, of the Public Prosecutor's Department, was asked over the phone if he would care to accompany the party, but cautiously declined on the ground that the Public Prosecutor's Office was not an office of investigation. Their work only began when all possible facts had been collected, then their job was to consider them and to prepare the case for presentation in court.

"Besides," he had added, "you'll find the bird has flown and the nest empty. The lady knows when to declare and when to pass— especially when to pass."

In this, however, Mr. Findlay was wrong in part, and he has always felt that even the bridge at his club with visiting experts, which, as a psycho-analyst might have guessed from his use of the card metaphor, was the real cause of his refusal, was hardly worth what he missed.

Darkness had already fallen when the two cars drew up in Mop Brow Terrace before a row of five houses, presenting as derelict and dismal an appearance as can well be imagined. They had been used for what is known as 'fly' bill posting. Chalk inscriptions had been scribbled on their walls. Windows were boarded up on the ground floor, on the upper floors they showed thick with the grime of years and often displayed broken panes as well. The woodwork had gone unpainted for so long that in places no paint was left and the bare wood showed signs of beginning to rot. In the areas, dead leaves, dirty paper, and so on, had accumulated. Only one sign of use and occupation was visible and that only to the observant eye. The door of the central of the five houses had a Yale lock that had plainly not been in position for long.

Knocking produced no answer. One or two passers-by informed them that no one was living there. The information was received without gratitude, but the chief constable began to be nervous lest a crowd should assemble. It doesn't take much to cause a London crowd to collect and all police have an ingrained dislike of crowds. Incalculable things, crowds. So he sent two of the party round to have a look at the back. They returned to report it even more securely fastened up than was the front. So then he reluctantly produced the search warrant with which he had provided himself, and said to Bobby:—

"Carry on."

Bobby went back to the car and found the jemmy they had brought with them. He inserted it between door and door post. The lock held but the unpainted woodwork soon gave way. Bobby pushed the door back and they all went in.

"Try to find a switch, the electricity should be on," said the chief constable.

The switch was soon found, but no answering light responded, for the very good reason that there was no bulb.

They had brought police electric lamps and by their light saw an unfurnished hall, the walls black with dirt, the floor boards uncovered and broken and splintered in more than one place. Plain traces of occasional passage along the centre of the hall to the foot of the stairs were visible. There were other stairs leading down to the basement, but cobwebs and dust gave proof that no one had recently gone that way. Bobby opened one or two of the doors near. They admitted into empty rooms where evidently no one had been for years.

"Try upstairs," said the chief constable.

Their steps loud on the uncarpeted treads, echoing through the silent and deserted house, they ascended to the first floor, silent themselves as the silence around, for a foreboding of strange evil lay heavily upon them. On the landing they paused. Everything here was in the same condition. Cobwebs and thick dust, a broken banister rail, paper peeling from the walls, great patches of damp where water at one time had seeped through from somewhere, a general air of desolation and decay.

The chief constable looked round. Since he began to climb the ladder of promotion he had done a lot of reading and he was not averse from showing it. He said now:— "Fit place for treasons, stratagems, and spoils, eh?" Then he laughed nervously.

The superintendent said:—

"Fair gives you the creeps, don't it?"

The chief constable said:—

"That's what I meant."

The inspector said:—

"Cleared out. We shan't get much here."

Bobby, who had found the electric switch, pressed it, again without result.

"There must be lights somewhere," he said, "if bills have been paid."

He pushed open the nearest door. This time pressure on a switch produced a flood of light. There was shown a bathroom, comfortably, even luxuriously, fitted up, and with traces of recent use. There were even clean towels ready. The water was evidently heated by electricity. Convenient cupboards held all accessories, which included a large jar of expensive bath salts.

"Quite dinky, eh?" said the chief constable.

Bobby opened a second door. It showed a well-fitted kitchen, with an expensive-looking electric range. Again there were signs of recent use, and there was a supply of tinned and other preserved provisions in the cupboards. There was even a small electric furnace for disposing of rubbish "Very nice, too," said the superintendent. "My old woman would appreciate it."

"Any one could have lain doggo here for long enough," said the inspector. "Must have got an idea we might be round."

Bobby did not say anything, but he wondered how that could be, since there could have been no knowledge that Lord Henry had lived to tell his story.

They went on to the third door. It opened on a large bed-sitting-room, again comfortably and even luxuriously fitted up. Everything was in the most modern style of glass and shining metal. The general effect should have been austere and cold, but somehow was not. For one thing the bed was a splash of colour with a great red crimson covering, and then the rich, heavy hangings on the walls were crimson and black.

"Very stylish," said the chief constable approvingly. "All the latest." He walked over to the gleaming dressing table and picked up a comb mounted in silver and mother of pearl. "Hair," he said. "Woman's. Been used recently."

"Too much like a dentist's, if you ask me," said the superintendent, looking round disapprovingly. "Smells, too," he added, and in fact there was a strong, slightly intoxicating odour of perfume in the air.

"A bit—what do you call it?—austere," said the inspector. "Not what you would expect for goings-on like we've heard about."

"Contrast is sometimes effective," Bobby observed. "Cold can burn, too. Touch metal at forty below and see." They all trooped back to the landing. Bobby opened the door opposite. It admitted to a large room, running the whole length of the house, from party wall to party wall, possibly originally intended for entertaining at a time when it was considered smart to have the reception rooms on the first floor so that the hostess could stand at the head of the stairs to receive guests and be seen by them.

Bobby found the switch and pressed it. There sprang into light all round the room a number of small electric candles fitted in pairs before a series of small brackets, like tiny altars. On each stood a framed photograph of a man, beneath each hung a piece of rare jewellery, shining faintly in the dim radiance from the little electric candles that only half illumined the enormous room, but showed so clearly each different photograph. In the middle of the room stood a great crimson divan. There was no other furniture. Great black velvet curtains covered the windows, the walls were hung in black, the rich, luxurious carpet was black, even the ceiling had been painted black. Around the walls twinkled the small candles, showing clearly the photographs they framed. Beneath sparkled and shone those different pieces of jewellery against the black background of the wall hangings. In the doorway stood that little group of men and stared and were silent—for how long they never knew.

The chief constable was the first to speak. He muttered:—

"Photographs... all of them... is it?... how many?—"

Bobby moved forward, his feet sinking deeply into the soft pile of that dark, luxurious carpet. He paused before the first.

"Byatt," he said. "Young Lord Byatt, I think. Those are the Byatt sapphires underneath."

He went on to the next.

"Mr. Andrew White," he said. "I've seen his photograph before. That's the great diamond necklace Higham's sold him hanging there."

He went on to the third.

"Baird," he said. "Diamond and ruby bracelet this time."

He came to the next—the last on that wall.

"I don't know who this is—a foreigner, I should think," he said, looking at it closely. "South American for a guess. Those pearls look good."

In fact the photograph was never identified, the pearls never claimed.

Bobby went on to the next wall.

"Henry Darmoor," he said, "but he's alive."

The next was a photograph that Bobby recognized at once, though he had never seen the original. But one like it had been circulated to all police forces, had appeared in all the papers underneath the caption: 'The Missing Chauffeur'.

"Ted Reynolds," Bobby said now. "Those are the earrings and the pendant he stole. He couldn't buy for her so he stole instead."

"Does it mean he's dead?" asked the chief constable. "No body was ever found, was it?"

"No, but I think I know where it is," Bobby answered. He went on to the next on that wall.

"Another I don't know," he said. "Looks young." Afterwards the photograph was identified as that of a young Englishman who had vanished in the Swiss Alps. His body has never been found. Probably it lies at the bottom of some crevasse. A consideration of dates makes it probable he was the first.

The inspector said slowly:—

"Hell."

The superintendent said:—

"God."

Perhaps they both meant the same.

The chief constable said:—

"If I can wangle it, I'll get permission to be there to see her hang."

Bobby said:—

"We haven't got her yet."

The chief constable glared at him. He said:—

"She won't get away with it, not if all the force do nothing else but chase her till they get her."

Bobby said:—

"I think there's someone else who wants her just as badly."

The chief constable said abruptly:—

"I've had enough."

He was, in fact, looking very pale. He went down to the waiting car and sat there. The others could carry on. They knew the necessary steps to take. Bobby came presently to the car where the chief constable was sitting. He said to him:—

"I have been trying to think where she may be."

"Run for it," said the chief constable. "Knew the game was up and ran. We'll get her."

"Yes, sir," said Bobby mechanically, because he always said 'Yes, sir,' to superiors, before he contradicted them. "Yes, sir, only what made her think the game was up? She didn't know Lord Henry was still alive to tell us things."

"There's that," agreed the chief constable. He added:— "That's right. This business has got me so I can't think straight. Well, where is she? There's all that jewellery she's got up there in that ghastly room of hers. You mean she'll be coming back for it?"

"It's possible," agreed Bobby. "Do you remember, sir, I said I was thinking of trying a spot of burglary?"

"Here?"

Bobby shook his head. He said:—

"I guessed she had a hide out. That flat of hers I went to once was evidently only a blind. But I never found this place. I was thinking of Mountain Street."

The chief constable said nothing. He was thinking it out for himself. He said presently:—

"I suppose I can guess what you have in mind."

"I was thinking of burglary because I wasn't at all sure," Bobby explained. "I feel more certain now. I thought if you would come, sir, and used your authority, we could persuade the caretaker to let us have the keys."

"All right," said the chief constable. "Jump in. Collect a uniform man or two first."

Bobby obeyed. He secured one of the uniform men—a sergeant. He explained to the superintendent what they had in mind, and that gentleman then went off back to the Yard, there to begin the organization of the nation wide, world wide search

Bobby in his own mind felt would be useless, but that nevertheless had to be begun because no possibility must ever be neglected. Then the chief constable's car started and they were so far in luck as to catch the Mountain Street hall caretaker in that brief interval he allowed himself between closing time and bed. But he was a good deal less impressed than Bobby had expected by the information that the tall, stout man in plain clothes was a chief constable. To the caretaker a chief constable was someone somewhere between an ordinary constable and a sergeant. The sight of the sergeant in uniform accompanying them was much more effective. Sergeants the caretaker understood, and on the strength of those three stripes he yielded up his keys.

To the hall therefore the three of them, the chief constable, Bobby, the sergeant, forthwith proceeded, and when they entered saw at first nothing in any way unusual or of interest.

"We'll have a look at the basement," Bobby said, and led the way.

He found the door at the head of the stone steps leading to the basement, and when he opened it—it opened towards him—he threw forward the light of the electric lamp he carried. As well he had remembered to be careful. A string was stretched across the head of the stairs, so that any one descending them without first looking would almost certainly trip and fall.

"What's that for?" the chief constable asked.

No one answered and they descended carefully. At the bottom of the stairs lay a woman's stocking, half filled with sand.

"I've seen one like that before," Bobby said. "Those stairs aren't very high. A fall might not be effective enough and perhaps a knockout was necessary, too. Nothing overlooked."

He found the light switches and turned them on. Lights sprang up.

What the darkness had hitherto concealed was now plainly visible.

In one corner the door of that small compartment walled off from the main cellar and hitherto kept locked, was now open. On the threshold lay open a big packing case that still seemed largely filled with lime. In the middle of the main cellar a dead man in a chauffeur's uniform was seated on a chair. A belt kept the body in position. In one dead, shrivelled hand had been placed the end of a rope. The other end was round the neck of Gwen Barton, who, her hands strapped behind her, her feet some inches from the ground swung slowly from one of those hooks in the ceiling beams that Bobby had noticed before.

## CHAPTER XXVI
## CONCLUSION

Once again Bobby was in Cardiff, and this time when he entered the little shop that did so good a trade in cigarettes and sweets, the woman behind the counter, though she had watched his approach, made no attempt at avoidance.

She had been busy dusting and re-arranging some of the stock. When Bobby entered she laid down the light feather brush she had been using and turned gravely towards him. For a moment or two they stood and looked at each other, her gaze as steady and direct as his. She was the first to speak. With a gesture that was half sombre, half mocking, she pointed towards the feather brush she had been using.

"My job is finished," she said, and then again: "I have done what I had to do." In the formal tone of the shopkeeper to the customer, she said:— "What can I get for you?"

Bobby said:—

"What job have you finished?"

She did not answer, but again their eyes met, and his were doubtful and questioning, but hers were dark and strange; and he had the idea that though it was at him she looked so straightly, it was something else she saw He said:—

"You are Mrs. Ted Reynolds. The first time I saw you you said your name was Jones, Jane Jones, wasn't it?"

"Did I?" she asked indifferently, and as though with an effort she withdrew her gaze from whatever it was she had seemed to see.

"You were pretending to be a street singer?"

"Why 'pretending'?" she asked. "It's what I was."

"A woman was murdered in London two evenings ago," Bobby told her.

"Was it a woman?" Mrs. Reynolds asked. "Was it a murder? Or do you mean a vampire was put out of existence?"

"I mean murder," Bobby answered steadily. "Except in self-defence, killing by a private person for private reasons is always murder."

"Have you come to tell me that?"

"No. To ask you where you were two evenings ago?"

"In bed," she answered promptly. "Influenza cold. Ask the police. We've had quite a lot of custom from them lately. Cigarette sales gone up a lot. Very nice, too. Sis tried to sell them sugar candy sometimes, but it was always cigarettes they wanted. Very often when they were in the shop, they heard me call from my room upstairs. 'There's Jinnie calling,' Sis would say; and as it was a policeman, she wouldn't mind leaving him alone for a minute or two in the shop while she ran up to see what I wanted. Very sympathetic those policemen were, wanted to know who my doctor was."

"Who was he?"

"I was never bad enough for a doctor. With what they charge for a visit, you think twice about getting one in. I'm not insured, you see. Sis looked after me herself, and old Mrs. Reynolds came in to help sometimes. She stayed the night once or twice. My mother-in-law, I mean, Ted's mother. She felt it a lot when Ted disappeared. You go to her. She'll tell you."

"What you are telling me," Bobby said, "is that you have an alibi."

"Oh, no," she answered. "Why should I want an alibi? But if I did, there's Sis, and old Mrs. Reynolds, and the neighbours Sis told about me, and the police who heard me calling—quite enough, I think."

Bobby thought so, too. The voice supposed to be hers the police had heard could easily have been arranged. Old Mrs. Reynolds, perhaps, or even such a cheap gramophone record as is often manufactured—'while you wait'—at popular seaside resorts or at country fairs. Direct testimony from the sister and mother-in-law as well, and very likely confirmatory evidence from neighbours. A watertight tale constructed by a very clever and determined woman, Bobby told himself, and when he looked up he saw how fiercely blazed those dark, gleaming eyes of hers, fixed full on his, almost like blows.

"All the same—" she said and drew a deep and gasping breath. More calmly, she said:— "Well, there's my alibi. Do you want to upset it?"

"I have my duty to do," he said gravely.

"I had mine," she answered.

"What was it?" he asked.

"I think you know," she said, and picked up her light feather brush as if she meant she had no more to say.

Two tiny children appeared, sticky pennies in their small, hot hands. With an almost unbelievable change in her manner, she leaned, smiling and gentle, over the counter to attend to them. It was Judith laying down the scimitar to soothe a crying baby, it was Jael putting away hammer and tent peg for some loving household task. Before so many and such dazzling treasures, the two infants remained in an awestruck hesitation. Gently she helped them to their choice, finally sending them off with a kiss and an extra piece of toffee each, the last as a bribe for permission to wipe small noses that certainly had need of such attention. Bobby had been watching. He said:—

"You have hurt your hands, Mrs. Reynolds."

She opened them and looked at them thoughtfully.

"The skin has got rubbed off in places," she said. "Why?"

"It looks as though they had been pulling hard upon a rope," he said.

A small boy appeared. He had brought a penny. It seemed he was bringing a penny every week for the purchase of a shilling box of chocolates he wanted for a Christmas present for his mother. Mrs. Reynolds took the penny, carefully marked another X on a dirty card he produced and he ran off happily.

"Isn't it nice of him?" Mrs. Reynolds said to Bobby. "I think I shall have to try to coax a two bob box out of Sis for him."

"Well, you won't," said unexpectedly a stern voice from within. "You'll ruin us the way you pet those children. This isn't a home from home for all the kids in Cardiff."

"That's Sis," explained Mrs. Reynolds. "She's worse than I am, really. They come in here, coughing as hard as they can, and buy a pen'orth of bulls'-eyes, so she'll give them liquorice or eucalyptus drops for their cold."

"I never," said the same indignant voice. The quiet-looking, elderly woman Bobby had seen on his previous visit, appeared at the inner door. " If I do, it's only business, so as not to lose their custom if they get laid up. It's you. We're getting notorious." She gave Bobby a hostile look. She said:— "Why don't you serve the gentleman and let him go?"

"So I will," Mrs. Reynolds said. "Shut the door, Sis, and then I will."

The other woman disappeared, banging the door behind her. Then she opened it again.

"You mind what you're doing," she said. "And you only just up after a week in bed."

She disappeared again.

Bobby said:—

"Strengthening the alibi. Quite effective. Will you answer some questions?"

"What do you want to know?" she demanded. "What shall I tell you? How happy we were together, Ted and I. We should have been happy still, but for her. I didn't know at first. I saw he was feverish and excited, but he was always trying to do things for me. If I had known, I think I could have stopped it. He told me there seemed to be a down on him up at the big house where he worked and that was what was worrying him. I was a fool not to see what it really was. How was I to guess she had got hold of him the way she had, when all the time he was never tired of doing things for me? I think it was his way of asking me for help, but I never guessed, I never knew. I was too happy, I think, thinking of him, thinking of my baby I thought was coming. He never knew that. I didn't tell him because I wasn't sure—not then. I never knew anything till the police came and said he had gone and jewellery was missing. I didn't know even then who it was. But I found out. It didn't take so very long."

"It seems you were a better detective than I was," Bobby said.

"Perhaps I wanted more," she said heavily. "It meant more to me to know. I knew it was one of those four, but I had to be sure which one. Do you know Lady May is married to Leonard Glynne? That was after he won a big football pool prize. He spent a lot of it on buying an awfully valuable ring for her. I suppose it will always be there as a reserve when he has muddled the rest of it away on those inventions of his. It didn't take me long to be sure it wasn't her."

"I felt that, too," Bobby said.

"First of all I thought it was Miss Hannay," she went on. "She used to go to Mountain Street sometimes and she was frightened her dad might find out, and so he did, and he was frightened worse than she was, because someone rang him up and asked questions about her—questions that were really hints. Questions about Lord Byatt and about Mr. Andrew White. Pretending to be the police, and, because it was a woman's voice, pretending to be a woman detective. All lies of course. Really her it was muddling things up. Colonel Glynne suspected Miss Hannay, too. Is his girl going to marry Lord Darmoor?"

"Henry Darmoor, you mean?"

"Isn't he Lord Darmoor? They've both been in hell, they'll understand each other. They've both known treachery, they'll be the better able to trust each other. I'm glad. I liked her the best of them. Because she had been through it, too, I daresay. Having the child stopped me doing anything for a long time. It was born dead. The doctor said that was worry, I had worried too much. Shock, he said. So that was her, too. Husband and son as well. Perhaps if the boy had lived, it might have been different. But he didn't live—born dead. Sis has a good living here and there's enough to keep us both busy. But I had to live while I was going about to find out what I wanted to know. So I tramped and sang for coppers while I was asking my questions." She paused for a moment and then resumed:— "Why shouldn't you gossip before the street singer you're giving a cup of tea to and some bread and cheese? Why shouldn't you answer her questions? I found out a lot. So did you.

I began to be afraid you would be first. I took a risk of spoiling my chance and helping you when I warned the man she was hottest after."

"Darmoor?" Bobby said.

She went on without making a direct answer:—

"I managed to get into her place in Camden Town. I cut out the lock of the area door of the next house and got in and climbed out of the skylight and in at the skylight where she was. One night I watched her. She sat on a big red divan in that room of hers, just sat there with the photographs all lighted up all round her—sat and looked at them and smiled. I saw her mouth all red and her crimson nails. I saw her smile. I wanted to strangle her then. But I knew she was as strong as I was and she had a little pistol she always carried with her. I had to be sure. So I waited." She paused again and said:— "I can see her now, sitting there."

So could Bobby. The picture drawn was clear and vivid to his mind. He did not speak. She went on:—

"But you won't find any finger-prints or anything. I had on gloves, I wore a man's bib overalls. And a boy's shoes. They've been got rid of long ago. Do you wonder how I got her to—to where you found her? I gave her a message—from you."

"From me?" Bobby asked, startled.

"She didn't suspect anything. I think it had happened before—I mean, a man never seeming to notice her much and then all at once thinking of nothing but her. She expected it. It happened like that sometimes."

"What did you tell her?"

"Just that you wanted to see her. Made her smile all over. Men were like that with her. One day they never thought of her at all, the next they thought of nothing else. I don't know why. I'm not a man. She had that power. That's all. I used to wonder sometimes if it would happen to you, too. When I gave her that message she thought it had. She was glad because she was beginning to think you were dangerous. So was I. I thought you might be first after all."

"First?"

"With her. Perhaps she did suspect just a little. She had a pistol all ready, and I knew she would use it quick enough. I could see she was watching me and wondering. When I opened the door to the steps that go down to the cellar she saw the string I had put there to trip her up. She saw it at once. Only too late. I was quickest. I gave her a push and she caught her foot on the string and she fell down the steps and I ran down after her, and to be sure I hit her head with a stocking I had filled with sand."

"As you did with Darmoor?"

"When she came round I had her under a hook in a beam in the cellar ceiling with her wrists strapped behind her and one end of a rope round her neck and the other end looped over the hook above her head. I got open the door of the small cellar where I knew she hid Ted's body after she killed him and I put him on a chair before her and I put the loose end of the rope in his hand—his dead hand. She was screaming then. I didn't mind. I didn't think any one could hear. No one did. I left them like that while I made a cup of tea. There was no hurry. I don't suppose she ever expected to see Ted again, do you? But he was sitting there, with the rope in his hand and the other end round her neck. It was all I could do to pull her up when I was ready. You can't think how heavy she was and what a time it took me. But I did it at last. Then I washed up the cup and saucer I had used and put everything straight and I came away, leaving them together. That's how you found them, isn't it?"

Bobby did not speak. But he nodded slightly. They were both silent, watching each other.

"That's all," she said presently. Then she added: "I've done the job I had to do."

Bobby was still silent. A child came in for chocolate drops. There was something wrong with the little one's collar. She began to adjust it, coming round the counter for the purpose. Bobby saw her hands, tender and gentle, move about the throat of the child smiling up at her, and he thought he saw those hands about another's throat, moving in another manner.

He turned abruptly and went away. There was nothing to be done. He was not sorry. It was all over. He felt the matter could best be left to higher authority—and by high authority he did not mean his own official superior not even the Home Secretary himself for that matter.

THE END